MW01087698

PRAISE For THE BACKWATER

"A completely gripping story, with two brave, tough and damaged women at its heart. Vikki Wakefield is a brilliant writer."
—Shelley Burr, author of *Wake*

"Vikki Wakefield's *The Backwater* gets under your skin. Two very different women are brought together in the search for the truth and something like justice. Covered in dog hair and splattered with river mud, this taut, muscular thriller absolutely delivers."
—Hayley Scrivenor, author of *Dirt Town*

"An original thriller full of empathy. Flawed and vulnerable, Abbie is so real. I was with her all the way."
—Sarah Bailey, author of *The Housemate*

"An atmospheric mystery with layer upon layer of secrets. Two flawed women discover how much they are willing to risk when justice is not equal and the system is not there to protect them."
—Dinuka McKenzie, author of *Taken*

"Heartrending and heart-pounding. At times beautiful and graceful, at times propulsive and frantic—just like a river."
—Michelle Prak, author of *The Rush*

PRAISE FOR *AFTER YOU WERE GONE*

"Elegantly written and utterly chilling. A dark and twisting novel of psychological suspense that will have you turning pages and checking your locks."

—Emma Viskic, author
of *Those Who Perish*

"Beautifully written and superbly unnerving, *After You Were Gone* is the very best kind of thriller: tender and wise as well as pulse-poundingly tense, with characters so real you want to linger with them even as you race through the pages, desperate to find out what happens. Absolutely wonderful: I could not have loved or admired it more."

—Anna Downes, author of *The Safe Place*

"Gripping, propulsive, and unbearably tense—the best psychological thriller I've read in years."

—Mark Brandi, author of *The Others*

"Spooky, believable, compelling. I kept turning the pages hoping for a way out."

—Leah Swann, author of *Sheerwater*

"Through captivating prose and an intricately crafted plot, *After You Were Gone* explores the complexities of what it means to be a mother: the joy, the rage, the floundering—and the desperate, unquenchable love."

—Amy Suiter Clarke, author of *Girl, 11*

"An elegant, powerful and utterly compelling thriller. The best book I have read all year."

—Lucy Christopher, author of *Release*

"*After You Were Gone* cleaves open ideas of friendship and family, revealing the complex inner workings of our closest relationships. Wakefield achieves what all good crime writers aspire to do: she forces the reader to stress-test their own sense of morality. She looks you in the eye and asks, *What would* you *do if the unthinkable happened? What would* you *sacrifice? How far would* you *go?* At once tense and atmospheric, *After You Were Gone* is also brilliantly plotted and populated with complex characters. An exciting new voice in Australian crime."

—J. P. Pomare, author of *The Last Guests*

"You'll be questioning every character, their motives and [their] memories… [A] great thriller."

—*Australian*

"A riveting read… Breathtaking."

—Sisters in Crime

"This is how to write a psychological thriller; stylish prose in a warts-and-all tale… Wakefield makes a seamless transition into the adult genre."

—*Herald Sun*

"A pacey and engaging thriller… The characters are well-developed and rich in detail… This is one for the beach or a long flight when you need something entertaining to sink your teeth into."

—*Courier*

"Chilling and laced with dark suspense."

—*Australian Women's Weekly*

ALSO BY VIKKI WAKEFIELD

THE
BACKWATER

A NOVEL

VIKKI WAKEFIELD

Poisoned Pen
PRESS

For Allayne

Copyright © 2025 by Vikki Wakefield
Cover and internal design © 2025 by Sourcebooks
Cover design by Alan Dingman
Cover images © Farion_O/Shutterstock, Howl/Stocksy, Sergey
Lukankin/Stocksy, Yuriy Mazur/Shutterstock

Sourcebooks, Poisoned Pen Press, and the colophon are
registered trademarks of Sourcebooks.

All rights reserved. No part of this book may be reproduced in any form or by
any electronic or mechanical means including information storage and retrieval
systems—except in the case of brief quotations embodied in critical articles or
reviews—without permission in writing from its publisher, Sourcebooks.

No part of this book may be used or reproduced in any manner for the
purpose of training artificial intelligence technologies or systems.

The characters and events portrayed in this book are fictitious or
are used fictitiously. Any similarity to real persons, living or dead,
is purely coincidental and not intended by the author.

Published by Poisoned Pen Press, an imprint of Sourcebooks
P.O. Box 4410, Naperville, Illinois 60567-4410
(630) 961-3900
sourcebooks.com

Originally published as *To the River* in 2024 in Australia by The Text
Publishing Company. This edition issued based on the paperback edition
published in 2024 in Australia by The Text Publishing Company.

Cataloging-in-Publication Data is on file with the Library of Congress.

Printed and bound in the United States of America.
SB 10 9 8 7 6 5 4 3 2 1

2007

TRAILER PARK INFERNO LEAVES NINE DEAD, SUSPECT AT LARGE

Fire claimed the lives of nine people, including three children and a police officer, when a section of Far Peaks Trailer Park burned to the ground late Sunday night. Following an arrest on suspicion of arson, a suspect was taken to Far Peaks District Police Station, from where she escaped custody.

Around 11:20 p.m. police were called to attend reports of a burning vehicle located in the main parking lot. A second explosion was heard minutes later, resulting in an intense fire that destroyed four residential trailers and burned through a patch of adjacent scrub. Police have confirmed both fires were deliberately lit, accelerated by gas cylinders and fuel stored at the location.

First responder Constable Tristan Doyle arrested suspect Sabine Marie Kelly (17), a resident of the trailer park, who was apprehended leaving the scene. Kelly was taken to the police station on Main Street, where she escaped. She was last seen running east along Cooke Terrace and may be driving a silver Commodore Wagon (SLE449), which was reported stolen this morning.

While the nine victims have yet to be formally identified, police have confirmed one of their own, Constable Logan Billson, died trying to save other victims. Billson was the son of Sergeant Eric Billson, a respected veteran officer who has served Far Peaks District for thirty-five years.

"This is a tragedy for our community and for my family," Sergeant Billson said during this morning's press conference. "I ask for privacy to grieve and for the community's support and vigilance. The suspect is injured, possibly armed, and very likely dangerous."

The tragedy has devastated the community. According to residents, the suspect's younger sister and mother, a known drug dealer, were killed in the fire, leading to initial speculation that the incident was connected to organized crime. The subsequent arrest of Kelly, a local teenager, came as a shock to many.

Several crime scenes located in and around Far Peaks Trailer Park have been cordoned off pending a full investigation. Sergeant Billson asked that those not directly involved with the investigation avoid the area. Police are calling for witnesses, particularly anyone who might have information that could lead to the arrest of the suspect.

Sabine Kelly is described as seventeen years old, five feet six inches tall and approximately 121 pounds, long curly blond hair and blue eyes, last seen wearing a white dress. It is likely she sustained burns during the fire and may seek medical attention.

"Anyone found to be hiding or assisting the suspect in avoiding formal charges will face charges too," Sergeant Billson said. "It can't be stated strongly enough—it's for the safety of the community that Sabine Kelly is found and returned to custody."

2019

SABINE

The cliffs at Shallow Bend are painted red and gold; the willows sweep the water with loose limbs as the river brings Sabine home.

It's the last day of summer and change is coming. Time moves slowly on the river—she hasn't seen her grandfather since late winter, but it seems like longer. Pop keeps an eye out for her, but his hearing isn't what it used to be, and he sleeps like the dead. Sabine has mastered the art of cutting the houseboat's engine, reading the current— her last visit, he didn't know she was there until she had steeped a pot of tea and set the mug in his hand. He won't call her, won't pick up if she calls. It's for her protection, he says. She thinks it has more to do with his distrust of technology. They have that in common. Pop believes microwave ovens can record conversations—he blames his cancer on the one she gave him. The cancer has gone, and he stashed the microwave in the shed, its inner parts buried in the midden for good measure. He eats his meals cold, straight from the can.

Blue sits in his usual spot at the helm. He turns his back on the land and stares wistfully at the water, as if to say, *This can't be right.* He's more seal than dog. Won't eat red meat, only fish and occasionally chicken. Kibble is an abomination. Sabine often catches him nosing dog biscuits over the side of the houseboat for the carp.

She looks around.

Pop's dinghy rocks gently in her wake and the orange flag tied to the jetty post reassures her the area is clear of surveillance. The houseboat drifts into a space near the opening of the backwater; a soft bump, and the rear swings around.

Blue loses his balance, his claws scrabbling on the deck.

Sabine laughs and Blue, indignant, barks once. She shushes him with one finger. His bark sets off the kennel dogs across the river, and for the first time, he shows interest in going ashore.

"Leave it," Sabine says softly, and he settles on his mat.

She leans over to scratch at the peeling lettering on the side of the houseboat. *Kirralee.* She wanted to rename her, but Pop said there were at least five other boats he knew called *Kirralee* and that was a good thing. Keep it simple, hide in plain sight, and all that.

She would've named her *Aria* if things weren't the way they are.

As houseboats go, this one is no beauty: a single cabin with a double bed, kitchenette, and couch, some cupboards for storage, and a toilet cubicle. Utilitarian. She floats. The deck is rotting in places, and a section of railing broke away last week, but it has near-new pontoons, and the engine runs like a dream.

The railing needs to be fixed. Noncompliance can draw attention from the water police, particularly during the last days of summer, when the townies are out and about in their speedboats and on their Jet Skis, stirring up mud. In a couple of days, there'll be fewer patrols—she'll be able to relax her vigilance.

Smoking a hand-rolled cigarette, her palm cupped over the glowing tip, Sabine waits until the sun slips away. She doesn't smoke often, and the tobacco is stale, fizzing like a sparkler. Sometimes she has to travel well after sunset to find the right place to moor, which can be risky. Tonight her timing was just right.

Blue dozes, head nodding, slit-eyed.

Pop's property isn't as secluded as it used to be. His triangle of land, five or so acres with a hundred yards of frontage, has been squeezed by development on either side: two- and three-story mansions, sloping lawns, towering lights that send fragmented beams across the water. Pop's riverfront is a black expanse in the center. No glimpse of the green weatherboard shack from here, apart from the aerial on the roof. He has let the blackberry grow wild to form a wicked hedge, like something from a fairy tale.

Pop likes to point his rifle at the kids who sneak through the fence to pick berries. Wouldn't shoot nobody, he says. The rifle is never loaded. He just gets a kick out of taking aim. Little bastards deserve it—they can read the signs. *PRIVATE PROPERTY. KEEP OUT. GUARD DOGS ON PREMISES. NO VISITORS. TRESPASSERS WILL BE SHOT. GO AHEAD, MAKE MY DAY.*

Sabine smiles grimly, worried this might be the time she turns up to find he's incarcerated, or dead in his chair. Three, maybe four times a year she checks in. Although there have been fewer raids over the years, the risk of surveillance is ever present.

The light turns deep blue and quiet falls. There's always a brief hush at this hour, changeover, when the daytime creatures clock off and the nocturnal animals start creeping about. She spots movement—a feral deer drinking at the river's edge—and claps her hands to scare it away before Blue takes off on a chase.

She checks the horizon. Dark enough now.

In the cabin she stuffs a bag with toiletries and a change of clothes; it'll be a luxury to take a bath. She locks the door behind her and disembarks to tie off. Blue hits the bank without getting his paws wet, but Sabine misjudges—her feet sink into the grainy sand and her shoes suck in water.

"Fuck it," she says under her breath.

"Mind your mouth and stay where you are."

Sabine's heart misses a beat before settling. "You gonna shoot at me too, you old bastard? I thought you were deaf."

"Can read your lips all right," Pop mutters, emerging from the murk. "Watch where you step—tiger snake's claimed that spot."

Sabine pulls her foot from the sand with a squelch. "He'll be curled up asleep, probably."

"The devil don't sleep," Pop says. He flicks on a flashlight and plays the beam over the bank to check. Just as quickly, he turns it off. "Come on then."

Blue waits. When Sabine clicks her fingers, he follows at her heels.

Pop leads the way. After seventy years on the same patch, he finds the path easily, even in the dark. The shack is on Crown land, and his is a life-tenure lease, but at seventy-two his life is running out. No Kelly in recent memory has lived past seventy-five. Sabine knows that's the thing bugging him lately: he's got nothing to leave her, apart from meager belongings and an ugly boat, and even if he did own the land, she wouldn't be able to claim it.

"Can't croak. Those vultures are waiting," he said once, narrowing his eyes at her. "Can't die peaceful-like until you get your shit together."

For Pop, getting her shit together would mean to properly disappear—obliterate her name, find a real man to take care of her, never come back here again. To Sabine, it means something else entirely. She has managed just fine for twelve years. Why stick your head up when you have everything you need in the hole? For now, she's just happy Pop's mean old heart is still beating.

"Sorry it's been a while," she says.

"The river takes; the river brings back. That's how it is." He stumbles and rights himself.

He's thinking of Nan. Sometimes the river only takes.

The shack looms ahead: an unfriendly building with a drunken lean to it, painted dark green without any bogging up or sanding back—every five years or so Pop just adds another layer to glue the place back together. He has a single propane lantern burning in the front window and three solar lights staked near the steps. Electricity's too expensive, he says, so now he runs gas and a generator only when he needs it, and he's going to need it now because Sabine has been dreaming of the bath for months.

"You'll want to soak yourself," he says, as if he can read her mind. "I'll crank the gas. Leave that dog out." He heads off to the shed.

Sabine settles Blue on the porch, slips off her wet boots, and lets herself inside.

Nothing has changed. The ancient floorboards throughout the cramped kitchen and living area have been mended in patchwork over the years, and she trips on a new section inside the door. The old couch is shaped like a hammock—Pop keeps it covered with layers of tartan blankets, not unlike the way he uses paint to keep the shack from falling apart. A film of coarse hair and dust coats everything. Pop only opens one window, and the air is stifling, flavored with the lingering odor of dog.

Blue's dam, Polly, died a few years back—she crawled under the rainwater tank after being bitten by a tiger snake. Pushing seven years old and scarred from the previous litter, she shouldn't have had her last: four fat pups, stillborn, and Blue the runt, barely breathing. Sabine blew in his lungs and claimed him as hers, lest he go the way of Pop's bucket. Polly had been bitten twice before and survived. The last litter drained the fight out of her, which accounted for Pop's hatred of tigers and his intolerance for Blue.

Sabine enters the bathroom. It's tidy but not clean, and the enamel is cracking. She wonders if the bath will hold water. Pop wouldn't know since he only ever uses the outdoor shower. She plugs the drain, runs the hot tap, hopes.

Steam rises. She adds more cold—it's still eighty-six degrees outside—but not too much. It's not really a bath unless you nearly poach yourself. When she looks for the shampoo to make bubbles, she finds a neatly folded towel and a lavender-scented bath bomb resting on the sink.

So Pop knew she was coming. *Fucking river telegraph.* Her eyes water, and it has nothing to do with the steam.

She closes the door and strips. The mirror is spackled with grime; she wipes a spot clean with a corner of the towel and peers at her blurred reflection. Lately her close vision isn't great. She can't read a book or a map without holding them at arm's length. Too many years scanning the horizon. She probably needs glasses. She bares her teeth: straight and white against her tanned skin, but with a chipped incisor that makes her look as if she has been in a bar fight. Her cropped brown hair is showing blond at the roots again. Is the suspicious mole on her collarbone turning black?

She shrugs. Couldn't be any more malignant than the past she keeps put away. Optometrist, dentist, hairdresser—add those to the list of ordinary tasks she avoids. She can manage a razor, scissors, and a pharmacy dye kit, but not doctor visits, beauty treatments, or any kind of appointment that might enter a system. Her skin is tanned and dry, and her muscles have become ropy from heaving and hauling, from riding the sway of the boat. She has too many scars to remember how they all got there, old cuts left unstitched.

She settles in the tub, shoulders submerged, knees protruding. The bath bomb fizzes on her belly. Pop will leave her as long as she needs, but she wants enough time with him to talk business, and he gets jumpy if she stays too long. Plus Blue needs feeding. And she forgot to bring the batteries up for a decent recharge.

She pinches her nose and ducks her head under. When she comes up, Pop is rapping on the door.

"Just a minute!"

"*Now*, Beenie," he says.

It's been so long since she's heard him call her that. She experiences the conflicting sensation of heat in her extremities and, deep inside, a cold spike of fear.

"What is it?"

She lurches from the water and levers her body over the side of the bath to sit on the mat, struggling to pull her underwear and shorts over her wet skin.

Blue's barking his head off. For some reason he's in the house.

Pop's slamming cupboard doors. Looking for something.

She snaps her bra, yanks a T-shirt over her head, and scrambles to her feet. Where are her boots? Outside.

She opens the door a crack. "Pop?"

"Out the back. Take the dog and go."

He's cradling the gun. The ammunition box is on the kitchen counter, bullets spilling across the Formica. Blue's barking has reached a pitch and tempo he reserves for pelicans and unwelcome guests.

"Go!"

Pop raises the gun and walks steadily toward the door, aiming through the screen at chest height. He won't let the person on the other side come in. She is terrified he won't let them leave.

Sabine enters the kitchen on all fours, spidering across the floorboards. She crouches behind the counter.

"Leave it," she hisses and runs her hand past Blue's nose.

On command, he drops and falls quiet. His eyes stay fixed on the screen door, still swinging after Pop barged through.

Outside the window, Sabine can see the silhouettes of two bodies, one pressing forward and the other backing away. Her palms are slick; water drips from her hair to pool on the floor, dark as blood. The air is heavy with humidity and danger. All signs are telling her to leave, like Pop said, but the realization that the trespasser is a woman makes her pause. A long-dormant instinct is taking over, one that goes back to childhood—distract, deescalate, protect.

With her hand, she stays Blue.

She crosses the room to the door and peers through the screen.

Her grandfather and the woman are moving slowly toward the far end of the porch. Yellow light from the lantern on the sill passes briefly over Pop's features before he fades into shadows.

Sabine reels in shock.

The woman's presence is disturbing enough, but Pop's appearance takes her breath away. In the dark she didn't notice the new lines and hollows, and his eyes, always bright, are now sunken and dull. In less than three months, he appears to have lost a quarter of his body weight, and he's moving as if each step is agonizing. Compared to the woman, Pop seems the lesser threat.

The cancer. It's back.

"Face the wall," Pop says through gritted teeth.

The woman does as he says. Her midlength dark hair is tied in a low ponytail, and she's wearing a white blouse and navy skirt. Her stockinged feet are coated in mud. Everything about her screams *desk job, government,* or *cop.* Pop has her by the back of the neck, the barrel of the gun pressed between her shoulder blades. She's trembling, her head ducked in a show of submission.

"Don't turn around," Pop says.

"Okay," the woman answers. "Okay."

"You've seen the signs," Pop growls.

She nods.

"Then you knew what you were getting into."

Sabine knows whatever happens next, they'll be coming for her. She cracks open the door, steps outside. She can't let them take him too.

"Pop."

He freezes, then jerks his head. "It's her."

The neighbor.

"Go back inside," Pop mutters.

But it's pointless—the woman has turned her head.

The tension inside Sabine releases. Pop is sick again. By the look of him, he's never been closer to death. There's only the inevitability of what will come.

She goes to her grandfather and presses down on the gun barrel, lowering it. For a moment he resists, but she puts her other hand on his shoulder and squeezes.

He's shaking. There's blood on his lips.

"Pop," she says. "Enough."

2019

—

RACHEL

On the deck, by the river, Rachel is celebrating with a bottle of champagne. Aidan has finally agreed to the terms of the divorce settlement. She got everything she wanted: the river house, the Audi, and the cat, while he keeps the town apartment, the Jeep, and his share portfolio. And *Nadja*.

Theirs is an old story. Woman, wife, mother reaches middle age, suffering resentment, loneliness, and exhaustion from being everything to everyone, while trying to keep her husband and her career. Man, husband, father can't keep his dick in his pants.

That's her assessment of the situation.

It's a still, humid evening; she's starting to sweat in her rumpled suit. She takes a cube from the ice bucket, rubbing it on the back of her neck until the cube melts away. When she tries to twist her heavy hair into a perky topknot, it immediately uncoils to slither along her spine. It's getting too long. Months have passed since she last bothered to color her roots, where the dark-brown strands are shot with gray. She doesn't need to lose any weight—the stress has taken care of those extra perimenopausal pounds—but a different hairstyle and some new clothes aren't a terrible idea. One of those studded leather jackets, some hippie-style skirts. A tattoo or a piercing. Rites, to speed up passage through the dark tunnel of divorce.

She laughs self-consciously. *God, Rachel, is this a celebration or a wake?*

Mainly she's relieved the painful yearlong mediation is over and it didn't involve the kids. Ben and Alexis are twenty-three and twenty-five, respectively—far more civilized about their parents' ugly divorce than she and Aidan have been, and more forgiving than Rachel about Nadja.

The champagne was a gift from her lawyer. Alexis left a voicemail message saying she'd see her in couple of weeks. Apart from that, there was no line in the sand, no real sense of letting go. For company, she settles for an unremarkable sunset, a glass of tepid champagne, and one pissed-off cat called Mo, who has been winding increasingly agitated figure eights around her ankles and needs to be fed.

She glances back at the house. It's too big for her on her own. When she and Aidan built it nine years ago, they envisioned weekends filled with kids, the extended Weidermann family and, in the future, grandchildren. When they separated it was like somebody died. Even Lex and Ben stopped coming.

She accepts that the marriage breakdown is partly her fault, but she can't get past Aidan's confession that Rachel bored him. They were together for twenty-seven years, and they barely spent any time together in the past ten—how could a person be bored by a spouse they rarely saw? That Rachel was tired, distracted, driven (most of the time), and distant (some of the time) she can believe. But boring? It hurt. It changed her self-perception, eroding her self-belief to the point that, when she was laid off from the newspaper six months ago, she felt like a senior on the verge of retirement, not a forty-eight-year-old professional woman who had it all and then suddenly, devastatingly, lost it.

Well, not everything. She looks back at the house.

How hard she fought for it—the biggest prize, a home large enough for a family of eight, with three double guest bedrooms and a master suite, three bathrooms, two living areas, and an expansive deck that steps down to the jetty. She has peace and quiet, freedom, independence, in an idyllic location. Then she thinks of the expensive solar panels and batteries that still aren't paid off; she thinks about the mortgage, eating into what's left of her severance package, her meager freelance income, and dwindling savings, before deciding not to think anymore.

The jetty. Mentally, Rachel adds that to her to-do list. She needs to arrange for it to be shortened by a yard, thanks to old mate next door.

Living on the river full-time took some adjustment, not least because of her nearest neighbor: Ray Kelly, batshit crazy, roaming his acreage with a .22 slung over his shoulder like some kind of vigilante hillbilly. He caused her no end of trouble with the council, lodging complaints about anything and everything: the proximity of the septic tank to the boundary, the wattage of the sensor lights, the color of the fence, and the length of the jetty. When a pair of Rachel's underwear blew over on a windy day, he brought it to her attention by impaling them on a pitchfork.

Now the last of the sun's rays are fading; any moment the deck lights Aidan installed will come on. On that she concedes Ray Kelly has a point—they light up the deck like a football stadium.

She throws back the last mouthful of champagne, goes inside, and turns off the main sensor switch. When she settles back in her chair to pour another glass, a houseboat chugs past.

It's after sunset—they're cutting it fine, she thinks.

As the houseboat passes, the lights turn off, and the engine sputters out.

Rachel leans forward in her chair, straining to make out the darkened shape as it drifts toward the bank on the other side of the fence. Every part of her is on high alert.

Is it her? Is she back?

Until four years ago, Rachel and Aidan were unaware of the

connection between their unpleasant neighbor and the fugitive, Sabine Kelly. Their busy lives meant the river house was mostly used as a weekender, but Rachel had decided to take a midweek break. It was the raid that tipped her off—the road choked with police vehicles, suited-up officers pawing through the bushland on the other side of the fence, dogs baying. At first she assumed it was drugs, but a little digging produced the link. She knew of the Trailer Murders case, but only in general terms. *A fire in a trailer park, nine people dead, a teenage girl on the run.* Back then crime wasn't her beat. But further reading led her down a rabbit hole, and it was then that things got interesting.

Rachel never forgets a face, and one look at a photo of Sabine Kelly gave her a jolt of recognition. She'd seen the girl before, a couple of years earlier, on the river—just a glimpse as she was leaving Ray Kelly's jetty.

Now she knows everything about the case. Her mild interest has grown into an obsession. It's the kind of story that could make her career, but years have passed since that first sighting, and she has almost given up hope that Sabine Kelly will return.

Rachel stands and peers into the dark. Her nerve endings are on fire.

Could this be her, after all this time?

She wouldn't call what she does surveillance. It started as a way to pass idle time, and she's had a lot of that since the separation and being laid off. She watches people—always an observer, uncomfortable with people looking in at her. Staring out at the river is like watching a series of vignettes of other people's lives. Families and friends. Lovers. Parties, fights, and near-death experiences, all rolling past like a show reel. On a clear day, she can overhear entire conversations.

She reaches for her phone, heads down to the riverbank, and starts a video recording.

The houseboat drifts closer to the bank near the entrance to the backwater. Its rear swings around. A slight figure steps out of the cabin. A dog barks, setting off the dogs across the river. As the sun sinks behind the cliffs, the figure slouches against the railing and lights a cigarette. Something in the easy way the figure moves about the boat reminds Rachel of a man, but it is the hips and the slender neck that tell her it's a woman. For a long time, the figure is still, waiting.

Rachel zooms in, but the image is too grainy. Her new fence stops five yards from the water—in accordance with council regulations— but Ray Kelly's barbed wire fence continues a meter in.

It isn't far. It isn't deep, she tells herself.

The usual panic rises, but her curiosity wins. She kicks off her heels and wades into the dark water, feeling her way along the wire until she reaches the almost-submerged post. Mud squelches between her toes. She hates the feeling, but forges on, scrolling through head-lines in her mind—an old habit she can't shake.

Bitter ex-wife wades into river to end it all.

Unneighborly feud ends in bloodshed.

Sad-sack ex-journalist drinks too much champagne and drowns.

Or *Body of woman in river remains unidentified.*

The last one's a winner. Everyone loves a Jane Doe.

The current is fickle in this part of the river, the curve of the bend sharpest here—all manner of flotsam washes up on her frontage. Once, she found a kayak, no passenger, with a lunch box containing a cheese sandwich and a minibar-sized bottle of Jack Daniels; another time it was the bloated, stinking carcass of a bull. Everything comes up to float eventually.

She takes another couple of steps, her blouse clinging to her sweaty skin. The water laps at the hem of her skirt, soaking the fabric and traveling to her hips—her no-nonsense, divorce-paper-signing, don't-fuck-with-me outfit. She's still wearing stockings, for God's sake.

She stumbles and drops her phone into the water. She snatches it before it sinks, but it's soaked. Tucking the phone inside her bra, she rounds the post, feeling her way to the bank on Ray Kelly's side. There's plenty of cover here, but it's hard going; woody blackberry bushes tear her skin, and she trips on twisted roots. She's worried about the dog on the houseboat; will it hear her?

Once her feet are clear of the water, she stands completely still.

"Fuck it." Clear as day.

Rachel crouches, all ears. There are two voices—the gruff grumble of Ray Kelly and another husky female one.

Her heartbeat quickens. It has to be her.

Typical. The story of the year washes up on her shore, and the only resources she has at hand are her stubborn ambition and an outdated iPhone. And she has backed herself into a corner here: the angle of view is obscured by foliage and the trees' deep shadows.

They're on the move now, their voices fading.

Rachel looks across the fence. The safety of the river house, lit up like a Christmas tree, beckons. She should go home, call the police, but then this might end up as someone else's story. She'll miss her shot, and in any contest Rachel always aims for the biggest prize.

It takes long arduous minutes to navigate her way through the dense shrubs to the rectangle of dead grass behind Ray Kelly's shack. A faint glow through the nearest window illuminates what looks like a living room and kitchen, and a hallway at the rear.

Hunched behind a bush, she watches as the old man emerges from the shadowy doorway of a shed to the right. He makes it halfway to the porch before turning back, muttering, and pulls the shed door closed to lock it with a key. He pauses, searching the darkness in her direction.

For a moment it feels as if they're staring at each other.

Rachel presses further into the bush, heart drumming.

Kelly climbs the steps to the porch.

Once he's inside, she releases her breath and slinks across the lawn, heading for the darkened window at the side of the house.

Too late, she remembers the dog. As if summoned, it appears as a silhouette, seconds before erupting. The barking sets off an echo across the river, and Rachel freezes, wondering if the animal smelled her fear before it heard her footsteps, and thankful that there is a door between them.

Suddenly the dog is hauled back, and the door swings open to reveal a more terrifying silhouette: Ray Kelly with a rifle.

Rachel scrambles to her feet.

Kelly moves fast for an old guy carrying a heavy weapon—he has her by the collar before she has taken five steps, her bare feet scrabbling in the dirt like the dog's claws on the floorboards. Her skirt rides up. She reaches behind her head, gripping his hairy wrists to relieve the pressure on her throat, choking out a protest.

"Let me go!"

Without uttering a word, he drags her across the lawn. At the porch he lets go, only to shove the barrel between her shoulder blades and force her to stumble up the steps.

Rachel spins to face him, hands up, and backs away to the far end of the porch. A dead end.

Kelly jabs at her with the gun. "Face the wall."

She does as he says. Automatically she places her palms flat against the wall and widens her stance, as if she's about to be frisked.

Kelly has one hand pinching the back of her neck. The other is pressing cold steel against a knob of her spine.

Rachel ducks her head. A tremor starts at her jaw and spreads, earthing through her feet like an electric shock. It's not her life that passes before her eyes, but her bloody, violent death.

Stupid. Stupid. Stupid.

"Don't turn around," Ray Kelly growls.

"Okay," she answers. "Okay."

"You've seen the signs."

She nods.

"Then you knew what you were getting into."

"Pop." Almost a whisper.

Under his breath: "It's her. Go back inside."

A mad pulse beats in Rachel's skull. Her bladder is ready to release. She looks down at her feet, pale and squashed inside the wet toes of her stockings.

"Pop," she hears. "Enough."

There's a heavy pause. Then the cold press of the gun loosens, and Rachel slumps against the wall. A sharp fleck of paint wedges under her fingernail.

A creak, followed by a slamming door. Now it's only the two of them.

"Take the gravel path. It'll bring you back out on the road." Kelly pokes her right glute with the gun. "Don't come here again, understand?"

Rachel nods.

She has been here before, snooping around. She knows the path; she knows the front gate is topped with razor wire, but there's a gap between the rails wide enough to slip through. She keeps her hands raised and moves sideways down the steps until she feels stones under her feet.

"Keep going."

Kelly follows her around the side of the house. She picks her way gingerly along the narrow path, flanked on both sides by dense shrubbery. Away from the dim light of the lantern, it's dark.

"I can't see where I'm going," she bleats.

He grunts. *Plink. Chick.*

Rachel recognizes the distinctive sound of a Zippo lighter. The path ahead is now illuminated, their long shadows merged into a single lumpy mass. Without turning around, she can tell he's listing to one side, limping. They emerge from the path onto an overgrown driveway. His truck, with a flat front tire, is parked on the other side of the fence.

"There's the gate," he says. "Show yourself out."

"I'll do that."

"I'd have shot you for trespassing. I'd be within my rights."

Rachel's first instinct is to set him straight about *her* rights. Beneath the terror is a welcome flicker of rage. She chooses to mitigate the danger by lying.

"I was only after your help."

He waits, the flame dying, as she climbs through the gap between the rails. When she turns around, he is smaller than she remembers. Thinner. He is no longer carrying the gun.

"What help?" he says and flips the lighter lid down to extinguish the flame.

Rachel can only see a golden halo on her retina; he's a disembodied voice in the blackness. "Rats. In my roof," she says.

That part is true.

His eyes fix on her, then lose focus.

Rachel has heard it too: the low rumble of an engine.

"Can't poison 'em," Kelly drawls. "You poison 'em, they'll die in your cavities, and you'll have to live with the stink. Then you'll get the cadaver flies—thousands of 'em. So many of the bastards, you'll think your house is possessed. Rats gone, but you'll have something worse. You've gotta cull your fruits—those pears you've got hanging there, the lillypillies, and them figs. That's why they're hanging around." He looks over his shoulder. "And they come for the scraps. You got chickens?"

"No."

She knows what he's doing. He has just babbled more words than she has heard him speak in a year—so his fugitive granddaughter can slip away.

"Right. What do you suggest?"

"Trap 'em."

"Like, in a cage?"

He nods. "It'll take a while—rats are suspicious, gotta get used to something new. Eventually they'll get curious and investigate; then you knock 'em on the head or drown 'em in a bucket."

Rachel's feet are bruised, possibly bleeding. Their next-nearest neighbor with a light on is a hundred yards away, further by road. She is not safe here. Her phone is ruined. She needs shoes.

"The woman—" she starts.

His expression is like a door closing. "I'll drop those traps around."

"I appreciate it."

Kelly spits to one side; then he's gone.

———

At the house, Rachel is grateful for the security system that tracks her movements. From the back gate, along the driveway, through the entrance, and down the hall until she reaches the kitchen, the lights switch on ahead of her and off again once she has passed. The outside deck is still a black spot; she turns the sensor switch back on, flooding the area with light.

Trembling all over, she pours a packet of arborio rice into a mixing bowl and buries her phone in the grains. Ben has assured her it works. She hopes so; otherwise she'll have to pray there was enough signal for an immediate backup to the cloud.

Call the police, Rachel.

And tell them what exactly? That she trespassed? That her neighbor pulled a gun on her? Reporting certainly won't help her get to Sabine Kelly.

Mo materializes from his cat igloo, tail twitching with irritation.

Equally irritated, Rachel presses the button on his auto feeder with her foot. He has never gotten the hang of working the damned thing. A handful of pellets shoots into the bowl, and Mo gives her another glare before deigning to eat.

She picks up the kitchen handset and dials.

"Lex?"

"Hey, Mum. You're on the landline? What's up?"

She registers the quaver in her daughter's voice and fears Lexi will forever be anxious about her calls. Rachel has drunk-dialed on more than one occasion; she has overshared—her anger over Aidan's cheating, her grief over the separation. She promised herself she wouldn't do it anymore.

"My mobile got wet. Everything's fine—I just wanted to hear your voice."

"Here I am!" Lexi says. "What are you doing?"

Rachel inspects her ruined pantyhose, the mud spattered up her calves, her bleeding fingernail. "Oh, I've been watching the sunset with my friend Veuve Clicquot," she says, too brightly. "I was thinking, I need a couple of days in the city over the weekend. We could house-swap? You can come up here with your friends?"

She has voiced her fear—that Lexi doesn't want to be at the river house while Rachel is there.

"It's a three-hour drive there and back. I can't afford the petrol," Lexi says. "Anyway, I've already made other plans. Sorry."

"It's fine. Another time."

"Sure."

"I'll let you go."

What a loaded statement, she thinks. *If you love something, set it free.*

"Bye, Mum."

"Bye, beautiful."

Rachel hangs up, leaving a smear of blood on the receiver. She turns off all the lights, checks the windows and doors.

There are too many. She pored over the design of the house, spending hours moving a chair into different positions and holding up a cardboard frame to find the right angle. The reward is the perfect panorama, a 180-degree view of the river's changing moods and colors.

The price is that everyone can see in.

2019

—

SABINE

Sabine moors the houseboat in Dixon's backwater—not too far along in case she needs to move again quickly. She has made it about three miles downriver from Pop's place in the dark, only the faint light of the moon to guide her. It's unlikely there are any patrols this late, and she hasn't received any callouts over the radio—locals, warning each other—but it's too risky to travel any further.

Like many of the locals, Dixon has put up his own sign to deter entry: *KEEP OUT. PRIVATE PROPERTY. SHALLOW WATER.* Although the sign is less hostile than Pop's, it's just as effective. This is council-owned land, and the backwater is deep enough, but few would have the balls to follow her in here. Dix likes to think this part of the river is his, repainting the sign whenever it fades so there's no confusion. This time of year, he'll probably be camping at the river's mouth, catching mulloway. If she wants, she could go up to his shack, find the spare key, and have a shower, but there's a chance he'll be there. When he's drinking, he can't keep his hands to himself.

Blue likes to sleep inside at the foot of the bed, but tonight she puts his mat on the deck so he can keep an ear out. When she closes the door on him, he turns circles, whines for a bit, and finally settles.

Her body is tired, but her mind is still whirring. She's worried about Pop. It's a twisting, constricting sensation inside her, one she recognizes as helpless panic.

She undresses, letting her damp clothes fall where she stands. The faint scent of lavender rises with the heat of her skin, and she finds undissolved bath crystals in her navel. She crawls slowly across the bed, unmade since yesterday, and pulls the curtains open to let the moonlight spill across the sheets.

She lies awake for a long time.

Pop is in danger because she was sloppy. Twelve years of chugging from place to place and evading detection has made her complacent. It doesn't help that the river is more populated now—the old shacks have been torn down and replaced by mansions, built by people who have nothing better to do than sit on their decks all day and poke their noses in other people's business.

Pop said the intruder was his neighbor. It's not enough by itself to send her back into deeper hiding, but there was something about the woman's demeanor that set Sabine on edge—she was too composed, too watchful, even with the muzzle between her shoulders. When Pop sent her packing, he probably thought that'd be the end of it, but Sabine has a radar for trouble, and she suspects there'll be some coming.

When she recalls the way Pop looked—shrunken, ancient, as if the life was being drained from him—she chokes up. She had a taste of this fear when Pop first admitted he was sick, but the last time she saw him, he said he was better.

He lied then, and he'll lie under oath before giving her up. She won't let him do it. However little time her grandfather has left on this earth, she doesn't want him spending any of it in jail for aiding and abetting a fugitive.

She should be on her way already—upriver, downriver, inland, anyplace but here—but the blood tie is too strong. It always pulls her back.

———

Sabine has always been a heavy sleeper, and Blue doesn't bark a warning, which is how Ryan makes it all the way to her bed before she wakes.

Through slitted eyes she finds the shape of him in the murk. For a split second, she wonders how he got in, what's happened to Blue, why she didn't sense him, before the rush hits and she kicks her way out of the tangled sheet. In one clean movement, she shifts to a crouch before launching herself at him, her legs a vice around his waist.

Now Blue barks—a series of excited yips.

"How did you find me?"

"Too easy," he says. "You're not far enough in."

He knows all her mooring places, and he knew she was headed down Pop's way. But he can't know what happened tonight, and she won't tell him. She doesn't like him to worry.

"Maybe knock?"

"Maybe lock the door?"

"If my knife was under the pillow, I might've stabbed you." She releases her grip and lets herself fall onto the bed. "And it's after ten. You shouldn't be on the river this late."

His eyes flick to the bedside drawer, where she keeps a knife—a filleting knife, but it would just as quickly gut a man as a fish. She raises herself to her elbows, lets her bare legs fall open, and that's where his eyes travel next.

"I've missed you," she says. "It's been three weeks."

"First chance I've had to get away." He kneels, bracing with one hand on the side of the mattress, the other running along her inner thigh.

Sabine shivers. Her head flops back.

He pulls her underpants to the side and strokes her lightly before peeling them down one-handed, alternating left and right until they slip off her feet. His hand is back, rubbing. He climbs onto the bed, positioning himself above so he can see her expression, gently sliding his middle finger inside her. He stays so still she forgets to breathe. She is full and empty at the same time. She squirms against him, but he clamps her down with his big palm and bends to kiss her lower lip. A sigh, and she gives in. He might hold her there for five seconds or five minutes—it depends on his need, not hers. It's been so long he could go either way: soft and slow because he wants her to be patient, or fast and hard because he can't be.

Sabine has to take herself somewhere else to wait for him—the place she always ends up is at the beginning: a single mattress in his bedroom, their bodies young and undefined, her response tentative, and his touch less sure but still a revelation. She remembers the feel of his adolescent stubble on her skin, and his expression when her breath quickened as he realized he was doing something right.

It's the same look on his face now. She has come, neither of them moving. He feels her tension and release on his finger, and it surprises him.

It doesn't surprise Sabine.

Dee put her on the pill at fifteen, said it would be shit the first time and probably the hundredth too, and warned her not to ruin her life by having a baby at sixteen like Dee had. Any relationship was hard enough all on its own; a baby was a passion-killer. Guys only ever wanted one thing. *Only give if you were willing to take too. Don't fall in love with the first guy you sleep with; hold something back.*

Dee said a lot of stuff that didn't turn out to be true and Sabine has never held back, not the first time and not since.

Ryan smiles and pulls away, delighted. His weight leaves her, but only long enough to remove his clothes. It isn't over. They have all night.

The way she feels about him—it never fades, never changes, never gets old. In some ways every time feels like the beginning. She knows he'll never be with anyone else, but she has to remind herself that one day it will end.

With Ryan it has always been easy. It's everything else that's hard.

———

As soon as she hears the magpies' predawn song, Sabine is awake. She has trouble sleeping in, even when it's still relatively dark, like it is now in the deep shade of the backwater.

They were up late. She stretches and yawns, her muscles throbbing with a pleasant ache.

Ryan is on his side facing away from her, his lower body covered with the sheet. He's just come off a ten-day straight shift at the mine. He probably won't wake for ages. Ordinarily she adjusts her rhythm to match his, even if it means hours lying next to him, watching him sleep. But today she's antsy. If she takes Ryan's tinny, it won't take long to motor back to Shallow Bend for a quick check on Pop.

She rolls out of bed.

Leaving Ryan makes her chest hurt, and the sentimental part of her wonders why love so often feels like pain. Her more pragmatic side knows why—love can kill you. To tie your life so completely to one person is not a wise strategy for survival.

She shrugs off her melancholy and kisses his knee, poking up from beneath the sheet.

Quietly, she grabs clean clothes, a large straw hat, and a bottle of water. Behind the privacy screen of the outdoor shower, she rinses, dries off, and pulls on a pair of shorts and a T-shirt, slipping an oversized cotton shirt over the top. The shirt makes her look bigger than she is. The hat will cover her hair and conceal much of her face.

She steps into the tinny and clicks her fingers. Blue follows. She uses the oars to paddle out of the backwater before starting the outboard and put-putting into the river proper. It's too early for much traffic, and she has this stretch to herself: the low bank to her right, the vertical cliffs to her left, a cloudless sky above. The air is still fresh with morning chill.

Blue splays his paws on either side of the bow and lifts his nose to scent the breeze, showing interest in some movement on the bank. Another deer, head up, nose twitching.

"Not today," she says.

Blue throws her a disgruntled look, but she can't have him off overboard when she has to keep moving. He's spoiled. Most days she's happy to sit in one spot for hours, letting him wander. It bothers her that she has so little awareness of time passing—days have turned into weeks, weeks into years. In another month she'll be thirty, not much younger than Dee was when she died. When you rarely talk to people or use technology and you don't read the papers, it's too easy to pretend the world hasn't changed.

The tinny comes around Shallow Bend. Pop's flag is still fluttering from the jetty post, but Sabine cuts the motor, readying herself to turn around at the first sign of unusual activity.

Everything is quiet.

At the joint adjacent to Pop's, she spots the light poles, taller than the remaining willows, and the rows of London plane trees planted along the curved driveway. She wonders how on earth permission was granted to remove the red gum that was there. It would have been over a hundred and fifty years old.

Money, she supposes. Rich people can get away with things poor people can't. Pop said the neighbor woman asked him to move his rainwater tank because it looked ugly next to her fence. Look at her jetty, sticking out too far, look at the sandbags she brought in to make her own private beach—doesn't she know the river will do what it wants?

Behind her the *Old Mary* paddleboat is heading upriver.

Sabine makes Blue drop to the bottom of the tinny and steers closer to the bank, cutting the engine to slip under the cover of the willow branches. Too late, she realizes the beach sand has eroded and piled up here. *Scrape.* The tinny bottoms out.

She'll have to get out and give it a push. *Fuck.*

When she throws her leg over the side, Blue takes it as a sign he should disembark too.

"In. *In,*" she hisses, but he has his snout in the shallows.

He comes up with an old tennis ball and bounds ashore to give his signature full-body shake.

The sound, thankfully, is drowned out by a blast of *Old Mary's* horn. When the paddleboat's wake slaps the bank, Sabine jumps out, turning the tinny and giving it a hard shove before hopping back in. She gives a low whistle.

Blue has disappeared.

As she looks back, a tortoiseshell cat shoots from under a boat trailer parked behind a shed.

She spots Blue on the beach, his tail stiff as a rudder.

"Leave," she shouts. "Blue, *leave it.*"

He's already off after the cat, which is airborne and clearly in fear for its life. Blue sends sand flying as he claws his way along the beach and up a steep retaining wall, yelping like his tail is on fire. Sabine knows there's nothing she can do but hope the cat is smart enough to find safety up a tree. Not that Blue will hurt it if he catches up, but the poor thing might die from shock in the interim.

The woman from last night is standing on her deck wearing a bathrobe, a mug in her hand.

Sabine turns the tinny around and pulls up alongside the jetty.

The woman is yelling, waving her arms. "Get! Get, you mongrel!"

Sabine jumps out to tie a quick knot and races up the path toward the house. By the time she reaches the back door, Blue is half-in and half-out of the pet flap, trying to follow the cat. She pulls him out by the hind leg and gives him a hard shove in the chest. Once she makes eye contact, he backs off, whining.

The woman has followed her and reaches down to lock the flap. "Lucky he didn't fit," she says, panting.

Sabine's hat has blown off during the chase. She keeps her eyes cast down. "I'm sorry. He won't hurt it—he only wants to catch it."

"It's not my cat I'm worried about. The last dog that took on Mo lost an eye." She crosses her arms.

"Sorry again. I'll get him out of here right now."

The woman's body language changes; she holds out her hand, smiling. "Rachel."

Sabine shakes her hand briefly, offers nothing in response. "You're Ray Kelly's—?"

In her pause is everything Sabine has been worrying about. Coming here was a mistake.

"I'm a family friend," she says. "I look out for him. Come on, Blue."

The woman—Rachel—gestures toward an impressive teak outdoor setting. "I've just made coffee. Would you like to join me?"

It seats twelve, Sabine notices. There's one mug on the table, and a lonely champagne flute with bright red smears around the rim. Sabine hasn't worn lipstick since she was seventeen.

She shakes her head. "Thanks, but we really have to go."

Blue is snuffling at the cat flap again. She taps his flank to get his attention and strides down the path, along the jetty, but once there she struggles to untie the knot.

"Fucking fingers," she mutters. "Blue, *in*."

"Wait," Rachel says. "Let's talk."

Finally, the knot loosens. "Nice to meet you."

She gives a limp wave, the foreboding so intense she shudders, and steps into the tinny. Blue jumps in at the last second and she guns the motor, swinging out across the widest part of the river, heading back to Ryan. It's too dangerous to hang around—Pop will have to wait.

———

Both river and sky reflect Sabine's mood: cloudy, unsettled.

She knows, she knows.

Blue senses her unease and lies low in the bow, nose between his paws. Every now and then he gives a single *whump* of his tail, hopeful he'll be forgiven for everything he has done to make her like this.

When Sabine reaches the backwater, she ties off the tinny and steps aboard the houseboat, setting off a gentle rocking.

She knows. But why did she want to talk? Why hasn't she called the police already?

When she ducks through the doorway, she finds Ryan still asleep—stubbled jaw slack, one arm flung above his head, the windows beaded with the condensation of his warm breath. For an awful moment, she hates him. What must it be like to close off his mind to everything, to sleep so deeply for the same number of hours he has been awake? She would have to sleep for years to catch up on her lost slumber, like a cursed character from a fairy tale.

Stifling the urge to startle him awake so she isn't alone, she props on the end of the bed and watches his chest rise and fall.

Even if the woman, Rachel, knows, telling Ryan won't fix anything. He will never truly understand how it feels to be hunted. They can only meet briefly in the in-between, a place where time doesn't matter. But something about turning thirty, realizing time hasn't stopped at all, makes her wonder if the way they live is enough for her anymore.

Last year they were separated for two months, while Ryan completed his training as an explosives technician and got a promotion at the mine—he joked about it being the perfect job for him, a guy who had no control over his own life and sometimes just wanted to blow shit up.

It's not the terrible loneliness that Sabine remembers now, but the minutiae of the discussions they had when he returned: how just the right kind of explosive had to be used, the exact amount, set in a precise location, taking into account existing fractures and weak spots and the preciousness of all life in close proximity.

Pop is dying. Maintaining the status quo is no longer an option. Change is coming, and not just the change of season.

If there is to be an explosion, it must be controlled. She knows what she has to do.

2019

——

RACHEL

Rachel opens her laptop for the second time this morning. It's almost 8 a.m. Apart from the brief encounter with her unexpected visitors, she has been working since five-thirty, when she startled awake, disoriented and sweating, as if woken from a bad dream. If it was a dream that disrupted her sleep, she couldn't remember it. The evening's events were nightmarish enough.

She cracks her neck from side to side.

Her body is stiff, aching, especially the spot between her shoulder blades where Kelly pressed the muzzle of the gun. She inspects her hands to see if the act of typing has stilled their tremor, unsure whether it's lack of caffeine and sleep that has been making them shake. More likely nervous anticipation.

She checks her phone. It seems fine—this morning when she powered it on and the Apple logo appeared, she punched the air. It's probably too soon for a response, but she goes back to her laptop to check her email.

Perhaps impulsively, she has sent a brief pitch to two contacts— just enough to imply a break in the Trailer Murders case, that she still has the jump. If the story breaks elsewhere, at best it would be a rolling series of pieces as events unfolded. But there's no reason to suspect anyone else knows where Sabine Kelly has been hiding. Waiting too long, however, has been her undoing before. She has to clinch a contract before word gets out, and she needs an arrest to close the story. Judging by her behavior earlier, Sabine Kelly is already spooked and might go underground again.

A question is nagging at her: Why did the girl risk coming back?

Rachel has always been methodical, practical, reliable, her research meticulous. She has never filed a story late. Six months ago she packed up her desk, accepted a tacky oversized *Goodbye and Good Luck!* card from her colleagues and transferred her life's work to her office at home. Now she understands how vastly unprepared she was for the precarious nature of freelancing: writing on spec, without a clear brief or the feedback of her peers. Without the backup of Legal.

In hindsight, her work has been *safe.*

The Sabine Kelly story feels dangerous. It has been on the simmer for four years—now she must pitch quickly, write fast, and run with the grainy photos taken on her phone. They're not ideal for the kind of in-depth, character-driven, long-form article Rachel planned to write when she had the time, but she did not expect time to run out. She has enough backstory. It's a matter of knocking it all into shape. If things play out the way she hopes, Rachel has the scoop, the climax, and following an arrest and resolution of the murder charges against Sabine Kelly, she will have an ending.

Her hands are definitely shaking.

She clicks on the working document. She has close to ten thousand words. For lack of any new information, she has been dithering on a page of reported sightings, mostly interstate and inland. Could Sabine really have been on the river the whole time, or has she only recently returned?

Rachel highlights much of the page, cuts and pastes the paras into a deleted text file. She will pick up where the story stalled: Sabine Kelly, escaping custody, on the run for the past twelve years. The last image taken of Sabine was syndicated across countless newspapers, appearing on the front page: a girl, seventeen, mouth slack, her white dress stained red brown with blood and gray with ash, her long blond hair singed to the scalp on one side—defiant in body language but, inexplicably and horrifically, devoid of expression.

It's an incredible shot, but copyright means she can't use it.

The photos she took with her phone last night and this morning aren't great, but she opens them on her laptop and scrolls through the images on the larger screen. She has only one good shot: the tinny leaving her jetty. It's a clear view of the hull identification number and a decent profile of Sabine Kelly's face. She is no longer wearing her hat—Rachel has it now, tucked inside a plastic bag to preserve the few short strands of hair caught in the weave. The dog is facing backwards in the boat, looking straight at the camera lens, his tongue lolling out the side of his mouth.

She compares the two images, taken a dozen years apart. There's no question in her mind that they are the same person.

"I've got you," she singsongs.

She zooms in and notes the HIN on a notepad. She'll get onto her sneaky contact for registration numbers. Whoever owns the tinny knows Sabine Kelly, or maybe it was registered under an alias. Borrowed? Or could it be stolen? She recalls the childlike way Sabine covered her face when her hat blew off as she ran after Blue.

Rachel suspects collaboration. Complicity. That would give another interesting angle to the story. Rachel has been on the receiving end of the river-folk shutout—they'd be adept at hiding one of their own. But it doesn't make sense in the interviews she has read over the years. Sabine was almost universally condemned by the people who knew her. *Cop killer. Child killer. White trash. Evil. Violent. Psychotic. She should be locked away and never released. She should get nine life sentences.*

That said, during Rachel's own research, there were just as many who declined to be interviewed, who clammed up. In her experience, the first people to offer information were often the frauds and fabricators, the drama queens and hangers-on. Rachel might have been laid off from her job, but she won't let that stop her from doing what she was born to do. She has a knack for divining truth, for getting to the beating heart of a story; she is tenacious, dogged, resilient. Her life might be a train wreck, but this story—her magnum opus, so to speak—has landed in her lap at just the right time.

She closes her laptop and puts it on the charger.

After drinking her second coffee for the day, she takes a long shower and washes her hair. She keeps her phone on voice control to record; her best thinking is done in the shower. And her best crying too.

———

Rachel is carrying a basket of washing to the laundry when a figure appears at the front door.

Through the smoky glass panel, she can just see the curve of the top of a head. The person is standing there, unmoving. When the knock finally comes, Rachel jumps, cursing the open plan of the garden and house; her unwelcome visitor could have approached from any direction, the road, the adjacent properties, the river.

"Who's there?" Her fingers twitch toward an umbrella behind the coat stand, the only object resembling a weapon within reach.

No reply.

A moment later, a female voice utters a short sharp command. "Sit."

She breathes out sharply. Sabine Kelly has come to her. It may only be to retrieve her hat, but Rachel's blood hums. She puts the basket down on the bench seat near the entrance and cautiously unlocks the dead bolt.

"Hello again." Rachel stands aside, gesturing for her to come in.

Sabine ducks her head as she steps through the doorway, the heeler right behind her, whining, scenting the air for cat. Rachel grabs for his collar, but the girl nudges him with her foot.

"Stay."

The girl, Rachel thinks ruefully.

Sabine Kelly is not a girl anymore. Any resemblance to the stock photos in the folder taking up near-permanent residence on Rachel's bedside table is incidental. Her hair is short, several shades darker. Her build is still slender, but lacking the softness of youth, and she seems taller, but that has everything to do with the rigid set of her spine. Her eyes, however, are unchanged—the palest blue, with that distant gaze light-colored eyes have.

Sabine takes everything in with a sweeping glance, and Rachel is taken aback by her wrinkled nose and down-turned mouth. "Do you want to lock the dog in the shed?" she offers.

Sabine waves her hand. "He'll wait outside."

"What about my cat?"

"Sounds like your cat can take care of itself."

Rachel beckons, leading the way along the hallway to the kitchen. They pass beneath an open archway and into the family room with its parquetry floors and concertina doors.

Again, Sabine ducks her head.

"Why do you, you know…?" Rachel mimics her action.

Sabine's expression is blank for a moment. "Oh," she says. "It's living on the houseboat—the doorways are so low I always hit my head."

Unexpectedly, she smiles, and Rachel is transfixed by a chip in her incisor. She is curiously well-spoken, her enunciation perfect, slightly British. How that's possible growing up in a remote mining town with a drug-addicted mother, Rachel cannot understand. She suspects it's another part of her disguise.

"I have a dent right here." Sabine takes Rachel's hand, presses her fingers to her scalp. "Feel it?"

Rachel nods. She can't feel much of a dent, but she does experience the sudden, painful memory of feeling her babies' pulses through their fontanelles. She yanks her hand away as if burned.

"Can I get you anything? A drink? Coffee?" She tries to sound casual, but electricity is zapping through her.

"I don't drink coffee." Sabine doesn't ask for anything else. Her gaze roams and settles on the wall of shelves at the far end of the room. "You have a lot of books."

Rachel shrugs. "I have trouble getting rid of things."

"Why would you, if you have the space for them?"

Sabine strokes the hide of the tan couch as if it were an animal. Aghast, Rachel watches as she bends to sniff it.

"Leather?"

"Yes."

Sabine sinks into the floral two-seater instead, drumming the slim fingers of one hand on the arm. Rachel suspects she finds all this tasteful opulence...well, distasteful. She should warn her guest not to touch any metal surface when she leaves that couch; it packs a brutal static shock on par with a defibrillator. Even the cat knows not to come near.

"Nice house."

Rachel chooses to take the remark at face value, and shrugs. "Glad you like it."

On the surface, the home would appear obsessively tidy, but it is simply undisturbed; there is only so much mess one person can make. Rachel has not changed the linens in the guest bedrooms for months. The downstairs bathroom hasn't been cleaned since the last tradesman left, and she dusts half-heartedly, skirting objects without lifting them. Her battered slippers stand pigeon-toed at one end of the kitchen counter, as if she were a time traveler who had been called to adventure without warning. Her dressing gown is draped across the back of the leather couch. Beneath the scent of a burning lemongrass candle, there is the greasy odor of oven-baked frozen food and cooking oil—she remembers there are four uneaten chicken nuggets petrifying in the oven. If her guest has any insight, she will register the low hum of the digital radio, set to an easy-listening channel, giving Rachel respite from the terrible quiet; she will notice the chalkboard on the fridge, the chalk fixed with hairspray to preserve a years-old message from Lexi, her last declaration of love.

She will surely sense the loneliness here.

But Sabine is interested in the books. She points to the second highest shelf. "I've read a few of these."

Rachel can't hide a sardonic smile. "True crime?"

Sabine's head snaps around as if pulled by a thread. "Nothing is ever all true. There's always stuff nobody can know, especially when people are dead and someone else is telling their story."

"Agreed," Rachel says, then leaves a long silence for Sabine to fill.

Sabine simply stares at her fingers, entwined in her lap.

Rachel changes tack. "What do I call you?"

"Emma. Emma Whelan."

"Really?"

"It says so on my license."

"That's how we're playing this?"

Sabine skewers Rachel with a glare. She has quick, darting eyes, like a bird's. "This isn't a game."

Rachel suddenly feels unsafe—alone in her home with a fugitive and murderer. *Alleged* murderer. She takes a step back and folds her arms.

"Why did you come here, Sabine?"

"*Emma*," she corrects. "I want to know what *you* want. Why were you at Ray's last night? What were you looking for?"

Rachel suspects Sabine would respect straight-up honesty over deflection.

"You."

Sabine's eyes follow the dog, snuffling along the bottom of the doors outside. Her brow furrows in confusion, and she swallows repeatedly.

"I'm a journalist," Rachel adds.

"Who do you work for?"

"Myself. I'm freelance."

"And you just happen to live next door to Ray?"

"I lived here for years before I found out about your story," Rachel says.

A derisive snort. "You don't know *anything* about my story."

"But I want to." Rachel shrugs. Her shoulders stay high and tense. "I tell the truth. It's my job."

"Your *job*?"

"My integrity is important to me."

It's pretty much all I have left, she thinks, but Sabine rolls her eyes.

"You write this story without me, you'll look like a hack," she says. "You'll get it wrong because nobody but me knows the truth."

Rachel's chin goes up. "You can give me an interview before—"

"Before you call the cops? That would be a mistake. I'm a killer, remember? A killer *you* let in your house." Sabine gives a forced laugh. "And I know exactly why you haven't called them already."

"Why's that?"

Sabine regards her steadily. Her stillness is unnerving.

"Because you want more than you've got."

To hide her discomfort, Rachel walks briskly to the kitchen and turns on the coffee machine, before remembering Sabine doesn't drink coffee. *Something harder? Something to take the edge off, loosen her up?* She glances over her shoulder at the clock on the wall—*Is it too early for booze?*—only to find Sabine is a few steps behind her. Heart thudding, she spins around. How did she move so quickly, so quietly, without Rachel hearing? In the tall white kitchen, Sabine is like an urban fox: shy, wary, out of place.

"It's not your story to tell."

All gutter speak now, the plummy accent gone.

"Someone will tell it, if not me." Rachel takes a deep breath. "But you are a wanted fugitive—I'll have to turn you in."

A hiss escapes Sabine's lips, and Rachel takes another step back, closer to the laundry door, the nearest exit.

"I won't hide you," she says softly. "I can't protect you."

"I know," Sabine whispers. "No one can."

Her eyes move from side to side as if she's searching for an exit too. Scared she might flee, Rachel puts out her hand. It is a gesture meant to calm, but Sabine grabs her hand, squeezing Rachel's fingers. A tremor passes from Sabine's body to hers.

"It's okay," Rachel says. "Everything will be okay." It's the kind of thing she used to say when one of her kids was hurt or crying— meaningless words, or at least not all true.

It seems to work.

Sabine releases her hand and folds her arms. "I'll give you the story—on one condition."

Elation makes Rachel's blood race. She gives a small nod.

"There is a way you *can* protect me—as a source."

The slyness in Sabine's expression tempers Rachel's excitement.

"Why me? Why now?"

"You found me. Others will too." Sabine looks away. "I want control over my own story. I want this to be over, but I need more time."

Rachel holds up a hand. "I can only protect a source if it's in the public interest. I can't if you present a danger to anyone. We'd be walking a very fine line."

"It's in the public interest, I promise you."

"As long as we have the understanding you'll give yourself up when this is done."

Sabine shrugs. "It's nothing I don't already have hanging over my head. So how do we do this?"

Rachel's legs go suddenly weak. "We start. We keep the plane in the air until we figure out how to land it."

Sabine waits.

It occurs to Rachel that she can wait too. Just minutes ago she was ready to turn Sabine in, but now she wants the dangling carrot, the promise of a bigger story. What's a few more days? Sabine is right. Technically, until she admits otherwise, she is Emma Whelan, simply a source.

But Rachel doesn't like to rely on technicalities, and already she is questioning her integrity. The emails have been sent. She needs to move things along quickly.

"The truth. All of it."

Sabine nods. "I need time. It's the only way you'll even get close to the truth. I have to be sure I'm safe."

Rachel has what she hoped for—or has Sabine planned this all along? Does it matter, as long as they both get what they want?

"Agreed."

"And, Rachel?" That cunning look again. "I'd like my hat back."

2 0 1 9

—

SABINE

Blue is poised like the figurehead on a ship as the tinny cuts a straight line upriver.

Sabine swings wide around the splintered bones of an old jetty and a lone kayaker bobbing near the cliffside reeds. She fails to slow to the four-knot limit, raising a hand in apology as she passes. The old miner's shack is to her left, one of the few low-lying buildings to survive the 1956 flood and hard to spot unless you know it is there. A squadron of pelicans circles above, riding the thermals. The sun is high and bright, the water glittering like broken glass.

One-handed, Sabine opens the tackle box beneath the seat, searching for a pair of Ryan's sunglasses to dull the glare. Her fingers touch a coil of fishing line, heavy sinkers, a feathery lure. A couple of inches to the right, and her hand closes on the velvet box. Inside is the ring, a smooth band with a single emerald-cut stone. It has been there for months, maybe longer, or it's possible Ryan doesn't leave it in the tackle box but takes it with him in case the time is right.

Sabine has never looked at the ring. She only knows its shape by feel.

It's not as if they could ever have a real wedding, but a quiet engagement would have been nice, something symbolic. Just the two of them, somewhere safe. She lets herself imagine a five-star hotel room with a king-size bed and a spa bath. They snuck away to a B and B once—two nights in the wine country, lazy mornings, cheap champagne, a complimentary basket of fruit and chocolates. But she couldn't sleep because the night sounds were different and the bed didn't rock. Like Blue, she is not a land creature anymore; she is lighter on water; when her feet sink into the earth, she feels its gravitational force. The atmosphere is changed; her spine is compressed. It must be how astronauts feel when they return from space.

Sabine opens the box, expecting the usual pleasant flutter in her belly when she touches the ring. It doesn't come.

She knows why: the timing could never be more wrong. If, as she suspects, Ryan plans to propose on her thirtieth birthday, there's no easy way to warn him that he's running out of time. Rachel has forced Sabine's hand, and Sabine has to follow through. Even if Ryan asked, would she have said yes? She can only feel relief that he hasn't—he needs to know the truth too.

It's almost midday, later than she planned. Ryan will most likely be awake. Since she left the jetty, her mind has been flitting from one unfinished thought to the next. Rachel gave her a blank notebook and a tricolored pen. The pen is tucked behind Sabine's ear; the notebook lies in the bottom of the boat, soaking in the puddle from Blue's dripping coat. She is supposed to create a timeline of events before they meet again tomorrow: red for dates, blue for names, black for description. A basic framework, Rachel said, a guide for the interviews. They'd fact-check and fill in the blanks as they went. Pretty straightforward. Sabine shouldn't be worried.

But she is. Where should the timeline begin? The blanks cannot simply be filled in; they are not memories that need to be coaxed forward, but vivid, painful images, strung together. Pull one and the rest will come, slithering and coiling.

She summons an image: Aria, Dee. A still of their faces the last time she saw them. It is like opening a children's book to a grotesque illustration, trying to gauge whether growing up made it easier to stomach.

She measures her response now. It is as visceral as it was then: shock, followed by a sick, hollowed-out feeling. It's her own fault for daring to hope she could take charge of her fate, buy more time with Pop and relieve her guilt simply by telling the truth. Maybe there will never be a right time for Ryan's proposal. Perhaps she'll never wear his ring.

The illusion of control is fading fast.

Sabine scoops a handful of cool water to splash her hot face. Cutting the engine, she eases the tinny into the backwater opening and drifts to bump the stern of the *Kirralee*. The blinds in the bedroom are up. There's a mug set on the card table on the deck, and the mud has been recently stirred. The kayaker nosing around the houseboat? Feral carp spawning?

She ties off and steps out.

Blue follows. He sniffs the air, whining, and turns his attention to the patch of scrub behind the houseboat. The ridge of hackles along his spine is raised.

"What is it, mate?"

She follows his line of sight and spots a hunched figure about twenty meters away, poking at something on the ground with a stick. It's not Ryan. Not his broad shoulders and tanned skin, his dark curls. This man has reddish hair, a slouched back, a pimpled neck.

"Hey, Dix," she calls out.

He startles and springs to his feet.

"What are you doing?" She swings her legs over the railing, strides to where he's standing, looks down. "Oh."

A deer, freshly and raggedly disemboweled with a blunt tool, most likely teeth. Young, not much more than a fawn.

Sabine puts a hand to her mouth. She can cope with the blood, the pinkish curves of bone, the fatty intestine and the excrement—but not the eyes, open in death. She bends to close them, feeling the feathery tickle of lashes on her palm.

"What happened?"

Dixon nudges the carcass with his foot. "Dunno. Trying to figure that out."

Sabine looks around. "Where's Ryan?"

"He's taken my utility vehicle to the general store. He said he needed a few things, and someone had nicked his tinny."

"Yeah, he was asleep when I left. Catch anything down south?"

A smile, nicotine yellow. Gaping spaces between his eye teeth. He's barefoot, wearing a blood-smeared nylon apron over jeans and a undershirt.

He glances down at the gore. "Mulloway times four."

"Nice."

Blue sniffs the dead deer and backs up, stiff-legged like a dressage horse.

Dixon jerks a thumb in Blue's direction.

Sabine shakes her head. "He's been with me. He chases deer, but he's not big enough to bring one down."

"First time for everything," Dix says. "Once they get a taste for it—"

"Not Blue. You must have a stray about, and a big one too."

"Well." He takes the deer by its hind hoofs and drags it back about five meters. "I'll roll it into the ditch where it won't stink up the place."

"I'll help."

"Nah." His eyes roam over her body. "Keep your pretty self clean."

Sabine squirms and tries not to show it.

Dixon is five or six years older than her; she's known him her whole life. He can't bring himself to call her by her new name, and it was only after the fire that he started looking at her this way.

Thankfully, he's sober now. He's always contrite after he's made a drunken pass, and Sabine always forgives him, but she finds herself looking to the spot on the ridge where Ryan will first appear when he returns. She might be able to trust Dix with her secrets, but one day his collusion might come at a cost.

"I'll be out of your hair when Ryan comes back," she says.

"No rush," Dix calls, panting and heaving. "Come up later for a drink, some fresh fish."

She waves and steps aboard. Already she is thinking of a different place to moor.

———

Sabine is sitting on the bed, knees drawn to her chest. The notebook is next to her, open to the first page, still blank. She knew it would be hard, but she wasn't prepared for the surge of hopelessness that leaves her drained of energy. Dates, times, places—it's not as if she has forgotten. The opposite is true: she can't forget.

The rear of the houseboat dips. She closes the notebook.

Blue barges through the dog door, tail spinning, bringing in the smell of mud and wet dog.

Ryan enters a moment later, carrying a box. He has bought bananas, apples, overripe kiwis, a liter of shelf-stable milk, and a fresh loaf of bread. He puts the groceries away, his expression dark.

"Thanks," she says. "Sorry I took off without telling you. I didn't want to wake you."

He nods. "I figured, but I still worry. Do you know how that feels?"

She stamps out her irritation. "I'll be moving berth later and picking up Pop's spare tinny from Sammy's," she says lightly. "Tow or follow?"

He shrugs. "I should get back. It's Echo's stag party tonight, remember?"

Sabine remembers Dave Echols—Echo—from high school. A skinny kid with an infectious laugh. All she knows of him now is what Ryan tells her, and she can't picture him at all. Ryan was thin and gangly back then too; now he's six-four and heavily muscled, hardened by years of manual work.

Her eyes trace the snake tattoo that writhes up his left forearm. The humidity has made his hair even curlier. He smells of citrusy deodorant and beer.

"I have to go—there's a full gas bottle for you in Dix's ute. I did a Swap'n'Go."

She pushes the notebook aside and rolls onto her stomach, her chin resting on her hands. "Kiss me."

"A quick one."

"A long one," she says. "I never really know if you're coming back. Do you know how that feels?"

"Fine," he grumbles, but he's smiling. "Touché."

When he rolls her gently onto her back, Sabine senses the split: her body receives his weight, softening, letting him sink into her, but her mind prickles with resentment. It has happened before; now it's happening again. She won't let it ruin the time they have, but the moment he leaves her to go back to his other life, she'll cry. Sulk for a while, kick something inanimate, then busy herself with practicalities.

She watches Ryan's head dip between her knees and strokes his head as his breath warms her inner thighs. These could be their last hours together; every minute has seemed fragile and precious, but none more so than this.

She tries to wipe her mind, to focus on the present, but thoughts rush in.

It's for the best that he's leaving. They have a pact: if Sabine is ever caught, it is Ryan's turn to disappear. She won't risk having him do time for her past mistakes, nor the ones she's probably about to make. She won't tell him about Rachel, in case things go wrong. Ryan has always been afraid of change, that their protective bubble will burst. He's right to be afraid.

As if to punctuate the finality of her decision, the notebook falls to the floor with a slap. Ryan tenses, raising his head, and Sabine guides his mouth back to her. This is the part she wants him to remember.

Outside, a magpie warbles. It's a long mournful call that could have come from her own throat.

———

Ryan left an hour ago, taking his dirty laundry, a clock radio that needed fixing, the tinny, and the ring. He's due on-site in five days' time; he said he'd be back before his leave ends. A few days to nurse his hangover and visit his parents—he'll see her on Tuesday.

It's the first day of autumn, but the feeling of summer lingers. A mild northerly carries the smell of smoke and dust. The heat doesn't bother Sabine, but the river needs rain; the levels are low, debris has collected in the bends, and many of the shortest jetties are marooned like shipwrecks. Above-average temperatures are predicted for the next week.

She opens every window to let the breeze pass through. The room is barely fourteen steps across and back, and she paces endlessly, scooping out a kiwifruit with a teaspoon the way she'd eat a boiled egg.

She's relieved that Ryan didn't misread the way her eyes traced every inch of him as he stepped into the boat. He seemed to sense it wasn't passion, but a wistfulness that made her clingy, something that was unusual for Sabine. If anything, there was quiet resignation in his expression, a knowingness—often he understood her motivations before she did. On any other day, the setting would have been perfect for a proposal. She's still grieving that it might never happen.

Blue lies on his mat by the door, nose between his paws, waiting for a trigger. If she takes her seat at the helm and starts the engine, he will move to his favorite spot on the bow; if she so much as touches a towel, he'll shoot through the dog door, jump into the river, and paddle circles until she joins him. For some dogs, the word *walk* sends them into a frenzy. For Blue, it's *swim*.

He raises his head, ears pricked.

Noticing his graying muzzle with a stab of sadness, she wonders if Blue can see inside her mind too. He's past middle age, fifty-something in human years, slow to build up to a run, and growing arthritic in his hind legs. He has saved her life twice that she can remember, more if she counts the mornings she wouldn't get out of bed if not for him.

When nothing happens, Blue sighs. He continues to watch her pace.

Sabine has picked up the notebook several times. She has even written something on the first page. Then her hand started shaking, wouldn't stop, and the pen slipped through her fingers. Is it the humidity making her sweat, or fear?

She opens it again, studying her handwriting: looping, childlike, stuck in time. Hearts for dots.

Aria is born, July 13, 2000.

Pop brought Aria home from the hospital—no baby carrier, just swaddled tightly in his warmest jacket, lying on the floor of the truck behind the passenger seat. She wasn't any trouble. *Not like Dee and Sabine*, was the implication. She slept the whole way, like an angel, but she was small, born three weeks early. Because of the drugs, she could end up not right in the head, or worse, she might not live. Everything he and Dee touched ended up broken, Pop said, so he warned Sabine not to love the baby too much too soon.

But her sister was whole and perfect. Pop showed her how to boil the bottles and how much to feed Aria and how often—after that he left her to it. Sabine was ten years old.

Dee reckoned that, because Aria spent her first weeks of life with Sabine, she thought Sabine was her mother. Dee was in a state after the birth, coming down off the drugs, bleeding, hooked up to a blood transfusion. Her placenta had ruptured. When she was told there would be no more babies and she'd likely need a hysterectomy, she went crazy, ripping the tubes from her arm, spraying blood everywhere.

Sabine always wondered about that—Dee never seemed to want the babies she already had.

She shakes her head. She only knows what Pop has told her, and there's no way of checking whether any of it is true.

In giving Rachel her story, Sabine is determined there will be at least some record of *her* side—a truer version of the events that will inevitably be twisted, obscured, and covered up when she's apprehended and brought to trial, or if her past catches up with her and she doesn't make it to court at all. A record to challenge everyone who condemned her because of her family's reputation. A record for Ryan, who believes she's innocent but asks the wrong questions. And a record for herself.

In slow, robotic movements, she packs up, preparing to move the houseboat first thing in the morning. She needs to stay close enough to Pop, to Rachel, but remain hidden for now. She has to be careful not to implicate Pop and Ryan when the time comes to turn herself in. The deal with Rachel means she will be leaving this part of her life behind forever, but she's ready. Like Ryan, Sabine has been waiting for the right time.

Hypervigilance has made her wary of people, but adept at reading them. She recognized the hungry look in Rachel's eyes—she's smart and ambitious, but for all her fine possessions, she is lonely and suffering too. Can she be trusted?

Sabine will tell the truth as she knows it—for the record—but she's under no illusion that Rachel is *helping* her.

They're using each other. They are not friends.

2019

—

RACHEL

Rachel wakes to a flurry of notifications. She went to bed early after drinking half a bottle of wine and without eating dinner. Her phone was switched on, but she slept surprisingly deeply, missing emails, a call from Lexi, and a text message from her husband—*ex-husband*, she reminds herself—asking her to remove him from the insurance policies on the Audi and the river house.

Both responses to the pitch emails have come through, and she experiences an anticipatory buzz. The next half hour will be an exercise in delayed gratification. Aidan can wait too, for an entire week if she feels like it.

She glances at the clock: 8:45 a.m.

Rubbing her eyes, she slips on her dressing gown and shuffles to the kitchen. The coffee machine spells out its belligerent message: *PERFORM DESCALING OPERATION NOW.* The battery warning light on the alarm panel next to the fridge has been flashing and beeping for weeks, and the gas bottles outside are running low. The quarter-acre garden, once lush and contained, has become woody and overgrown. Thankfully, the gardener is due today or tomorrow.

Her possessions are conspiring against her, she's sure of it.

She bypasses the message on the coffee machine for the hundredth time, makes a double-shot espresso, and sips it, grimacing at the bitterness. She calls Lexi first. The phone rings forever and goes to voicemail. When she tries again, her daughter answers, sounding as if she has just woken up.

"Mum, I have a problem," Lexi says.

"What is it?"

"I got another speeding fine."

Rachel groans. It's Lexi's third in eighteen months, along with a fine for running a red light.

"I have four weeks to pay or sign a statutory declaration, but if I pay, I'll lose my license."

Rachel knows what's coming.

"Can you take the points? Say you were driving? I promise it won't happen again, but I need to get to and from work. Please—I know what you're going to say, and I'm asking you not to say it."

Lexi knows what's coming too.

"What do you think I'm going to say?"

A pained sigh. "That I am free to make choices, but I am not free from the consequences of my choices," she says in a robotic voice. "I know, but *please*. It won't happen again, I promise."

"That's what you said last time."

"Last time I wasn't driving."

"But you let someone borrow your car. Again, your choice." Rachel knows the process: indignation, followed by wheedling, then crying. She cuts her off. "Don't push me on this, Lex. We'll both end up in tears, and I don't have the time or the energy."

"But you have *zero* demerit points—"

"Exactly. Because *I don't break the law.*"

"But—"

"And don't you dare go behind my back and ask your father. We might be divorcing but the same rules apply." Before Lexi can respond, she says, "Hanging up now. Make better choices. I love you."

"Mum!"

She hangs up.

Rachel's tough love is legendary. Aidan was always the good guy. She will call Lexi back in an hour, by which time she will be resigned to her fate: three months of catching public transport to her job at the call center and burning the goodwill of friends. This time she might learn a lesson.

The half hour is up. She settles on the couch and opens the first email response to her pitch—from her ex-boss, senior editor Sophia Bennett. She scans the first line, smiling. A bite. Sophia wants an urgent meeting—on-screen if Rachel can't make it into the office. It's annoying that it took Sophia so long to respond to such a time-sensitive pitch, but at least she's interested.

The second response, from Miles Cooper, features editor, is smarmier and more demanding. It's the one Rachel wants, a chance to write the long-form article for the weekend pull-out section. But Miles wants to know what she's got. He wants proof, and by 10 a.m. this morning, if he's to commission the piece.

Rachel swears under her breath. She came out of the gates too early. She should have waited, sent him a sample of the full scoop. All she has is the photo and a shaky verbal agreement with a criminal.

She rereads the email from Sophia, noting the formal language, the standoffish tone. They didn't part on great terms. Rachel was incensed about her layoff, and Sophia hadn't gone to bat for her. Why? The great unanswered question, since Rachel had been a model employee. She suspects it was a case of woman-eat-woman—she and Sophia had been vying for the same positions since they were interns.

She opens the folder containing her research notes and clicks on the photo of Sabine. It's a perfectly clear, publishable shot, but without the full story and more evidence, it's not groundbreaking. Sending the photo to Miles as proof will buy her time and clinch the commission, and a commission will clear the way for her to smash the ball back to Sophia:

I appreciate the opportunity, but the article has been placed with another publication and is no longer available. All best.

The coffee goes cold on the table as Rachel drafts her response to Miles Cooper. It begins with a cutthroat list of demands: a negotiable deadline, minimum eight thousand words, a long byline, a dedicated photographer, the works. She proofreads carefully and doubles her per-word price because she can.

In answer to Cooper's biggest request—*Please confirm that this is an exclusive with direct quotes from the subject*—she replies yes. She cuts and pastes several paragraphs from her work in progress. There's a moment's hesitation when she attaches the photo, but she reassures herself that Miles knows the deal—he has everything to lose by leaking this story, and nothing to gain.

Miles gets what he wants. Rachel gets what she wants. Sabine gets what she wants. Everyone's happy.

Feeling exultant, Rachel presses send.

———

By 11:30 a.m. Rachel has showered and dressed; she has been shopping at the local weekend produce market, bought wine, and prepared an impressive platter of cheeses, dips, dried fruits, stuffed olives, breadsticks, and crackers; she has descaled the coffee machine and set up the dining table with her research notebooks, laptop, and video recording equipment. If Sabine has completed the timeline of events, they can launch straight into the recorded interviews.

Everything in readiness, she waits.

Despite her earlier annoyance, she calls the insurer to request the necessary forms. She texts Aidan.

Have requested a switch to a single policy.

Immediately, he sends a message back.

Thank you. A reminder that the septic was due to be pumped out at the end of last month and the gas heater needs servicing before winter. Assuming you haven't done either.

She hasn't, but both chores can wait another month or two—summer has just ended, and it's not as if there are four people wiping their arses anymore. Just one.

Already done. But thank you for your concern.

Liar, liar, pants on fire.

You're welcome. Take care.

His tone, it hurts.

They were strangers once: two ambitious students eyeing each other in the university bar, drunk on watered-down shots. Two years later they were graduates, engaged to be married, and Rachel was pregnant. Soon enough, they were parents, sharing a one-bedroom apartment with a baby who didn't sleep, struggling to pay the bills, working long hours in shitty jobs for low wages. Next, an unplanned second pregnancy, more years of scraping by, passionate fights, and make-up sex on the couch because the kids were asleep in their bed. Then, out of the blue, an unexpected windfall from Rachel's dead unmarried aunt, a promotion at work. Their first house and a second car. A partnership for Aidan at the law firm. Another home, bigger. A holiday home on the river. Five years ago, they renewed their wedding vows—at sunrise on a jetty in the Maldives, for God's sake.

Now they are strangers again.

Mo brushes against her legs. He wanders over to bat at the auto feeder with a paw, and Rachel gets up to push the button with her toe. Out of the corner of her eye, she spots a shadow moving on the driveway, a figure pushing a wheelbarrow stacked with tools. Wrinkled khaki shorts, strong brown legs, mustard-colored boots.

The gardener. Josh.

Rachel raises the blinds so she can watch him through the kitchen window.

He doesn't look older than thirty. He never knocks to announce his arrival. Today he gets straight to work on the English box with the hedge trimmer, shaving off sections of dying foliage.

She's not sure he knows what he's doing (should a hedge be pruned in summer?), but it doesn't matter—from the neck down he's a solid eight and a half. A nine right now, with his deep tan accentuating muscles carved from rock. But he has an unremarkable face compared to her ex-husband, whose classical features were so Rob Lowe perfect she never tired of looking at him. Then again, Aidan was now balding, and his body has softened and paled over the past decade. The last time she saw him wearing shorts, she was both fascinated and repulsed to notice he was knock-kneed. As a senior partner, he spends too many hours sitting, drinking too many cups of coffee at his desk under fluorescent lighting, attending too many boozy lunches on Wednesdays and Fridays.

Except, according to intel from Ben, Aidan now goes to the gym every morning with Nadja, who is twenty years his junior and so bloody nice it's impossible to hate her.

Rachel reserves her meanness for Aidan.

She is self-aware enough to admit she has let the First Wives Club down and let herself go. No body transformation, no new clothes or fresh hairstyles for her. She doesn't go out. She knows it's pathetic to sit here alone day after day, sticking pins in a figurative straw doll and placing bets on the rapid disintegration of Aidan and Nadja's relationship, but she's not hurting anyone by hoping for this shared gym ritual to reveal something revolting: Aidan's hairy back, a stray testicle. She hopes he sharts when doing squats.

Josh spots her gazing through the kitchen window. He waves.

Rachel blushes and waves back. She runs the cold-water tap, splashes her blushing cheeks.

She's a hypocrite, objectifying a man twenty years her junior. It's not a revelation—she has been doing it monthly for a few years, even when Aidan was around. *Especially* when he was around. Another minute and she would have been lost in one of her lush fantasies where Josh comes looking for a cool glass of water, only to find Rachel in the shower, the door open.

She never so much as peed or shaved her legs with the door open when Aidan was around; she never spoke about her fantasies with him, never masturbated in front of him. She worked to keep her private habits private. *Maintain the mystery!* Instead Aidan was drawn to Nadja's youthful, crass exuberance. In comparison, Rachel was boring.

This is the thing that cuts deepest: Aidan will never really know her, and now it's too late. Her children don't know her either. When Ben and Lexi look at her—with the cruel arrows of disdain aimed so unerringly by fledgling adults at their aging parents—she wants to shout in their faces: *You didn't invent flares or weed or dancing; you weren't the first do the walk of shame!*

The alarm panel emits another tiresome *beep*.

She makes a milky latte and checks the clock on the wall. If she's on time, Sabine will be here in half an hour. Rachel is looking forward to her company, however guarded and sullen a companion Sabine might be. Her mood lifts a fraction.

Josh has moved to the square of yellowed lawn below the second-level retaining wall. He starts the lawnmower, leaning into the push-pull of it. Sweat has formed dinner-plate-sized patches under his arms, and his calves are bunched with the effort.

Rachel sighs.

Even her fantasies are now in tune with her self-loathing. It's getting harder to summon the exquisite longing she used to feel whenever she allowed herself to think of being alone, the sheer delight of having nothing to do, nowhere to be, no one's needs to satisfy. It's like finally arriving at her dream destination to find the pictures in the brochure were airbrushed, the five-star reviews fake, and there's nobody to pick you up from the airport.

Coffee shoots from her nose. At least she can still make herself laugh.

———

Rachel is sitting on the end of her jetty, checking her phone, swinging her legs, when she hears a familiar voice coming from near the house.

What started as a promising morning is rapidly going downhill: Miles Cooper has not replied to her email, Sabine is late, and now her psychotic neighbor has waylaid Josh, probably whining about leaves blowing over his side of the fence.

She has resigned herself to the possibility that Sabine is not coming. She has had more than twenty-four hours to take herself as far from here as possible—she could be anywhere by now. Maybe Ray Kelly has come to rub her nose in it.

Muttering, she hauls herself up.

At least there's a witness, so he's not likely to shoot her, but by the time she makes it to the house, Kelly has gone, and Josh is packing away his tools.

"Friendly chap," he says without a trace of sarcasm.

"What did he want?"

He gestures at the fig tree near the boundary. "Said I need to prune your fruit trees back, that way you can use netting to keep the vermin and birds away."

Rachel cringes. He's dead sexy until he opens his mouth.

"Oh. What do you think?" she says.

"He has a point, but you'll lose next season's fruit." He slides a rake into the trailer. "Can't do it now anyways. Got a hot date tonight."

He gets in the ute, grinning, a wad of gum oozing between his teeth, and there goes any last vestige of mystery.

"Okay, maybe next time. My direct credit still goes straight to your account, right?"

"Yup."

"Thanks so much. See you next month," she says.

He pulls away, spraying gravel onto Rachel's shins. She turns, swearing, to find a cardboard box on the step by the front door.

As she gets closer, she puts a hand to her mouth and nose—it's the stink of something rotten. She snaps a twig from the nearest tree, pokes open the flaps to find two metal cages with spring-loaded doors. At the same time, she hears a dog barking and high-pitched whine: a boat, smaller than the one from yesterday, approaching the jetty. Inside the cages are rat traps, complete with desiccated cheese and disturbing clumps of soft gray fur.

2019

SABINE

abine puts the time at around half past two when she reaches Rachel's house at Shallow Bend. She passes Pop's place, scanning the long stretch of bank for signs of life. As she steers toward the jetty, she half expects a welcoming party of police, but there's only Rachel, standing near the house, using her hand as a visor. It's impossible to tell if she's pleased to see her or angry she's late.

Sabine spent the morning moving the *Kirralee* a couple of miles downriver to a concealed mooring spot adjacent to a patch of council-owned land. The backwater was unexpectedly shallow, only half a meter deep—all the houseboat needed—but a drop in water level could leave her beached in mud. She had to hope that wasn't on the cards. From there, it was a sweaty walk through dense bushland, a tiring swim across a wide point in the river—Blue hindering her efforts, trying to save her—and another long walk to the riverfront marina. There she picked up Pop's spare tinny from Sammy's Boat Shed, where it was stored in case she needed it. It's a risk; the boat is registered to Pop. Maybe it's unregistered—Pop's memory for details isn't great these days.

An uneasy feeling has followed her since this morning, when she discovered a second dead fallow deer on Dixon's land, this one a young doe. Its injuries were typical of canine attack—torn abdomen, shredded jugular. But Sabine heard nothing of its struggle in the night. Blue didn't bark. Tracks in the dirt showed it had been dragged almost forty meters from the site of the kill to the steep bank near the houseboat. Sabine almost tripped over the carcass, spread-eagle on its back like an offering.

She shrugs off the foreboding. She has no idea what the killings mean or what their proximity has to do with her, but she will have to be more careful. After she's finished with Rachel, she will check on Pop.

Rachel meets her at the jetty, barefoot, wearing a paisley-patterned maxi dress that shows the outline of her figure against the sun. Her body language and expression give nothing away.

"I'm sorry I'm late." Sabine steps out and ties off.

Rachel looks her over. "What happened to you?"

Sabine runs a hand though her stiff hair and glances down at her shins, covered with scratches, her white T-shirt and denim shorts rumpled and stained brown. She probably smells like dead fish.

"Sorry," she says again. "It's been a busy day."

Rachel surprises her by taking her hand and leading her up the steps.

"Where are we going?"

"You need a hot shower."

Sabine isn't about to argue. She gives a sharp whistle, and Blue bounds along the path, overtaking them.

It's cooler inside the house. Rachel shows her to a bathroom on the ground level—all white, apart from a timber vanity unit with two sinks and gold taps. Not real gold, surely. They look like real gold, and the shower, which includes a tiled bench seat on one side, is big enough for two people.

Rachel opens a cupboard in the hallway and hands her a stack of three towels, varying in size. "Here."

"I only need one towel," Sabine says.

Rachel rolls her eyes. "Take your time. Use anything you like. I'll leave some clean clothes outside the door."

Sabine opens her mouth to protest, but the door closes on her.

———

Clean, pink-skinned and smelling of a citrus-scented body lotion she found in the bathroom cabinet, Sabine carries the wet towels to the kitchen.

She used all of them: one for her body, one for her hair, and the smallest one to slough dry skin from her face and neck. Absolute luxury. She's wearing a soft pale-gray T-shirt dress over daisy-print cotton underwear and bra—all with the tags still attached. Everything is a size too big, but they're the nicest things she has worn in a long time.

Who keeps brand-new clothing on hand for guests? Rich people, she supposes. But she's a kind rich woman. A kind, sad rich woman. She wouldn't call her old, but she does seem worn down.

She searches the house for Rachel, but she is not inside, or at least not downstairs. Through the wide glass doors facing the river, she spots her, sitting on the end of the jetty, her feet dangling in the water, Blue by her side. A Jet Ski passes, and their heads turn in unison to watch.

Sadness hits her like a dull punch; she has not thought about Blue in all this. What she's doing will affect him. He's just a dumb dog, a dog who won't understand why she's left him. A dog who is better than most people on their best day.

She makes her way down the path.

"Does everything fit?" Rachel says without turning around.

"Yes, thank you." Sabine stands next to her.

"My daughter's," she explains. "They were things I bought before

she moved out, but for whatever reason, she never wore them. She's
about your size." She looks up. "We should get started. Did you bring
the notebook?"

"No."

"Why not?"

She didn't bring the notebook because she has not written anything beyond the date of her sister's birth.

"I didn't know how to begin."

Rachel shrugs. "It's okay. We'll manage."

Sabine paces up and back along the jetty. "Look, I don't even
know how to have this conversation."

Blue bumps against Rachel's back and she stiffens, drawing her
knees up to her chest. Sabine notices the way Rachel's fingers hook
into the cracks between the boards.

"You don't like the water?" she asks.

"No."

"You don't swim?"

"No."

"Never?"

Rachel shakes her head. "Not anymore. I used to water-ski. I've still
got a boat license, but I came off one time and that was it. After that,
I was afraid. I think it was something to do with having young kids—
like, it was my job to stay alive until they could look after themselves."

Sabine doesn't get it. "You can jump in right now. I'll save you."

Rachel smiles wryly. "I could live at the base of a mountain and
admire the view every day without ever having the urge to conquer
it. It's the same with the river. It's beautiful, when I'm not in it. Those
catfish…" She shudders.

Sabine laughs, then realizes Rachel's smile has faded. She feels
bad. She's not mocking Rachel—it's just confounding that she wants
to be so close to something that clearly terrifies her.

"It's not about conquering anything; it's about letting it get under your skin. A place becomes part of you—you can hear it calling, even when you're not there," Sabine says. "But if you're afraid—"

Rachel hooks her arm around Blue's neck as if he were an anchor. "I know. I mean, the logical response would be to stay away from the thing you suspect wants to kill you, or at least to try to overcome the fear. But no, I like to sit here and look at it. This is as close as I'll get."

Sabine frowns. "The river is an ecology, a system, not a *thing*. It's not trying to kill you."

"What the mind perceives as a threat can be powerful, even if it's not a real threat."

Sabine tries to think of a fear they might have in common and can't. She's not afraid of water, heights, bugs, snakes, spiders, the dark, or being alone. The only thing that terrifies her is the fear of being locked away without a fair trial, of dying before she can reveal the truth—and of living with so much guilt it feels as if it has eaten a hole through her middle.

"People with easy lives can get too civilized," Sabine says. "You need rewilding; then you won't be so scared."

"Maybe. Every time I tell the story I am a little less afraid."

"What story?"

"I went in, once, when we first bought this land nine years ago." Rachel's hand sweeps the air behind her. "There was nothing here, just flattened dirt. Council gave approval to take down the trees, all except the big gum out near the road, and there was an Indigenous consultant present, in case any bones or artifacts were unearthed. Every scoop of dirt sifted and scrutinized." Rachel glances at Sabine. "They didn't find anything significant, but ever since I've had this irrational fear that we did something wrong, that the river didn't want us here and there would be some kind of reckoning. A payback, you know?"

Sabine winds a stray hair around her finger and yanks it. *Why is*

Rachel telling me this? She isn't used to such intimate talk, certainly not between women. It makes her squirm.

"So the block was bulldozed and scraped clean, ready for the concrete slab, and we all came here for a picnic, a celebration for breaking ground." Rachel laughs. "It was a dusty, empty paddock. The kids were swimming. God, they were teenagers, and I made them wear life jackets. They were so annoyed with me, but I was convinced if I let them out of my sight, one of them would be taken as an offering."

A healthy respect for the river is necessary, but a reckoning, an *offering*? It sounds like superstition. Ridiculous. "The river can be dangerous," Sabine says evenly.

Rachel snorts. "Do you know what a self-fulfilling prophecy is?"

"Not really," Sabine admits.

Rachel spins around on her bottom to face Sabine. Her brown eyes are warm but too direct. "It's when you strongly believe something will happen, and you behave to make it happen."

The woman is talking in circles. Sabine is one for straight talk. An unpleasant feeling unfurls inside her. Rachel makes her feel vulnerable. She hates that.

"I've got things to do," she says. "Can we get on with the interview?"

Rachel goes on as if Sabine hasn't spoken. "I was sitting on a deck chair, right there." She points to the bank. "Aidan, my ex-husband, had gone up to the car to fetch some cold beers. The kids were splashing around, yelling. I thought I'd get it over and done with—I'd confront the fear, banish the thoughts; then I'd be okay."

Sabine nods.

"So I got up and waded in. It was so bloody cold. I mean, it was ninety-seven degrees in the shade, but the water was freezing."

"Snow melt," Sabine says. "From upriver."

"I didn't know it would drop off so suddenly. Five steps in and

I was under." Rachel looks across the river and shudders. "It's the memory of water closing over my head. I couldn't see a thing. I didn't even fight it; I just sank like a stone."

"Someone needs to teach you how to float."

"I couldn't. It's like I was paralyzed. Something had hold of me, like I was being pulled—"

"Tree roots," Sabine offers. "Fishing net or something. People leave their crap lying around; they chuck it overboard. Things disappear forever down there. Sure, it looks pretty, but it's a junkyard underneath."

"No," Rachel says. "*Pulled* isn't the right word. Sucked, like quicksand."

Sabine shakes her head. "Geologically that's not poss—"

Rachel shuts her down with a glare. "Sabine, you're looking for answers before I've finished telling the story. Sometimes there are no answers."

A horn blasts; a paddleboat is making its way upriver on this perfect, cloudless day. It's Saturday, and the paddleboat is crammed with people. Sabine automatically lifts her hand to cover her face. It has been this way for too long.

After a short pause, she says, "Can you please avoid saying that name?"

"You're right," Rachel says. "I'm sorry."

"I'd like to go inside."

Rachel launches to her feet. She clucks her tongue and strides up the path, Blue at her heels.

Sabine follows. At the house, she is shocked to find Blue inside, tail whipping circles, his snout shoved in a plastic contraption on the kitchen floor.

Rachel smirks. "Mo took off into the shed. I think his feelings are hurt."

"What's Blue eating?"

"Cat food."

Sabine picks an errant biscuit off the floor and sniffs it. "Oh, that's why. They're fish flavored."

Rachel opens a double-door stainless-steel fridge and takes out a bottle and a tray wrapped in plastic. "Is it too early for wine?"

Sabine doesn't reply. She's busy taking in the carefully set table: computer, notebooks, a two-inch-thick blue folder. The cover has curled, revealing sheafs of newspaper clippings and photographs inside. The urge to open it is like the urge to tear off a broken finger-nail—an ignored compulsion is more unpleasant than pain.

She reaches for the folder.

Rachel swoops, shoving a wineglass in Sabine's hand and gathering the folder to her chest. She bustles about, clears away a dirty mug, and sets the tray on the table. "Help yourself to the food." She pulls out the dining chair at the head of the table. "Can you sit here? I'll set up the webcam, and we're good to go."

"I thought you were just going to record me speaking?"

Rachel plugs a small black camera into the laptop, angling the lens to face the chair. She takes the seat opposite and opens the laptop. "Pretend the camera isn't there. We can stop at any time; just say the word."

Sabine sits in the designated chair. Despite the new clothes, she feels naked. Her scalp is sweaty and itchy. She takes a sip of wine, eyeing the camera lens; in it is an upside-down reflection of her silhouette.

"Let's just try one question. Would that be okay?"

"Fine."

"The theory was that you escaped interstate or overseas. Were you always here?"

"Where else would I be? I can't drive. I don't have a driver's license, let alone a passport."

Sabine realizes what she has admitted—ostensibly she does have a license, in the name of Emma Whelan. But Rachel doesn't pounce.

"Twelve years, and you've never been found?" she asks.

"That's two questions already."

Rachel goes quiet, her gaze unwavering.

Sabine reaches for the glass and takes a deep swallow. Blue has settled under the table, his head resting on her foot. The silence is unnerving; her legs are shuddering.

"Look, I've had some close calls. A couple of license and compliance checks. But there are hardly any water police patrols in the off-peak—it's probably easier to hide on the river than it is on land."

Rachel opens the folder. "Have you ever seen this?" She holds up a photo, then slides it across the table.

Sabine picks it up. It takes all her concentration to keep her hand steady.

She's seen the photo before, a newspaper copy, not a glossy print. As she inspects her own blank expression and the patch of singed hair on the side of her head, her hand shoots up to feel for the scar covered by a flop of heavy fringe—a fifty-cent-sized untreated third-degree burn. The hair never grew back, and the patch is faded now, the scar concave and insensate.

"I've seen it," she says.

"And how does it make you feel?"

Like falling, like spinning off into space. Rage. Pain.

What hurts is seeing the faces in the background of the picture, enlarged and in full color. Whenever she looked at her newsprint copy, she hoped it was wrong—a few misplaced dots of ink might change a person's expression, make them look angry. But this photo tells the same story: the mob outside the police station was not screaming for justice for her or her family. They knew nothing about what really happened, but she had already been judged and condemned.

"The way they looked at me—they hated me. How could they believe I killed my mother and sister? They didn't know me. They still don't know me. Nobody does."

Sabine registers the change in Rachel's expression; she seems satisfied, as if she has solved a puzzle, cracked a code.

"Keep going."

"Is it recording?"

"Yes."

The lens is a small malevolent eye.

"I don't know how."

"Sabine, you know how to have a conversation—we've just had one, down there, on the jetty. You're just telling me a story, and I'm just listening without expecting answers. If there are no answers at the end, I'm okay with that too."

Sabine now understands what Rachel has done. Oddly, she doesn't feel manipulated, but understood. She is afraid, but not of Rachel—of herself.

"I'll need another drink," she says. "And I'm still not sure where to start."

"It's simple," Rachel says. "Just tell me what I don't know about you."

2000

—

SABINE

Sabine was under the house, digging, when she saw something she wasn't meant to see.

Dee had dropped her off at Pop's that morning and gone again. Sabine didn't know where her mother went, but wherever it was it seemed to make her happy. She rarely bothered to get out of the car anymore—she just leaned across Sabine to open the door and nodded for her to go inside. But today Dee had spotted Pop on the porch and stepped out of the car, leaving the engine running. She came around to the passenger side and pulled Sabine close, leaving the flowery taste of her perfume in Sabine's mouth; when she let go, brittle strands of her long blond hair were caught between Sabine's fingers. A swirling wind whipped up her sundress, revealing her brown legs and the tight ball of her belly. Dee had grown fat over the summer.

Was it Sabine's imagination, or did Dee stroke her belly, smiling? Did Pop bare his teeth?

Pop's manner with people warmed by degrees depending on whether he thought you were a useful human being. With Sabine he was curt, easily annoyed when he was busy and mostly indifferent when he wasn't. If he was inclined to show her something—how to fix a leaky tap, how to prune the apricot trees or kill a snake—Sabine had one shot to do it right before he threw up his hands. Like the dogs, Sabine learned to stay out of his way unless summoned.

With Dee, Pop was cold. Dee had done something bad, and he'd never forgiven her. Sabine didn't know what it was, but even as a child, she could sense the danger when the two of them were alone in the same room.

"See you soon, baby," Dee said. "Be good."

Soon could mean two days or two weeks, but Sabine liked being with her grandparents. She preferred the steady flow of life on the river to the dust bowl of Far Peaks Trailer Park, where she and Dee lived amidst the constant noise and changing faces. She had grown accustomed to leaving her bag packed and enjoyed sleeping in the single bed on the shack's porch, listening to the rush of the river and the music of crickets. On the river, she could forget to worry about Dee—her wildness, the unpredictable way she swung from loving Sabine too much to not enough. Life was simpler on the river: Sabine, Nan and Pop, the shack, seven Australorp chickens without names and the ever-present dog, always a heeler.

Occasionally relatives turned up, mostly when there was a death: great-uncles who smoked and drank and fished, great-aunts who cooked and whisked away empty beer bottles and did as they were told. Dee's surly cousins brought older children who mostly ignored Sabine, except when they were making fun of her or sending her on dangerous missions. Once, they had dared her to swim out to a moored paddleboat across the river to steal cigarettes from the day-trippers. She had made it back with two packs between her teeth, only to find they'd forgotten about her and walked to town to get ice cream.

Her grandparents' shack was built on poles to escape the flood-waters. The space underneath was a couple of feet deep—enough room for a skinny nine-year-old to crawl in and do her digging with a dessert spoon. Sabine was burying the bones of a red-bellied black snake she'd found on the riverbank weeks earlier. There were similar graves all over the crawl space. Whenever she found a dead animal, she'd first place its body near the bull ant mound out near the road and wait for the bones to be picked clean, then bury it in her graveyard.

When she'd collected the snake that morning, she had made a fascinating discovery: its curved ribs held a perfect miniature skeleton inside—the snake's last meal, a skink. Like one of Dee's babushka dolls.

As she carefully arranged the bones and scooped dirt on top, Sabine heard a thud. She peered through the slats. Nan had dropped the washing basket to the ground and was hanging wet clothes on the line: Sabine's cotton underwear, Pop's Y-front jocks, and her own droopy white knickers—*smalls*, Nan called them, though Sabine didn't understand why because they were huge.

Sabine cannot picture Nan's face. What she remembers of her grandmother is abstract, pieced together with fragments of memory: soft graying hair worn in a bun, floral dresses, and slippered feet, machine-gun smacks when Sabine didn't do as she was told. Hot meals, even in summer, and always served with Pop's favorite barbecue sauce. Her light touch at bedtime, as she tucked the sheets around Sabine's body and drew them to her chin. Rules. Routine. Long silences. A different kind of love from Dee's.

She went back to digging—quietly, because she was not supposed to go under the house—when a soft clomp made her look up. The soles of Pop's boots were directly above. His frozen state was an ominous sign; he was so rarely still. The screen door hadn't creaked, which meant he hadn't let it go. He mustn't have wanted anyone to know he was there.

Sabine understood this without knowing how she knew. Instinct told her to break cover and announce her presence, but the moment passed, and it was too late—Nan did something inexplicable.

She held up a pair of Pop's underpants, pinched between her

fingers. A quick flick to shake out the creases, just like every other pair, except this time a terrible choking sound came from her. She cupped the fabric in her palms and spat into the folds, twice. Sabine watched in horror as her grandmother rubbed the spit, knuckling the fabric until it had soaked in. Another flick, and she pegged the underwear on the line as if nothing had happened.

Sabine shot upright, hitting her head on the boards above, but the noise was smothered by the sound of Pop's boots as he launched into explosive movement: three long steps from porch to washing line, arms flailing, to whip the offending underwear from the line.

Ping-ping went the pegs. He balled up his underpants.

Nan spun around, recoiled, fell.

The terrible silence of them both as Nan curled like a possum cornered by one of the dogs, while Pop repeatedly punched her face and chest. Nan bore the blows, her dress riding up and the pale flab of her belly rippling. She may have screamed, but it was impossible to tell because Pop had stuffed the soiled underwear in her mouth.

Pop stopped suddenly, panting, yelling something about a second bastard child. Then strode inside, this time letting the screen door slam.

Nan got to her feet. She pulled the underwear from her mouth, strung with spit and tears, smoothed her dress, and swayed toward the river like a drunk person.

Sabine covered her eyes, biting down on her dirt-covered fist.

———

When she left the crawl space, enough time had passed that the drone of boats had ceased and an orange sunset was turning the trees to silhouettes. She went inside to wash up in the bathroom, passing Pop slumped in his chair, the dog at his feet, staring into space, an unlit cigarette in between his fingers.

Pop must have made Sabine dinner, put her to bed, because she never saw Nan again. Later, Pop went out for an hour or more, flashlight in hand. When he returned, Nan's slippers were back in their place outside the bedroom door.

Sabine didn't ask questions—all she knew was something frighteningly adult had taken place. When she heard Pop's snore that night she crept out of her bed, knelt on the floorboards, put her hands together and said a clumsy prayer for Dee to come.

And she did, the next day. Around lunchtime, Sabine heard the car pull up. She gathered her things. Pop told her to wait until she was called, but she crept around the side of the house.

Dee's eyes shot to where Sabine stood, but she didn't give her away; Pop said something to Dee, but his back was turned and Sabine couldn't make it out. Then Dee, her face pale and her mouth tight, swung a closed fist at his face, stopping just short of hitting him.

Pop didn't flinch. He went inside without saying goodbye.

"It's just you and me, kid," Dee said.

2019

—

RACHEL

I found a body in the river once," Sabine says.

She seems unaware of the camera now, barely drawing breath between ending one story and beginning another. For a moment, Rachel thinks she has missed something.

"You mean a dead body?"

"Is there another kind?" Sabine sniffs. "It was a couple of years back. A teenage boy. He'd been missing for three days—jumped from the top deck of a houseboat while his family was on holiday and didn't come up. It was in the papers."

"What did you do?"

A shrug. "I untangled him and dragged him ashore."

"Did you call the police?" Rachel says.

"No. I sat with him, stroked his face, talked to him. I held his hand."

"That's it?" Rachel is taken aback.

"I left him where he would be found quickly. It was only a few hours."

"How did the discovery make you feel?"

"I cried. I mean…obviously he was gone and there was nothing I could do, but that was the first time it hit me about Nan. I'd always thought of her as old, but…sitting there next to him, I did the math. She was only forty-nine when she walked into the river."

Forty-nine. Not much older than Rachel is now.

"What was the finding? Suicide?" she asks.

"No, it was an accident, obviously."

"Not the boy. Your grandmother."

Another shrug. "I guess. Her slippers were on the bank."

Rachel tries to disguise a shudder. "Was it reported? What about her body?"

"Not everything floats, Rachel."

"So it wasn't reported?"

Sabine shakes her head.

Rachel is struggling to comprehend Sabine's responses to these traumatic events. She was a child when her grandmother disappeared in violent circumstances, a teenager when she lost her mother and sister and was accused of murder, a fugitive when she discovered the boy's body. But how, Rachel wonders, could a person go missing—and a missing person turn up—and Sabine do nothing? It wasn't a normal response in either situation.

The image of Sabine stroking a dead boy's face is disturbing, but her expression is now more so—it's almost serene.

"What did you say to the boy...the body?"

Her lips twitch. "I can't remember."

Rachel makes a note about the twitch for later. Perhaps it's Sabine's "tell"—something that will give her away when she's not telling the truth—because Rachel is almost certain she's lying.

"So you just let your grandmother's disappearance go?"

"I never talked about it. Not with Dee, not with Pop. Anyway, things happened fast after that."

She waits, but Sabine is somewhere else. By things "happening fast," Rachel assumes Dee had given birth to the child she was carrying, Aria. Sabine would have been around ten years old; the dates corresponded.

She changes tack. "Does your grandfather know you're here? Does he know what we're doing?"

"Not yet." Sabine flicks her hand. "He doesn't trust anyone. He's old-school. Carries a lot of guilt around with him. I think he's just waiting to die."

Rachel presses. "Guilt?"

Sabine's eyes snap back. "I'm a ghost. Everyone else is dead. It hasn't been easy on him."

"It's clear he cares about you."

"Of course he does." Sabine looks at her hands, clasped in her lap. "I know what you're thinking—Pop can't be a good man because he hit his wife. It's not that simple where I come from."

"I'm not thinking that," Rachel says, but she does think of her ex-husband, who was like the shifting sands of a desert, a landscape that could change overnight. But for all his changeable moods and question-able morals, he never raised a hand to Rachel. She was never afraid. It was pretty black and white to her: hit a woman and you're a piece of shit.

"No one is all good or all bad," she says smoothly. "Everything is shades of gray."

Sabine raises an eyebrow. It's a trick Lexi has perfected, effectively calling Rachel on her bullshit without saying a word. Lex thinks her mother has impossible standards, and she might be right.

Blue comes from under the table and tries to squeeze through the cat flap, rump wiggling. Sabine's attention turns to him, and she starts to fidget, scratching at her neck. Her hand comes away with the dress tag. She pulls, snapping the string.

Rachel gets up to let the dog out. She senses she's losing Sabine and fires another question. "Your grandfather took Dee and Aria's deaths hard?"

Sabine's head jerks as if someone has yanked her hair. Something cold slips into the room.

"Dee, not so much. She made her bed." She closes her eyes for a full five seconds.

Another tell—this one for emotional pain. Rachel wonders if Sabine is aware how much she is giving away through her body language.

Rachel has a file on Dee Kelly too. Not many photos, but plenty of character testimony and none of it glowing. A drug addict and dealer, a liar and thief, promiscuous behavior and several arrests—no convictions, interestingly—and a history of ducking and diving to avoid Child Services. Dee had been notorious in the small town of Far Peaks; the Kelly name in general made people huff and tut.

Rachel notes Sabine's curled lip. It seems she is not particularly forgiving of her mother's behavior either.

"And your sister?" she asks gently.

"Aria was a child, an innocent." For the first time, Sabine's composure truly slips. Her eyes dart in all directions; she bites down on her lower lip. "She never asked to be born. She didn't deserve what happened to her."

"No one would argue with that. Some might argue you were an innocent too."

Sabine hisses through her teeth as if Rachel has aimed a weapon at her and missed. "You can turn that thing off now."

"Would you like another drink?"

"No, thank you."

Rachel closes the laptop. "Okay."

"I'm going."

"Where?"

"To save your cat for starters." Sabine gets up. "Can I use the bathroom again?"

"Of course. You don't need to ask."

At the door, Sabine pauses. "What do you call it when women do what men expect them to do? You know, like, they put up with men's shit because that's the way it has always been?"

"Docile? Biddable? Submissive? Compliant?"

"Bigger."

"Do you mean the patriarchy? Misogyny?"

"You know a lot of words."

"It's my job to know a lot of words—and to tell the truth." Rachel taps the table with a fingernail. "So you can't leave anything out in all of this. Or it'll blow up in our faces."

It'll ruin what's left of my career.

"And is there a word for a woman who cracks because she can't take it anymore?" Sabine says quietly.

Rachel searches, but she is distracted by the realization that Sabine understands more about her grandmother than she has given her credit for. Maybe her passivity is a front, her reserve a way of protecting herself—or someone else.

"Shades of gray," Sabine says over her shoulder. "I hope there are more colors than that."

———

Rachel has taken the laptop outside to the table on the deck. It's past six and the sun is sinking, the river aglow with a wash of pale gold. Another couple of hours and it will be dark.

Sabine has been in the bathroom a long time, and there's no sign of the dog, or Mo. Could she have left without Rachel noticing? No, the boat is still there. It's a different one from yesterday's—older, with a rust-colored stain on the bow. Or the hull? She should know these things.

She lines up her phone and snaps a photo of the boat, then opens the video recording of their conversation to check the sound and picture quality.

Sabine was under the house, digging, when she saw something she wasn't meant to see.

It was strange at the time—Sabine spoke in the third person, never wavering from that point of view. Now Rachel finds it unsettling. Was it a deliberate device to avoid the recording ever being used as a first-person account or confession, or some kind of cognitive dissociation, a defense against reliving trauma?

On-screen, slouched in the carver chair at the head of the table, where Aidan used to sit, Sabine looks like a waif, despite her sharp blue eyes and determined chin. But, Rachel suspects, underneath her fragility is cunning and strength. She'd told the story of her grandmother's disappearance impassively, but on the video, Rachel can see her hands, like claws, clutching and releasing the arms of the chair.

For all her claims that she didn't know where to start, Sabine seems to know exactly what she's doing, skirting around topics that might reveal more than she's ready to disclose. Is she steering Rachel toward a predetermined conclusion? What's her agenda? Is Sabine *using* her? Something doesn't feel right. Her fear is that Sabine does not intend to tell the truth at all.

Every interview is subjective; it's up to Rachel to maintain objectivity and distance. She's a professional. She will not be manipulated.

She checks her emails.

Miles Cooper has responded, agreeing to her terms—all but one. He has set a hard deadline for the piece, six days from now, and he wants to book dates and times for a photographer. There's a contract attached to the email.

"Shit," she mutters.

Given Sabine's reserve, this might be the first deadline Rachel will miss. Her patient approach isn't going to work; the timeline will need rejiggering.

Where the hell is she?

As if she can hear her thoughts, Sabine appears at the top of the path, Blue by her side. She has put her mud-stained clothes back on.

"Where have you been?"

"I was…unwell. It must have been the wine on an empty stomach."

She does look washed-out under the tan.

"Can I get you anything?"

"I'm fine now."

From the corner of her eye, she spots the cat slinking past the shed, his back arched and tail bristled in alarm. When he sees the dog, he completes a semidignified turn and heads back to his hiding spot.

If Sabine accepts the proposal she's about to make, Mo might never recover.

"I don't know where your houseboat is, but wouldn't it make better sense for you to stay here? While we're interviewing? I have plenty of room."

Sabine's expression doesn't change.

"And if you're okay with it, I'd like us to go to Far Peaks. To the trailer park."

Not a flicker.

"Tomorrow," Rachel adds.

She's astonished when Sabine agrees.

"Okay. I'll go and pull the boat up."

"Where?"

"Pop's. There's a dirt ramp. I'll hide it in the trees."

Rachel gets up. "It'll be heavy—I'll help you."

Oh God, does she mean get in the water?

Sabine looks at Rachel's dress with an open-mouthed grin, revealing her chipped tooth. She raises her arm and flexes a tanned bicep. "I don't need help."

"So you'll stay?"

A nod. "Just for tonight. Then I have other plans."

"You'll be safe here, I promise."

Sabine smiles again, but this time without humor. "But are you safe with me, Rachel?"

She's already striding to the jetty, the seat of her shorts stained with dried mud.

As Sabine unties the boat, Rachel slips inside, taking the laptop with her. The scent of orange blossom lingers—a body lotion she has only used once because it gave her a headache. Lexi's dress is folded over the back of the couch.

How long was Sabine alone in the house? Ten, fifteen minutes?

The folder is still on the table. She opens it, riffles through the pages and images; she is so familiar with its contents she would know in a heartbeat if something was out of place. Nothing seems to be missing, but another wave of suspicion surges through her.

There isn't a lock on the office door, but she can hide the folder and laptop away in the floor safe. She will remember what Sabine has been accused of. She will sleep with her bedroom door closed tonight.

2019

—

SABINE

R achel is cooking penne carbonara on a stainless stovetop with eight gas burners. She has reopened the bottle of white wine from earlier and filled two glasses, occasionally splashing generous amounts from the remainder of the bottle into a pan of sizzling bacon and onion. Disco music plays from a digital radio as she moves from sink to fridge to stovetop, singing along, dancing lightly on her bare feet.

In the *Kirralee*, Sabine has a single-burner butane stove Ryan bought to replace the cooktop when it stopped working. She's used to living on sandwiches and toasties, overripe Riverland fruit from roadside stalls, canned food, and one-pot meals. She is overwhelmed by the smells emanating from Rachel's kitchen.

"*Don't blame it on the sunshine…*" Rachel sweeps her arm in an arc. Another sweep, horizontally. She spins around and thrusts her hips, hamming it up. "*Blame it on the boogie.*"

Sabine gives a strained laugh.

"You missed out on the seventies!"

"Yep."

Rachel's behavior is freaking her out. She knows most of the songs and some of the lyrics, and there's a clear invitation to sing along—but Rachel is trying too hard, and someone who tries too hard to win Sabine over is a potential threat. Kindness makes her nervous. Too many people have smiled at her just before they stabbed her in the back. She'd like nothing better than to drink enough wine to soften the sharp edges of her anxiety, but she needs to keep her guard up.

This is not exactly a sleepover among friends.

"I haven't cooked for anyone in a while," Rachel says. "I miss it. I've been living on frozen or fried food."

"It smells really good."

She picks up the packet of pasta. "How hungry are you? Scale of one to ten."

"Nine," Sabine says, and she means it. "How long will it take?"

"About twenty minutes."

Sabine squirms. She's not sure of dinner etiquette, but she suspects she's about to be rude.

"I thought I'd go and see Pop. He might spot the tinny and worry."

Rachel sets the pasta down. "It's fine. The sauce can sit awhile." When Sabine doesn't move, she flaps her hand. "Take the dog with you so I can find Mo and feed him."

"Sorry. I'll be quick."

Blue has been lying outside on the mat, a wet nose pressed to the concertina door, his breath fogging the glass. Sabine didn't trust him not to jump up and snatch food from the counter, although right now Rachel probably thinks Blue's manners are better than hers. When she opens the door, he shoots straight down the path to the jetty, only to skid to a stop when he realizes there's no boat.

"Here! Come!" She heads up the steep driveway and onto the road.

For years now she has only approached Pop's place from the river. Everything is new: the bright streetlights, the shiny letter boxes with brass numbers, the boat trailers and picket fences, and the rows and rows of council bins. The old road has been widened and freshly graded; the recently built shacks on the opposite side are stacked and squeezed on tiny lots.

Pop must hate this.

Blue has found his way through the slackened fence and is already waiting on the other side of the front gate. If he wasn't sick, Pop would have fixed that—tensioned the strands, added chicken-wire patches or barbed-wire traps. In the beams of light from the house across the road, she can see other signs of neglect: ruts in the driveway, grass shooting from the gutters of the house, a flat rear tire on his beloved ute.

Blue runs off.

"Dammit," she says.

She whistles, but he's gone, probably straight to the midden to roll in something foul. He'll upset Pop, get a boot for his trouble.

She walks along the driveway and around to the porch. The street-side door hasn't been used for decades, not since Pop started using the hall to store old furniture. He's not a hoarder, but he never buys anything new, and he's not the least bit sentimental. He refuses to throw perfectly good furniture away.

She steps onto the porch and sees him through the dirty window, sitting on the couch. For a moment he's perfectly still, arms slack at his sides, staring at the TV; when he hears the steps creak, he turns his head slowly and glares at her.

Sabine opens the screen door and goes inside.

"Thought your dog was Polly," Pop says, his gaze faraway. "Thought you was Dee."

Sabine runs a hand through her short hair. She looks less like her mother since she cut it off. Has she missed it—misdiagnosed his agitation in recent years? Is he getting the old timer's disease?

"Don't pull that face. I'm not losing my mind," he says. "Just jump back sometimes."

The TV volume is turned down. An empty can of Irish stew lies on the kitchen counter, crawling with ants.

"Sit," he says.

"I'll clean this up first."

"Do what you have to do," he mutters, reaching for the old tobacco tin he keeps stuffed between the couch cushions. He rolls a cigarette and flicks his Zippo.

Pop never lit up inside the house when Nan was around. Only ever on the porch. Smoke rises and creeps along the low ceiling. Sabine is dismayed to discover it smells sweeter than tobacco.

She puts the can down. "I know it's back."

He grunts.

"Pop, the cancer is back, isn't it?"

"It never went anywhere."

"But you told me the doctor said—"

"I never saw no bloody doctor." The bristles on his chin glisten with spit.

"Where is it?"

"All over." He gestures at his body as if it is a broken, useless thing. Sabine chokes out, "Does it hurt?"

"Not at this precise moment in time," he says, inhaling.

"Who's getting the weed for you?"

He doesn't answer, but she knows. It's not that she begrudges Pop finding relief any way he can, but if Dixon is supplying, it means he's likely growing it on Pop's patch again, snapping a few buds here and there and giving Pop a blokey pat on the back. *There you go, old fella.* Zero risk and all the reward.

"I wondered why you let the blackberries grow wild."

"You shouldn't be here." Pop points through the window. "Her Highness next door. She's got something to say about everything, and I gotta be nice to her because of you."

"About that," Sabine says.

"Yeah, I wondered what you were up to. I heard you picked up the spare tinny."

"She's a writer. For the newspapers."

He shakes head. "Don't trust that woman, Beenie."

"I have to tell someone. If he comes after me—if he finds me—there won't be a living soul left to make it right for Aria and Dee."

Pop puts up a hand to shush her. "What I don't know won't kill you."

His eyes are red and watery, and it's not the smoke.

"She knew it was me, Pop. I had to buy us some time. And anyway, we can't live like this anymore. It's not living."

She touches his shoulder, a gesture of reassurance. She expects him to shrug her off, but Pop just looks defeated. Or maybe it's relief, a giving in. If he didn't have her to worry about, he might crawl off someplace to die without a fuss, like an animal.

"There are things I have to tell you," she says. "And a few things I need to ask."

"Before I cark it, you mean."

"Before—" She stops.

"Over my dead body." He wheezes a laugh.

Sabine doesn't find any of it funny. Pop doesn't look after himself because he's too busy looking out for her. If he suspects things are about to blow up, he's likely to go off and do something reckless, like shoot someone for real. All that target practice—he's not going to miss.

"Me and Rachel, we made a deal." When he shakes his head, Sabine says, "I had to, Pop. It's the only way to make sure someone else knows, someone outside all of this. I have to believe there are good people out there too."

"And you think she's one of them? Like you're such a fine judge of character."

"She has integrity."

He whoops and slaps his knee. "Integrity! Same thing our fine boys in blue are supposed to have?" He snorts. "They look after their own; you know that better than anyone. We look after our own too. Remember that."

"Have you counted lately? There aren't many of us left."

Suddenly he reaches up and grabs her hand. "There's a yellow envelope in your nan's dresser. Go and get it."

Sabine can't remember the last time Pop touched her that wasn't in anger.

Reluctantly, she lets go and heads down the musty hallway that runs through the middle of the house. The dresser is at the end, barricading the front door. She notes the layer of grime coating the warped timber top. Memories rise and settle like the dust; here are the pale rings left by Nan's cups of tea, her jewelry box, her paddle brush, still tangled with strands of her hair.

The yellow envelope is in the top drawer, on top of Nan's underwear.

She gasps, then coughs and breathes deeply—if she shows she is upset, Pop will be upset.

The dust tells her the envelope has been in the dresser for some time. It's not thick, a few sheets of paper, maybe four. When she runs her fingernail under a corner of the flap, the seam of spit and glue cracks open.

"Bring it here!" Pop yells.

She tucks the flap inside and takes the envelope to him, hands it over.

He thrusts it back. "If you trust her so much, give it to her next door."

"What is it?"

"It's legit, signed by one of those JP people. Two witnesses."

In that instant she knows what it is. His confession.

"Same deal—something happens to you or me, she opens it. Her, not you. Understand? I'm too goddamn tired to argue."

Resigned, she nods. "Why are you doing this now? It won't change anything."

He butts out the joint. "Because I don't want the cops getting their hands on it before you do."

He's right. Although she was never here to witness the raids, he has told her about them. The image of Pop cuffed to the porch post while Sergeant Billson and his cronies tear the place apart is as vivid as if she had been there too.

"And because I'm dying," he adds.

"I know." Again she struggles to hold back tears.

"Why are *you* doing this now?"

"Because you're dying," she chokes out.

"You should just go, girl," he says gruffly. "Start your life again someplace else."

"I can't start anything until this is finished. I can barely live with myself now."

"And what if it doesn't change anything?"

"It will, Pop. It has to."

A kind of weary understanding passes between them.

"I'll see you off." He struggles to get up from the couch.

"Don't get up. I'll be fine. I could bring you some leftover dinner later?"

"Don't bother. These days it all goes in and comes out looking the same." Again, he waves at his wasted body. "Before you go, you'd better tell me what you need me to do."

Sabine's heart flaps like a wounded bird. He's so frail, so impossibly vulnerable, and he's trying not to let her see. She has experienced many different kinds of love; Pop's is as rigid and scarred as the old newel post outside, the one with Sabine's and Aria's heights etched in the wood. Like the post, it has always been there.

He won't let her hug him, and she's not sure she would know

how. She does know he needs her assurance that—this time—she won't run.

"You don't need to do anything," she tells him. "I'm stronger this time."

"That's my girl."

There's a glimmer of his old spark. Despite her fear, she convinces herself it will all be worth it.

———

Sabine sees Rachel before Rachel spots Sabine. She's standing inside the glass doors, looking out at the moonlit river. The curtains are not drawn, and it appears she has turned on every light on the lower story. Her eyes are wide, and Mo is pressed against her legs, the tip of his tail wriggling like a worm on a lure.

The outside light switches on; when Sabine reveals herself, Rachel and the cat jump and separate.

Sabine is irritated. *Why is Rachel afraid? What does she have to be afraid of, living in her mansion with all these sensor lights and high-tech security?* But beneath her irritation, Sabine is surprised by how badly she wants it—a life like this, a home that stays in one place.

Rachel unlocks the door and slides it open. "You were a gone a long time. I was worried I'd have to come looking for you. Is your grandfather okay?"

Her face is slack with relief, and Sabine's annoyance fades. Rachel seems genuine.

"He's fine," she lies.

"Where's Blue?"

"He takes off sometimes. He knows how to find me. He'll turn up when he's ready."

On the coffee table in the lounge, Rachel has arranged two bowls of steaming pasta, a salad, bread. More wine.

Sabine chooses the floral couch again. She doesn't like the sensation of leather, the sticky rub of skin on skin, and she hasn't the heart to tell Rachel she no longer has any appetite. Reluctantly, she pulls the yellow envelope from her back pocket and slides it across the table. She leaves her hand resting on top.

Rachel raises one eyebrow. "What's this?"

"Pop gave it to me. He says you're to open it, but only if something happens to me or him."

She frowns. "What might happen?"

Sabine doesn't reply. Rachel will find out soon enough.

"Do you know what's in it?"

"Yes."

Their eyes meet in a moment of complicity. Rachel's are bright with curiosity, Sabine's with unshed tears.

"Should we?" Rachel asks.

Sabine almost gives in, but what is in that envelope will only test Rachel's integrity further.

"Not right now. Keep it somewhere safe."

Rachel inclines her head and tucks the envelope in the blue folder. "We can talk while we eat. If it's okay, I'll just record the audio this time?" She pushes a bowl toward Sabine, taps on her phone, and sets it down on the table. "Where were we?"

"My mother," Sabine says. "Now I should tell you about Dee."

2000

SABINE

There was no mistaking Dee's mood on the drive home to Far Peaks. She turned up the music, wound down the windows, and smoked cigarette after cigarette, swerving across double white lines to overtake slower vehicles. A trip that should have taken just over an hour turned into three as she took detours along the backstreets of various small towns. When Sabine asked the inevitable question—*Are we there yet?*—Dee turned to her with a mystified look, as if she had forgotten Sabine was there.

Sabine, still confused about what had happened between her grandparents, was furious with her mother for driving like a lunatic. *What is up with her? Why doesn't she want to talk? How can she be fat and thin at the same time? Why is her body shaking?* And Sabine was scared; she sensed the danger was following them home.

Tired, hungry, and anxious, she crawled over the console onto the back seat and fell asleep.

Sometime later she woke alone, her bladder bursting.

It wasn't the first time Dee had left her alone in the car, but this time it was parked behind a service station she didn't recognize. Dee was nowhere to be seen.

Sabine fidgeted, remembering Dee's rule that she should never leave the car, but she couldn't hold on, and the toilets were right there, less than ten steps away. She'd be quick.

She got out, leaving the interior light on.

The toilet door creaked open, and she checked behind it, the way Dee had shown her. Four cubicles, two on each side; three open doors, one closed and engaged. She bent down to peer underneath—no visible feet. Perhaps kids had locked it and climbed over to get out.

Sabine went into an end cubicle and let her bladder go with a sigh. Once she'd finished, wiped, and flushed, she went out to wash her hands. When she turned off the tap, she thought she heard a cough, followed by silence, the loaded kind. Like a held breath.

"Dee?" she whispered.

No reply.

She opened the exit door and let it go but stayed inside. Seconds later, another cough. Sabine did what a boy did to her at school: she stood on the adjacent toilet and peeked over the partition.

Dee was huddled on the closed seat, a glass pipe grasped in her hand. Her eyes shot up, and she whipped it behind her back.

"Get out, get *out!*" Dee screeched. "I told you, *never* leave the car!"

Sabine climbed down, overcome with shame, embarrassed for Dee. "I needed the toilet."

"I was sick," Dee said. "Everything will be fine in a minute. Take five dollars out of my bag. Buy a drink or something to eat, and wait in the car."

It was twenty minutes before Dee returned. The shaking had stopped. When she got in the car, she pulled Sabine close, stroking her hair; she kissed her neck and sang *sorry sorry sorry*.

Dee was fine, like she promised. She was better than fine.

———

The next time Sabine woke, the car was parked in a bay outside the trailer park. It was getting dark, and the kiosk had closed. Dee believed superstitiously that you should never wake a sleeping baby. But Sabine was not a baby anymore, and she was beginning to wonder if Dee let her sleep because there were things she didn't want her to see.

Like whatever she had been doing in the toilet.

She popped the trunk release and hauled her bag from the car. Though she usually avoided it, she took the shortest route to the residents' section, past the rows of trailers that housed off-shift miners—cranky men who drank in the morning and sat around playing cards, who yelled at the kids if they played nearby.

When she reached the van, everything was dark. She switched on the night-light by the annex door and crept inside.

Dee was lying on the double bed behind the curtain, flat on her back, snoring. Her dress was drawn tight, her swollen belly like a hill. Sabine reached out to turn her over, but Dee stirred and rolled toward her.

Fascinated, Sabine took a risk: she placed her hand against Dee's belly and pressed. It was firm, not the same as the bloat after a meal, and she noticed several things at once: a flutter, a ripple under her taut skin; the glass pipe on the table next to the bed; a sweet smell, like the trailer park toilets after they were cleaned.

Perhaps the danger was Dee.

It was months before she saw Pop again.

The residents' section of Far Peaks Trailer Park was close to the noisy freeway. It resembled a shanty town, and Dee's van was the worst: a rusting 1971 Viscount Explorer set on cinder blocks, with a leaky gray canvas annex and a three-yard TV antenna that spun like a windmill in bad weather. Dee had plugged the holes in the canvas using a bike-tire repair kit she'd found left behind in an on-site van (always worth checking the cupboards and drawers when guests left), but it still rained as much inside as out in the annex.

The van didn't cost Dee a cent, not in real money. She kept Arnie the caretaker "fixed up," and he "overlooked" the rent. *A mutually beneficial arrangement,* Dee called it. Arnie was all right, just a bit sad and lonely, and Dee was difficult to refuse. On her good days, she was hard to look at directly, like the sun.

But Dee lost her mind after Nan disappeared. She got angry over little things; she locked Sabine out of the van for hours at a time, claiming she had to sleep. Though Far Peaks Area School was only a fifteen-minute walk from the trailer park, Dee forbade Sabine to walk there alone. Sabine's attendance dropped, and she fell behind. Dee scratched until she bled, she forgot to buy food, and her belly got bigger while the rest of her shrank. And her eyes—she looked as if something was eating her from the inside.

Sabine understood it was her fault. Dee said it was too much, looking after Sabine all the time. She needed the occasional break, time away, and she didn't mean for one night. She wanted days or weeks, and since Nan was gone and she wasn't talking to Pop, she had to find another solution.

That was when she started being nice to the neighbors.

Bram and Faith Mitchell were both in their late seventies and long retired. Their on-site van was almost new, attached to a solid annex with a concrete foundation. Inside, there were shiny appliances and frilled curtains Faith had made herself, and an en suite bathroom. In the area around their van, she had planted flowering bulbs in raised garden beds and hung wind chimes and bird boxes from the trees.

Dee said they were busybodies, but Sabine always smiled and said hello. Faith had a nice face, kind and interested. Bram was good with his hands; he could fix anything. He'd offered to fix the aerial: *It's basically a propellor that will take somebody's head off during a strong wind*, he said. Dee told him to fuck off. She called him a kiddie fiddler behind his back. Sabine knew what a kiddie fiddler was, and she knew Bram wasn't one.

But one day Dee cornered Faith, turned on her million-dollar smile, and asked if she could keep an eye on Sabine.

"I've got to run some errands. Maybe you could make sure she eats dinner and goes to bed on time?"

"You're leaving her overnight?" Faith said.

Dee shrugged. "She's all right by herself. She's a smart kid."

Faith frowned at Dee's belly. "When's the baby due?"

"Three months."

It was the first time Sabine had heard Dee say anything about the baby.

"Right-o. You leave Sabine with me."

Faith made up a bed in her annex and walked Sabine to school the next morning. Dee was gone three days. Faith made breakfasts, bacon and egg rolls or fluffy pancakes, which they ate on the way to school, and she packed lunches with sandwiches and fruit.

"Tell me about your mum," Faith said on the second morning as they walked. "She's a hard one to get to know."

Sabine stiffened. She was embarrassed—Dee swore a lot and banged about, and sometimes she smelled bad—but Sabine was protective of her. Dee said family had to look out for each other because they had no one else.

She pressed her lips together and stared at the ground.

Faith let it go. "What about your friends at school? Tell me about them."

"I've got lots of friends, but Taryn is the best."

"That's a pretty name. And what do you want to be when you grow up, young lady?"

"Rich," Sabine said. "Rolling in it."

A wry smile from Faith. "And what will you do with all your money?"

"I'll build a big house by the river, and I'll look after Dee."

Faith was quiet after that, squeezing Sabine's hand until it hurt.

After Dee came back, Faith still made Sabine's lunches and walked her to and from school. Sabine insisted she was fine to walk on her own, but Faith said she needed the exercise to loosen up her bones. For the first time, Sabine had near-perfect attendance.

The next time, Dee disappeared for a week. When she came back, she was different. She seemed content, as if her worries had disappeared. She was more tolerant of the Mitchells, allowing Faith to mother Sabine, letting Bram potter around without spitting her usual insults. And when the policeman came to do his checks, which seemed to be happening with more frequency, Dee was calm, in control. She opened the van door, offered no resistance, spoke to him with respect. Started calling him *Logan*. Sometimes there was yelling and the van shook, but Dee said she was onto a good thing and Sabine shouldn't worry. By now the baby was the size of a basketball under her dress.

One afternoon Sabine and Faith returned from the grocery store on Main Street to find the unmarked but recognizable police four-wheel drive in the outside parking lot, an officer in the passenger seat. As they drew closer to Dee's trailer, the door swung open. Dee appeared briefly, her hands clawing at the air, before a closed fist yanked her back inside by the hair. The door slammed.

Faith took Sabine into her van and used her mobile phone to call Bram. When she hung up, she made hot chocolate and set a plate of biscuits on the table.

Sabine started to cry. "Is Dee in trouble again?"

"I don't know, honey." Faith stroked her cheek. "Why do you think the police are here?"

"He's doing his checks," Sabine said. "That's what Dee says."

"Okay. Drink your chocolate."

Minutes later, Dee was outside, eyes wild, breathing heavily. Her right cheek was red and puffy. "Where's Beenie?"

Faith opened the door wide. "She's right here."

"I need her with me."

Faith shook her head. "What she needs is—"

Sabine never found out what she needed.

"Mind your own business!"

Dee pushed Faith aside so roughly she staggered and banged her hip on the corner of the table. By the time she'd righted herself, Dee had pulled Sabine from her seat and shoved her out the door.

Once inside their own van, Dee locked the door and performed her rapid switch from hostility to elation. "We're going to be fine now," she said, and fanned out a wad of cash on the quilt. "I've got us sorted. We're rolling in it."

Sabine had never seen so many fifty-dollar notes. "Where did you get all this money?"

Dee winked. "Suitcase by the side of the road."

"Are we allowed to keep it?"

"Sure. We can buy anything we want."

"We should buy a new bed and diapers for the baby," Sabine said. "Can I have a brand-new bike?"

"Maybe an old one."

"New clothes?"

"We can only have nice things *inside*." Dee grabbed Sabine by the shoulders. "Don't let anyone in the van know, not even Faith. You can't tell anyone about the money, or they'll take it away."

"Okay."

Dee bought a big-screen TV that she mounted on the wall at the end of her double bed, and a DVD player. Sabine couldn't see the screen unless she was lying on the bed too, which Dee only allowed when she was in a good mood. The picture was so bright and close, it made Sabine squint.

For a while things were fine again. Sabine didn't even mind when Dee locked her out of the van so she could take her naps—she had a secondhand BMX, and Faith was there when Dee wasn't.

The morning Dee went into labor, Sabine woke to the sound of a plate smashing on the floor.

Dee had one arm curled under her belly, bracing herself on the table with the other. She bent double. "Oh, Jesus, not now," she moaned.

"What's wrong?"

"Go next door."

"Faith and Bram aren't there. They've gone on holiday, remember?" Sabine said.

"They live on fucking holiday—can you stay at Taryn's?"

"Not if you're going to be gone a long time, Dee."

Dee's expression hardened. She swore again. "You'll have to call Pop."

Sabine picked up Dee's mobile from the table.

"Not that one. Ask Arnie if you can use the office phone."

"What do I say?"

"Tell him he needs to come pick you up from the hospital. You'll have to stay with him until I come home."

"How are we going to get to the hospital?"

Dee let go of her belly long enough to pick up two pillows from her bed. "How old are you?"

"Ten."

"How old was I when I learned to drive?"

"Ten."

"How many times have I showed you how to drive the car?"

Sabine thought about it. "Exactly ten."

"See? Ten is our lucky number. Now, let's go before I drop this puppy on the floor." She thrust the pillows at Sabine.

Sabine was blubbering now. "I can't, Dee!"

"You have to."

"I can't. I'm scared, and you're bleeding everywhere." She pointed to the linoleum floor.

Dee looked down. "Oh, shit. Seriously, get the car, Beenie."

"Okay," she sobbed.

"That's my girl. You can do it."

"I can. I can do it."

"Yeah, you can."

———

When they took Dee into the operating room, the doctors told Sabine to sit in the waiting room, and a nurse let her use the landline phone to call Pop. He took so long to get to the hospital she had decided he wasn't coming. The first she knew he was there was when she woke to a finger poking her ribs.

"It's a girl," he said. "Your mum's got some trouble. They've gotta keep her here."

"What's wrong with her?"

He shrugged.

"I'll help look after the baby, Pop."

"Not yet. They're keeping her too. You can come home with me for now."

They made it almost the whole way to the river without speaking. Pop kept chewing his tongue—something he did when he was out of tobacco or trying not to swear in front of Sabine.

They pulled up at a set of lights.

"It'll be okay, Pop," Sabine said. "Dee will be all better now the baby's out."

He sighed. "It wasn't the baby making her sick." Pop turned. "You've gotta take care of your baby sister. She's not bad like the rest of us. You've gotta protect her."

"From what?"

Sabine knew there were all kinds of bad people: cops, teachers, social workers—anyone with a badge or a gun. Pop's look meant he was serious. She'd better not mess up.

"From Dee," he said.

2019

—

RACHEL

Rachel wakes from a broken sleep to the familiar stillness and silence of the house.

It takes her a few moments to remember she has guests. She allowed Blue to sleep in the downstairs bedroom with Sabine, but only if she kept him there with the door closed. That way Mo could come and go as he pleased. Given the stricken expression on the cat's face every time he turned a corner to find the dog still there, she doubts he came into the house at all. She has long suspected he moonlights as a stray anyway, begging for food from the neighbors.

She puts on her dressing gown and slippers and scuffs downstairs. At the end of the hall, the guest bedroom door is open, the queen-size bed neatly made. In the kitchen, last night's dishes are washed and drying on the rack, a tea towel spread over the stack like a blanket.

From outside comes a steady thud, like a drumbeat.

She hurries through the sliding doors and spots Sabine under the branches of the apple trees, tossing windfall apples into a bucket with perfect aim. She's wearing Lexi's gray dress. The front is marked with beads of blood from her scratched arms.

As Rachel approaches, Sabine says, without turning around, "I set a trap for you."

"A trap?" Rachel frowns.

Sabine faces her, brushing her damp fringe to the side. "For the rats."

Rachel steps forward to peer through the branches at the trap, mounted in the *Y* of the trunk and secured with cable ties. At least half a block of her most expensive cheese is sitting inside the cage, sweating in the morning sun.

"Well, Bruny Island saffron-infused cheddar should do it," she says.

"I couldn't find any peanut butter."

"What happens if I catch one?"

"Knock it on the head with a brick."

Rachel's smile disappears. Her hand flies to her mouth. "Oh, I couldn't."

"Then tie off the cage and dunk it in the river for half an hour." Sabine hands her the bucket of rotting apples. Most of them have been hollowed out, leaving skin and browned core. "You have to get rid of these or they'll keep coming."

It's exactly what Ray Kelly had told her.

"Fine, but I can't kill anything," she says. "It's not in my nature."

Sabine regards her with a hint of impatience. "Think of it as a mercy killing."

"Rats are supposed to be very intelligent."

"If they're so smart, they'd know it was a trap." Sabine ducks under a low-hanging branch. "You'd kill if you were starving, threatened or desperate. After the first time, flesh is just meat."

Rachel picks up the bucket. The first time? Are they still talking about rats?

"I'll put these in the green waste and make us some breakfast," she says.

Sabine looks pale. "I'd rather just get today over with, if you don't mind."

Rachel struggles to work out what has triggered her apprehension, then remembers: they're heading to Far Peaks. Back to the scene of the crime.

"Well, *I* need coffee first. And you need a change of clothes."

Sabine looks down at the bloodstained dress. "Oh, sorry."

"No problem. We'll find something else in Lexi's wardrobe, I'm sure." A thought hits. "Where's your dog?"

"Pop will look after him for the day. I can't trust him to stay here."

Rachel has turned to head up the path when Sabine calls out. "Rachel?"

She looks back. Sabine has her ankles crossed, her arms spread— she looks like a scarecrow. Or a person prepared for sacrifice.

"Do you think we could try to make me look...not like me?"

———

In the spare room, Rachel slides garments on coat hangers along the rack, discounting them one by one. Nothing she owns will fit Sabine, and Lexi's leftovers are all of a type: stretchy material, muted colors, elasticized waistbands and flowing cuts. The shelves are stacked with oversized T-shirts, leggings, jeggings, and baggy jeans. In the drawer there are neat piles of pure-cotton full-brief underwear and half-cup bras in floral prints.

No wonder Lexi left all this stuff behind. Rachel has completely missed the mark, trying to dress her sophisticated adult daughter like a middle-aged woman.

"Take whatever you want. It'll only end up going to the thrift store."

It comes out more sharply than Rachel intended and Sabine freezes, hovering uncertainly by the door.

"Here, fill this up." Rachel hands her an empty beach bag with rope handles.

Sabine moves slowly to the wardrobe. She inspects the clothes, pulling each garment from its hanger and holding it to her body for size. She discards a paisley beach dress, then folds a pair of ripped jeans and a white short-sleeved tie-front blouse and places them on the end of the bed. Not much goes back into the wardrobe. Judging by the expression of wonder on her face, all her Christmases have come at once.

"Thank you. This is too much. Really."

Sabine chooses a matching set of underwear and turns to face the wall. She pulls the T-shirt dress over her head and reaches behind her back. Her bra, gray and sagging but loose in the cups, stretches too tightly across her back. Her skin is deeply tanned all over but marred with fresh bruises and old scars. Her body looks strong and fragile at the same time.

The gray bra drops to the floor. Sabine crosses her arms to cover herself.

"I'll leave you to it," Rachel says, closing the door.

Flushed with shame, she goes to her office to gather everything she needs for the day. Without saying a word, Sabine has a knack for making Rachel check her privilege. When she was only seventeen, Sabine had lost her mother—was there enough time to receive the knowledge passed from mothers to daughters? *Feel your breasts for lumps. Don't leave a tampon in too long. Always pee after sex.*

She packs a carry-on suitcase with her laptop, SLR camera, and the blue folder. From the drawer under her desk, she retrieves two enlarged detailed maps.

Rachel grew up on the coast; she spent most of her adult life living in the city and suburbs. Shallow Bend and the wider Riverland district had seemed remote at first—140 miles from the city, no convenient chain stores, over half an hour to the nearest hospital. But traveling to Far Peaks, a further ninety miles inland, squarely in the arid zone, had put things into perspective.

The map of Far Peaks shows a typical rural town grid, the main street a backbone down the center. The police station is located on the major intersection opposite a BP service station. At last check, the town's population had fallen from around six thousand during the mining boom in the nineties to just over four thousand at the last census, three years ago. The map of the trailer park is a copy of a relic from around the time of the fire. Rachel has drawn up a legend and marked the map with eleven points of interest, numbered and circled in red:

1. Kelly, residential site 112 (bodies of Dee and Aria Kelly found inside)
2. Mitchell, residential site 113 (Faith Mitchell found alive/body of Bram Mitchell found outside, closer to 112)
3. Shoosmith, residential site 111 (bodies of Ellen, Gary, Michael, and Jack Shoosmith found inside)
4. Residents' camp kitchen and toilet block (body of Constable Logan Billson found on path)
5. Adjacent to residential site 111 (unoccupied), propane tanks x 6 in locked(?) cage (location of second explosion at approx. 11:21 p.m.)
6. Sites 40–54, donga accommodation
7. Trailer park office (Arnold Willis, caretaker, asleep in private accommodation at rear)
8. Main parking lot
9. Dee Kelly's Toyota Camry parked here (location of first explosion at approx. 11:15 p.m.)
10. Secondary trailer park exit leading to Windy Bridge (Sabine Kelly apprehended here by Constable Tristan Doyle)

Rachel has walked these maps before during her earlier investigations, including the area surrounding the police station and the dusty dead-end streets along which Sabine Kelly had made her escape twelve years ago. But never with the full cooperation of a single resident or witness, and certainly not with a guide, one who might hold the missing pieces.

Will Sabine tell the truth? Or will she twist it?

"What do you think?"

Rachel startles. Reflexively, she holds up her hand as if to hold Sabine back. She can't come in here. Another two steps and she'll see it.

"You look great."

"Thank you. These are nice." Playfully, Sabine pokes one finger through the ripped denim and wiggles it. "They feel good on my skin."

Rachel glances at her bare feet. "I probably have some shoes for you. Let's have a look in my room."

Sabine hasn't noticed her agitation. She twirls. A bit of a performance considering she's wearing jeans, not a skirt. The tie-front blouse makes her look like tomboy from the fifties. A decent haircut, a bit of makeup—she would be arresting if not conventionally pretty, but all Rachel can think is that she still looks very much like herself, and that she must not see the wall of the office.

"We should make tracks."

But Sabine has spotted Rachel's diplomas, two of them, in the usual black frames.

"How much school did it take you?" she asks, as she strides to the desk to squint at them.

"Two degrees, two children. Over twelve years."

Sabine hooks her thumbs in the belt loops of her jeans. "You must be really smart," she says.

Rachel would demur, say something about late nights and hard work, but she's too desperate to get Sabine out of there. In the time it takes to wonder how to distract her, Sabine has turned in slow motion, exhaling as if she has been punched.

"*Oh.*"

Rachel says, "I'm sorry. I didn't want you to see any of this."

She knows how it looks—like something from a B-grade thriller. Like the rambling mind of an amateur detective and obsessive conspiracy theorist has been translated into a gory montage.

"Don't look at it."

But it's too late. Sabine is frozen to the spot, her eyes glassy.

Dominating the center of the montage of victims: an 8-by-10 color photo of Dee Kelly, laughing and very much alive, sitting in a deck chair with a beer can in one hand, a cigarette in the other. Even pixelated and in 2D, her life force is undeniable. In horrifying contrast, the photo next to it shows her burnt body, rigid, arched, her hands to her throat as if she'd choked on the smoke before she ever felt the flames.

The Shoosmith family, a mother, a father and two sons under ten, are together in life and in death. The first image shows them huddled around a campfire, their faces aglow. In the second there is only a blackened lumpy mass as evidence they tried to take shelter under a table. The gas bottles were next to their trailer. They never stood a chance.

Faith and Bram Mitchell, the immediate neighbors, tried to save Dee and Aria Kelly. When the gas bottles blew, Bram died quickly. Faith lasted a little longer after the ambulances arrived, but the damage to her airway was catastrophic. She died en route to the hospital.

Constable Logan Billson, the first responder, took the full force of the blast. He was torn apart by the explosion, his body incinerated by the flames. The only pictures on the wall are his high school graduation and official police officer photos. These were the images released to the media, showing him young and good-looking in the way of a fresh recruit: clean-shaven, buzz-cut blond hair, direct blue-eyed gaze. He had served almost ten years to the day when he died in the fire. He'd been in line for a promotion.

Rachel can only stand aside as Sabine moves toward the wall the way a mourner might approach an open coffin. Her hand reaches to touch the school photo of her sister, but when she draws closer, she pulls it back.

Aria was five years old when the photo was taken, pale, dark-haired and dark-eyed, smiley and gap-toothed. More solidly built than Sabine and bearing little resemblance to her mother and sister. Far smaller but more heartbreaking is the crime-scene photo of her tiny body, curled like a sleeping cat at the foot of a burnt bed. Liquified and turned black.

Over the years Rachel has developed an immunity to the horror; now she is seeing them all as if for the first time. To Sabine, it's probably akin to having her nightmares made real.

For obvious reasons, many of these images were not released to the public. Most of them Rachel regrets not having torn down long ago. It was bad enough that she'd blown up an image she'd found as a header to a podcast: a moody shot of an old trailer, a ghastly orange sunset behind it, photoshopped flames shooting from the windows, THE TRAILER MURDERS painted on the side, styled to resemble the words written in blood during the Manson Tate-LaBianca murders.: DEATH TO PIGS. RISE. HEALTER (sic) SKELTER.

And most damning of all is the way the wall has been divided: photos of the dead on one side, the now famous image of Sabine Kelly covered in blood and ash on the other, surrounded by the usual choppy sensationalized headlines cut from the newspapers. Rachel has written VICTIMS in black. KILLER in red.

"I'm so sorry," she says softly.

Sabine seems to visibly collect herself, wiping her eyes and nose with a fist. Her stance widens; her mouth sets. She removes the push-pin holding the picture of Constable Logan Billson and holds the sheet of paper at arm's length, staring at his image. Her blank expression gives nothing away.

On a hunch, and to break the excruciating silence, Rachel asks, "What came first with your mother—the using or the dealing?"

"Logan came first," Sabine says quietly. "Before him it was only booze, cigarettes, and weed. Then the using, and then she started dealing."

"He was corrupt?"

"Bent as an elbow."

"Do you think they had a sexual relationship?"

"I know they did."

"Consensual?"

"Violent. But Dee loved him."

"Was he Aria's father?"

Sabine shakes her head. "No. He may have had other brats running around town, but Aria wasn't one of them."

"So who—"

"Look, I'll never know who my father is, and I have no idea about my sister's. Dee never said, and she's dead. It's not important. All this"—she stabs a finger at the wall—"just tells me you're not on my side. And that's okay. We don't need to be friends, but we do need to be partners. You obviously know things about the investigation that I don't, and I need to know, so let's get this done."

"What do you want to know?"

As if she might turn to stone doing it, Sabine takes a quick look at the wall. "What evidence do they have that I started the fires?"

"There were dozens of witnesses who saw you running from the main parking lot toward the residents' section," Rachel says. "And, of course, there's your confession."

She holds out a hand to take the photo, but Sabine moves the sheet to the side where her own image has stood alone under the headline *KILLER*. Slowly, deliberately, she places Billson's image over the top of hers, securing it with a pushpin through one eye.

Such a simple gesture, but one that instantly alters Rachel's perception of Logan Billson's clean-cut image—and the changing shape of this story.

"What are you trying to say, Sabine?"

"I'm not saying anything." Sabine turns from the wall. "I'll show you."

2019

—

SABINE

The inside of Rachel's car smells of leather and something plasticky and sweet. Sabine takes everything in: a dashboard display as complex and neon-lit as the cockpit of a plane, a cube-shaped box of tissues in the center console, along with a packet of wet wipes, a pen holder, a blister packet of tylenol, a compact mirror, and lipstick, all neatly organized. When Rachel types the address on her phone, a screen pops up from the dash to display a detailed map, and a posh computerized voice asks her to confirm the route.

Sabine can't stop thinking about her new clothes, neatly folded inside the beach bag on Rachel's dining table. She takes off the pink rubber flip-flops Rachel gave her, kicking them aside in the footwell. How will she explain the gifts to Ryan?

A cold blast hits her feet, raising goose bumps. She's not convinced they're caused by the freezing air.

The same thing happened when she took Blue to Pop this morning: as she entered the shack, a shiver ran down her spine. Dread followed, the feeling that this would be the last time she'd see either of them. While she resisted the urge to embrace Pop, she pressed her face into Blue's ruff and squeezed him so tightly, her tension passed from her body to his. He growled at Pop and tried to follow her.

"I run hot," Rachel says. "If you're too cold you can adjust your individual temperature here." She leans across and turns a dial on

Sabine's side: the number fluctuates between sixty and seventy degrees.

"I'm fine," Sabine says.

"It'll take us about an hour, I reckon. What kind of music do you like?"

"I don't mind."

"Come on, but don't tell me you're a country fan."

"This station is fine."

Poppy eighties or something—Sabine isn't really listening. Cars make her nervous, and this one automatically locked the doors once they hit twenty miles per hour. Sabine feels nauseous. The tree-shaped deodorizer hanging from the rearview mirror does not smell like a tree.

They pull onto the freeway. The car moves smoothly to the speed limit, and the display shows a countdown of the number of miles until they reach their destination.

Sabine doesn't need a GPS to tell her exactly how far it is to Far Peaks: fifty-three miles, almost a direct line inland from the river. She has traveled this route more times than she can count, but not since the fire. By car it should take them under an hour; on foot, the journey would take roughly five days. She knows this because she has walked every mile. Back then, she stole fruit from trees, water from garden taps, and she slept under bushes. Until a year ago, she had kept the goose-down jacket and hiking boots she'd taken from someone's porch during a night when the rain came in sideways and the temperature dropped below zero. Bone-tired, sunburnt, with bleeding feet and a swollen tongue, she arrived at the place where her grandfather somehow knew she would go. No question she wouldn't turn up, no chance she'd lose her way. Pop was waiting for her—he knew the river, and Sabine, too well. He'd evaded the police swarming Shallow Bend and lying in wait at the shack. The *Kirralee* was waiting too, stocked with food and medical supplies. When Pop shoved her off two hours later, he said he'd meet her at a precise location, at a precise time, in three weeks. Until then, she shouldn't speak to a soul. She couldn't trust anyone.

His advice has kept her safe.

She glances at Rachel now. Has she made the right choice?

The questions keep coming, but not the ones Sabine suspects Rachel wants to ask. Maybe Rachel is nervous too.

"What's it like? Your hometown, I mean. You haven't said much about it."

Sabine shrugs. "It's dry, dusty."

"That's it?"

"Cheap living for fly-in, fly-out workers and prospectors. Tourists. A truck stop, pubs, casinos—you know." She tugs at her seat belt. It feels like a straitjacket. "It's like Kalgoorlie; people come for the gold."

"Do they find it?"

"In the nineties a guy dug up a nugget worth about fifty thousand, but he was just lucky. Getting gold out of the ground is hard work."

"But it can be lucrative?"

Sabine's mouth twists. She spent plenty of time mooching about and kicking the dust in Far Peaks—she never unearthed anything that might have taken her to a better place. Apparently all that guy had done was dig a hole to bury his dog's shit, and *eureka*.

"Honestly, you can make more per ounce dealing drugs. And they're easier to find."

"I've been to Far Peaks," Rachel announces. "About four years ago, I did some research and interviews there."

Sabine turns to face her. "So why are you asking me what it's like? I haven't been back since the fire."

"I mean, I know what's *there*. I was asking you about the demographic, I guess."

"Poor people," Sabine says. "Sad people. Drunks and drug addicts and miners."

Silence.

Sabine breaks it. "What did you find out?" She's not sure she wants to know, but the question clawed its way from her throat.

"Well, the people aren't too friendly, I'll say that."

She's holding something back.

"Who did you speak to?"

Rachel waves a dismissive hand. "The pub owner. A few locals. And the woman who owns the IGA, Rita something."

"Bennett," Sabine supplies. "Who else?"

"Arnie—"

"Willis." Sabine looks down at her hands. "What did Arnie say?"

The posh voice interrupts, instructing them to turn left. They enter a picturesque town with alfresco cafes, bric-a-brac stores, and antique shops. All around, lush vineyards curve and wind across the surrounding hills.

Rachel slows to fifty. She seems to be ignoring the question.

"Rachel, what did Arnie say?"

She sighs. "He was pretty hostile, to be honest. Told me to get the fuck off his property."

Sabine swallows a sob, and a single tear leaks from her left eye. Rachel has unwittingly relieved her of a burden she has carried for years. She lets the tear fall rather than have Rachel see her brush it away.

———

Thirty minutes later, Far Peaks materializes through a hazy red cloud.

Since leaving the last town, Rachel's incessant questioning has ceased. Sabine relishes the silence, staring out at the changing landscape—it has certainly changed over the years. The narrow single-lane road that once cut inland has been redirected and is now a double-lane highway; the once-bare brown hills to the west have been revegetated with trees and dotted with rows and rows of wind turbines, which Sabine finds alien, yet strangely beautiful. Twelve years ago, the farms where she sought shelter marked a parallel line to the road; now they have disappeared into the trees.

If Rachel asked her to retrace her journey to the river, she could not do it. She would be lost.

But the town ahead is almost as Sabine remembers it: dead flat, although now it sprawls on both sides of the highway, as if the new road has been built straight through, without regard for life or property. There are still large blocks with peeling weatherboard houses, like tiles on a Scrabble board, the yards mostly covered with white scoria, glittering under the beating sun. The airstrip, visible in the distance, is still an ugly scar on the land. It appears not much thrives here on the outskirts; then again, it never has.

"You weren't wrong," Rachel mutters. "It's bloody dusty this time of year."

"The trucks make it worse," Sabine says. "They're supposed to slow down, but they don't."

As if to prove her point, a double tractor trailer overtakes them, sending up tornadoes of dust.

"When I came it was greener."

Sabine snorts. "This place has never been green. It hardly ever rains, but there are definitely more trees than I remember."

"Do you want to go straight to the trailer park?"

"I didn't want to come here at all, Rachel."

Main Street takes them off the highway, past the two pubs on opposite corners and a collection of drab shopfronts: the Far Peaks Bakery, the grocery store, a newsstand, Renfrew Hardware, Baz &

Son Butcher. Sabine guesses it would be the son now—Baz would have to be at least seventy-five. Halfway along, in the middle of the street, the leaf-shaped park area contains the oversized bronze statue of William the miner, pickaxe thrown over his shoulder. And the rotunda. Somewhere, on one of the heavy overhead beams, Sabine's name is etched into the wood. Maybe the chewing gum she stuck under William's armpit is still there; maybe the friendship ring Ryan gave her is still rusting away in the flower beds where she'd lost it. The plane trees lining the street are now fully grown, their tall canopies hacked straight across at the top to keep them clear of the power lines, but everything else looks much the same. Going by what Rachel said, Rita Bennett still runs the IGA, the place where just about every employable Far Peaks teenager has worked at the till. The familiar supermarket smell comes to her as if she's standing right there: lemon-scented floor polish and overripe fruit.

And the other thing that strikes her: Far Peaks is like a ghost town. She searches the faces of the few people they pass, terrified someone will see her, equally terrified she won't recognize anyone from her childhood.

As they cruise past the police station, Sabine slips further down in her seat. "Don't speed."

"I'm not."

"God, I feel sick."

Rachel slows down. "Do you want me to pull over?"

"No, not here! Take your next right."

Rachel turns sharply. "The trailer park is in the other direction."

"I want to see something." Sabine sits up, peering around. "Next left."

"This one? Barnard?"

"It's a cul-de-sac. Turn around at the bottom and keep going. Don't stop."

A dead-end road—a single entrance and exit. Sabine's nails bite into the armrest and the familiar panic creeps in.

Ryan had told her Taryn was married with three kids and lived in one of the brick homes on Barnard: L-shaped three-bedroom houses on large lots, built in the seventies, and not much nicer than the typical weatherboards in the area.

"What are we looking for?" Rachel asks.

"An old friend," Sabine says.

As they turn a slow circle at the end of the street, a black cat shoots across the road in front of the car, and Rachel mutters, "That doesn't bode well for us."

Two cars are parked on the street, one a four-wheel drive utility crusted with dried mud, the other a white Commodore Wagon.

"Reports said you stole a car," Rachel says. "One just like that." She points to the wagon.

Sabine frowns. "Why would I steal a car?"

"A Commodore Wagon was reported missing the morning after you escaped. They said that's probably how you got away so easily."

"Do you know how many cars are stolen in Far Peaks every week, Rachel? It used to be a lot," Sabine says. "I didn't steal anything. I walked."

Rachel gasps. "All the way?"

Again Sabine's body conjures horribly real sensations, like the ghost of a missing limb. The tightness of her sunburnt skin; the ache in her muscles; her blistered, bleeding feet. She feels the cold biting her bones. The night of the fire, a chasm had opened up inside her, and she's not convinced she has reached the bottom yet.

"All the way," she says. "To the river."

Rachel lets go of the steering wheel, pressing her palms to her cheeks. "Oh, Sabine."

It's been so long since anyone other than Ryan and Pop have

called her by her name. She should remind Rachel how dangerous that is, especially here, but in a way now, it's comforting. She has not completely disappeared.

"I don't know which house is hers. Let's just go."

"Are you sure?"

Sabine nods. "If you turn left, we can get to the trailer park without heading back along Main."

Rachel follows Sabine's next directions without speaking. When they reach the road leading to Windy Bridge, she breaks her silence, appearing to measure her words. "Sabine, how did you get away? Why did you run?"

Until now, it seemed important to tell Rachel everything in order, the way it happened. Sabine is scared she'll forget things, skip the parts that only make sense if they're allowed to fall like dominoes. One after the other. But, she realizes, Rachel is already judging her. And that's exactly why she ran in the first place.

Sabine holds up her hands, wrists pressed together. Her hands are small; her wrists are thin. "The cop, Doyle—he felt sorry for me. My skin was burned. He left the cuffs loose."

"You got out of them?"

The sensation of cold steel scraping singed flesh. Every nerve ending on fire.

"He left me alone in the back of the car. The crowd out the front of the station was getting out of control. Everything was crazy."

"Why did you run?"

They're approaching Windy Bridge. On one of the east pylons, near a concrete slope where Sabine kissed Ryan for the first time, she had drawn a heart with their initials inside it. Once in a blue moon, when the dry creek flowed, you could paddle in rock pools as clear as any lagoon pictured in a holiday brochure. Right now, the drop beneath the bridge is a dry ravine.

Again, Rachel seems to choose her words before she speaks. "All you have to do is tell the truth, Sabine. Justice will take care of the rest."

They drive across the bridge. Sabine presses a button to lower the window. The air is warm and sweet on her face, and the bridge seems smaller, the ravine below less terrifying. Like many things from her childhood, Sabine's memory of it has shrunk.

Perhaps the chasm inside her isn't as deep as she fears—if she jumps, she might survive the fall.

"There's justice for the powerful, and there's justice for the powerless," she says. "If you don't know the difference, Rachel, it means you're powerful. Dee didn't teach me much, but she taught me that."

2019

—

RACHEL

A round fifty meters past the other side of the bridge, Sabine motions for Rachel to pull over.

She parks the car under the shade of a tree in a gravel turn-out. There seems to be nothing but impenetrable scrub on either side of the road, no indication that there's a trailer park nearby. And only the rattle of cicadas and Sabine's quick, shallow breaths.

"I can't see an entrance."

"It's here," Sabine says, frowning. "It must be." She leans forward, gripping the door handle.

Rachel reaches across the console to the back seat. She scissors the trailer park map between her fingers, pulls it from her case and unfolds it, spreading it over the steering wheel. She taps the spot where the bridge is marked and looks around.

"This is roughly where you were arrested by Constable Doyle. He was parked here?"

"Yes."

"He chased you down, right?"

"No, I wasn't running away."

Rachel tries to hide her surprise.

"I went *to* him." Sabine's tone is bitter. "I thought he would help."

"Why was the police car here? Why not the main entrance, where your mother's car was parked?"

Sabine's mouth curls. "This is the way Logan came and went if he wasn't on"—she pulls air quotes—"*official business.*"

"But the first explosion *was* official business. Wouldn't they have checked out the burning car first?"

"Maybe they did. I don't know—I wasn't here. Dee's car was already on fire when I arrived."

"What about the second explosion? Where were you when that went off?"

Sabine is far away, reliving a scene Rachel can only guess at. She is reluctant to break the spell. Were repressed memories coming back to her? But they need to go back to the start; this isolated spot by the side of the road was the beginning of the end.

Rachel changes tack. "Doyle's statement said you were catatonic, that he shook you. When you finally responded, he asked the whereabouts of Constable Billson, and you said, *He's dead. They're all dead. Oh God, it's my fault.*"

Sabine's gaze snaps back, then slides away. "I did say that."

"Those exact words? What did you mean by them?"

"Slow down," Sabine mutters to herself. "*Think.*" Realizing she has spoken aloud, she adds, "I have to be sure of everything. If I get anything wrong, they'll use it against me. They'll say I lied."

"Of course, take your time." With the ignition off, the car is warming up under the sun. "Are you sure you remember where the entrance is?"

Sabine nods.

"Walk me through your movements that night." She pulls out her phone. "Is it okay if I record?"

Sabine says through gritted teeth, "Okay. But we have to be careful. Someone might see me."

"It was a long time ago—it would have to be the worst kind of luck." Rachel thinks of the black cat, feeling silly. "Just tell me what you think happened."

Sabine corrects her. "I'll tell you what I *know*. I hope, as you say, justice will take care of the rest."

She gets out of the car and steps slowly toward the edge of the scrub.

Rachel considers using her SLR camera, but it would be too unwieldy. Her phone will have to do—she can use stills from the video footage if needed. She puts her phone and a bottle of water in her bag and locks the car.

Sabine approaches a small grove of paperbarks. She lifts the tree branches to duck underneath and stops; with her other hand, she touches one of the trunks, tracing a line from the pink-white section of new growth to where the bark has turned to a deep carbon black.

Rachel starts recording.

Sabine stays there for a long time, her face blank. Even on the small screen Rachel can see how she might have behaved if she was in shock: her movements are sluggish, puppet-like.

Somewhere in the distance, a child screams and Sabine snaps out of her trance.

"This way." She pushes through the dense scrub.

Rachel follows. Most of the trees here have blackened trunks. Not recently burnt, she assumes—this must be the section where the fire spread.

Less than a dozen steps in and the scrub opens up to a clearing; beyond it, a six-foot wire fence and a padlocked swing gate. On the other side of the fence, she can see the row of miners' dongas that correspond to the fourteen red squares marked on the trailer park map. On her previous trip, she had gotten as far as the office before Arnie Willis had turned her away.

"The gate's locked," Rachel says.

"It only looks like that." Sabine tugs at the padlock—sure

enough, it isn't secured. "It's to keep people from sneaking in to use the showers."

An unholy screech, and the gate swings open. Sabine shuffles through, head ducked, arms held stiffly by her side. She stops to check along the row of dongas.

To Rachel they appear unoccupied. There are no parked vehicles. The roller shutters are down and the umbrellas in the center of the outside tables are closed.

"It's quiet this time of year," she says.

Sabine presses a finger to her lips. "Shift workers. They might be sleeping." She moves on, taking the right-hand path.

Rachel doesn't need to look at the map—she has it memorized. This road leads directly to the residents' row and intersects with the other path at the residents' camp kitchen and shower block. She can see the building appearing through the trees: dirty-white cinder block and, by the look of it, decades older than the modern camp kitchen near the main entrance. Straight across from the shower block was the site occupied by Dee Kelly; next to that, the Mitchells; alongside the toilet block, the Shoosmiths.

As they approach, Sabine appears calm, but Rachel can sense her distress. Her steps slow and grow shorter, her eyes move around, taking in what Rachel suspects is a changed landscape. The nearest residential site is now at least forty meters away. There are none where she had marked red crosses on the map, only a stretch of well-tended garden. Fresh mulch. Nine rosebushes planted in a semicircle and, at the base of each bush and partially hidden by leaves and blooms, nine small white crosses. No names.

Rachel points to a bronze plaque inlaid in stone. "This says the Rotary Club built it."

After the fire. In memory of the innocent lives lost on October 14, 2007.

"But our van was here." Sabine spins, seemingly disoriented.

Rachel opens her mouth to point out the obvious: the van would have been nothing but warped metal and sodden ash by the time the fire was extinguished. There was next to nothing left.

Sabine is scraping the soft mulch underfoot, looking for something. Another scrape. She kneels to look closer. A concrete slab. With a stick, she traces the edge of the slab to the furthest corner and uses her hands to sweep the dirt aside.

Rachel zooms in with her phone camera. Scratched into the concrete are the words *Beenie + Dee 1997.*

"Before your sister was born?"

A nod. "This was the slab for our annex."

"And a point of ignition for the fire," Rachel says in as neutral a tone as she can manage. "I've seen a copy of the report."

No response, unless Sabine's composure can be considered a reaction.

When a stout older woman carrying a toiletries bag and a towel exits the shower block, Rachel ends the recording and lowers her phone. The woman glances at them curiously as she passes, rubber thongs clacking. Far from hiding her own face, Sabine searches the woman's—her hopeful expression changes to one of desolation.

Sadness, perhaps, that she does not recognize the woman? Or is she seeing ghosts everywhere?

A sudden breeze disturbs the stillness, rustling leaves.

Sabine shivers and looks away. She gets to her feet, shielding her eyes from the sun, and surveys the area. Her gaze settles on a wooden seat to her left. She heads toward it.

From where she stands, Rachel can't make out the inscription on the seat's plaque.

"A bench," Sabine says. "He got a white cross, a medal and a bench."

Her face contorts and Rachel is taken aback—it's hard keeping up with Sabine's constantly changing emotions.

The older woman has gone. Rachel starts recording again. She zooms in.

It's a compelling if disturbing picture: Sabine, hands on hips, face screwed up with contempt. *In remembrance: Constable Logan Billson 1979–2007.* The bench seat is worn and smooth on one side, as if someone comes here often.

"Can I ask you something? Those photos on your wall," Sabine says abruptly, "the pictures of them all burnt." She takes a deep breath. "They were taken while they were still here?"

"Yes, before the bodies were removed from the scene."

"What about pictures from after? You know, when they cut them open?"

"I don't have any pictures, but I can show you the report. There was an inquest. The coroner ruled the victims were, in his words, *killed by fire, explosion, or secondary effect*, like smoke inhalation."

Sabine frowns. "They held an inquest without a trial?"

"An independent inquiry." Rachel waves her hand at the area behind the camp kitchen. "The proximity of the gas bottles and fuel, the lack of safety and firefighting equipment—an inquest was held to prevent a tragedy like this from happening again." Quietly, she adds, "If there had been a trial, you might only have been charged with arson and manslaughter, not first-degree murder. Or maybe the finding would have been that it was all a terrible accident. You were a minor, a child. Did you consider that before you ran?"

She expects an emotional denial, but Sabine laughs bitterly.

"It wouldn't have mattered what I said. If you had seen the looks on the crowd's faces—if you had heard what Billson said to me, you would have run too."

"Sergeant Billson? What did he say?"

"He told Doyle to let them get a good look at me on the way in. He said I would go down for what happened to his son."

Rachel's first reaction is to feel empathy for Billson—if her own son had been killed trying to save others, she would be vengeful too. Something tells her to keep it to herself. If she had any doubts about Sabine's guilt before they'd met, they were only compounding now that she suspected that Logan Billson had played a part in the tragedy. But she has almost reached peak frustration—Sabine is withholding information, and if Rachel doesn't file the story before the deadline, it might be taken out of her hands. No decent editor would risk it breaking elsewhere, and Miles Cooper is not a fool.

She snaps out of her reverie to find Sabine watching her, a cat watching a mouse.

"Why did you agree to come back here, Sabine?" Rachel gestures at the white crosses. "You have to give me something to go on."

"I'll give you some answers. But I can't give you all of it, not yet."

"Why are you holding back? We're going in circles, and we don't have a lot of time."

Again, that unnerving scrutiny. "Because if I tell you everything, you won't need me anymore. And I'm not done with you yet, Rachel."

A shudder runs down Rachel's spine. "I'm not your enemy. You won't be helping yourself by lying to me."

Sabine's gaze is steady. "I won't lie to you. Ask me what you want to know, but no more recording."

"Okay." Rachel turns off the phone and slips it in her pocket. "Did you light the fires?"

"No."

All the unasked questions come in a rush.

"Did you kill your mother and sister, either intentionally or by accident?"

"No."

"Did Logan Billson die trying to save the victims?"

"No."

"Did he light the fires?"

"Yes."

It's like an extreme version of the game Hot and Cold. But instead of finding treasure, Rachel knows she is drawing inexorably closer to something horrific.

"Why did he light the fires?"

"He had to destroy evidence."

"What evidence?"

The first crack in her composure. Her lower lip trembles. "*Us.*"

Sabine is transfixed by the square of concrete. She nudges dirt over the names with her toe, squares her shoulders and looks up. And up. Her eyes fix on something.

"Smile and wave, Rachel."

Rachel traces the direction of her stare: a camera, cleverly camouflaged among the wires and connections of an electrical box on the side of the toilet block. A robotic eye on a swiveling arm, the kind that follows you when you move.

A prickle, like ants crawling on her skin. She turns her back to the camera, but it's too late—there's no way out for her now. If the camera has been set up by police, they will have proof she has been far more complicit than simply investigating a story.

"Rachel, I need you to do something for me."

"What is it?" she mutters.

"Go back to your car, and wait for me there."

"Where are you going?"

"There's something I need to do before we go." Sabine's gaze snaps back from the camera. "I hated Logan. He terrorized us for years, and I threatened to expose him—I thought that would make him let Dee go and he'd leave us alone, but I should have known better."

She thumps her breast with a fist. "*I* was the motive. *They* were the evidence. They died because of me—it was my fault."

The hairs on Rachel's arms stand up. *New twist in Trailer Murders case. Brave hero or killer cop?*

But she's not convinced. "If you were the one who threatened him, why didn't he kill you too?"

Sabine touches the scar on her scalp. "He tried. I wasn't meant to live." She brushes past, striding in the direction of the main office.

The camera tracks Sabine until she is past its range of motion, then swings back to Rachel.

She stands there, fear and guilt rooting her to the spot. All she knows right now is this is very, very bad. Worse, she can't shake the feeling that Sabine knew the camera was watching the whole time.

2019

—

SABINE

Sabine makes her way along the main path to the trailer park office. Parts of the place are unrecognizable—not so much individual things, but the shape of the whole: familiar yet strange, like a time-lapse photograph. The log fort and a rusting metal swing and slide combo—Faith had called it the Death Trap—has been replaced by a fenced playground with rope bridges and a climbing wall, and the ground covered with some kind of rubber mat. Safety barriers everywhere. When she was six, Sabine fell from the old fort and broke her wrist; Aria split her eyebrow on the swing. They'd both lost a lot of skin. Whenever they came home covered in blood, stinking of creosote, Dee told them off and sent them to the showers.

She tells herself to walk faster, to get this done quickly. But she feels dizzy, untethered. She can't escape the memory of bright-hot flames and blistered flesh, of blood and rage.

A man sitting on a deck chair gives her the one-fingered wave as she passes.

Absentmindedly, she waves back.

She's thinking of Rachel, her expression when she saw the camera watching them, as if she'd been betrayed. Even though Sabine didn't know about the camera, she isn't surprised. She trusts Rachel will do as she asked: wait for her at the car. If she were to follow, everything might come undone. Then again, it was misplaced trust that had destroyed lives twelve years ago, and it's trust in Arnie Willis that brings her here now. Is it misplaced too?

As if she's summoned him, Arnie appears on the path ahead, loping toward her. When he sees Sabine, he stops. She gives him a wide unguarded smile, but he avoids her gaze and turns sharply, heading back to the office.

"Arnie, wait!"

He's gone.

When she reaches the office door, the sign is up. *Back in fifteen minutes.* She goes around the side, pushes through the gate and lets herself in through the unlocked back door leading to the caretaker's accommodation. She cuts through the kitchen and down the hallway.

Arnie is waiting in the office. "Well," he says. "Look what the wind blew in."

The last time she saw him, he'd saved her life.

Sabine opens her arms to embrace her old friend. After a brief hesitation, he hugs her in return. He's frail under his baggy shirt. She can smell alcohol on his breath.

"You shouldn't have come. It's not safe for you or me."

"Things have changed."

"Wasn't sure it was you at first," he says. "You look different. All grown up."

They pull apart.

Sabine attempts a smile. "What, have you been sitting here all this time, waiting for me?"

He shrugs. "Nothing better to do. You're lucky it was me that spotted you and not the copper. Sometimes he waits on the bench. Sometimes he sits here"—Arnie points at the security monitor on his desk—"watching."

"He still thinks I'll show up?"

"You did show up," he points out. "And when he gets here and eats my biscuits while he trawls through that footage, he's gonna know you showed up."

A knock on the office door. They both jump.

Arnie looks through the glass. "Kids. Probably wanting ice cream. Can't read the bloody sign, just like you never could. They can wait."

Sabine needs to think fast. "When does he come?"

"Once a week, maybe. You were lucky—he was here yesterday. He fast-forwards the footage until he sees someone hanging around. And you two were there a long while." He frowns. "Who's the woman?"

"Rachel? She's helping me."

"Helping you do what?" At her silence, he slumps. "You can't rip the scab off a wound that won't heal, Beenie. You must have a life happening out there somewhere. You wanna risk that?"

She sets her shoulders. "It's not the life I want."

"It's better than what's coming for you if you do this."

"Maybe." She grabs his hand. "Arnie, I hate asking—can you delete the footage?"

"Don't need to." He grins. "The camera malfunctioned."

"When?"

He thinks. "About fifteen minutes ago."

The relief is so overwhelming, she can't hold it in. He has kept her secrets for twelve years, and he's still protecting her now.

"Hey." He rubs the tears from her cheeks. "That woman had better be looking out for you."

Rachel? Looking out for her? Rachel is only looking out for herself, but in a way it's all part of the plan.

"You know what I'm asking for next," she says shakily. "You've still got it?"

"You know where you'll end up if I give it to you? I can't do it."

"You have to. It's the right thing." She holds out cupped hands.

He searches her face. Eventually he sighs. "In the freezer with my lamb steaks."

Sabine checks over her shoulder and stifles a hysterical laugh. Arnie keeps a chest freezer in the office, within arm's reach of the desk where the security monitor sits.

When he hands her a ziplock bag, the lightness of the object inside it surprises her. Back then it had felt so heavy.

"And the jerry can?" she asks.

"Bagged. In the ceiling above the rec room."

"I can't take it with me now. When the time comes, I'll tell them where it is. Arnie, *I* put it there, not you. Don't trust anyone, not even Rachel. Okay?"

Air hisses between his teeth. "I'm old now. I don't give a shit what they do to me anymore."

"I have to go." She tucks the bag into the waistband of her jeans, sucking in her stomach at the touch of freezing metal. "I owe you everything. I'm so grateful. You'll never know how much. Maybe one day you'll visit?" She gives him a brief, tight hug and leaves.

———

Rachel is scribbling notes when Sabine returns to the car. She jumps when Sabine opens the door and climbs in.

"I was worried. Where did you go?"

"I'm sorry. I had to collect something."

The ziplock bag is warm now, sticking to her sweating skin. She has moved it around to her back, and the awful rod inside is making her sit awkwardly upright.

Rachel is looking at her with suspicion. "What?"

"Later," she says. "Let's go."

"Okay, but first tell me about the camera." Rachel's eyes narrow further. "Are we on the same side or not? Did you set me up?"

Sabine holds up a hand in protest. "I didn't know about the camera, and you can stop worrying. There's nothing to prove we were here."

"What did you do?"

"Arnie. He stopped the recording. Please, can you just trust me on this?"

"Trust you?" Rachel snaps. "Why is the caretaker helping you? Is he involved? Have you gotten something on him?"

"Because he's my friend," she says, her voice cracking. "*Please*, can we go now?"

Rachel starts the ignition, puts the car into drive and does a careful U-turn. They cross over the bridge and head back toward the town, her hands white-knuckled on the steering wheel.

Sabine just wants to get the hell out of Far Peaks as quickly as possible, but Rachel stops at the pedestrian crossing outside the Queen's Head Hotel. The lights turn red, and two women pushing prams step off the curb.

Sabine is hit with a jolt of recognition. It happens so quickly she forgets to hide her face, forgets to avert her gaze.

Taryn.

She has put on weight. Her hair is shorter and darker; her clothes are not as tight or short as they used to be, more hippy-bohemian. Her bare arms are tattooed. The child in the pram—a boy, around two or three years old—looks just like her when she was younger. She looks past Rachel and locks eyes with Sabine.

Almost immediately Taryn turns away, continuing to chat to her friend, walking on as if nothing has happened. For a moment Sabine thinks she hasn't recognized her, but Taryn falters as she steps off the crossing, her mouth slack-jawed—the recognition is mutual.

Sabine's first reaction is a hollow feeling that deadens everything else, including the fear. She has already grieved losing her friend the same way she mourned Aria and Dee.

But why didn't Taryn acknowledge her? Why didn't she stop?

Common sense kicks in; had Sabine called out, Taryn would have stopped. She walked on because she hates her—because Sabine broke a promise all those years ago.

With a last, furtive look over her shoulder, Taryn steers the pram into the mall entrance and out of sight.

The light turns green.

Rachel glances across. "Are you okay?"

"It's nothing," Sabine says. "Just memories."

———

They pull up at the last stop sign on the outskirts of the town. On the surface Rachel seems calm, but Sabine senses her emotions are as turbulent as her own. Rachel's mind must be buzzing with new ideas after the revelations, while Sabine's is stuck on repeat, going over and over old pain.

On both sides of the highway the plains spread out like a dirty patchwork quilt. Although there's no traffic in sight, Rachel waits at the stop sign for a full five seconds before turning. Out here the speed limit is 110, but she sets the cruise at one hundred.

"Have you done anything really bad, Rachel? Like, ever?" Sabine asks.

A long pause. "When I was fifteen, I stole a mascara. It was in the bottom of the basket, and the sales assistant forgot to ring it up. I took it home." Her cheeks flush. "Not gonna lie—I got a bit of a thrill."

Sabine rolls her eyes. "So it wasn't really stealing. You just took an opportunity."

"It was still theft."

"And when you didn't get caught, did you think of doing it again?"

Rachel barks a laugh. "God, no! I couldn't sleep. It wasn't worth it."

"And now?"

Silence.

"It must be hard for you, protecting someone like me. Is it a—what do you call it?"

"An ethical dilemma." Rachel's mouth twists. "Yes, it is. But that isn't what's worrying me."

"What is?"

"I've been thinking. If your claim that Logan Billson lit the fires to destroy evidence is true, it changes everything. Now we're talking police corruption, and if I'm completely honest, that terrifies me." Rachel's fingers drum the steering wheel. "I can protect you as a source, Sabine—I'm just not sure how to protect myself."

Rachel's admission is troubling. So much for a controlled explosion. The camera, Arnie's involvement, Taryn seeing her, and now Rachel pushing back—Sabine is numb and exhausted from trying to clear the area before detonation.

"I want justice for my family, but not at the cost of anyone else getting hurt," she says quietly. "I don't want you to sacrifice your integrity for me."

Rachel snorts. "I can only write the truth if you give it to me. You asked me to trust you—well, honestly, I don't right now."

"I *am* telling you the truth."

"You're giving me the slow reveal," Rachel says. "And I don't know why you're doing it, but I'm losing patience." She turns up the volume on the radio.

Sabine blocks out the music, thinking of Taryn: their friendship had been a lifeline, but their breakup was an anchor, dragging Sabine under. Without Taryn, she had felt so alone. And then everything came to a head: Dee lost her mind, Sabine met Ryan, and things were never the same.

It's all there, on the tip of her tongue, but there's no going back once she lets it all out. And the lack of trust between her and Rachel is mutual—until she's sure about Rachel, the focus has to be on Logan. It's all that matters. She *is* holding back, and for good reason. Rachel needs context; she has to know what it was like for Sabine.

She leans across to turn the volume down. The truth is, she's scared to finish her story—she knows there won't be a happy ending.

2007

—

SABINE

S abine had put on makeup and blow-dried her hair hours earlier. She'd been lying still on her bunk for the past hour so she
wouldn't mess it up. Dee was passed out on the double bed at
the other end of the van, fully dressed, her long hair fanned across the
pillow. Aria was asleep on the top bunk above.

Right at 9:45 Sabine got up and set the blue bucket on the floor.
Dee probably wouldn't wake until morning, but Aria might; if she
needed the toilet, she'd look for her sister to take her to the toilet
block, but when she realized she wasn't there, she would know to use
the bucket. The deal with Aria cost her five dollars.

In the annex, Sabine wriggled out of her pajamas and put on
skinny blue jeans, a pink crop top, and her puffer jacket. Leaving
the trailer door unlocked, she quietly opened and closed the annex
zipper and tiptoed barefoot to the end of the residents' row, her black
suede flats in one hand. When she reached the unpowered sites, she
slipped them on.

The trailer park usually emptied out at the tail end of the July
holidays, but there were a few townies still hanging around until the
weekend was over. They left their crap behind, and the overflowing
rubbish bins reeked. You had to queue to take a shit. Dee mostly hated
the holidays because she couldn't sleep as long or as often as she liked,
but Sabine didn't mind so much. There was music; there were new

faces, parties, different boys—boys who never called once they'd left, but still. When the townies left, it was depressing, just the old folk and families like hers, who couldn't afford private rent or had nowhere else to go. The holidays were good—Sabine stocked up on expensive hair products left behind in the toilet block, and she and Aria regularly found unopened snack food in the bins. Occasionally Sabine got lucky and, on the washing line, found brand-name clothing that fit.

Honestly, the stuff rich people threw away.

Most of the year-round residents hated the holidays. Faith and Bram Mitchell had been threatening to move for years, but they stayed. Some days Sabine thought it was because Faith couldn't bear to leave her garden. Other times she thought it was because of Aria and her.

Sabine snuck past a group of townies drinking, their camping and prospecting gear spread over the recently vacated sites on either side. Tomorrow morning they'd pack up; by afternoon they'd be gone.

Arnie Willis was sitting in his deck chair outside the trailer park office, an old zapper hanging above his head, clogged with dead bugs and smelling like fried hair.

"Where are you heading off to this late?"

Sabine waved. "Town. Anything good in lost and found?"

He shook his head. "Some pool toys and a pair of kids' floaties. Check back tomorrow."

"Right-o."

She tried to grab the ten-dollar note he whipped out of his shirt pocket, but he held on. "It's okay," he said. "I won't tell Dee." He let go.

"Thanks, Arnie. See ya."

Sabine changed her mind and doubled back. She passed the dongas, left through the rear exit, and crossed Windy Bridge—not the most well-lit route to town, but it was the quickest. Fewer people might see her. It was a full moon, and Sabine felt reckless. Wasn't even sure she wanted to go back to school in two days. Dee said she could leave if she had a full-time job, but not if she was just going to hang about and cause trouble.

She met Taryn at the Mobil. Right after they bought one-dollar slushies, it closed for the night. They took their drinks to the rotunda on Main, tipped half out and topped them up with the quarter bottle of vodka Taryn had stolen from her older sister's room.

"Won't Lauren notice it's gone?" Sabine asked.

"She'll think she drank it."

Taryn was wearing her favorite off-the-shoulder white spandex top and a pair of tight black jeans Sabine hadn't seen before. She lived with her dad and her nineteen-year-old sister in a semidetached house just outside town, near the disused train tracks. It was bigger and nicer than the van, but not by much. Her dad drove a truck six days a week, including a couple of overnight stopovers. Lauren was supposed to look after Taryn and make sure she went to school, but both girls pretty much did what they wanted.

"New jeans?"

"Yeah. Dad brought them back. Lucky they fit."

"Lucky he brings you stuff." Sabine lay back on the bench and slurped her drink. "I haven't even met my dad."

"Your mum's cool though. At least she's around."

Dee, *cool*? Dee was an embarrassment, but she was untouchable, and she wielded some power in the town. If Dee got angry, she cut off supply, and nobody wanted that.

"Think we'll get in tonight?" Taryn said.

There were two pubs: the Queen's Head and the Highway Arms. The Arms was Dee's spot—dilapidated, terrible food, but good for dealing. The Queen, where they were heading, was for rich locals and tourists, but the publican was hot on kicking out unsupervised minors after 10 p.m.

"We'll go in through the back and hang in the beer garden. Play some pool."

"Did you have to pay Aria again?"

Sabine nodded.

"She'll be taking over the family business soon," Taryn said.

Sabine's face turned hot.

Instantly contrite, Taryn pressed her forehead against Sabine's. "You can legally leave home if you want to. I'll ask Dad if you can live with us."

"I won't leave Aria."

Taryn's face dropped. "Yeah. I know. It would be fun though."

"When I turn eighteen, I'm out of here. I'm taking Aria with me."

"And me."

"And you. We'll live on a boat on the river. No one will find us there."

Taryn gave a theatrical shudder. "I was thinking an apartment with an indoor pool and a gym."

"*Anyplace but here,*" they said at the same time.

"*Jinx.*"

"*Double jinx.*"

A flurry of hands. "*Pinch, poke, you owe me a Coke.*"

Taryn collapsed, laughing. "What's after that?"

"No idea. We're officially one person now."

Her friend turned serious. "Don't you dare run away and leave me here on my own."

"Never," Sabine promised.

———

In the beer garden at the Queen, Taryn told Sabine to bag a spot on the pool table and went inside to get a cue.

Two locals had just started a game. Sabine set her coins on the corner of the pool table and took a seat at the edge of the dance floor under the grapevine. When Taryn hadn't returned after a few minutes, she approached a group of four men she didn't recognize, drinking and smoking. They looked like typical blow-in prospectors: around thirty, wearing dusty shorts and steel-capped boots.

She held out Arnie's ten-dollar note to one of the men. "Mister, could you buy me and my friend a drink?"

He looked her up and down, waved the note away. "What are you having?"

"Vodka and lemon squash. Two?"

"Well, sure." He went inside to the bar.

Usually she and Taryn double-teamed. It was the first time Sabine had scored free drinks on her own. Taryn would be impressed.

The man came back carrying two tumblers and two shot glasses. She pointed to the shot glasses. "What's that?"

"Bourbon chaser." He smiled, revealing greenish teeth. "Go on—it'll put hair on your chest."

Sabine had tasted bourbon only once before—sitting in a tight circle of teens, a quick sip she made look like a gulp, her tongue pressed against the rim of the bottle. This shot burned all the way down.

"That's disgusting." She mimed a retch and slugged a mouthful from one of the tumblers. It tasted strong, like it might be a double shot of vodka.

The four men laughed.

She finished her drink and started on Taryn's as the pool game concluded. Someone turned on the jukebox; a few couples drifted outside to dance.

"Looks like you're up," the guy said, nodding at the table.

"I'm waiting for my friend. She's gone to get a cue."

"I'll take you on."

He disappeared inside and returned with a cue.

The second bourbon shot went straight to her head. Nasty stuff. Grimacing, she took the cue in his hand. She lined up and broke, but it slipped off the white and stabbed the felt.

"Do-over," she said and reset. "Local rules."

"How old are you?" the guy asked, and when she told him seventeen, he reversed, his hands up. "Woah, woah." But he came back, put a hand on her leg and rubbed his thumb in slow circles. "She looks like someone." He looked around for confirmation. "Doesn't she look like someone? Don't you think she looks like someone?"

"That's Dee's kid. You don't want to mess with her, mate," one of the locals offered. He finished his beer, gave Sabine a warning look and left.

"Oh yeah, Dee. I know Dee," the guy hooted. "*Everyone* knows Dee."

Sabine took that to mean he didn't know Dee at all and slapped his hand away. "Why do you keep repeating yourself?" she said. "It's like you're stuck." She knew she was treading a fine line between getting a few free drinks and being expected to put out for them.

The guy pinched the skin of her knee through her jeans. "You look like that chick in that old mermaid movie. What's her name? Daryl Hannah. Yeah, that's it."

Sabine wriggled free. "Touch me again, and I'll shove this cue where the sun doesn't shine."

More laughter.

Sabine took aim at the white, but the alcohol had seriously kicked in. The ball ricocheted off the corner cushion and bounced across the dance floor. When she bent to retrieve it, the guy picked up the cue, flipped it, and drew the handle back and forth between her thighs.

Sabine straightened up and spun around.

The laughter was uncomfortable now.

"Another drink?" The guy smirked. "Might improve your game."

One of his mates shook his head. "Leave her alone, Tone. That's jailbait right there."

"Old enough to scam drinks? Old enough."

"I offered you the money," Sabine said. "I never asked for free drinks." With shaky hands she reset the white ball and stood back.

A tray of drinks appeared, and Tone placed another bourbon next to her empty glasses.

"No, thanks."

He kept his eyes on her as he downed the shot instead, smacking his lips.

A slower song came on. The dancing couples returned inside, leaving the five of them. Sabine looked desperately at the door, but Taryn was nowhere to be seen. *Where the hell is she?*

After he'd taken his extra shots, he passed her the cue. She laid it on the table.

"The game's not finished," Tone said.

Sabine stuck out her chin. "I'm going to find my friend."

He picked up the cue and tossed it to her, tip pointed upwards, but she missed the catch. The cue clattered to the ground and broke, leaving a splintered end.

"Now you owe me twenty bucks for the deposit," he said.

"Technically you broke it, and I only have ten." She tossed her hair, slung her bag across her body and rummaged inside. "There." She dropped the ten-dollar note on the table and turned to leave.

He grabbed the strap of her bag. As she struggled, the strap slipped from her shoulder to her neck. He reeled her in like a fish.

Sabine twisted and worked free of the strap. Her bag fell, scattering lipstick, coins, and her flip phone, which smashed and broke into two pieces. She backed into a corner, teeth bared.

"Jesus, Tone, what the fuck?" One of his friends tried to scoop her things into her bag. "Hey, are you okay?"

"Thank you." She took the bag as he held it out to her, then retrieved the missing half of her phone from under a plant pot.

Tone was leaning against the pool table, watching her.

Sabine couldn't speak. For a moment she wondered if her drink had been spiked, but decided she was in shock.

The guy who'd helped her glanced over his shoulder. In a low voice, he said, "Let's go, mate. I'm not spending the night in the clink for your pathetic ego."

Sabine looked up.

Tone's gaze radiated pure hatred. He lurched at her, eyes bulging, then stopped inches from her face. Leaned back again. Crossed his arms, leering at her.

Everything was white noise. Sabine knew that expression; it awakened her instincts as if he'd hit her and was about to hit her again.

She could feel the smoothness of maple wood in her hand before she lunged and took hold of the end of the broken cue; as if she was outside her body, she saw herself raise it two-handed, like a stake. She brought the splintered end down into the flesh of his thigh and stepped back, exhilarated.

The cue didn't stick and fell to the ground; the cut was probably not deep. There wasn't much blood. Tone's reaction was slow; his eyes slid from the wound to Sabine, then to the doorway leading to the bar.

Constable Tristan Doyle appeared, hands on his belt. "What's happened here?" He directed his next question to Sabine. "Is there a problem?"

Sabine sucked in a breath. Constable Logan Billson was right behind Doyle. His eyes met hers and something unspoken passed between them. She was supposed to pretend she didn't know him well—not because he'd told her, but Dee had. It was hard.

Tone gestured at the bloody cue. "She attacked me. She's nuts."

Doyle prompted her gently. "Want to tell me what happened, Sabine?"

His tone made her blink, holding back tears, but her eyes stayed on Logan.

"Did you attack this man, Sabine?" Doyle asked.

She turned and stared at Tone in horror. Blood was now running down his leg.

Logan interrupted, looking Tone over with disgust. "First things first. Name?"

"Antony Russo."

"Got anything illegal on you, Russo? Did you purchase alcohol for a minor—maybe solicit sex from an underage girl?"

Sullen now, Tone shook his head.

"Witnesses might say otherwise. I'll have to search you." Logan pulled his notebook from his top pocket. "But you are within your rights to press charges if, like you say, this skinny kid stuck a pool cue in the leg of a fully grown man who should fucking know better." He smiled. "It's been a quiet night. I'd like to keep it that way."

Tone's hand moved to cup the wound on his thigh. "No."

"No, what?"

"I don't want to press charges."

Logan put the notebook away. "Well, that's generous of you." He cocked his head toward at the exit. "Night's over, boys."

As they moved away, Tone shot Sabine another look, one that promised a different ending if they should ever meet again.

Doyle took her by the elbow. "Are you hurt?"

"I'm fine. Taryn's in the bar. I need to find her."

"Your friend was kicked out an hour ago, as you should have been." Doyle let go. "You know how this could have ended, right?"

She nodded.

"We'll make sure you get home safely."

Logan stepped in. "Close call, Kelly? Your knees still shaking? What the hell were you thinking?" To Doyle, he said, "You finish the pub rounds. I'll take this one back."

Doyle hesitated before nodding. "Right." He turned on his heel and went inside.

"Car's out front. Let's go." He took her elbow, his grip a lot less gentle than Doyle's.

"I need the toilet first," she said. "Please."

"Hold it," he said. "Piss in the car, and I'll rub your nose in it."

Frightened and helpless, Sabine's temper flared again. "I'll tell Dee."

Mistake. He ran his cold gaze over her, and she pulled up her top to cover her bare shoulder.

"Logan, *please*."

To anyone watching, it would seem he placed a courteous hand on top of her head as she got in the back of the police car; anyone who knew him would realize he had a fistful of her hair.

As the car pulled away from the curb, Sabine wrapped her arms around her body to stop the shaking. She knew Logan well enough to read his composure for what it was: a prelude to violence. He would use what happened tonight at the Queen against her family.

To threaten Aria, to punish Sabine, to control Dee.

He adjusted the rearview mirror so they could see each other's reflections. He blinked like a reptile and smiled. That was when Sabine knew for sure he wouldn't be taking her straight home.

2019

—

RACHEL

As they enter the same pretty town they passed through on the way to Far Peaks, Rachel has the sense of emerging from the dark into light.

The violence in Far Peaks permeated everything, like an odor you couldn't wash off. She smelled it the last time she was there; it clung to her now, and the statistics on crime in the district only validated her feelings. High on the list: domestic violence, sexual assault, and drugs. Drug manufacture, drug distribution, drug use. Crimes like robberies and break-ins were less frequent—anyone who worked in the mines was rich, and drugs were cheap and plentiful. Her research had shown that even the policing culture was different in an isolated town like Far Peaks; similar to prison culture, it was geared more toward maintaining equilibrium than cleaning up the community. Let enough drugs in to keep the inmates in line; better still, run things yourself by controlling the distribution, thus preventing the inmates from killing each other.

Rachel is not surprised by Sabine's revelation that Logan Billson was involved with the distribution of drugs through her mother, Dee. She's not shocked by allegations of police corruption in general. She is, however, terrified that she won't be able to contain this story. It might blow up to be bigger than she can handle.

Since telling Rachel about Logan Billson driving her out to the middle of nowhere and leaving her to walk home alone, Sabine has been quiet, pensive. Understandable that she'd feel drained after reliving it—Rachel is running on empty too. But Sabine seems intent on going over disparate scenes from her childhood in exhaustive detail, whereas Rachel needs the whole picture if she's going to pull this story together before the deadline.

Before Sabine realizes that she already sold her out.

She bites at a fingernail until it bleeds. As always when she's stressed, she's suddenly starving.

"We could stop, grab some afternoon tea," she says. "Look, there's a bakery." She points and swerves neatly into a vacant parallel parking space. "You coming?"

Sabine shakes her head.

"You're not hungry?"

"I'll just wait here."

Realization hits. "Oh. I'm sorry—I didn't think."

She gets out of the car. At the door of the bakery, she glances back. Sabine has slid so far down in the seat, the top of her head isn't visible.

In the bakery, Rachel pays for a couple of double-cut veggie sandwiches and two bottles of tropical juice. On impulse she grabs a loaf of fresh bread, a large vegetarian quiche, and a tray of Florentines from the counter display.

Back at the car, she hands over one of the sandwiches and a bottle of juice.

Sabine eats fast and two-handed, her body curled protectively around her food as if it might be snatched from her. A clump of mayonnaise slides from her lip to her chin, but she keeps tearing and chewing.

Rachel smiles. "Is it okay?"

"It's good," Sabine says, cheeks bulging. "Thank you." She

swallows, cracks the seal on the juice bottle, and washes the food down with a giant gulp.

"There are some more things in the bag. Take them home with you. I figured you don't get fresh baked goods often."

Rachel pulls a tissue from the box in the console and deftly wipes the mayonnaise from Sabine's chin. Sabine's body tenses; in contrast, her mouth trembles.

"I'm sorry. I didn't mean to embarrass you."

Sabine waves a hand and turns to face the passenger-side window. Without looking at the sandwiches on her lap, she rewraps the uneaten half in its paper.

A noisy group of teenage girls has congregated on the benches outside a Subway.

"They're like starlings," Rachel says. "A murmuration."

"Another big word," Sabine mumbles.

Rachel looks across at her but continues. "All that darting and swooping in unison, but you have no idea who's leading."

Sabine takes her literally. "The red-haired girl. The one wearing the NY cap."

"How do you know?"

"Watch her."

The girl is wearing an oversized T-shirt, short shorts, the cap. She sits apart from the rest, surveying them with a bored look. But Sabine is right; when another girl unwraps her sub, she leans across, takes it, breaks off half, and hands it back. Not a peep or a frown from the girl whose six-inch Subway sandwich has been reduced to three.

"I wouldn't have picked her. She seems separate from the others," Rachel says.

"It's the dominance hierarchy, part of the social order. The leader eats first."

She recognizes that it's judgmental of her, but Rachel is taken aback. "How do you know this?"

"We all send out signals—I'm pretty good at reading them," Sabine says. "People are just animals wearing clothes."

"Are you—were you—a follower or a leader?" It's a clumsy question, and Rachel wishes she could take it back. She rushes on. "Your friend Taryn, the one who left you at the Queen—what was the friendship dynamic between the two of you?"

The name had popped up during Rachel's research, but she wasn't able to locate Taryn for an interview. Could she be the person Sabine was looking for when they took the detour?

Sabine is still staring at the girl. "Taryn." She stops, as if an answer is still coming to her. "No, we were more like this." She hooks her thumbs together, flaps her fingers. "One."

"Did you stay in touch?"

Another quick shake of the head. "Not possible. Not after what happened. Anyway, we fell out before that."

"Why?"

"Taryn thought *I* left *her* that night—I tried to tell her about Logan, but she didn't believe me." Sabine gives a helpless shrug. "I still can't explain it. It was like she used it as a reason to freeze me out. And if my best friend didn't believe me, I knew no one else would."

"You must have felt so alone."

Another shrug. "I'm used to it."

"Have you made other friends? Under your new identity, I mean?"

"Too risky because of the reward."

Rachel nods. A hundred thousand dollars is a lot of money.

Sabine laughs and there's no humor in it. "I don't trust many people, although Ryan would argue with me about that."

"Your boyfriend?" Rachel had interviewed the boyfriend four years ago. Tall, well-built, good-looking. Seemingly guileless. The conversation had only lasted a few minutes before Rachel was convinced he had moved on and knew nothing about Sabine's whereabouts. "Are you saying you're still together?"

Sabine registers her shock. "You don't need to talk to Ryan. He doesn't know anything. Leave him out of this."

"I've already spoken with him," Rachel admits. "Years ago though."

In turn she registers Sabine's surprise and—was it hurt?

"He didn't mention it," she says eventually. "He doesn't like me to worry about things I can't control."

"But it must be difficult, managing your relationship while you're on the run. Have you discussed things like marriage or starting a family?"

"I can't have children," Sabine says.

"Medical reasons?"

Sabine slumps and straightens as if something has jabbed her spine. "I *won't* have children. Not with Ryan or anybody else."

"Okay. You've obviously thought about it."

"Some bloodlines should end, Rachel."

It's said so coldly, a shiver passes through Rachel. She is becoming familiar with Sabine's defensive mannerisms: the twist at the corner of her mouth, the flare of her pupils. She can read signs of avoidance or deceit in most people, but Sabine gives little away.

———

They arrive back at the river house just before six. Within seconds of Rachel pulling into the driveway, Blue barges through a gap in the dividing fence and scrabbles at the passenger-side car door until Sabine gets out. He's all over her, yelping, trying to lick her face.

Immediately, her guard goes down. "Hello, you. Did you miss me?"

"Can't say Mo gives me the same reception," Rachel says dryly.

Sabine grins. "You know what they say: dogs have owners; cats have staff."

Rachel unlocks the front door and pushes it open. "He can come inside. Something tells me I couldn't stop him if I tried."

Blue shoots down the hallway, sniffing every corner and doorway, and Sabine follows, trying to shoo him out of the bedrooms.

"I need to use your toilet," she says.

Rachel turns on the living-room lamps. She slings her suitcase on the dining room table and goes to the kitchen to switch on the coffee machine. Deciding she needs something harder, she takes last night's open bottle of wine from the fridge, pours two glasses, sets one on the counter, and slugs from the other.

They haven't discussed whether Sabine will be staying tonight. She's not sure she'll offer. Despite the scrappiness of her notes and the gaps in Sabine's story, she needs to get to work. Given today's developments, the entire piece will need restructuring. Meeting Cooper's deadline is looking unlikely, if not impossible. It's too much. She will email him in the morning to ask for an extension.

Or—she can pull the story. Let Sabine go and pretend none of this happened.

The thought is a welcome one, giving her instant release from the building anxiety.

Sabine enters and wanders the perimeter of the room, trailing her fingertips over objects: a ceramic wren, a silver antique platter, a dusty bowl of potpourri. Her hand settles on a school photo of Ben and Lexi, aged around nine and seven.

"Cute kids. They look really happy."

"They're grown-up now. Moved out."

"I don't have anything left from my childhood." Sabine is unmoved by her own declaration, or else she's good at hiding it. "No photos, no knickknacks."

Rachel watches the way Sabine studies the faces of her children. In the photo, Ben and Lex are bright-eyed and rosy-cheeked, but Rachel remembers they were both coming down with something that day; the next they'd spiked fevers.

Photos can be deceiving.

"You lost everything in the fire?" she asks.

"Yes."

"What about your grandfather? He didn't keep anything?"

Sabine shrugs. "Nothing to keep. When we visited, we played outside or on the river. We didn't draw or make things, and Pop never took pictures. We ran wild."

"That must be tough. Trying to remember your life without photos, I mean."

Sabine picks up the frame. "I don't have any trouble remembering what happened. I only have trouble with people believing me."

They're obviously not talking about childhood memories anymore.

Rachel carries her glass to the table and sits. "You said after Logan Billson put you in the back of the police car at the hotel, he dropped you roughly five miles from Far Peaks and left you to walk home alone. Why do you think he did that?"

"To teach me a lesson. He wanted to scare me."

"Were you scared?"

"Of course. I was drunk and confused. It was dark. I followed the road back the same way the police car went, but it wasn't until I reached a crossroad that I realized I had gone the wrong way. It took me another two hours to get back to the trailer park."

"And his partner went along with this kind of behavior?"

"Logan's father was the sergeant. I don't think Doyle had a choice."

"Well, that kind of thing probably wouldn't happen these days," Rachel says. "Police wear body cameras. They're miked up."

Sabine seems interested in this information. "Miked?"

"Microphones."

She frowns. "Wouldn't they just turn the cameras off?"

"If they did, it would imply wrongdoing."

"What do they do with the recordings?"

"They can be used as evidence in court." Rachel tries to get the conversation back on track. "Did Logan threaten you? Attack you?"

Sabine shakes her head. "I was in the back. He was quiet. He kept looking at me in the rearview mirror, but that was it. Eventually he stopped the car and told me to get out."

"You didn't ask him to take you home?"

"No. I got out like he said. I flipped him the finger and screamed that he was a bastard, but he didn't stop, of course."

"Why do you think he wanted to scare you? A tough love kind of thing? Teach the wayward teen a lesson, something like that?"

"No. He was just... There was a meanness in him. I used to sass him, and he didn't like it."

"Pretty extreme reaction, if you ask me."

"He was an extreme guy. He got buzzed on inflicting pain."

"And you didn't report the incident?"

Sabine gives a humorless laugh. "Dee would've lost it. I wasn't meant to be out that night. If she knew I'd pissed him off... She warned me to stay out of his way because she didn't want me to ruin her good thing."

Rachel refills her glass. Sabine hasn't touched hers.

"Look, straight up—if you were supposedly framed for the fire, how deep does this go? Was it just Logan? Was it his father the sergeant too, or are we up against the whole bloody force?"

"I never said I was framed, Rachel." The shadows under Sabine's eyes are ghoulish in the lamplight. "I get why Billson wants me to go down—the evidence points to me. That's why I need you to tell my side."

"I'm bound by truth, accuracy, and impartiality. I can't choose sides. Your side will come out in court."

"No, it won't," Sabine says with exaggerated patience. "It'll get covered up to protect Logan's memory. Billson needs to know what his son did. Back then he may have turned a blind eye to some things, but I don't think he had anything to do with the drugs, or Aria and Dee. I don't know for sure. I don't even care anymore—I just want Logan's life destroyed the way he destroyed mine."

"He's dead," Rachel says quietly. "Isn't that enough?"

"It's not enough. I didn't get the chance to say goodbye to Aria and Dee. I never saw them go in the ground. Sometimes I dream they're not dead and it's all a big conspiracy, and I'm walking along the street one day and there they are. I need some kind of closure on this. Since I never got to go to their funeral, I want…this." Until now Sabine has been hugging the picture frame to her chest. She sets it on the table and regards Rachel with wary eyes. "If you use everything I tell you, it'll create some kind of doubt about their version of events. The more you learn about me, the more you believe me, right? The same goes for the public. I just want a chance to tell my side."

"I understand," Rachel concedes. She rubs a hand over her face. "I do believe you, but I'm not sure I'm up for this. This isn't just your story anymore—it requires a full internal investigation."

"Internal? You mean the police investigating the police?"

"Yes."

Sabine's expression turns bleak. She grabs the beach bag and bakery goods from the table and gives a low whistle, prompting Blue to appear.

"Thanks for these." She holds up both bags. "I should go."

Rachel tries to hide her relief. "It's been a long day. Get some rest. I have things to do in the morning, so—"

She walks down the hallway. Sabine and Blue follow.

Already Rachel is drafting an email in her mind—not to beg for an extension, but to back out of the story entirely. Everything about it feels dangerous; just a few more steps, a question asked of the wrong person, and she could be in over her head. The thought of backing out promises peace for her, but where does it leave Sabine?

Exposed. Vulnerable. But that's not Rachel's problem, and it sure as hell isn't her fault. *Is it?*

She opens the door. "I'll be in touch."

"Will you?" A quizzical smile. "How?"

"Carrier pigeon, smoke signals. I don't bloody know."

She's dog-tired. Right now she just wants to crawl into bed.

Sabine is still standing outside on the doorstep, looking at her expectantly. "So that's it?"

"It's a lot. I need some time to think."

Sabine shrugs. "Maybe you're too smart, Rachel. You're worrying about all the big stuff, like nuclear war and all the rules you have to follow and what color rug you'll buy to replace the one my dog just pissed on. Me, I'm just a dumb hick. I crawl out of my cave every morning, and I stretch, and I think, *How will I survive today?*"

A flash of disgust in her blue eyes, and she's gone.

2019

SABINE

Rachel is going to back out. It was Sabine's last thought before she went to sleep, and it's the first to surface when she wakes. Rachel will pull the pin. If not today, then soon, and not because the story isn't as big as Sabine had promised but because she's scared. And she doesn't even know the half of it yet.

She sits up, dizzy. Her head throbs. It's after eight, much later than she usually wakes, but yesterday's events drained her.

She jumps when Pop's tinny bumps against the bow of the *Kirralee*. A wake, washing into the backwater, no doubt. If there's a boat passing nearby, she can't hear it. She throws off the bedcovers and swings her legs to sit on the edge of the mattress, waiting for the dizziness to pass.

The river and this wonky little houseboat have been her home for so long. She has relished her freedom. She looks out the window next to the bed. A perfect cerulean sky broken into puzzle pieces is visible through the tree canopy; a light breeze ruffles the curtains. Autumn is her favorite time of year—cooler temperatures, a cleaner scent. Strange, then, that the cabin walls press in as if the room is shrinking, and all she can smell is mud, blood, and smoke.

She stands, feeling woozy, hungover, although it was Rachel who drank the wine.

She's going to back out.

Suddenly the door flies open. Instinctively, Sabine rolls like a stuntwoman across the bed to the other side, before realizing it's Ryan. *Shit.* That makes it twice in as many days that he's crept up on her.

He fills the space, breathing heavily, eyes wild. With fear or anger, Sabine can't tell. *Both*, she decides.

She presses a palm to her chest. "You scared me! I wasn't expecting you until tomorrow."

"There's blood on the stern—lots of it," Ryan says. "What the fuck is going on?"

"I don't know. I just woke up." Her body floods with adrenaline while her brain struggles to catch up. "Where's Blue? He didn't want to come inside last night."

She'd left him to sleep on the deck.

Oh no oh no oh no.

When she tries to push past Ryan, he holds her back. "I'll look for him. You stay here."

Gratefully, she sinks onto the edge of the bed again. Her bare knees knock together. The pain barely registers. She waits and waits and tries not to cry.

What did he get himself into while she slept like the dead? Did a farmer shoot at him? Did he crawl back for help, and did she snore through it? Stupid bloody animal. Her best friend. *Dumb fucking dog. Beautiful boy.*

The houseboat tips.

Ryan is kneeling in front of her. He puts both hands between her knees to stop the knocking.

"It's not him," he says. "It's something else."

He seems rattled.

"Let me guess," she says flatly. "A deer."

He nods. "Young. Maybe it tried to cross the backwater, got caught in the mud, and panicked."

"And gutted itself?" She shakes her head. "Not likely."

His gaze sharpens. "How'd you know it was gutted?"

She shouldn't have opened her big mouth. She can't tell him about the other deer—there are too many questions she can't handle right now. If she tells him, he won't leave her. Things will be taken out of her hands.

She pushes his hands away. "I'm going to find Blue. Let me put some clothes on."

"Not exactly what I had in mind, but okay." He smiles and gets up, knees cracking.

He has caught too much sun recently: his shoulders are pink, and he has a sunglasses tan. He also has the beginning of an erection, and he's not bothering to hide it. Any other time she'd follow up on the invitation, but she can't shake the feeling that something has happened to Blue. It's not like him to stray far—if he was nearby, he would have heard Ryan arrive and returned straightaway.

"Not now," she says, averting her eyes. "Jesus."

A corner of Ryan's mouth twitches. "I've missed you too."

Aside from worrying about Blue, another thing is bugging her. "But how—?"

The *Kirralee* was well hidden. Unless he got lucky, it should have taken him a whole day of exploring every backwater in the area to find her. But when he glances guiltily at the side table next to the bed, she runs a hand behind it. Her fingers find a clean white charging cable emerging from a hole in the back of the drawer, tangled with the lamp cord and plugged into the wall socket.

"The phone's at the back of the top drawer," Ryan says. "I thought you would have found it by now."

He'd tried to give her a phone a couple of years ago, but she threw it in the river.

"It tells you where I am?"

"There's a tracking app." He puts up a hand. "Before you throw this one overboard too, hear me out. It's not listening to you or recording your conversations, and it doesn't tell anyone but me where you are. It can't be traced."

"*You* traced it! How long has it been there?"

"Couple of months," he admits, red-faced. "It doesn't have a PIN—you can set your own. It's for emergencies. I did it because I love you."

So that was how he found her so easily—not because of some kind of deep and profound connection. She's so *stupid*. The first time was forgivable; the second is not. She feels betrayed.

"Fuck's sake, Ryan. Everyone knows the new phones listen to whatever you say."

He laughs. "Everyone? Who's everyone?"

"Pop said."

"You're as bad as him. Bloody paranoid."

"I'm careful!" she shouts. "That's why I've never been caught!"

In a flurry of furious energy, she strips naked and throws on clean underwear, a tank top, and a pair of denim shorts. She grabs her sneakers from under the bed, but her fingers feel like thumbs, and she can't undo the laces. She swears and stuffs her feet into them, the backs folded under her heels. Ridiculous—she won't be able to walk.

"*Fuck.*" All the fight goes out of her.

Ryan kneels and gently takes off her sneakers. He unties the shoelaces, loosens them, and puts the shoes on properly, as if she's a child.

"All these years, and you've never once asked me if I lit the fires," she blurts. "You've never asked me if I killed anyone."

"I never needed to," he shoots back.

"You didn't need to ask? Or you don't want to know the answer?"

Ryan holds her accusing stare, but it's taking all his concentration.

She wonders if he is experiencing the unsteadiness too—as if the deck has tilted and they are about to slide off.

"Why are you doing this?"

She lowers her eyes. "Doing what?"

"You're up to something." He points at the empty paper bag sitting on the kitchen counter. "Pretty far from the river, isn't it? And maybe a bit close to home?"

The bakery's logo is on the side of the bag.

"A family left it behind on a table in the reserve. Seemed a shame to throw it in the bin."

God, when did they start lying to each other? After the last time, he knew how she felt about phones. But he's done it again. And she can't tell him about Rachel—he'd lose it. He doesn't trust easily. Until recently, neither has she.

"Why now, when things are going well?" he says.

"Things aren't perfect, Ryan, and I'm not the person you think I am."

Before he can react, Sabine leans across the bed, grabs the cable, and reels in the phone from behind the side table. She rips out the cord. The phone looks new, expensive, and she has no idea how to operate it. When she raises the phone, the screen lights up, revealing a photo of a woman. Just the back of her: cropped dark hair, slightly built, sitting on the end of a jetty.

Another woman. The *other* woman.

It's Sabine, of course, but a different version from another time. She has never had to worry if there was anyone else. She doesn't know what jealousy feels like, but she figures the feeling of betrayal comes pretty close.

"Take the phone with you when you leave," she tells him.

He reaches for a rope lead from the shelf above the sink. "Let's go and find your dog."

It's as if she hasn't spoken.

———

A few hours later, they're dusty, sweaty, and the cool morning is turning into a stinking hot afternoon. Ryan has dragged the deer carcass far enough inland that the flies won't bother them. Moving around inside the cabin is like wading through soup.

Still no sign of Blue.

Sabine undresses and runs the outdoor shower. She closes her eyes and turns her face to the spray. A moment later Ryan joins her. They stand under it together, close but not quite touching. Despite the heat and tepid water, she's shivering.

"We should have checked the property up on the hill. He might have gone sniffing around the working dogs. Maybe there's a bitch in heat."

"You would never have risked that a week ago," Ryan says, shaking his head.

"I'm desperate," she says miserably. "People do crazy things when they're desperate."

"He'll turn up. He's probably having the time of his doggone life."

She laughs, and he pulls her into his arms. They stay like that for a while, water pooling between her breasts and his chest, her small feet between his. This is where she has always felt safest.

"It's already been a couple of days," he says. "You need to move to another berth. Maybe you should head back upriver, nearer the border."

It's an uncomfortable reminder that he's been tracking the houseboat's location for months. But he hasn't been tracking Sabine, though he must assume she has been here too. She's not really angry at him anymore, just sad.

"I can't go that far," she says.

"Why?"

Because of Rachel, and Pop, and Blue.

She only mentions Blue. "If Blue comes back and I'm not here, he'll think I left him." She holds up a finger. "Don't you dare say it."

But he does. "He's a dog."

She pulls away, steps out of the cubicle, and wraps a towel around her body. "You don't understand. He's the only thing I've ever managed to save. He's the only thing I've kept alive."

He turns off the water and catches the towel she throws. "You've got me. I'm still here. But you make a good point about your houseplants."

He always does this—a neat pivot around serious topics.

"I know, but aren't you tired of living like this? Of thinking every time we say goodbye, it might be the last time?"

His voice is muffled by the towel as he dries his hair. "I don't think like that. I can't."

"Yeah, well, I can't help it." She scowls. "It's fucked. Everything is fucked."

He loops his towel around her neck and pulls her to him. "Even when I don't get enough of you, it's enough. I love you."

"I love you too," she says hopelessly. "I always will. But maybe we need to let each other go, and soon. On *our* terms."

"Never," he says with quiet conviction. "Not while either of us is still breathing."

Would he still love her if he knew? If she gave herself up, would he wait?

Ryan is a good man. Why wouldn't he be? He's surrounded by good people. She's the only bad thing that has happened to him in his life, and she's wrong to hold on to him. But show her a person who would give up their last loaf of bread if they were starving.

It seems obscene to make love when Blue is missing, when everything is poised on a knife edge.

As usual, Ryan falls asleep straightaway. She has always envied his ability to do that.

She wriggles from the stifling heat of his body to turn on the overhead fan, but it whirs for a few seconds then stops. Without running the engine regularly, the deep-cycle batteries lose charge, and she can't install solar panels without an expensive upgrade to the system.

Goddamn it.

She longs for another cold shower, but the pump won't work now.

Ryan is snoring, oblivious to the unbearable heat and her misery.

Pop is dying.

Blue is gone.

She can't count on Rachel anymore.

Should she stop now? Disappear for good?

But it's too late for that. Taryn has seen her, and it's possible Billson knows she has surfaced. The pendulum is already in motion. If she never sees Rachel again, she has the added challenge of recovering the ziplock bag she's hidden under the sink in the guest bathroom. And she needs to get hold of Pop's envelope.

In the wrong hands, both items could be used against her.

2019

RACHEL

Rachel finally snaps out of her stupor and turns off the shower taps. She has been standing under the hot water for twenty minutes, rotating like a chicken on a rotisserie—that's how long it has taken for her to feel almost human, and to process her thoughts about Sabine Kelly.

Her mobile is ringing in the kitchen: House of Pain's "Jump Around." An incongruous song selection for her ringtone—her son's attempt at being ironic a few months ago. She hasn't bothered to change it.

She dresses quickly in a shapeless beige linen dress and unplugs her phone from the charger in the bedroom. Eight-thirty. She has missed two calls, one from her son, the other from an unknown caller.

Ben's voicemail message is something about borrowing money to pay out his phone contract so he can upgrade to a new model. Like clockwork, he does this every eighteen months. He should know better than to ask. She'll reply later with her usual advice: *If you can't afford to have it now, you can't have it; if it ain't broke, don't ditch it; only use credit for needs, not wants.* Some version of one or all of them.

Her stomach rumbles. She pads barefoot to the kitchen, pours milk into a bowl of bran flakes, and waits for the cereal to disintegrate the way she likes it. She opens the missed-call log and dials the unknown number, expecting a recorded message from a scammer about an Amazon purchase she's never made.

A man picks up. "Hello?"

"This is Rachel Weidermann returning your call."

A pause. Then, "Rachel, thanks for calling back."

"Who is this?"

"I need to speak with you about your progress on the Trailer Murders story. What have you got?" His tone is abrupt.

"Look, I'm not—"

He interrupts. "Let's save ourselves the banter and get down to it. I know it's not ideal, and you've probably invested a lot of time on this."

"Of course," she says, disquiet fluttering in her belly. "What are you trying to say?"

"I'm offering you a kill fee."

"Why?"

He mumbles, "Higher-ups. Conflicting stories, overassignment—you know, the usual. We can't run it."

"I'm sorry, I didn't catch your name," she says.

"You can expect fair terms and a generous payment for the work you've already done on this. You'll find the paperwork in your inbox. Sign it, and I'll arrange an immediate transfer. One of the terms is you can't publish the story with any other publication, online or in print." Another extended pause. "It's a generous payment. I strongly urge you to accept it."

"Are you threatening me?" she squawks. "Who have you spoken to about this—is it Miles Cooper? Who wants to kill it?"

"Every two hours the payment will halve."

Her phone beeps. The line has gone dead. *Bastard.*

Fumbling with her phone, she opens her mailbox. The email is there, as promised, but it's not in the same thread as the other correspondence with Cooper. It has come from a Gmail address, one so generic it could be spam. She opens the attachment: standard non-disclosure stuff. But the figure makes her gasp.

On wobbly legs she moves to sit at the table. She reads the through the contract again to make sure she's not hallucinating. Surely she has misread, added a zero.

Fifty thousand dollars. Twenty times more than any kill fee she has ever accepted.

It doesn't look like a kill fee. It looks like hush money.

An hour later, Rachel has downed two double-shot espressos and is still sitting in the same spot.

She hasn't signed the contract; she hasn't rejected it either. Her severance package is already committed to paying the mortgage, and the divorce settlement, while fair, has left her asset rich and cash poor. Cash flow is precarious on a freelance income; selling the river house is the only way she'll be able to stay afloat.

Fifty thousand dollars is a lot of money, enough to keep her solvent for at least a year.

The man on the other end of the line—what if he isn't affiliated with the newspaper at all? The terms of the contract are questionable; the amount he's offering is obscene. It doesn't sit well with her. But she's so close to dropping the story anyway.

Sign the bloody contract, Rach.

A small but insistent voice is growing louder. *What about Sabine Kelly?*

She might as well take the kill fee out of the equation, because the story is already dead—Rachel killed it when she closed the door on Sabine. Without Sabine there is no story. And Rachel has no way of contacting her. Even if she could just pick up the phone, she wouldn't know what to say to make things right.

So sign the contract. Take the free money.

But is it free and without strings? If it is legit, wouldn't Cooper have called her himself?

She checks the time. In fifty minutes, the payment will drop to twenty-five thousand.

"Shit!"

When she calls the newspaper and asks to be put through to Miles Cooper, the receptionist asks for her name. Her old instinct kicks in and she makes one up, says it's regarding a tip-off for a breaking news story. She waits.

"Cooper."

"It's Rachel."

He sighs. "Take the kill fee, Rachel."

"Just tell me—who's paying, Miles?" she says.

He muffles his voice. "If we printed, we'd end up in court for so long you and I would be wearing adult nappies and eating our food through straws. You won't get a better deal."

This doesn't make sense. "But you don't even know what the story is about."

Silence.

"Miles? Who did you speak to about this? You knew my pitch was confidential." The signal appears to drop out. She opens the sliding door and moves outside. "Miles? Are you there?"

He has hung up on her too. "*Goddamn* it."

Cooper spoke to someone about the story. Or maybe it wasn't him—it could have had gone through several people, and he's been warned off too. Either way, it's a breach of privacy. But there's no way she can accept the money now with a clear conscience, not if it means Sabine is telling the truth and someone wants to shut her up.

She squats on the step, hugging her knees. It's almost half past ten. She's tired. Emotional. Scared. And epically pissed off.

Mo rubs against her legs and slinks past. When he spots something in the direction of the shed, he creeps down to the retaining rocks and switches to stealth mode, rump wriggling, ready to pounce.

Rachel tries to work out what he's after. Her eyes land on Ray Kelly's trap, cable-tied to the apple tree. Her first thought: Ray Kelly must have a way of contacting Sabine, surely? Her second: she has caught a rat.

Warily, she approaches the trap. The poor thing is huddled in a corner, eyes bulging. Mo, thwarted, stalks away. When she gets close, the rat starts running mad laps and clawing at the mesh.

What did Sabine tell her? *Hit it with a brick.*

This was the kind of stuff Aidan would sort out, along with spiders, snakes, cleaning gutters, negotiating the price of a new car—their gender-based roles were clear-cut. It's times like this she feels his absence most acutely, which only affirms she doesn't need a husband—she needs a handyman. She's a bad feminist.

Drowning! Drowning is supposedly a peaceful death once you get past the thrashing part.

She opens the shed and finds a pair of gardening gloves and shears on the bench. She puts on the gloves and goes outside, sidling up to the cage. The rat is back in its corner, watching her with evil eyes. Shuddering, she snips the cable ties and, holding the cage away from her body like a dirty sock, heads down to the jetty. She doesn't overthink it, doesn't make any further eye contact with the rat in case she changes her mind.

It's only after she has dropped the cage over the side that she realizes she should have tied it off to the jetty post. The bloody thing doesn't sink the way it's supposed to. Aghast, she watches it drift away like a tiny boat before lodging in a clump of reeds about six meters away.

She runs back along the jetty and down to the bank.

The tray at the bottom is filling up; the cage tips and begins to sink. The rat is frantic now, emitting heartrending squeaks and hanging like a trapeze artist by its tiny humanlike hands.

After the first time, flesh is just meat.

There will be no second time. It's all too much. Rachel kneels in the mud, covering her eyes. She can't watch, and she doesn't have the courage to jump in to save it.

She counts to thirty and peeks through her fingers: nothing but bubbles. Despite the perfect weather, the river is brown and murky, rippling with strong current underneath. She feels just like the poor rat. And she's lost Ray Kelly's trap—that'll be grounds for murder.

She looks up. Halfway across the river, something is cutting its way through the water. Jesus, a bloody snake—that's all she needs right now. She jumps to her feet and up onto the steps, but the thing keeps coming like an arrow pointed straight at the jetty. As it gets closer, she can make out two dappled ears and a pink nose.

It's Blue.

Her heart still pounding, she searches for any sign of Sabine. The river is clear of traffic in both directions. When Blue reaches the bank and drags himself ashore, she heads back down the steps to meet him.

"Where did you come from?"

He responds with a half-hearted tail wag and a shake, spraying water on her. At any other time, she would say he looked like a drowned rat, but the idiom has taken on a more literal meaning. He's clearly exhausted, and there's a weeping cut under one eye. How far has he swum? And the bigger question: Where is Sabine? Has something happened to her?

Blue wanders down to take up a position at the end of the jetty, staring across the river like a fisherman's wife in mourning.

A feeling of dread comes over her. If Sabine doesn't arrive in another fifteen minutes, she'll raise the alarm with Ray Kelly.

She checks her phone. Twenty past eleven. The payment has already halved, and it'll halve again soon. In not choosing to accept or reject the offer, she has made a decision. One she can live with.

She makes her way down to the jetty.

When she sits next to him, Blue shuffles closer, and she uses a corner of her dress to wipe his bleeding eye. He licks her face once and returns to his vigil.

She wishes he could talk. Maybe he knows something she doesn't.

Rachel puts her arm around the wet dog and cries.

2019

—

SABINE

It's almost one o'clock in the afternoon before Ryan leaves, and only then because he has been called back on shift a day earlier than expected.

Sabine's voice is hoarse from calling for Blue; her eyes ache from holding back tears. For lunch, they ate the quiche Rachel had bought. They threw the rest away, along with most of the contents of the fridge. With the batteries dead, the fridge has stopped working and the food is beginning to spoil. Ryan asked Sabine repeatedly where the bakery goods came from, but she stuck to her story.

"I'll see you in a week," he says. "Try not to worry. Blue will turn up, I promise."

They kiss, but it's more bared teeth than soft lips. He is suspicious; she's angry, but not at him, not anymore. Digging up the past has brought her hatred to the surface—it's as bright and hot as it ever was. For a dead man, Logan Billson still wields power over her life, or lack of a life.

Before Ryan has disappeared around the nearest bend, she has the *Kirralee* locked up, the tinny ready to go. She won't move berth in case Blue returns, but she can't sit around waiting either. She has to charge the batteries and dispose of the rubbish before it stinks up the place. Ryan refused to take the phone with him. Should she risk keeping it, or ditch it overboard between destinations? Undecided, she tucks the phone in her shorts pocket.

The current is brisk, and it's hard work steering upriver. She cuts as close to the bank as she can in case Blue is nearby. Every now and again, she whistles for him, but the only creature to respond is a tame magpie who hitches a ride for a couple of miles, perched on the bow.

It's Blue's spot—she has to resist the urge to shoo it away. When she reaches Dixon's backwater, the magpie flies off.

She ties up the tinny and, carrying the rubbish bag, makes her way up the path.

Dixon's shack is an extension of one of the originals, built in the late 1800s. Set on a gentle rise beneath the cliffs, the lower story is little more than a stone hut with a dirt floor, and is susceptible to flooding. Inside there are tidemarks on the walls, like the rings of a tree. In 1956, the roof had gone under; Sabine struggles to imagine the water so high. Back when Dixon's old man was alive, Pop had brought her and Aria here; she remembers dozing on a camp bed in the shack while the men drank themselves comatose by the campfire.

She has always been fascinated by the history here: relics hidden in the cracks between stones, bones beneath the dirt, initials carved into the cliffs. As a child, before she knew better, she would spend hours sifting through the layers of the old midden to find treasure. Now the midden is roped off, protected as a heritage-listed site.

To distract herself from a wave of melancholy, Sabine focuses on the building appearing through the trees. The upper story of the shack was built around the mid-1970s and has basic modern conveniences. There is no easy access, and it's a steep walk along the cliff path to the road—one of the reasons she feels safe here: she knows all the exits. And Dixon has guns. A lot of them.

Ordinarily, Blue would announce their arrival by bounding ahead. Now she calls out to warn him she's coming.

"Dixon!"

No answer, but the generator is running so he must be up at the shack.

She climbs the steps and checks the door handle. Unlocked. "Dix?" She enters, leaving the door open. "You here?"

She sniffs. The kitchen is a mess of dirty plates and saucepans. She picks up a bag of weed. He's that confident nobody will trespass, he leaves his paraphernalia lying all over the place: baggies, papers, a Coke-can bong, whole branches of buds hanging out to dry. It's not an entirely unpleasant smell, and smoking marijuana isn't the worst crime, but Sabine doesn't discriminate. She hates all drugs. She hates what they do to people.

"Yo, Sabine." Dixon is standing in the doorway.

"Hey. I've left some rubbish at the bottom of the stairs if that's okay."

"I'll get rid of it." He gives her a lazy grin. "Unless you've got body parts in there."

"Nah, not this week." As for exits, he's got the only one here covered. "And I need to charge a battery."

"Again?"

"Yeah, it's getting old. Runs out real quick."

She has different voices for different people. The rough twang is some kind of self-protective reflex. She loathes it, but she has to remind Dixon she's his people, otherwise he forgets.

"Well, okay, then. No problem," he says.

It's not really the time for a confrontation, but she might not get another shot.

"I know you're growing on Pop's patch."

"Ray's okay with it."

"How many you got?"

A defensive shrug. "Under ten."

"So, like, two? Or nine? Because there's a big difference if he's caught."

"He won't get caught." He takes a few steps toward her.

She stands her ground. "Pull 'em out, Dix. He's got a record—he'll die in jail if they catch him. He's sick. But you already knew that."

"He told me not to tell you. Fuck's sake, Sabine, the stuff's mostly for him. He goes through a bag a day." He gives her a mock bow. "But whatever you say."

"Thanks. Appreciate it."

"Beer?" He pushes past her and opens the fridge.

When he hands her a bottle, she takes it. *Play nice.* "Hey, Dix, I need a gun," she blurts.

If he's surprised, he doesn't show it. "What kind?"

"One that shoots."

"Funny," he drawls. "One that makes a big messy hole, or a tidy little one?"

"Tiny gun, tiny hole." She gives him her widest smile, followed by her biggest chug. "Please."

"I've got a record—I'll die in jail too if they catch me supplying a weapon to a murderer."

"*Accused* murderer," she snaps.

"Oh, excuse me. *Accused.*" He laughs. "Your pop gonna shoot me when he finds out?"

"Only if you mention it."

He regards her for a moment. He's drunk and stoned—a dangerous combination.

"All right. Wait here." He goes into his bedroom. A minute later, he calls her.

With some trepidation she follows, keeping her eyes averted from the bed.

He places a black handgun in her palm. "Beretta, ten-shot. Should do nicely."

"That's a lot of shots," she says.

"Not if you miss nine times." He gives her a box. "Ammo. Who you planning to shoot?"

"It's just for protection. Maybe a bit of persuasion."

"You need me to show you how to use it?"

"I know how," she says. She doesn't need ammunition, but she doesn't want to tell him that. "I'll give it back when I'm done with it."

He hoots a laugh. "I'm not getting pinned for anything you do with it. You take it, you bought it. Eight hundred." When she flinches, he says, "Fine, I'll spot you. I know where to find an easy hundred grand if I need it."

He's joking. And threatening. It's not the first time.

"Sure you know how to point this thing? Look. I'll show you." He comes around behind her.

"I've got it."

He puts one hand on her hip; the other reaches for the gun. "Give it to me."

He's too close with his hot breath on her neck; his sweat reeks of hops and dope.

Sabine's blood drums to a familiar warning beat. She spins on her heel, cupping the butt, her finger resting on the trigger. She aims at his groin. "Like this?"

"It's not loaded." He bares his teeth.

"Are you sure?" she says coldly.

He's not sure. He puts up his hands and backs away.

To conceal her shaking hands, she lowers the gun. "Dix, I owe you big-time. If things don't work out, I'll let you know—you can walk me into the station and claim the reward yourself."

While he contemplates that, she takes the weapon and the bullets and slips away.

———

Sitting low in the water, buffeted by the current, the boat seems sluggish during this next part of Sabine's journey upriver. Every thought finds its way back to the unbearable weight of missing Blue.

It takes her a full ten minutes to realize she forgot to charge the battery, thirty miles sitting in the hull, weighing the tinny down. Or maybe it's all the rage she's carrying. It has been like this since she developed breasts, keeping men in general—and Dixon in particular—at arm's length.

When she was twelve, she and Taryn were walking past a parked car on their way home from school when a man called out to them. They turned to find him masturbating. At fourteen she ran home from a party when a guy put her hand down his pants and tried to force her to jack him off. At fifteen, she was swimming in the public pool when the older brother of a friend cornered her in the deep end—at first she was flattered, but then he peeled her bikini bottom aside and stuck his finger inside her. With each assault, she froze, numb with shock, and later wondered what she'd done wrong. How did they always find her? Was it somehow her fault?

Until the night at the Queen, when she fought back. Even then, Logan took that away from her.

These days her rage is a simmering, seething thing, like an evil twin kept in the cellar. Dixon has no idea how much strength it takes her to humor and placate him, to resist succumbing to her fury. She's so tired of being afraid. But not of him or anyone else—of what she might do.

Of course, she doesn't have to do anything. She has Ryan. She has the river to take her wherever she wants to go. She'll find Blue. She could return the gun to Dixon, demand Rachel forget everything she has told her, and accept her life as it is, however limited.

But she keeps going back to the first time she met Ryan and the weeks after. Not even three months between the night at the Queen and the night of the fire, when everything changed. She had been on her way to writing a different ending when Logan ripped the last pages from her book.

No, it's not enough that he's dead.

Now she's an accused murderer with a gun.

2007

—

SABINE

aria Pike's eighteenth birthday party was all anyone had talked about for weeks. Sabine and Taryn had planned their *D*-themed costumes months in advance and changed their minds a dozen times. Taryn had finally decided on Daphne from *Scooby-Doo*. Sabine was convinced nobody else would think of Day of the Dead. But now she and Taryn weren't speaking, and her excitement about the party had turned to apprehension.

A Dracula opened the door and ushered Sabine inside. The moment she walked into the house, she felt eyes on her. She heard the whispers. The only reason she'd decided to go at all was because she'd spent fifty bucks on renting her costume, plus the fifty-dollar deposit. The whole thing cost her weeks of babysitting so Dee could head off on one of her benders.

She felt sick. It was a mistake to come.

School wasn't Sabine's favorite place at the best of times, but over the past two weeks, she'd simply stopped going. She and Taryn had had their arguments before, but this was different. Taryn's popularity soared when she started talking trash about Sabine, and it took Sabine the longest time to figure out why her own had taken a dive. To make things worse, Faith kept getting on her case about missing school. Predictably, Dee acted like she'd won a bet.

When she entered Daria's living room, there were three other

girls who looked just like her: bright dresses, skull makeup, crowns of
flowers. Heads turned; the crowd parted. Groups of friends huddled
and whispered; dancing couples broke eye contact to point and stare.
It was like they were trying not to be infected by her. No one could
catch what her family had. Violence. Poverty. Addiction. Neglect.
Everyone in the town had something to say about her family. It was
easier to ignore when it was said behind her back, but much harder
when they did it to her face.

She steeled herself and kept walking. The house was packed, the
music too loud, the air too close. Thankfully she couldn't see Taryn
anywhere. She went out through the back door, helped herself to a can
of Coke from an old washing machine being used as a cooler, while
her classmates continued to move around her.

A few were getting braver. One girl muttered, "Skank," and the
others laughed.

A reputation is a strange thing, Sabine thought. *It can grow without
you feeding it. You will shrink to fit it. It allows you access to some places,
keeps you out of others. It will define you if you let it, and there's no control,
no second chances, no escape.*

Maybe it wasn't all Dee's fault, but it was Dee she blamed at times
like this, when nothing ever seemed to go to plan.

Or would she have ended up at exactly this point anyway? Maybe
it was something in *her.*

She wandered to the end of the garden, where a few people were
sitting on deck chairs around a smoking fire pit. Globes were strung
along the rear fence, throwing a dim blue light. In the adjacent shed,
she could hear others playing pool and dance music blasting in the still
night. How long would it be before the cops came to shut it down?

Rhiannon McBride, one of Taryn's new confidants, got up from
a guy's lap. "Wow, you've got balls showing up," she slurred. "We all
thought you left town."

Sabine was suddenly tired of everything. She didn't want to fight. There was enough of that at home. She should leave.

"Hey, Daria!" Rhiannon waved the birthday girl over. "Look who's here. Thought you should know."

Daria looked Sabine over and gave a theatrical shudder. "I don't remember inviting *you*."

"Well, you did," Sabine said cheerfully. "It's fine, I'm leaving. Happy eighteenth, Daria."

Daria caught Sabine's arm. "Wait. Where's my present?"

Sabine blushed. She hadn't brought anything.

"How rude."

A crowd formed around them. It appeared Taryn had been the only person standing between Sabine and the wolves. Now the pack was closing in.

She could feel her makeup sweating down her cheeks—before she could stop herself, she rubbed her eyes with her fists. Immediately, they watered and stung.

As if performing for the crowd, Daria gave Sabine a hard shove in the chest.

Sabine stumbled back and righted herself. Her eyes were streaming so badly she could barely see. Someone tore the crown of flowers from her head, ripping out a clump of hair in the process. Hands on her body. Cool air on her skin as the elasticized neckline of her costume dress was pulled off her shoulders. All she had on underneath, she remembered, was an ugly strapless bra.

Her temper flared; she swung wildly but hit nothing.

The music stopped. Nervous laughter.

"What the fuck, you guys?"

A man's voice. Youngish. Authoritative. Sabine fumbled for her dress and tried to yank it up, but she was standing on the hem.

"Everyone, back off. Give her some room."

Sabine found the sleeves and slipped them on. She swiped at her eyes with the material. Gradually they stopped watering, and the scene came into focus.

It was easy enough to guess who the voice belonged to: the only person not in costume, and so tall she had to look up to see his face.

"Why are you here?" Daria whined. "Did my parents send you? Are you spying?"

The guy took in her horns, forked tail, and suspenders. "What are you supposed to be, Daria?"

Her lips flattened. "I'm the devil, *obviously.*"

He grinned but didn't respond, which said everything. Sabine ranked it as one of the most satisfying moments in her life. Her temper was cooling, but his perfect disdain was having the opposite effect on her racing heart.

"Are you okay?" he asked.

Sabine ducked her head to hide her flaming cheeks. "I'm fine."

"At least all your guests dressed to your theme, Daria—I've never seen so many drunk dickheads at one party." He threw a look of disgust at everyone standing around. "You all need to take a good hard look at yourselves."

Daria skulked away with her forked tail between her legs, signaling the spectators to disperse. The music started again, at a lower volume, and the guy showed a sudden interest in something lying in the burnt grass at the bottom of the garden.

Sabine stood there, half naked, clutching her dress to her chest. She felt horribly exposed and alone. After a moment, she gathered what was left of her dignity and left, pushing her way through the crowd in the living room, most of whom seemed oblivious to what had taken place outside. Her humiliation was complete—or so she thought.

Just outside the front door, she realized her dress was torn and her crown missing. If she didn't return the costume in good order, her deposit wouldn't be refunded. Fifty bucks, gone. No way was she going back in there.

She started walking home.

The door opened behind her. "Hey!"

She was already on the footpath when he caught up. She had been about to let her tears fall. She sniffed deeply and held them back.

"Hey, wait!"

She stopped. "I'm fine."

"You left this behind." He brushed off the crown and handed it to her. A few of the fabric flowers were singed at the edges. "It landed in the fire—it's a bit worse for wear."

"Shit," she said. "I mean, thank you."

"Ryan," he said, reaching out.

For a second she thought he was about to shake her hand—instead, he plucked away a leaf that had stuck to her makeup. Embarrassed, she yanked back the hand she'd offered in return.

"Sabine."

"You go to school with Daria?"

She nodded.

"My family are friends with the Pikes. They were worried about leaving the house tonight, so I said I'd sneak over and check out the party. Make sure things didn't get out of control." He leaned close enough to ruffle her hair with his breath. "I'm undercover."

Despite her self-consciousness, she smiled. "I think your cover's blown."

He looked down at his T-shirt, shorts, and thongs. "Yeah. They might have bothered to mention it was a costume party."

He didn't talk like anyone she knew, but she wasn't uncomfortable with him. And she didn't feel as if she needed to keep up her tough act.

"What happened back there?" he asked. "Apart from the *Mean Girls* parody, I mean."

She laughed. "You're right. That's exactly what it was."

"Daria can be impossible sometimes. I'm sorry they did that to you."

She smiled. He sounded much older than he looked. "It's okay. I'm used to it."

"My money's on you if you want to finish the fight."

She shook her head. "I'm going home, actually. This is not really my thing."

"Mine neither. Can I walk you?"

She'd let her defenses down. Now they were back up. The last thing she wanted was for him to see where she lived, but she didn't want the conversation to end so soon.

"Maybe a little way," she said. "For all I know you could be an ax murderer."

He turned out his pockets and showed her his phone and keys. "See? No ax. *You*, on the other hand—frankly, you're scaring me."

She touched her sticky face and tucked a strand of hair behind her ear. She must look like the walking dead. "I'm normal under all this, I promise."

They had just crossed the road when Sabine saw lights strobing on a corrugated-iron fence. She knew those lights; she was intimate with that shade of iridescent blue.

The police car pulled up alongside them. The sirens were off, and there was a familiar profile in the driver's seat. Logan got out first, one hand on his baton as if there was some kind of imminent danger. Doyle followed.

"Well, look who's here." Logan's eyes ran over Sabine's costume and makeup. "Nobody told me it was Halloween."

"Constable Billson," she said.

Doyle glanced at them, then muttered, "I'll do a sweep." He crossed the road, strode to the front door of the Pikes' house, knocked, and went inside.

Immediately, the music stopped, and a chorus of groans resounded.

"Isn't this an eighteenth birthday party?" Logan said. "Are you eighteen yet, Sabine?"

She kept her expression carefully blank. "No."

"Have you been drinking?"

She went to hold up her can of Coke as evidence, but she'd left it behind. "No."

"We had a phone call about a disturbance."

"I didn't do anything wrong," she said sullenly.

"Oh, you're on good behavior tonight? That's a first."

"*I didn't do anything wrong*," she repeated.

She shot a look at Ryan, who seemed to register the undercurrent of the conversation.

He spoke. "Everything's fine in there. I checked. The music will be shut off at twelve—I'll make sure of it."

Logan's frigid gaze swiveled toward him. "And you are?"

"Ryan Franklin."

"How old are you?"

"Twenty."

"Sabine is underage. She tell you that?"

Logan knew damn well how old she was.

"I'm seventeen," she mumbled.

"Is there a curfew for seventeen-year-olds I don't know about?" Ryan said. A beat, then, "Sir."

Logan gave Ryan the once-over and dismissed him. His scrutiny returned to her. If things went the way they often did, Sabine's night was far from over.

"Where're you headed, Sabine?"

She sighed heavily to mask her growing agitation. "Home."

"You can go," he said to Ryan. "She's not your problem."

"It's no problem," he replied in the same measured tone. "I'll make sure she gets home."

"No need. We'll take her." Logan took her by the elbow, pressing hard in the exact spot where she had a near-permanent bruise. "It's a well-worn route."

Sabine was used to Logan's possessive manner, but Ryan frowned. Logan was getting wound up, and that guaranteed someone would get hurt. She didn't want it to be Ryan.

"I've changed my mind. I'll go in the car." She took two steps toward the police car and stopped. "Thanks for taking care of me, Ryan Franklin."

His frown deepened, his confusion evident. "I don't think this is a good idea."

"On your way," Logan said. "Before you get a free ride too."

Sabine stood by the rear passenger-side door and waited. If Ryan wasn't still standing there watching, she would have curled up in a ball and howled.

Doyle came back. "A bit of underage drinking going on, I suspect, but nothing worth the paperwork." His eyes flicked between the three of them, gauging the tension. "What's going on?"

"We're taking Sabine home," Logan said.

Doyle froze, then snapped back to his usual smiling, amiable self. "It's a long shift. Let's go then."

The moment he said it, a second police car pulled up. Immediately, the two officers stepped back. Sergeant Billson heaved himself out, hitching his pants under his big belly. Sabine had never seen father and son together, wearing the same uniform, in the same place.

Billson eyed her. "Do we have a situation?"

Before she could think better of it, Sabine took a deep breath and spoke in a rush. "They're trying to make me go with them, and I don't want to."

Billson addressed his son. "Did she tell you she doesn't need a ride home?"

"She's fine with it," Logan muttered.

"I don't want to go," Sabine said in a loud, clear voice.

"Any reason why we should detain this young person, Constables?"

Logan and Doyle both stared at the ground. "No," they said in unison.

"And the young man over there?" He nodded at Ryan.

Silence.

"On your way, Constables."

Billson stood watching until the other police car had gone. To Sabine, he said, "Is there anything you'd like to tell me about tonight, young lady?"

She glanced at Ryan. "No, sir," she said.

"Are you sure?"

When she nodded, he took a notebook from his top pocket and wrote something down. He tore off the page and handed it to her. "This is my number. You call me if you change your mind."

She took it. "I will."

"Give my regards to your mother, Sabine," Billson said. "You can go. And stay out of trouble."

Later, Ryan would say it was when she threw her wild punch that he knew he was gone. It was the fierce set of her mouth as she swung, and the fury she held contained as she walked out of the party. It was the way she kept him at arm's length for weeks before letting him touch her.

For her it was the opposite. It was his openness, his gentleness.

The way he looked at her, as if she was something precious he might break. It was the way he defended her, every time, without question. Nobody had ever done that for her.

2019

—

RACHEL

Rachel wonders at what point exactly she stopped being afraid of Ray Kelly. It's been less than a week since he held a rifle to her spine—now she's contemplating getting into the smallest boat in the world with him *and* his gun. On the *river*, this wide brown ribbon of terror. She's definitely still afraid of the water.

She has one foot on the edge of the boat, the other submerged in mud. "Maybe I should wait here?" she says. "In case she eventually turns up?"

Ray grunts and nudges her backside with the gun. Not as a threat this time, she decides, but simply as an extension of his free arm—he's trying to hold the boat steady with the other arm so she can climb aboard. Chivalry is not dead.

"Fine."

She swears under her breath and gets in, scrambling to grab on to the aluminum seat as the boat rocks under her weight. Blue jumps in to settle at the bow. Ray Kelly lays the gun in the bottom of the boat and walks out until the water laps at his shorts; he turns the boat, then hoists himself inelegantly over the side to take the seat at the rear.

Already nauseous, she spots a filthy life jacket under the seat and yanks it out.

"Can I put this on?"

"Suit yourself," he says.

All it had taken was for her to knock on his door. He took one look at her expression and glanced at Blue sitting on the porch step behind her. "Something has happened to Sabine," he says.

So far he hasn't asked her a single question.

Rachel has many, but she gets the impression Ray blames her for this turn of events. Perhaps this is a form of punishment. At the back of her mind, she does feel responsible; it's pretty clear to her now that Miles Cooper has told someone else that Sabine is her source, and that someone might be looking for her, and they might have found her.

Ray steers the boat away from the jetty into deeper water.

Rachel closes her eyes. Spray hits her face and arms, but if she doesn't look, she can almost pretend she's riding in a convertible without a seat belt. It's a prospect infinitely less terrifying than imagining what lies beneath. After a few minutes in the full sun, she's enjoying the cooling spray. The chop-chop rhythm is hypnotic, and she finds herself almost relaxing. At least she has a life jacket.

She opens her eyes.

The view is spectacular: lush green foliage presses in on both sides; sunlight catches on the waves. Every now and then a bright spot of color: a bird, a buoy, a kayak. She has been on speedboats and paddle steamers, but never something this small. It sits so low she worries the water will rush in if they stop.

Out here, Rachel has little concept of the time passing or the distance traveled. She guesses they've been moving for five minutes or so. For an old guy who's pretty wobbly on land, Ray is nimble on the water. The river must be his natural habitat. Occasionally he gives a hacking cough and spits over the side.

"You know, this would be easier if you people had mobile phones," she says. "How do we know where to find her?"

"We don't," he says. "*He* does."

Blue stares straight ahead, his ears pinned. At first she's unsure what they're looking for, but when the dog's ears prick forward, Ray slows down. Blue shows some interest in a couple of backwater openings but holds his position. It's only when they near a vast stretch of land unbroken by jetties or beaches that his body language changes: he stands with his front paws on the bow, muscles bunched as if he might jump overboard.

"Right-o," Ray says and slows the engine. "Here."

Blue stays put, but he's prancing and whining now.

It's a narrow opening, and Rachel can tell by the clumps of reeds at the edge that the water is shallow. Ray seems wary of taking the boat much further. He lets it drift, craning his neck. Another meter and the dirty-white *Kirralee* comes into view.

"There it is!" she says.

Ray is less animated. After a moment she can see why. The houseboat gives off an air of forlorn abandonment. Blue has already lost interest.

"Blood." Ray frowns. "On the stern."

Rachel is suddenly faint. "Is it—"

"Can't tell, but my tinny's not here," he says.

"The tinny?"

"My other boat." He gives the motor a quick squirt to bring them alongside the houseboat. He points to an aluminum ladder. "I can't get up there. Bung knees. You'll have to check."

Rachel opens her mouth to argue—whatever is inside the cabin, she doesn't want to be the one to see it. But Ray's bright eyes and grim expression tell her he would if he could.

"Okay." She kicks off her sneakers.

The second she reaches for the handrail, Blue launches himself out of the tinny. By the time she has climbed the bottom two rungs, he's waiting for her on the houseboat, panting.

She pulls herself up onto the deck. The timbers are warm and smooth underfoot. There is no sound or movement from inside the cabin, and the curtains are drawn.

She tries the door handle. "It's locked," she calls out.

"Won't take much," Ray says. "Kick it in."

She thinks he's joking, then remembers he's not the joking type. She nudges the door with her shoulder. It gives a little. Another shove and the wood cracks. A third and the door flies open.

There's so much crammed into the small space, Rachel doesn't know where to start. And it's a *mess*. The fridge is wide-open, empty except for a carton of shelf-stable juice. Clothes are strewn everywhere, and the bed looks like there's been a brawl between the sheets. She checks behind both doors on the opposite side of the room: one is a toilet, the other a storage cupboard.

Thankfully, no blood and no body. She closes the broken door as best she can and goes back out on the deck.

"She's not here," she says breathlessly. "But there's stuff everywhere—it looks like the place has been ransacked."

Unbelievably, Ray laughs. He doesn't elaborate.

"What about the blood? Could it be from the cut on Blue's eye?"

He shakes his head. "Too much of it."

"So what do we do now?"

"Stop talking, woman, so I can think."

Rachel backs down the ladder and takes her seat in the tinny.

Blue jumps in, mud-streaked and stinking of something foul. Ray takes a leather pouch from his shirt pocket and draws out a hand-rolled cigarette. He lights up and takes a luxurious drag.

Frustrated, she shouts, "I'm trying to help her!"

"You're only out to help yourself." He spits in the water. "Why are you here? What's in it for you?"

She refrains from pointing out that he made her get in the boat.

"Nothing," she says. "I'm no longer writing or publishing the story."

"Ah." He squints at her. "You mean she gave herself up for you, and you've given up on her. Well, that's just great."

"Sabine was driving this," she says indignantly. "She said she wanted justice for her mother and sister. I'm not sure how my story would have achieved that, but that's what she wanted."

"She said you were smart—guess she thought you'd figure it out." He starts the motor. "Maybe she knows it won't change anything, and she just wants to be heard."

"Who's after her, Ray?"

He sighs. "It's Billson, innit? He hasn't stopped in twelve years, and he ain't gonna stop now."

"So what do we do? Where do we go next?"

He flicks his butt overboard and takes hold of the rudder. "Home. Nothing we can do."

"Something is clearly wrong. We can't go home."

Ray guns the motor, turning so sharply that Blue loses his balance and Rachel is thrown sideways. She rights herself, rubbing her elbow.

"I don't understand how you can just give up!"

He glances back at her. "Let me spell it out for you. Sabine's not here, the tinny's gone, and the mess in there is just how she lives now. The dog's not acting funny, and now you've told me you're not going to tell her side of the story, so I've only got one conclusion, right?"

She's not sure she wants to know. "What's that?"

He looks at her as if she's the stupidest being on the planet. "A smart animal always builds a burrow with more than one exit. Best thing you and I can do is stay out of the way."

Rachel is lost in her thoughts when Ray steers the boat up to a shady beach on the other side of the river. A rough concrete boat ramp slopes down to the water in front of a building, just visible through the trees below the cliffs. If they hadn't stopped, she wouldn't have known it was there.

There's no jetty—Ray simply drives the boat into the mud until it stops.

"I won't be long," he says. "Stay in the boat."

He gets out and limps along an overgrown path in the direction of the building, wheezing in pain.

If Ray's command was for both of them, Blue is the first to disobey. The moment Ray is out of sight, he jumps out. Straightaway he picks up an interesting scent and follows it, snuffling along the ground in a zigzag pattern, tail wagging.

Rachel waits for almost half an hour. It must be ninety-five degrees in the shade, and her linen dress is drenched in sweat. She needs to pee.

She hesitates a minute longer, then climbs out. There are a number of well-defined shoe prints in the mud; other people must have been here recently.

Further along the bank, she finds a bush with enough cover.

After peeing, she whistles for Blue, who has disappeared along the same path Ray took. If neither of them returns from wherever they've gone, she's stranded on the wrong side of the river with a tiny boat she has no idea how to operate and a gun she couldn't use if her life depended on it.

"Great, just great," she mutters.

She follows the path to a small clearing; beyond it she can make out the lower level of the building, an old open-fronted sandstone structure the same color as the cliffs. Above it is a ramshackle upper extension with mismatched windows and a narrow balcony, accessed by a steep set of stairs on the side.

A few steps closer, and she hears raised voices. Much closer, a rustling sound.

Ray's gravelly tone. "What for?"

"I don't know. Like I said, I gave it to her, and she left." A different man's voice. Younger.

Ray again. Indistinct.

"How would I know?"

"You see her, you tell her—"

"Yeah, yeah. She's a big girl, Ray. She's gotta do what she's gotta do."

The voices seem to be coming from somewhere behind the building. The rustling is Blue; he has his whole head inside a plastic garbage bag at the bottom of the stairs. The area around him is scattered with rubbish and food scraps.

Rachel grabs him by his ruff and tries to pull him away. He resists—he's found something good at the bottom. She manages to get his head out of the bag, but he refuses to spit out whatever he has in his mouth.

"Drop it," she hisses.

One last baleful glare, and he coughs up a twisted piece of cling wrap filled with what looks like scrambled egg and pieces of ham.

Rachel's skin tingles with recognition. She sees it now: the bakery bag, strewn amongst the rest of the rubbish. Was Sabine here? Is she *still* here? No, she decides. If she was here, Blue would be less interested in quiche.

She runs back toward the river, patting her thigh to encourage Blue to follow. They make it with seconds to spare before Ray Kelly appears, walking as fast as his bung knees will allow.

Rachel is still out of breath. Blue has egg on his face.

A shrewd look from Ray. "Thought I told you to wait in the boat."

She bows her head. "I am in the boat."

"There's been a development. She's been here."

Okay—so she doesn't have to make the decision whether or not to tell him.

"And?"

"Took a bit to get it out of him. Dixon gave her a gun."

"Who's Dixon?"

"An old friend." He rubs a gnarled hand over his face. "Look, the upshot of all this is we won't find her unless she wants to be found. That envelope—give it to the police. I'm almost dead anyway."

"What's in it? How will it change anything?"

"I'm a coward," he says. "I'm finally doing what Dee asked me to do, just twelve years too bloody late."

Rachel swallows hard. "It would really help if you'd tell me what the hell is going on, Ray."

"Fair chance you know more than me." He looks beaten. "Now, get out and help me push."

2019

—

SABINE

Sabine's eyes are swollen, and her voice is hoarse from calling for Blue. She half hoped he had found his way back to Shallow Bend, but the door to Pop's shack is wide-open. Nobody inside. She didn't pass him on the water, but the tinny is gone, which means he's either upriver or along a backwater somewhere. An odd time for him to go fishing.

On the boat ride here, she tried to figure out how to fix the mess she has made, or at least minimize the damage. Her deal with Rachel has left all of them vulnerable. She was never completely honest about what Rachel was getting into; it's only right that she should drop the story and Sabine should let her off the hook. Would Rachel let her off too?

Rachel's car is in her driveway and so is the cat, stretched out on the stones, sun-baking. Her knocking goes unanswered; she checks every door—and there are a lot—but they're all locked.

"Dammit!"

If Rachel were home, this would have been so much easier. She'll have to break in. Assuming the alarm system is activated, she'll have to be quick.

She tries the smallest window above the downstairs toilet. It's open an inch, but something prevents her from sliding it further. A rod, jammed in the track. She heads around to the laundry to assess the glass panel on one side of the door—perhaps the least amount of damage she can do. Add breaking and entering to her list of crimes.

She picks up a rock from the garden bed and taps the panel, wincing at the noise as the glass cracks. A second hit punches out a triangular piece, leaving a hole big enough for her to reach through to unlock the back door. She lets herself inside, braced for the screech of an alarm, but everything is quiet. A silent alarm? How long before someone comes?

She scrapes the glass shards into a corner with her foot and heads down the hallway to the bathroom. She kneels, reaches under the sink for the ziplock bag, and draws it out.

The weight of the thing inside makes her shudder: the screwdriver, one of two crucial pieces of evidence that Arnie has kept hidden. He's smarter than any of them gave him credit for—in the hands of the police, one or both might have conveniently disappeared. Along with the envelope, the screwdriver was meant to remain in Rachel's safe-keeping, but the script has changed. The jerry can is safe—for now. She'll have to hide the screwdriver somewhere else.

She knows next to nothing about preserving DNA and finger-prints. Now that the bag is out of the freezer, she's worried about deterioration and contamination—already black flakes have fallen away from the metal and collected in the bottom.

She goes into the office. Rachel's laptop and the blue folder are lying on her desk in plain sight, but when she flicks through contents of the folder, her grandfather's yellow envelope isn't there. Nor is it in any of the drawers. Further inspection reveals a heavy floor safe with an electronic keypad in the bottom of the built-in wardrobe.

Sabine swears under her breath. The moment Pop told her the document had been witnessed, she guessed it was some kind of con-fession about Nan. If the envelope is in the safe, there's nothing she can do. When he gave it to her, she didn't want to know the awful details, and she still doesn't. She can't save Pop from his conscience. One day they will both be accountable for their sins, and that day is getting closer.

She tucks the blue folder under her arm. In the hallway, she pauses. If the alarm is silent, she's running out of time. She has what she needs, but the compulsion to erase as much of herself as she can is too difficult to ignore.

She finds garbage bags in one of the kitchen drawers, tears two from the roll, and places one inside the other.

Back in Rachel's office, she begins. First, the entire blue folder—in it goes. Next, the photos from the wall and everything surrounding them. She doesn't look directly at the pictures, but she tries not to crease or tear them—to do so would feel like an act of desecration. Her hands are shaking uncontrollably. The papers feel smooth and warm, like skin.

Soon there are only the corkboard and pushpins left. She's careful not to disturb anything that doesn't relate to the story, but she's conflicted about taking Rachel's laptop. It's her livelihood. And anyway, Rachel will have duplicated her records and videos. What she's done is a symbolic act to help exorcise the horrific montage from her memory. It would probably be more effective to burn the house down.

She leaves the laptop where she found it and returns to the kitchen.

Without Rachel, the river house seems cold and empty. The air-conditioning is on full blast. A congealed bowl of cereal is on the kitchen counter, and Rachel's handbag is lying on the table.

Where could she be?

Her own internal alarm is going off—she's imagining a different scenario, one where Rachel and Pop are in some kind of danger because of her. She was wrong to involve either of them. The less they know, the better off they'll be when she turns herself in.

Close to tears, she shakes off the feeling and leaves the house the same way she entered.

———

Sabine stashes the garbage bag under the tinny's seat and pushes off with the oar to drift downriver.

There's no avoiding it—she has to recharge the battery. Even half an hour should be enough to get the *Kirralee* going; after that the inverter will do its job. It'll mean another delay, but it's a risk she has to take.

Deliberately, she runs aground at Pop's ramp. She carts the battery up the path to the shed and plugs it into the charger. There's still no sign of Pop at the shack. She hopes her unease isn't a premonition.

Back down at the river's edge, she scans the bank for signs of disturbance. It can't be hard to locate Dixon's horticultural project amongst the acres of overgrown bushland on Pop's patch; all she has to do is follow and eliminate the tracks originating from the riverfront, and think like a self-serving redneck.

Some tracks are well-worn and familiar, leading from the jetty to the shack and the sheds. Others are clearly animal made. As each trail peters out, she turns back to start again. Finally, when she pushes through a particularly deadly patch of blackberry, she notices the telltale signs: a trail of sawdust and a pile of recently cut branches, hacked away to allow sunlight to pass through.

Bingo.

She counts the cluster of plants, well over a meter tall and startlingly close to the boundary between both Pop's and Rachel's properties. *Fifteen.*

Once over her shock, she's relieved she didn't wait for Dixon to follow through on his promise, if he ever intended to. Pop's is the first place they'll start looking for her when she blows her cover—a supplier's quantity of marijuana is enough to put him away long enough that he could take his dying breath in a cell.

There are too many plants—the best she can do is dump them in the river, which is technically not Pop's property if they're found.

Furiously, she starts pulling. As each clump of roots comes away from the dirt, she scours the hole left behind. When there's nothing, she releases her breath.

It has been like this since the day her grandmother disappeared—living with the fear that she might finally unearth something. It had never stopped her digging though. As Sabine grew older, the search perimeter widened; she progressed from burying bones under the house to investigating every mound, every patch of disturbed dirt, every area that remained suspiciously green in summer. There are holes all over Pop's land now, but she has never found anything. What would she do if she did?

Twenty minutes later she makes the final trip, dragging the already wilting plants through the undergrowth. She waits for a speedboat to pass, then adds the last few plants to the pile in the water and weighs them down with a log. They'll be nothing but rotting vegetation in a couple of days.

As she heads back up to Pop's shack, a lull in the corellas' screeching allows her to hear the stealthy crunch of tires out on the gravel road. A car traveling slowly, pulling to a stop. From her cover behind the corner of the shack, she can see the rear of a four-wheel drive parked near Rachel's gate. A police car, or a security vehicle?

No time to find out. She must have triggered the alarm. *Shit*.

She dashes to the shed, unplugs the ailing battery, and hauls it back to the tinny. Her tired muscles cramp with the effort. Ten percent charge will have to do. She can never stay in one place for too long. If there's one thing she has learned since the day she made it back to the river, it's that she has to keep moving.

The only way now is forward. She can never go back.

A bird trills above her, and Sabine looks up. Dotted along the branches of the oldest trees are several boxes Pop installed to entice the possums away from his roof space. She has to leave the evidence somewhere safe but easily accessible—a box will have to do.

She stands on her tiptoes and reaches to feel inside the nearest box; apart from a few twigs and leaves, it's empty. Carefully, she pushes the ziplock bag inside and jams a small log in the hole to deter the possums.

She stows the battery, steps into the tinny, and pushes off. Her mind is a jumble, but a few minutes back on the water has its usual effect: her heart rate slows and the brain fog clears.

Who will be the first to turn her in and claim the reward? Taryn, who doesn't owe Sabine anything, let alone her silence? Dixon, who was becoming less good-natured about her rejections, whose plants she has just ripped up and drowned in the river? Rachel, who has spent years working on the story? Or will Sergeant Billson, whose hate never seems to fade, find her first?

Sabine doesn't hate him. She and Billson have more in common than he probably thinks. They're both driven by a desire for justice—except he has the law in his corner, and she's on the wrong side of it—and Sabine knows, perhaps better than most, that love does not diminish because the people you love are *bad* people.

The only way to make it right for Aria and Dee is to tell her story, to *make* somebody listen. And before she turns herself in, she has to turn over the evidence to someone she can trust. But who? She is finding it harder to trust anyone.

A slow tear works its way down her cheek as she remembers Blue is still missing. From here, every move she makes will take her further from him, wherever he is. In some ways it would be easier to know he's dead, rather than constantly imagining him hurt or trapped somewhere.

She shakes her head to banish the thought.

She knows herself better than this. Nothing about grief is easy—it can be a trigger for worse. She's starting to question if it's justice for her family that she still craves, or if it has become its cruder cousin.

Reckoning. For herself.

2019

—

RACHEL

Rachel expects the dog will stay with Ray Kelly when he drops her off at her jetty, but Blue jumps out and races toward the house.

"Hey! Where do you think you're going?"

They both ignore her.

Ray is already pulling away, his back hunched in pain. Since leaving Dixon's, his cough has worsened, and his skin has taken on a grayish pallor. He reeks of sweat. If it's true he's dying, he'll leave a restless, vengeful spirit, but he does seem to care about his grand-daughter's well-being. Her current whereabouts and why she needs a gun, not so much.

When Rachel considers the developments of the past couple of days, she grows more convinced that her decision to back away from the story is the right one. She doesn't have the guts for it. And what will she do about the dog?

She takes her phone from her pocket and checks for a response about her lack of action on the kill fee. Nothing. She has missed a text from Ben asking for an answer on the loan, and Aidan called but didn't leave a message. Gingerly, she touches the sensitive skin on her neck and shoulders. Sunburn. Her head aches. Even her toes are burnt.

She walks up the path to meet Blue, who is waiting at the sliding door. He's stiff legged, growling.

Poor Mo. He's been overthrown. Usurped.

Still looking at her phone, she turns the key in the sliding door to find it's unlocked. In her earlier rush, she must have forgotten to lock up properly. A welcome blast of cool air hits her. She'd left the air-conditioning on high.

Blue barges past her as if he owns the place. Like a canine vacuum, he sniffs a trail from the living room to the hallway.

In the kitchen, Rachel pours a glass of water and gulps it down. She goes to return Aidan's call, experiencing brief satisfaction when she can't recall his number and has to find it in her contacts.

He picks up on the first ring. "Rach."

"You called?"

"What the fuck are you doing?"

She's taken aback by the coldness in his tone. "Standing in the kitchen."

"You're still on the Trailer Murders story? You have an *informant?*"

Though she can't see him, she imagines him pulling air quotes on the word. That was how he commonly conveyed disdain. Aidan had warned her off the story before, calling her obsessed, saying she'd never make a living if she continued to waste time and resources on a story that had no legs. But what business is it of his? Why is he getting involved?

Her skin crawls. Someone got to him.

"Why are you calling me?" she says evenly. "You're corporate law, not criminal. Who contacted you?"

"A colleague, doing me a favor." He sighs. "Listen to me—if your source is the Kelly girl, you're in danger of crossing the line between protecting your source and putting the public in danger. A judge will most likely order disclosure. If you stand your ground, I *know* you can't afford the fine or the time. It's not worth it, Rachel."

"I'll take my chances."

He snorts. "Don't be naive."

"Who was it?"

"I can't disclose that."

"Some colleague," she spits. "Have you asked yourself why they're contacting you? It's a backdoor threat, Aidan. They offered me fifty grand to kill the story. *Fifty grand!* This whole thing stinks worse than a body in a dumpster. You and I never agreed on everything, but I honestly believed your ethics were more solid than that."

"This has nothing to do with my unquestionable principles and everything to do with your stubborn ego, Rach." His voice rises with every word. "Maybe your *informant* is using you—have you thought of that?"

She snorts. "Tell your *colleague* I'm about to pour myself another glass of chardonnay and kick back on my sundeck while I wait for the court order."

"Listen, babe. Please." Here comes the smooth wheedling she despises. "I'm just trying to protect you from making bad choices, both professionally and personally."

"Yeah, *babe?* Well, fuck you very much." She ends the call and bashes the phone on the counter in frustration. "You piece of shit!"

For all his so-called principles, they didn't seem to apply to her, his wife. Now ex-wife. Aidan wasn't above lies and manipulation. He'd moved Nadja into the town apartment during his and Rachel's trial separation, at least six weeks before asking for a divorce. When Rachel confronted him, he told her he was subletting to a colleague who was in a tight spot, and that they needed the extra money since Rachel's career wasn't going anywhere.

It turned out *colleague* was a stretch. Nadja worked in the coffee shop on the ground floor of his office building. No doubt the *tight spot* was her vagina.

She picks up her phone to inspect the damage: a minuscule crack in the glass protector, that's all. She resists the urge to throw it across the room and finish the job. She needs to figure out who sent the first email. There has to be more than one person involved in this scare campaign; there are too many tentacles. To come at Aidan under the guise of protecting his ex-wife is underhanded, but artful. They know the system. Do they know *her*?

Reality hits. *Shit.* What has she done? Now they'll really come after her, whoever they are. She looks around, fear mounting. Her skin prickles.

Perhaps they have already been here.

Her handbag is lying on its side on the table, where she left it. On closer inspection, it looks as if the contents have been pawed through and put back haphazardly. She opens her purse. It's all there: her ID, license, credit cards, cash. But not her keys. Her keys are in her pocket—where she put them *after* she locked up the house this morning.

But the sliding door was open when she got home. If that was how they got out, how did they get in?

Cautiously, she moves to check the front entrance. It's locked.

Upstairs, the guest rooms appear undisturbed, but not her bedroom. To anyone else nothing would seem amiss, but she is embarrassingly compulsive about straightening crooked frames and making sure the furniture is at right angles. When she looks closely, several drawers in the tallboy aren't fully closed.

She opens the top left to find her jewelry box intact—her wedding and engagement rings and her mother's necklaces are there. But the next drawer down, the one where she keeps her underwear, has been touched. Just enough to suspect someone had lifted her things to run their hand underneath.

Rachel's breath catches. Her heart flutters.

She's not afraid of anyone still being here—Blue would have

raised the alarm—but she's torn between abject fear and savage rage at the violation of her safe space.

She heads downstairs and turns into the hallway. From here she can see all the way through to the laundry: a triangle of glass is missing from the panel. And Blue is pawing at her office door. She rarely closes doors—she's all by herself in this enormous house with its enormous windows and its state-of-the-art security system that she forgets to turn on.

She's positive the office door was open when she left.

"Blue, come here."

He stops scratching and looks at her as if to say, *Hurry up, open it.*

She moves forward. A shadow darkens the gap underneath the door: someone or something is moving around, but Blue doesn't seem overly agitated. Could it be Sabine? Is she hiding in there? Is she hurt?

She turns the handle and opens the door, just a crack. When nothing happens, she pushes it a little wider, lets out a scream, and jumps aside when the cat shoots for the gap, yowling. Mo exits through the cat flap in the laundry. Blue, surprisingly, doesn't chase after him. He's more interested in something inside the office: a scent that sets his tail wagging.

Rachel's initial reaction is to lean against the doorframe for support and burst into relieved laughter. But when Blue nudges the door further, it becomes apparent that the cat is not responsible for what has happened in here.

The wall has been stripped bare. Her blue folder with hard copies of her research and interviews is not on the desk where she left it. And her laptop is missing.

———

Just after eight-thirty, the sky turns dark. A howling northerly tears leaves from the European trees outside, raining them against the windows.

Too rattled to take a shower, Rachel is in bed, her pink skin slathered in aloe vera gel. It's too early for sleep, but she couldn't stand being downstairs a minute longer. She can't help wondering if she's being watched.

Before bed, she checked every window and door and turned off the interior lights. The alarm is connected to the external reed switch sensors, while still allowing her to move freely inside. There was not much she could do about the broken panel in the laundry. The alarm will go off if anyone tries to enter. She has a heavy Maglite flashlight under the pillow on Aidan's side, a carving knife on the table next to her. She's not sure what she'd do if she was pressed to use either of them, but having them there makes her feel better, as does Blue, who is curled up next to her on the bed, his head resting on her shin. A dog's hearing is apparently four times as sensitive as a human's, and they can detect sounds at higher frequencies and at much lower volume. But mostly she's grateful for his company, even if he stinks like fish.

Without her laptop, she is forced to squint at her phone.

She scrolls through the junk mail to make sure she hasn't missed anything. It was easy enough to locate the IP address of the device used to send the email offering her the kill fee, but that's as far as she got. She does have the nefarious contacts to push for an identification, but she doesn't have the time or the money. It would be easier to press Miles Cooper or Aidan for more information, but she'd be up against the boys' club and their code of silence.

Blue raises his head, ears pricked.

It's so odd that he's here. Unless something has happened to Sabine, she can't imagine her leaving him behind.

She wipes some gunk from his weeping eye with a tissue and

places her hand on his head. "What is it, mate?"

Satisfied there's nothing to investigate, Blue drops his head and closes his eyes.

Rachel watches him, knowing sleep is a long way off for her.

Seconds after the shock of realizing the office wall had been stripped and her laptop was missing, her immediate response was to call the police. Report the break-in. Seek justice. But if whoever wanted to kill the story was responsible for stripping her office, they will have a vested interest in finding Sabine before she is brought to court. And if what Sabine said is true, Rachel's only reasonable conclusion is this: the party with the vested interest *is* the police.

The police are the neck of the funnel, the conduit leading to the vast network of the justice system. How could someone like Sabine Kelly access that network when the conduit is closed to her?

Rachel gets up and starts pacing the room.

She has never questioned her trust in the system before—it leaves her feeling powerless.

Good intentions aside, Rachel knows she has done nothing but expose Sabine and propel her deeper into trouble. She has to find her, warn her that the transcripts of the interviews are in the hands of whoever took her laptop and folder. There might be something in there that compromises her safety.

If Rachel does nothing, it will haunt her forever. The guilt will eat her up inside, and so will the rage. How could anyone believe she could be scared off, paid off, that she'd just get on with her life? And surely whoever broke in isn't stupid enough to think she doesn't keep backups?

It's a warning, and it's having the opposite effect.

Whatever Sabine is up to, Rachel wants in.

2019

SABINE

The horizon is showing a pale stripe of blush pink when Sabine sets off.

The color makes her think of cotton candy and sherbet, of Aria's pink phase, when she wore the same outfit for two weeks, wouldn't take it off, and Dee said she could stew in it despite Sabine begging her to let her run it through the wash. It had been a three-way standoff, each of them stubborn and hotheaded. Now she thinks Dee might have been right when she told Sabine to save her best fighting for the wars, not the petty arguments; otherwise people learned your moves in advance. Be nice, she said, until they're standing close enough that you can't miss.

Sabine has always loved the midnight colors: deep blues and purples, a few shades before they turn black. Sometimes she wonders if she might have been the kind of girl who pierced her nose, painted her fingernails black, wore studded collars and wristbands, leather platform boots. A punk, or a goth. One day she might have worn heels and business suits, like Rachel. Or she might have ended up here anyway, bare feet, tough skin, broken teeth, and all; maybe she's living her best life, and she doesn't know it.

If there was a phase that might have fit her, she wouldn't know that either—she went from teenage girl to fugitive so fast her head is still spinning. It feels as if she has been fighting the same battle for survival her whole life.

Then again, she's not even thirty years old. She might still have time. Aria will be seven years old forever.

The unsettled feeling that began at Rachel's the previous afternoon has stayed with her through the night and into the morning. Blue hasn't come home, and when she returned yesterday to find a broken lock on the cabin door, it only compounded her unease. She has torn the cabin apart and checked every inch of the boat looking for recording equipment or a tracking device. Nothing. The phone Ryan gave her is turned off. She wants to believe it was an opportunistic break-in, most likely kids. It has happened before, but it's suspicious timing. Her paranoia is at an all-time high.

She has barely slept. The shelf-stable, canned, and packaged food left in the cupboard is unappealing in her current state of hyperalertness. Worried that the battery will fail again, she has been running the *Kirralee*'s engine for an hour, burning up precious fuel. Ryan won't be back for a week, and by then she'll be in custody. She'll have to make do with what little fuel and food she has in the coming days.

She reverses from the backwater, disturbing a pod of pelicans roosting on a log. She checks that the river is clear before pulling out.

"Okay, let's do this."

Without Blue to talk to, her voice is raspy from disuse. Of all the everyday tasks she has avoided, all the normal things that normal people do, the one she regrets most is not having him registered and microchipped. If someone found him and turned him in to a vet or the council, he'd be euthanized. Nobody wants to adopt an aging heeler—the breed has a bad reputation for being hardheaded. Aggressive when they're afraid, destructive when they're bored.

If Pop knew what she is about to do, he'd tell her Blue is better off dead. It's the not knowing that breaks her heart. Perhaps an amputee feels this way—the constant ache of a missing part.

At just after seven, it's still too dark for the *Kirralee* to be on the water, but Sabine is glad she decided to get moving upriver early.

Pop's tinny bobs on the tow rope behind the houseboat. In another hour the locks and weirs will be operational. She has traveled around five miles, passing through Shallow Bend ten minutes back—it's not as if there's another way around—and she was relieved to see no action at either Rachel's or Pop's. Fifteen miles to go, a trip of around three hours, taking into account the lock delay, and if she travels a bit over the seven-knot limit.

If she had a teleportation device to take her anywhere, just once in her life, she'd use it now. The length of this journey feels like tempting fate—she has never traveled this far in a single day, preferring to make shorter trips that keep her off the river proper during peak times.

It's going to be a beautiful, clear day. The current is slow and lazy. Sabine forces herself to eat some dried fruit and nuts, chewing and swallowing without tasting much of anything.

She surveys the riverbank as she passes, noting the worsening cracks and erosion with dismay. Human intervention damages the river, changing its course, and this year has shown record low water levels. Native fish are dying; the European carp have taken over. Irrigation sucks up precious water, and further climate change will only make the river drier.

It's heartbreaking to see.

She wonders how many thousands of hours she has spent at the helm of the *Kirralee* over the years; the wheel is an extension of her body, the wood worn smooth by her hands, the seat compacted to her shape. Her blood has spilled and dried between the cracks on the deck. The entire houseboat is a floating petri dish of evidence that she exists, though sometimes she feels as if hers is a parallel universe.

She's tempted to use Ryan's phone to call Pop, but her limited knowledge about phones makes her wary. She'll keep it turned off unless it's an emergency.

There is one person she needs to contact, and soon.

She can't get Taryn out of her mind. Ryan knows the guy she married, a worker from the mines. He told Sabine that Taryn wasn't the same brash kid she remembered. She was the one with a reputation now, for drinking too much when her husband was away, for sleeping around. Rumor was her kids spent more time with her sister than they did with their mother, and her husband got a little rough sometimes.

What he described reminded Sabine of Dee, the way she seemed to cave in on herself once the drugs got her. Not that she suspects Taryn is on something, but drugs were only part of it—the town itself could do that to you if you stayed. Dee was a good example of the way its decay could get under your skin. She could have been anything. She could have been amazing.

———

By the time she passes through Lock Two, Sabine detects a stutter in the engine. The *Kirralee* is running on fumes, made worse by having to travel against the current. It's only when she reaches the shade of the cliffs that she relaxes.

She'll make it, but only just.

Her destination is around the next bend: Malachi's Reach, a sprawling thousand-acre property with around six miles of river frontage. While much of the farmland further inland is leased and run by an agricultural syndicate, the old homestead and its surroundings have been left to rot. The cliffs opposite mean there are no immediate neighbors and, with the nearest riverfront towns over ten miles by road in both directions, it's private and secluded.

When she headed for Malachi's Reach the night she escaped custody, it was safety she was seeking. Now it's something else.

The *Kirralee* rounds the bend in the river, and she sighs. The red-gold cliffs are on one side, the earthy hues of the homestead on the other; along with the purest blue sky reflected on the water, the colors are more vivid than any postcard. Scenery like this never fails to leave her speechless and grateful for what she has. Sometimes she dares herself to think that, if she had done her time at the beginning, she might be coming home to this instead of leaving it.

Ryan once asked her whether, if she could do things over, she would still run.

The truth is she would run faster, further, sooner. She doesn't regret what she did, and that must be proof she's a bad person. All her life people have either promised to help her but let her down, or tried to help and failed.

No one can help. No one can protect her. She is alone. She has always been alone.

She shrugs off her melancholy, cuts the engine, and spins the wheel.

A man-made spit runs parallel to the riverbank, and a rough single-lane dirt road cuts through the center. Houseboats often moor near Malachi's Reach, but rarely on this side of the spit—the water in the lagoon looks shallower than it is, and the entry is narrow, tricky to navigate, a deterrent to recreational boaters.

She eases the *Kirralee* through the opening, making sure not to bump against the jagged stones piled up to retain the banks. Only a light scrape along the bottom before she reaches deeper water. Once inside the lagoon, the height of the spit forms a protective barrier, and the *Kirralee* will be hard to spot from the river side. Except for fresh food, Sabine has everything she needs here: water, access to power from the wind turbine, shelter from passing traffic.

She will have time to prepare.

She lets the houseboat drift into the cove near the rocky beach and wades into the water to bring the tinny around. Once ashore, she ties them both off to an overhanging tree.

When her toe unearths something from the mud at the water's edge, she brings it up to find an empty spirit bottle. She surveys the area, noting dozens of scattered bottle tops and melted plastic bottles; higher up, there's a fire pit in the sand. On closer inspection, the charred wood left behind is crumbling—it must have been some time ago, but others have been here.

Sabine heads up the hill. She needs to take a look around before she settles in for the night.

The house looms ahead. As always, she's struck by its solidity, as if it has been carved from one giant piece of sandstone rather than constructed with blocks of it. It's a monument to the patience and craftsmanship of the time: walls over a foot thick and foundations sunk deep into the earth. A small oval plaque at the base of the steps reads: *The first stone laid by Malachi Johnstone, 1902.* The stones are worn smooth by feet and time, though some have been etched more recently by vandals.

She has seen photos taken during the 1956 flood when the water reached the top step, just inches from the wraparound veranda. The natural cycle of things means Malachi's Reach will likely flood again during her lifetime, but given the unnatural changes to the river's course, nobody will be able to predict where the water will flow.

The tidemarks in Dixon's basement are proof that the river does what it wants. For all the advances humans have made, stupid people still make their expensive houses out of sticks. All the new mansions along the riverfront are at risk. The old tin shacks sitting lightly on the land are part of it. But each time an ancient tree is cut down in the name of progress, they leave behind vast systems of rotting roots that destabilize the riverbanks, and the tons of high-nutrient soil people cart in to grow their fancy European trees soak up water like a sponge. Even Rachel's river house, set high on the hill, could go under.

The more you have, the more you stand to lose, Dee used to say.

Sabine found the key to the house easily the first time she was here and each time since. People leave signs, and homeowners are nothing if not predictable. She reaches into a space under the bottom step for the box, extracts the key, and opens the heavy wooden door. A blast of warm, musty air makes her nose wrinkle.

Even in its ramshackle state, the house is built solidly enough to stand for another century at least. A long hallway runs through the middle like a main artery, branching off into six large bedrooms and a small living room that leads to an enormous kitchen spanning the entire width of the house. Every room has a fireplace—all but the one in the kitchen are boarded up to keep birds and vermin from getting inside.

The first time at Malachi's Reach, with Pop, she'd found it weird that there was no bathroom or toilet in the house. *In those days, folks didn't shit where they ate*, he told her. It was before Aria was born—she must have been around eight or nine. Pop showed her other things too: the pump sheds and race, the pig pens and shearing sheds, all scattered with rusted vintage machinery and animal bones. It was here that her childish fascination with skeletons began.

She steps into the foyer and makes her way to the kitchen, glancing into each of the bedrooms.

Things have changed. The fireplaces have been opened up, and the rooms smell faintly of woodsmoke. The beds are made up—not with modern quilts but tasseled bedspreads in muted colors. She notices the different furniture, also not new. From the sixties, maybe. The walls have been stripped of the old peeling wallpaper. Beneath the smell of dust and mildew, she detects the plasticky odor of fresh paint, but the walls still look dirty.

A Formica table in the kitchen has a stack of papers in the middle, sticky rings on its surface. Sunny yellow curtains hang from the windows. On the counter is a modern kettle and toaster and several dirty wineglasses sitting in the sink. Through the window she sees a portico that wasn't here before—when she bolts through the back door, she realizes it's fashioned from old pallet wood and only painted white on one side.

It's as if multiple time periods overlap, and the changes seem recent.

Heart beating madly, she follows the stony path past the washing line. The bathroom and laundry are in a separate building, thirty or so yards from the main house, as is the pantry cellar, a long, narrow underground space with rough-cut stone walls and a solid cast-iron gate. The key to the gate is in the lock.

The cellar is part of the reason she's here, but these signs of recent occupation make her uneasy. Whoever has been here might come back.

She lets herself back inside the house and gulps water from the tap. Then she sits because her legs won't carry her anymore. The *Kirralee* won't take her far on the fuel she has left. Plan A won't work without Rachel. Plan B won't work without privacy. There is no plan C. There has to be another solution, but her mind is so muddled she can't think of what to do next.

She picks up a sheet of paper from the stack on the table, idly reading the first lines, and the world snaps back into focus. It's a run sheet for a film, dated two months ago. The changes in the house are for a set. The paint and furniture and curtains are only props.

She laughs.

It's funny in a way. She's planned her performance too. And she has her script. She has her props: the gun, the evidence. And, out of desperation, a new plan is forming, one that might salvage some good from the whole sorry mess that is her life. The only things that haven't gone to plan are Blue going missing and Rachel backing out of finishing the story.

Both might be for best.

Rachel's life is already perfect; she never needed anything from Sabine. She only thought she did.

In the end, death will be kinder for Blue. Some creatures can't be locked up.

2019

RACHEL

As she nears the freeway exit, it occurs to Rachel that she has plunged back into this investigation with very little to go on. It's not only concern for Sabine's welfare that brings her back to Far Peaks. She's livid about the violation of her space, ashamed of her own fear. And if there's one thing that drives her toward something, it's a man—even a faceless, nameless one—warning her to back off.

She pops two paracetamols from the packet in the console and swallows them dry. She has a mild headache. Her eyes are gritty from lack of sleep. She spent the hours before dawn trawling through archived notes and emails, trying to track down details that would have been readily at hand had her folder of notes not been taken. The process has forced her to look at things differently, to reassess. Some details she marked as irrelevant have become pertinent; several witnesses she discounted have reemerged at the top of her list. Everything bears closer scrutiny.

She left home early, the cat locked in and the dog outside with a bucket of water and the cat feeder, which is full of fish-flavored biscuits. Blue mastered it in three seconds flat. As she drove off, he was hitting the button with his nose, repeatedly and delightedly. She figured he'd either eat until he was bloated and sleep it off, or he'd get lonely and wander next door.

Rachel takes the turnoff, shielding her eyes from the sun.

The shops are just beginning to open. Every second shopfront has boarded-up windows—she wouldn't be surprised to see tumbleweeds rolling along the street.

Far Peaks is not a small town, but it has the small-town mentality: rumormongering among the locals, zipped lips for outsiders. She needs to be discreet. But if Ray Kelly doesn't know where to find Sabine, that leaves her boyfriend, Ryan, and Arnold Willis, the trailer park caretaker.

Both appear to be allies, not enemies. Then again, this story only gets murkier the deeper she goes.

She found the boyfriend in the witness statements: Ryan Franklin, twenty years old, living with his parents at the time of the fires and the murders. Years ago, she discounted him as a useful witness. He said he knew nothing about what happened after Sabine had left his house on the night of the fires. He couldn't even say what time it was, or why she'd left. His parents—fine, upstanding citizens, by all accounts—corroborated his statement. They shielded him from the subsequent media circus.

Ryan Franklin, thirty-three, still lives in Far Peaks. His childhood home is listed as his current residential address. Rachel assumes he bought it from his parents when his father retired from the mines, though why he'd stay there if he has regular contact with Sabine, who lives a transient life on the river, is only one question she'd like to ask him.

She drives along Main Street, past the police station.

As much as she wants to request a meeting with Sergeant Billson, it's not an option. Sabine is afraid of him and probably for good reason. If he's desperate to protect his son, he has a motive for the break-in at Rachel's house, and for killing the story. Under the guise of protecting the public from a violent offender, he also has the power to subpoena Rachel to make her give up her source. Not that she would, but serving jail time isn't high on her bucket list. And if she's wrong and he's not already aware—through the boys' club channel—of Rachel's investigation and her "source," speaking to him will only tip him off.

She turns toward the trailer park instead.

———

A bell tinkles when she opens the park office door. Arnold Willis is a thin, balding figure hunched over a desk in the corner. He appears to have lost weight since she last saw him.

He gets up and turns around at the sound of the bell. "Checking in or out?" he says.

She takes off her sunglasses. "Mr. Willis? It's Rachel. Rachel Weidermann."

His expression changes, like shutters closing.

"Do you remember me? We spoke briefly a couple of years back."

He shuffles behind the counter and leans against it with his palms flat. "I'll say it again—I don't know anything about a girl."

"I don't recall mentioning one."

"You did last time."

"Can we please speak in private?"

"I don't see no one else here." He looks around. "Do you?"

"I'd like to ask you a few things."

He waits with the resigned air of a man used to questions. He's going to be hard to crack.

"I was here with her the other day."

He pauses, then nods. "Yeah. I recognize you."

"Who set up the camera? The police?"

His cheeks and nose, already mottled with broken capillaries, are rapidly turning an even unhealthier shade of red. She feels terrible for pressing him, but if he isn't going to let down his guard, she has to keep going until he makes a mistake.

He glances at the door. "The copper, yeah. There's no video, so you can go now."

She leans closer. "I only want to help, Arnie, but to do that, I need to find Sabine. She's gone missing."

"Missing?" His mouth twists. "If you don't know where she's at, it's because she doesn't want you to know. She doesn't go missing—she hides."

"What if she's in trouble?"

He snorts. "That kid's been in some kind of trouble her whole life."

Rachel surprises herself by saying, "I think a lot of people who should have been looking out for her let her down."

"Didn't say it was trouble of her making, did I?" The whole time, his hand has been inching closer to the mug sitting on the counter. He picks it up and takes a long swallow. "If you keep digging, lady," he says, and she smells the bourbon on his breath, "you'll say the wrong thing to the wrong people, and it'll get her killed. Is that what you want?"

"Of course not." She lowers her voice. "It's why I'm here, talking to you."

He laughs. "You think she trusts me? She doesn't. She doesn't trust you either. You should know that."

Rachel smiles in return. "Maybe she pushes people away to see if they come back."

A car towing a camper trailer pulls up in the parking lane outside. Arnie frowns and says, "I've got work to do."

"One more thing—"

"It's never one more thing with you people. Anything I say can be used against me, so I'm not saying anything else. I can't help you."

She picks up her bag and slings it across her shoulder. "Just tell me, do you think she's okay?"

Arnie's expression softens. "Put it this way—if she's not, I'll find out, and I won't stop until I make things right."

Chatter from the family outside takes his attention.

Rachel speaks in a rush. "She wanted a chance to tell her side of the story—I'm here because I want to give her that opportunity. Arnie, I have information that might help her, and you have information that might help me. Doesn't it make sense to put those pieces together?"

He's wavering. But no—the shutters come down again.

She reaches for the door, frustrated. At the same time, she has to admire his integrity.

"I think she does trust you, Arnie. Thank you for not letting her down." She goes to leave.

"Wait."

She turns.

"I'll tell you this," he says. "Sabine already has the pieces. I'm just the caretaker."

———

The Franklin place is on the nicer side of town, if there's such a thing. Greener, at least. It's as if all the residents on the same block signed a Tidy Town agreement to plant lawns, mow them regularly, and water the grass twice a week. The house is double-story, a high-rise in a row of flat-roof contemporaries, with a landscaped garden and security shutters on all the windows.

Rachel parks on the street and waits. Her attention is caught by a patch of blue; she can see the glimmer of a pool through the bars of a side gate. That deep sapphire color seems out of place here, a veritable oasis in the desert.

She is having second and third thoughts about approaching the boyfriend.

Rachel has considered the logistics of their relationship and struggles to understand. Judging by the solid middle-class appearance of the house, Sabine and Ryan come from the same town but different worlds. From the information she has gathered, Ryan holds down a lucrative full-time job, plays cricket and football for the local team, and chooses to live almost ninety kilometers from the river and his lover. If he and Sabine spend time together, it must be difficult to manage—it's not as if their relationship could ever be *normal* while Sabine is on the run. How have they managed to stay together for so many years?

Is Ryan Franklin being careful, maintaining this life to protect Sabine and avoid suspicion? Even if he doesn't know anything about the story or Sabine's part in it, he must know something about her movements. Either way, there's a strong chance his reception will be as inhospitable as Arnie's.

She gets out of the car and locks it.

She raises her finger to press the doorbell, but there's a piece of electrical tape over it. She spots a handwritten sign on the front window: *Don't knock. Shift worker asleep.*

What the hell—she's here now, and it wouldn't be the first time she has ignored a sign. She peels back the tape and presses the button.

A dog starts yapping. Eventually the barking stops, and she hears a snuffling sound at the bottom of the door. A shadow appears, and the door is opened by a woman wearing cotton pajama bottoms and a tank top, her dark hair in a sloppy bun.

Immediately the dog, a cavalier spaniel with gummed eyes, shoots past her feet and out into the front garden. Rachel tries to grab his collar but misses.

"I'm sorry; do you want me to catch him?"

The woman waves a free hand. "It's fine; let him go. Can I help you?"

It's then that Rachel notices a sleepy toddler on the woman's hip, her head lolling on her shoulder.

She's taken aback. "I was after Ryan Franklin. Do I have the right place?"

"Oh, he's not home. He's on shift for the rest of the week."

"And you are—?"

"Katie Franklin."

The toddler lifts her head to regard Rachel with wide brown eyes. She reaches out with a chubby fist, rendering Rachel speechless. Her mind shoots off in several different directions. So this is why Ryan Franklin stayed in Far Peaks.

He has a whole other life, a wife and daughter.

"Do you need me to leave Ryan a message?" Katie says. "He's on base, but I can call him after hours."

"No, thank you—it's not important," Rachel says. "I'm so sorry to have bothered you."

Her legs can't carry her fast enough back to the car, away from the beautiful wife and the baby with the deep brown eyes. Of all the things she hoped to discover by coming here, this was not one of them.

Rachel is surprised by the pang in her heart, by how gutted she feels for Sabine. Does she know?

She hopes so. She hopes not.

2019

SABINE

A t the hottest part of the day, Sabine takes a break from clearing out the cellar to cool off.

Above the soft white sand at the bottom, the water in the lagoon is a murky green, ten degrees warmer than the deep river. She could almost convince herself that she's floating on her back in a far-off tropical paradise, but she feels choked with misery. Swimming was vigorous exercise with Blue around, not relaxation. By now he would have brought her a stick, and she'd have to swim away to escape the sharp end of it. He'd have nudged her from underneath like a seal or tried to drag her ashore to save her life. It's too quiet without him.

She closes her eyes and lets her body drift.

The amount of junk she found in the cellar was worse than anticipated: a mess of rusting wire, old furniture, broken machinery, and rotting carpets, twisted together like a hideous sculpture. So far, she has untangled and arranged them in neat stacks along the stony path. When the sun goes down, she'll finish carting the junk to the old hay barn, where an even bigger pile has amassed over a century or more. It was as if the cellar had been used as a dump, but she needs it to be clear.

A kite whistles overhead, searching for prey, and Sabine opens her eyes to find she has drifted almost to the spit opening. It's possible she has even fallen asleep for a minute or two. She can hear voices— another houseboat has pulled into the bay on the riverside.

What wouldn't she give for one of Dixon's signs right now.

She scrambles up the sharp rocks and onto the dirt road in the middle of the spit. From here she can see the houseboat: a sleek eight-berth at least, smoky windows, a full-length sundeck, three Jet Skis tied to the back, and three men in the spa, drinking beer.

It's definitely a rental—she can spot them a mile away, and the name isn't one she recognizes. *Endless Summer.* She breathes out. It means they're probably not loca,l and it's unlikely they'll find her presence suspicious, but they will drive her mad with their Jet Skis and dump their rubbish; they'll reel in carp for sport and leave them rotting on the banks.

Dee used to call people like that rich trash—far worse than poor trash. They had deep pockets and short memories, and they could afford to pay more for things, which pushed up the price of every-thing, including drugs.

These guys might not question why Sabine is here, but that's only one problem solved. They look like they've settled in for the night. So much for privacy.

A fourth man, early thirties at a guess, is climbing the spiral stair-case leading to the sundeck. Well muscled, with a beer gut and neck tattoos.

Sabine approaches and calls out. "Hello."

The man pauses midway and looks up. "Hi."

"You can't moor here," she says. "It's private property."

He frowns. "Nothing says we can't."

"No, of course not. But—"

"It'll be one night, lady."

She points. "There are better spots further up. Please, I'm asking you to move on."

He takes in her wet T-shirt and holds up a beer bottle. "Or you can hop in the spa with us."

Raucous agreement from the others.

Sabine doesn't react. She's had plenty of altercations with guys like these, but never at such a critical time. It's not safe for her if they're here.

He grins. "Come on—one drink? And a hundred bucks if you take your top off."

"I'll pass."

There's not much she can do without escalating the situation. She tamps down her irritation.

"You'll be gone by morning then? Keep the noise down, hey? Great. Thanks." She waves.

By the time she swims across the lagoon and makes it back to the *Kirralee*, the music has started. Add that to the screeching of a flock of corellas in the gum trees, and her peace is shattered. She can only hope they don't fire up the Jet Skis while they're drinking.

She enters the cabin, gasping at the heat trapped inside.

She opens the top bedside drawer, takes out the phone, and powers it on. It has fifty percent charge. She's not sure how long it will last, but the deep-cycle battery on the houseboat might have enough grunt left to give it a boost. It looks nothing like the flip phone she used to have, more like a computer.

She touches the images on the screen until something happens. By turning the phone on and off, she eventually figures out how to open and close the various applications. As well as installing a tracking app, Ryan has entered five contacts. Three she can understand: his own mobile and work numbers, her grandfather's landline, and the general phone number for police assistance.

Haha. Funny, Ryan.

She chokes up when she sees other two. The first is someone she doesn't know, but it's obvious why he's there: *Mark Hermann, Criminal Lawyer.* That's Ryan for you—always prepared. Knowing him, he has this lawyer briefed already. He's probably paying him a retainer.

Her finger hovers over the last contact: *Justin Case*.

She recognizes it—not the name, which is obviously a cheesy play on words, but the number. It's a number she has kept stored in her memory since childhood.

She's not sure whether to laugh or cry. Ryan is so intuitive to her needs. They've talked about it—he knows losing contact with Taryn is one of her biggest regrets; he knows if something bad goes down, there are things she needs to say. What he doesn't know is that she's getting frighteningly close to that moment.

There's another number she has kept in her memory too. She presses the new-contact button and types the number in.

———

After carrying the rest of the junk to the hay shed, Sabine heads back to the lagoon to rinse off.

It's taken her two hours. Her hands are cut from handling barbed wire and splintered wood, and she's so hungry her belly has started to cramp. She needs a nap, but there's no way she'll be able to sleep with all the noise.

She wades in. The water is too warm to be refreshing—she swims to the spit opening to check on her unwelcome guests. The Jet Skis have stopped, but it's rap music and drunken wrestling in the spa. While she watches from the cover of tree roots, the men climb out of the spa and form a line along the guardrail.

Oh no, they're not.

They do, taking aim and urinating over the side at the same time, trying to see who can piss the furthest, cackling when their streams cross. One of them throws his bottle in the river and they take aim at it. When they've finished, they climb straight back in the spa.

The bottle floats downriver, past where Sabine is hiding. She fishes it out and leaves it on the bank to dispose of later, her skin crawling with revulsion.

She ducks underwater, kicking hard until her outstretched hand touches the stern, then bobs up next to the open rear deck. As quietly as possible, she pulls herself onto the platform. Using a damp towel flung over one of the Jet Skis, she dries her body and squeezes the water from her hair. Then she mops up her wet footprints and enters through the sliding glass door.

Four bedrooms, each with an en suite bathroom. The master and queen have waterbeds, something she has heard of but never experienced. She lies on the king, arms and legs spread like a snow angel. *A waterbed on the water.* It feels almost like floating. She could get used to this in another life.

Reluctantly, she gets up, smooths the sheet, and moves to the main cabin.

With its custom-fit interior and a stainless-steel kitchen that looks like something from a sci-fi movie, the *Endless Summer* is more like a hotel than a houseboat. She opens the fridge. Unsurprisingly, the shelves are ninety percent full of beer, but there is a tray of barbecue meat and a container of ham rolls. She takes a beer and a ham roll for later, keeping an eye on the stairs in case anyone comes.

A phone on charge is lying next to a sink filled with scummy water. She pulls out the cord, dangling the phone in the sink as she counts to twenty. After drying it off with a tea towel, she plugs it back in.

In the master bedroom, she resists the urge to lie on the bed again and peels back the bedsheet and mattress protector. Using a skewer from the kitchen, she pierces a hole in one corner of the bladder. Water bubbles out, soaking into the marine carpet under the base. She watches it leak, remembering the first time she swam across the river to steal cigarettes for her cousins. Back then she was clumsy, lucky not to get caught. The trick is to take just enough that nobody notices, to do just enough damage that it could be coincidence or their own negligence, and to leave no evidence behind. It'll be hours before anyone notices.

Pocketing the skewer, she picks up her lunch and slips out through the sliding door.

Back on the rear deck, Sabine unties one of the Jet Skis from its mooring. With great satisfaction, she gives it a shove and watches it drift, slowly at first, until it's picked up by the current and disappears around the bend in the river.

If they're smart, they'll recover it easily enough. If they're not, they'll be paying a hefty excess on their insurance.

She lowers herself into the water without a splash. With the beer tucked in her waistband and the ham roll between her teeth, she swims back to the spit opening to pick up the empty bottle. After checking that they're not looking in her direction, she wades through the lagoon and makes her way up the hill toward the house.

———

Back at the cellar, Sabine looks around, making sure everything is in place.

About two meters inside the opening, there's a chair, a bucket on the floor, and two bottles of water on the table. It's cooler than outside, thanks to the thick stone walls and the cellar's position below ground level. The key to the gate is now hidden under a rock near the entrance.

She listens. Nothing but birdsong and the wind in the trees. Her unwelcome guests are quiet now; they must have worn themselves out. It's been a long time since she has knowingly taken a risk like that, but she knows what can happen when she lets her anger build for too long. Petty revenge has served her well in the past.

She sits in the chair, munching on the ham roll and sipping her cold beer, looking out through the bars of the gate. From here, the panorama is reduced to a postcard-shaped view of the bare wheat fields and the tree line beyond.

It's quite beautiful, really. There are worse places to be locked up.

2019

—

RACHEL

Rachel has seen plenty of dead ends and heartbreaking revelations during her career, but when she leaves the Franklin house, her dejection is at an all-time high.

She's all set to turn around and head home when she passes the side street Sabine pointed out when they were last here. Following her earlier hunch, she slows and turns the wheel. *Barnard*—that's it. But which house? They all look much the same: brown brick, wastelands for front yards, broken toys lying everywhere, curtains twitching.

She does a U-turn in the tight cul-de-sac at the bottom and parks midway along the street. After ten minutes without any sign of life, a postman arrives to do his rounds. When he pulls up next to her, she calls out through the window.

"Excuse me? I'm looking for Taryn—"

"Williams," he supplies. He points to a house on the opposite side. "Right there. Number twelve."

"Thank you."

She grabs her handbag and locks the car. Not that there's much inside to steal, but if she's parked here any more than fifteen minutes, she reckons everything will be gone. Twenty, and they'd have her shiny wheels for sure.

God, this place is depressing.

She heads along the driveway, stepping carefully over the uneven cracks in the concrete. An early-model silver Camry is parked less than an inch from a roller door. Judging by the bowed profile of the door, it gets used often as a bump stop. There are two baby seats in the back, little handprints all over the windows, and the rear end is blackened with exhaust fumes. Someone has written *slut!* on the trunk lid.

She raps on the screen door and waits. Inside, a child is crying.

The woman who answers seems to be around the right age. Early thirties, a pretty but tired-looking face, straight shoulder-length dark hair. She has a number of small fine-line tattoos on her hands, bare feet, wrists, and ankles, the kind that take less than half an hour and cost less than a hundred bucks. The rest of her is covered by a stained oversized T-shirt and a long denim skirt.

"Taryn Williams?" Rachel says.

"That's me. Hi there." Taryn doesn't ask her name in return—she just flings the screen door wide-open and stands aside, as if she's so damned happy to have company it doesn't matter who Rachel is or why she's knocking. "Come on in. Excuse the mess," she throws over her shoulder.

Rachel follows her into a crowded living room.

The sensation of sticky carpet underfoot makes her cringe, as she works her way through an obstacle course of toys and piles of clothes. The combined odors of cigarette smoke, burnt cheese, and nappies soaking in bleach bring back the worst memories of motherhood, although the smoke isn't strong enough to indicate an indoor smoker—more likely one who stands outside the back door, puffing madly to preserve her sanity, while everything goes to hell inside.

Down the hallway the child is still crying.

Rachel feels a surge of compassion. "You have a baby?" she asks.

"He's two," Taryn says. "Toby. Tobes when he's good." She tosses her head. "Tobias when he's pissing me off, like now. Conor and Reagan are at school."

"Do you want to see to him?"

"He'll stop soon. Ignore it if you can." Taryn scoops a pile of clothes from a gray pleather couch and adds it to another stack. "Have a seat. Do you want something to drink?"

Rachel sits, crossing her legs. "No but thank you. I suppose I should tell you why I'm here."

"Oh." Taryn screws up her nose. "You're not from the housing commission?"

"Sorry, no. My name's Rachel. I'm a journalist."

She lets that sink in.

Taryn doesn't seem fazed. "Whatever you want, can we stretch it out for half an hour? I haven't sat down all morning." She perches on the arm of the couch opposite and flexes her bare feet, groaning.

"Actually, I'm here to ask you about Sabine Kelly."

"I haven't spoken to her in twelve years."

She says it so fast, Rachel thinks it's a lie. And if that's the case, it means Sabine lied too.

She opens her mouth to fire the next question, but Taryn jumps up and sashays to the kitchen.

When she returns she's holding two beers, tops off. She offers one to Rachel. The glass is warm. Warm beer reminds her of uni bars and hangovers of the worst kind. It's barely lunchtime, but what the hell.

"Thanks." She takes a sip. "So if you haven't seen her—"

"I didn't say that," Taryn interrupts. "I said I haven't spoken to her... Wait." She tips the bottle in her direction. "That was you in the car with her."

"Here, you mean?"

"Yeah, in Far Peaks. On Sunday." Her eyes sparkle with curiosity. "What's going on? Where has she been? What's she doing back here?"

Rachel has been avoiding any mention of knowing Sabine

personally, but there's no point now. "She's not with me. She's gone back into hiding."

Taryn squints. "Then how did you find me? And why? I don't know anything. Sunday was the first time I've seen her since that night… Well, technically I didn't *see* her, but she was at my house."

Rachel's mind scrambles to catch up. "She was here the night of the fires?"

"Not here—my old house. She knocked on my bedroom window."

"What time was that, Taryn?" She rummages for a pen and whips out a pocket-sized notebook from her handbag.

A blank look. "It was a long time ago."

"Can you try?"

"My sister picked me up from a friend's house, and we got home around half past ten. I showered, and I'd just gotten into bed, so it would have been just after eleven. That's all I know."

"You didn't speak to Sabine? Let her in?"

She shakes her head. "We weren't talking. When she knocked, I pretended I was asleep. I felt bad and I texted her, but she never replied."

"What time did you send the message to Sabine's phone?"

"It was right after she left—she probably hadn't even reached the end of the street. Then all that stuff happened at the trailer park and all those people died, so in a way I'm glad I didn't let her in."

"Why?"

"Maybe she was going to kill me too."

Interesting. "She was your best friend. Do you honestly think she was capable of that?" she asks.

Taryn slaps her knee. "Hell, yes. She was a crazy bitch, just like Dee. Everyone said so."

The baby's incessant crying has subsided to the occasional plaintive wail.

"Crazy *how*?"

"The thing is, sometimes Sabine made shit up. It was like, I would say, *Oh, this happened to me and it was bad*, and then Sabine would say, *Well, this happened to me and it was worse*. My life was good and hers wasn't, blah, blah, blah. I got sick of her drama." She wipes her nose and sniffs. "For a long time, I believed everything she said, but then she went too far."

"Too far? What happened?"

Taryn curls her lip. "She told this bullshit story about stabbing some guy at the pub; then she said the cops kidnapped her, took her out of town, and dumped her by the side of the road."

"You think it was a lie?"

"I know it was. The pub was packed that night. I asked around afterwards, and nobody saw anything like that." She finishes her beer and holds up the bottle, raising her eyebrows.

"No, thanks. It's a little early for me." Rachel scribbles some notes. "Can you tell me what you remember about Logan Billson?"

Taryn's gaze sharpens. "Right. She got to you too."

"I'm not sure what you mean."

"I told you. She's a liar."

Sabine's manner when she spoke about her old friend was warm, nostalgic, misty-eyed. *We were more like this. One.* But Taryn's eyes are glassy with the kind of fervor Rachel associates with TV evangelists. If she had to pick the unreliable witness right now, her money would be on Taryn.

Or, as Taryn claims, Sabine is a consummate liar and a murderer, and Rachel's instincts are way off.

"Can you think of any reason why Sabine would have killed her mother and sister?" she asks.

Taryn contemplates the question for so long Rachel assumes she can't. True to her promise, the baby has gone blessedly quiet. The silence stretches between them.

"It's okay; you don't have to answer that."

"No, I want to," she says. "Sabine hated Dee. Like, *really* hated her. She was always telling me that when she turned eighteen, she was getting out and taking Aria with her. I think she would have killed anyone who stood in her way—I think she hurt Aria by accident, but she killed Dee on purpose. She ran because Aria was dead, she had nothing left to fight for, and she knew she was going to prison for the rest of her life." She slaps her leg again as if she has just scored a slam dunk.

Rachel takes another sip of warm beer. "Did the police interview you after the fires?"

"Once. I told them I hadn't spoken to Sabine for ages. Until the other day, the last time I saw her was outside the police station."

"You were there when they brought her in?"

"Yeah. Word got around really fast. Me and Lauren went down there to see what was going on."

"Lauren?"

"My sister." She points to the wall above the television, where there's a photo of a woman wearing a wedding dress standing next to a man in a tuxedo. "I don't see her much. She got out of this shithole."

"And what time were you both at the station?"

"Around midnight. We got there just when the car turned up."

So between leaving Ryan's and arriving at the trailer park, Sabine came to Taryn's window. If Taryn sent a message seconds after Sabine had left, the message would pinpoint the time Sabine was at her house, give or take a few minutes. It's a tight time frame. Could a proper investigation reveal the actual time it was sent? If it turns out it was after 11:15 p.m., Sabine couldn't have set the first fire because she wasn't at the trailer park yet.

"Can you tell me what it was like?"

"It was nuts. People everywhere, shouting and pushing to get at her."

"How did they know what had happened? Nothing was reported until the next day."

"Like I said, word gets around. We all knew she lit the fires."

Rachel is shocked by her vehemence. "How could you know that? She was a child."

"*Because she did it before.*"

Rachel flops back in her seat.

Early in her research, she immersed herself in the psychology of the arsonist. Offenders are often seen as violent, remorseless criminals responding to an irresistible compulsion to destroy, but fire setting is a complex disorder, often connected to mental illness and past trauma. In adolescents, it's recognized as a predictor of schizophrenia. Less is known about female arsonists, particularly in adolescence, but studies found that more female offenders than male ones were diagnosed with substance abuse, depression, and personality disorders.

One thing that struck Rachel during her initial investigations: Sabine Kelly did not fit the profile neatly. If Sabine had a motive to light the fires, it was unclear. Where the media saw a lack of grief and remorse, Rachel kept her mind open. Lindy Chamberlain, Joanne Lees, Kate McCann—all women who were judged for not responding the way society believed they should, women who were condemned because they did not share their trauma and grief with the world.

"There's no police record of Sabine Kelly committing previous arson," she says weakly.

"She didn't tell you?" Taryn smirks. "Of course she didn't. There's probably no record of her keying Logan Billson's Harley either, or putting sugar in his fuel tank."

"The first fire?" she prompts.

"Some old guy, a local, used to sit in his car and wank off when we walked home from school—the next time she saw him, Sabine lit a whole box of jumbo matches and threw them in his back seat. Like I said, she's crazy."

"How did the police handle it?"

"It's a small town. The cops dealt with us juvenile delinquents in their own way."

"And what way was that?"

"I got caught shoplifting at the BP once. Billson Senior made me stack shelves there for nothing every weekend during school holidays." She shrugs. "I never did it again."

Rachel nods. "That's entirely different from leaving a minor miles from home in the dark."

"It didn't happen. Tristan Doyle would have told me."

The baby's shrill cry makes them jump.

Taryn gets up. "Look, everyone knew Dee would eventually push Sabine hard enough that she'd crack. I don't blame her, really—I used to think Dee was cool, but now I know why Sabine wanted so badly to get out. When Sabine gets angry, God help anyone who gets in her way." She sighs. "Sabine always thought the cops were the problem. The *Kellys* were the problem. Did you know her grandfather killed her grandmother? It runs in the fucking family."

Rachel recoils from the spit that flies from Taryn's mouth.

"One last thing—can you give me your previous phone number and address? Is it close by?"

"Everything is walking distance around here."

Rachel hands Taryn the notebook and pen, and pulls out a business card. "Will you contact me if you remember anything else? If she calls you?" She offers the card, pinched between her fingers.

"Sure. I'll add it to my collection." Taryn takes the card and writes down her old number and address. "She won't call me, you know. She's smarter than that."

I hope so, Rachel tells herself.

"Thank you. See to the baby—I'll let myself out."

Rather than heading down the hallway, Taryn goes out the back door, letting the screen slam. She lights a cigarette.

This time Rachel doesn't feel an ounce of compassion, only assurance that her instincts about Taryn—and the people of Far Peaks—are spot on. It has obviously never occurred to Taryn that she might be Sabine's alibi. Since she's an expert at it herself, Rachel can spot blind self-righteousness a mile off. Sabine said she ran because she would never have received an unprejudiced trial. She made a fair point.

Then again, the crime of premeditated arson is almost universally recognized as an expression of powerlessness and a weapon of revenge. Rachel has to admit Sabine Kelly's possible motive is taking shape.

But she has a bad taste in her mouth, and it isn't the beer. Something doesn't feel right.

Four years ago, her rudimentary interviews had revealed little, and frustrated, she'd given up too soon. But back then she'd sensed the dark heart of this community, and talking with Taryn has only confirmed her suspicion: judging by the mob mentality of the people in this town, Sabine was right to run.

2019

—

SABINE

The house is spooky in the fading light, but Sabine isn't afraid. She doesn't believe in ghosts, at least not the dead kind. If the purpose of a vengeful spirit is to haunt a person who has harmed them, she'd have experienced visitations long before now. There's nothing here of the people who came before, other than skin cells and hair fallen through the cracks, and faded photographs on the walls. Bones beneath the floorboards, maybe. Malachi himself is rumored to be buried under the old red gum by the riverbank, but his headstone is long gone.

In the kitchen, Sabine unscrews the cap on the five gallon water container she'd brought up from the houseboat. She turns on the tap. While she waits for the container to fill, she watches the black hole of the doorway leading to the hall. The longer she looks, the more her mind plays tricks, conjuring shapes from the shadows.

If Dee came back, she'd be a ghost who wailed and slammed doors and pushed ornaments from the shelves. Aria would be a shining orb of phosphorescent light; Faith, a weight at the bottom of the bed, a gentle touch while she was sleeping. Pop, when he goes, will be sighs and creaks and groans.

Logan would be a malevolent presence, as he was in life, a negative energy that sucked the air from a room and made it hard to breathe. Sometimes she wishes he wasn't dead. Death wasn't his punishment—it was an exit. If time has made her realize one thing, it's that it isn't possible to exorcise him from her life completely without surrendering it.

"I'm coming for you," she says to the dark space, willing his figure to emerge.

The container overflows, splashing into the sink. She dashes to the tap to turn it off. When the water stops, she hears ringing. Not in the house, but somewhere outside.

The phone. She left it on the veranda post.

By the time she makes it down the hallway, the ringing has stopped.

She picks it up. The screen reads: *You have missed a call from—* followed by a phone number. She doesn't recognize the number. It could be Ryan calling from one of the base phones, but she's still wary of answering if it should ring again.

While she's deciding what to do, the phone beeps.

Another row of text on the screen, this one telling her the same number has left a message and she can tap to hear it. Her thumb hovers over the button. She's afraid to give away her location before she's ready. Ryan promised her the phone couldn't be tracked. But what happens if she calls *him*? Is Billson watching Ryan the same way he's watching through the camera at the trailer park?

It's all too confusing. Too many unknowns and variables. Her strategy, until now, has been simple—avoid contact with anyone but Ryan. But Ryan was right: she's getting as paranoid as Pop.

She carts the water container back down to the lagoon and steps aboard the *Kirralee*. A cool breeze is blowing from the south, and the heat inside the cabin has dissipated. She throws back the quilt and lies on the bottom sheet.

———

Sabine is asleep when the phone rings again.

She sits straight up in bed, as her mind struggles to catch up. Her skin is clammy with sweat, and her hands are shaking so badly she drops the phone several times.

This time she presses the green button to accept the call but doesn't speak.

"—me." The voice breaks up.

She has to be sure, so she waits.

"It's me, babe. Say something so—"

Ryan. She breathes out, letting her hand fall to her chest in relief, before pressing the phone to her ear again. "Hi."

"Where are you?" He sounds as if he's breathing hard.

"You can't ask me that."

"Wait…outside…reception." A shuffling sound and a door slamming. "Is that better?"

"Yes. I can hear you."

"I mean, I can see roughly where you are on the map, but why there? Are you okay? What's going on?"

She shouldn't have turned on the phone. Damn her lack of technology smarts. She wants to scream, but the day-trippers are just on the other side of the spit.

"Nothing's going on. Things are fine. I'm mooring here overnight because it's too busy downriver."

A pause. "It's just—something strange happened today. Apparently a woman came to the house, asking for me."

"So?"

"So it's weird, right?"

The strain in his voice is out of proportion to what he's telling her. Ryan doesn't freak out easily—he's calm and methodical and it takes a lot to upset him.

"Well, what did she say? What did she look like?" She walks out on the deck.

"Dark hair. Forties, maybe. Official-looking." He clears his throat. "Look, I think I should come there and be with you."

"No. Don't do that!" She lowers her voice. "Aren't you on shift? You can't suddenly change your routine. We agreed."

He goes quiet. The signal must've dropped out. She shakes the phone and holds it up.

"—feeling about this."

"What? I can't hear you."

"I said I've got a bad feeling about this."

She goes back inside. "You know I don't like talking on the phone. You're scaring me."

"You're scaring *me*. Why would some random woman turn up at my house? What are you up to? What's changed?"

The answer comes to her so suddenly, she almost says her name. *Rachel.* She must be snooping around again. But why? She made it clear she wanted out, and Sabine made it very clear that Ryan was off-limits.

Good question. *What's changed?*

Ryan is at the mine—unless there's an emergency, there'll be no flights until morning. Even if he could find her, it would take him the best part of the next day to get here. The best she can do is reassure him, so he doesn't feel like she's in any danger.

"I promise you, I'm okay." Now she wants to stay with him on the line. She can't. "The battery's almost dead. I have to go."

"Charge it and leave it turned on," he says. "I'll need to find you when I get back."

"I will." *I won't.*

"I love you."

You're the best thing that ever happened to me. If everything goes to hell, at least I've got that. Will you wait for me this time? Or is this the end?

All she says is, "I love you too. I'll see you next week."

———

An hour later, Sabine is still wide-awake.

Earlier she found the dry remnants of a pouch of tobacco in a cupboard. She rolls a loose cigarette and lights it. The smell of tobacco smoke reminds her of Dee, long gone, and Pop, closer to death than life. When she's anxious she can't help herself. She can't afford cigarettes—if it wasn't for Ryan paying for everything, she'd be homeless or taking from Pop's measly pension. It makes her squirm to think of Ryan buying her tampons and birth control pills.

Tomorrow, it all ends. Right now she's free, but the walls are pressing in on all sides.

She sits on the deck watching a perfect moonrise, mirrored on the water. It's a still night and the smoke lingers, forming wisps like a cirrus cloud.

Grief is tidal; it ebbs and flows. She hasn't allowed herself to feel it properly for a long time. There are triggers she avoids; she has become adept at dancing out of reach before it can pull her under. But she needs it now. After the grief, the fury will arrive, followed by the cut-glass clarity it brings.

Everything that happened happened because of what she did. She sits and lets the grief come.

2007

—

SABINE

Two weeks before the fire, Dee got sick. Genuinely sick, not drug sick. By now Sabine knew the difference and insisted she see a doctor—the diagnosis was some kind of infection or inflammation in her bowel. Dee spent four days in bed, only moving to dash to the toilet block or vomit in a bucket. She lay there, not eating, barely drinking, delirious.

Sabine stayed home to look after Aria, who was remarkably well-behaved and compassionate for a seven-year-old. She played quietly in the annex, or next door with Faith. Dee's sickness scared Aria—she thought if she was good, Dee would get better.

Sabine, on the other hand, rinsed the bucket when Dee threw up, made meals for Aria, and changed the sheets when Dee left the bed; she watched her mother thrash and mumble in her sleep, all the while brewing resentment, and guilt for feeling resentful. She missed being with Ryan, but she wouldn't let him come to the trailer park. Her life, which had been good for the first time since forever, was on hold.

On the third day, she sat outside the van smoking a cigarette she'd stolen from Dee's bag.

Dee seemed better today, but still unable—or unwilling—to get out of bed, and Sabine was growing more alarmed at the number of times Dee's phone buzzed and she didn't pick up. She didn't seem to care anymore, not about her kids, nor about what Logan would do to them if she kept ignoring his calls.

Sabine butted out the cigarette halfway and left it under the step for later. Her body ached. Her hands shook from the rage that had been building like a storm inside her head. Was this how Dee felt whenever she took off? Like, if she stayed, she'd tear the place apart in a fit of anger or, worse, hurt someone? Was everything she hated about her mother already in her, a destructive program running in the background?

She fought the urge to pack her bag and run as far away as she could.

"I'm hungry."

She spun around. Aria stood behind her in her pajamas, her hair floating in a staticky cloud.

"Do you want some toast?"

Aria nodded.

Wearily, Sabine went into the kitchen and pulled the toaster from under the sink, but the cord got caught, and she dropped it on the linoleum.

The noise woke Dee, who sat up swearing. Her eyes were sunken and red. "Jesus! Keep it down!"

Sabine, at the end of her tether, yelled back. "I'm making breakfast for Aria. Deal with it! Or would you rather we starve?"

Against her better judgment, she bashed a plate on the counter and rummaged in the top drawer, clattering the cutlery.

"I swear, if you don't shut the fuck up, I'll—"

"You'll what?" Sabine snarled. She picked up the nearest knife and waved it around. "What will you do, Dee?"

Aria pushed past her and clambered onto the bed next to Dee. "Don't, Beenie."

Sabine felt their accusing stares like a punch. No matter how bad Dee got, Aria always took her side. Aria treated Sabine like her mother and Dee like her sister; Sabine made rules, and Dee let Aria break them because Dee hated being the bad guy. Here they were, huddled together as if *she* was the threat. Everything was messed up.

She put down the knife. *It's a butter knife, for God's sake.*

Dee burst into tears, and Aria, always sensitive to her emotions, hugged her.

Sabine pulled Aria away. "Go and brush your teeth."

"I haven't had my breakfast."

"Go and brush your teeth!"

Aria sulked but did as she was told.

"Leave her alone." Dee reached for the overhead cupboard where she kept her drugs. "Why do you have to ruin everything? I just need a hug from my baby."

"She's a kid. It's not her job to make you feel better."

Dee ignored her.

Sabine came up behind her and snatched the pipe from her hand. "For fuck's sake, stop smoking and dealing that shit, Dee. You're killing yourself."

Dee whipped around. "Don't tell me what to do. You don't know what it's like."

"I don't know? I live it every day. So does Aria. We've got to get out of here."

"We can't get out. We've got nothing. Do you know what'll happen to us if we try to leave?" Her voice was getting louder.

Sabine sensed Faith would be listening next door—any minute Bram would come knocking.

But she couldn't stop herself. "I don't know about you, but Aria and I will go and live with Pop and have a *normal* life, because *normal* people don't have to take drugs to feel *normal.*"

That hurt, and Sabine was glad.

"Fuck you, Sabine."

Sabine was just tired of it all. "Fuck you too," she said, but Dee hit her, quick as a snake, and Sabine cupped her burning cheek.

Dee was a yeller—she had never hit before.

"Sorry, baby. I'm so sorry." Her eyes brimmed with tears, but there was wicked delight in her expression. She lived for extreme emotions.

Sabine understood there was no coming back from this. If she didn't force Dee's hand now, they'd still be here in another year, another five, another ten. As much as Sabine yearned to leave, she wouldn't. Not unless Aria came with her.

While they faced off, the phone on the side table rang again.

Dee glanced at it, but stayed where she was.

"Answer it."

"Get out," Dee snapped. "Let me deal with this."

Sabine moved fast; she elbowed her mother out of the way, grabbed the phone, and answered it. "Logan."

Dee froze. She shook her head wildly, lunging for the phone.

"I know you're there."

Finally, he spoke. "What the fuck are you doing, Sabine? Put Dee on."

"She's sick." The fury raced through her veins; the blood rush left her hearing muffled, as if she was underwater. "She's sick because you're making her sick. You make *me* sick. You're not a cop, you're a pig, and if you come near my family again, I'll blow your fucking life up."

He said something, but she couldn't make it out.

"Stop talking. If you leave us alone, I'll keep my mouth shut. If you don't, I'll talk and you'll go to jail. That's the deal. If you come near us again, I'll burn it all down."

She hung up.

"Oh." Dee collapsed on the edge of the mattress, but it was like marshmallow, and she slid onto the floor, eyes wide like a hunted animal. "I'll fix it. It's okay; I'll fix it."

"I don't want you to fix it," Sabine said. "If you let him back into our lives, I'll—"

"You'll what?" Dee mimicked. "Oh, you think you got rid of him? What makes you think he's gone?"

"Because—"

"Because a *kid* threatened him? Because you keyed his Harley out of *spite*?" She nods. "Oh yeah, he knows it was you. You don't get it—cut off one head and another grows back, Beenie. You have no idea what you've done."

Sabine grabbed an empty shopping bag and began stuffing things inside, just in case Dee kicked her out. No way would she leave though. She'd keep watch, all night if she had to. She might have no idea, but she definitely had no regrets.

After so many years feeling powerless, all she felt now was elation.

"I mean it, Dee. If you let him back in, I'll tell them what you and Logan are doing, and they'll take Aria away from you." She put one hand on the door. "Maybe I'll do that. I'll call Sergeant Billson—I've got his number."

"Billson?" Dee laughed. It was a hopeless sound. "Jesus, you're so naive. Go right ahead."

Sabine stuck out her chin. "He helped me before."

Dee slowly pulled herself off the floor, moving like a woman twice her age. She had no fight left. That was the thing that burst Sabine's bubble of elation and made her afraid.

"It doesn't matter what you do," Dee said. "We're already dead."

2019

RACHEL

The mild headache that started this morning has turned into a nauseating throb behind Rachel's eyes. A list is queuing in her mind: retrieve old backups, check and cross-check details, input new information and make more backups. And she has actually contemplated preparing an "In the Event of My Untimely Death" document for her lawyer. It all feels like the sort of manic, disorganized cramming she used to do before an exam, only there's so much more at stake. She's no further along in her efforts to locate Sabine.

Before leaving Far Peaks, she'd timed the walk from Ryan Franklin's house to Taryn's childhood home, and from there to the trailer park—a few minutes either way could exonerate Sabine from lighting the first fire, or point the finger right at her. The question is, why did Sabine walk home that night, and so late? If she had stayed at her boyfriend's house, she would have had an airtight alibi.

She pulls into her street as the sun is going down, feeling despondent. Neighbors have left their boat trailer parked on the road, and a blue Prius is double-parked near her gate. She recognizes the car. Her initial flutter of alarm turns to irritation.

She edges between both, trying to avoid hitting them with her side mirrors. Keys in hand like a weapon, she gets out and heads to the front door.

Out of nowhere, Blue shoots around the corner, snarling.

"Hey, I live here," she grumbles. "This is my house."

Blue isn't growling at her. His attention is on the gap beneath the front door. He prances from side to side as if to hurry her up, and it gives her the greatest satisfaction to open the door and watch him shoot inside with a zigzag of hackles raised along his spine. She follows at leisure, hoping to give him enough time to scare the crap out of her unwelcome visitor.

When she reaches the lounge room, he's standing with his back to her and looking through the collection of mail on the kitchen counter. She takes in the familiar shape of him, noting the crisp creases in his trousers and the whiteness of his shirt. His skin is dewy, as if he's just stepped out of the shower.

In contrast, she's crumpled and sweaty and needs a good lie-down.

"What the hell, Aidan?"

He turns, unfazed by Blue, who is blocking the exit, his tail tucked between his hind legs. Not making a sound but showing all his teeth.

Rachel holds up her hand the way she's seen Sabine do it. Remarkably, the dog obeys and sits, keeping sharp eyes on the intruder.

"Good boy. Leave it." She pats his head. "For now."

"I thought you were a cat person," Aidan says. He holds up an envelope and squints at the small print. "Where *is* the cat?"

Her ex-husband doesn't much like animals in general, and Mo in particular. As an act of self-preservation, the cat always reserved a cool disdain for him.

Rachel adopts the same strategy now. "Can I offer you some reading glasses while you go through my mail?"

He smiles. "Don't be snide, Rach. It doesn't suit you."

"You can't just let yourself in and wander around as if you own the place."

He raises an eyebrow. "Technically my name is still on the title."

"Mine's on the apartment title, but you won't find me reclining on your chaise longue in my silk pajamas anytime soon." She sighs and puts her bag down. "What do you want?"

"I was passing. Thought I'd collect my mail."

Passing. Hah!

"Find any?"

"No."

"Bye then." She switches on the coffee machine and busies herself emptying the grounds container.

She's not sure why her hands are shaking. The feeling of poison running through her veins, maybe. Hot off the revelations about Sabine's cheating boyfriend, she's faced with her cheating ex.

He's still standing there, a pitying look on his perfect face.

"I said *bye*."

"I came to make sure you're okay. Lex said you sounded funny on the phone the other night."

The other night? When did she call Lexi? Oh, the night she was nearly shot—a lifetime ago already.

"I'm fine. What do you really want, Aidan?"

He shrugs. "I see you've taken down the wall of horrors. Does that mean what I think it means?"

"You went in my office?" Blue, who had flopped into fitful sleep, stands to attention. "That's it. Get out." She points. "I mean it. Go!"

He comes so close she can smell his new aftershave. It's nice. It makes her head swim.

"I don't think you know how close you're skating to a subpoena, Rach."

She breathes in and out to calm her racing pulse. "Someone really wants to find Sabine Kelly before she talks, right? You know what they say: where there's smoke, there's—"

He throws up his hands. "Oh, save it. Your sanctimoniousness always got in the way of any meaningful conversation. I'm not sure why I'm bothering—you're so focused on doing what's right instead of doing the right thing."

She reels away, stung. "Is there a difference?"

"Of course there is."

"You've been reading too many men's magazines on your path to enlightenment. Do they hand you a stack during your rub and tug sessions?"

"If you think I'm going to bail you out when—"

"I don't need or want your help!"

He squeezes his eyes shut in frustration.

"Oh, I'm sorry. Am I *boring* you?"

God help her, she can feel every ounce of blood pumping through her vascular system. Her breasts are heaving. She can't make up her mind if it's desire or a desire to commit murder. *Somebody, get this woman a dose of HRT,* stat.

But there's something comforting about having him here, standing in her kitchen, something freeing about being around a person who knows her so well she can behave like a raving lunatic, and he'll just stand there while she works through it.

"Sorry. It's been quite a day." She sits heavily in her usual chair at the dining table, rubbing her eyes.

"Let's talk," he says.

"I will if you'll answer my questions too."

"I'll try, but I'm bound, Rach. You know that."

"So am I."

He throws up his hands. "Why are you protecting this girl? Why is this so important to you?"

"I don't know. There came a point when I wasn't writing the story for me anymore. I was doing it for her."

It's true. She's not sure when it changed from her and Sabine using each other, a quid pro quo arrangement, to a kind of pro bono defense. Maybe there wasn't a single moment, but a slow turning as Rachel got to know Sabine—where she has come from, what she is up against.

"If she turns herself in," Rachel continues, "she knows she won't get a fair trial. Like she said, you shouldn't judge a person without hearing their whole story."

"So you believe she's innocent?" he asks.

"Not innocent," she admits. "At least, not in the sense that she hasn't done anything wrong. But a killer? No. I don't think she has it in her."

"A court will decide that."

She sighs. "Don't placate me, Aidan. And don't pretend to be idealistic."

"If she is telling the truth, how is *you* writing *her* story going to help?"

"It'll mean the truth will come out even if something happens to her. At the very least, it'll give her peace."

"Peace?" He turns incredulous eyes to the ceiling. "She should be on trial for killing nine people, Rach. It's justice for the victims that counts, not repentance for a killer."

"Exactly," she says. "You don't find it suspicious that an alleged criminal wants the truth to come out, and the supposed upholders of the law are hell-bent on keeping that from happening?"

"Now who's being idealistic? Nothing is black and white, least of all the law," he says, tight-lipped.

He won't look at her. The lawyer who used to rail at the inequities of the so-called justice system is now so deeply entrenched in the problem, he's not only turning a blind eye; he's *defending* the system.

"Who got to you?" she asks. "I'm not accusing you of anything—I just need to know so I can do the right thing by everyone involved."

Incredulous now, he rolls his eyes. "It's obvious, isn't it? What do you think happens when a murder suspect becomes a fugitive? The police set trip wires, and people trip on them."

There's that supercilious expression she hates. Here it comes. And three, two, one—

"People being *you*."

"It was a confidential pitch, Aidan."

"It was dumb, Rachel. You let your ambition get ahead of you."

Movement in the corner of the room. Mo has emerged from his hiding place to assert his supremacy, and miraculously, Blue watches him saunter past, making no move to attack.

That's what she needs, a bit of Mo's sass.

"I'm doing my job," she says. "There are laws to protect me so I can do that objectively and with impunity. So if you get in my way, I'm going to forget you're the father of my children."

He stands. "You're hardly objective, Rach. If you want to save people, you should've become a paramedic."

"I want the truth. That's why I became a journalist."

"A laid-off journalist," he says viciously. "The personality traits that keep you clinging to this story like a life buoy are the same ones that lost you your job. You're not a team player. You're a lonely—" He stops, shaking his head.

"Get the fuck out," she says as coldly as she can manage with her cheeks on fire.

He picks up his wallet and keys. "Take the kill fee. If you've still got the bug, turn Sabine Kelly in and claim the reward. *That's* your story. Let it go."

As much as Rachel would like to think he'd take her side if he was forced to make a choice, she knows he wouldn't. He's all about backing winners.

"Aidan, look at me." She gets up. She holds his chin between her thumb and forefinger. "She's gone. I don't know where she is. And you can tell your contacts I'm not writing the story anymore." *But I am investigating it.* "You're the one who needs to let go."

He searches her eyes. Finally, he nods. He believes her, because the upside to being sanctimonious is that Rachel doesn't lie.

———

After a hot shower, a slice of toast, and two glasses of wine, she makes herself a coffee and heads to the office.

She turns on the printer, opens the relevant album on her phone, and queues fourteen images for print. The printer whirs; one by one the photos spit out in full color. While she waits, she tucks her notebook away in the floor safe. When the printer stops, she collates the sheets.

What was it Sabine said? She wants the chance to look Sergeant Billson in the eye and tell him the truth about his son. Is that what she's planning? What makes her think confronting Billson will give her peace? Or is it really that simple: a chance to be heard? But off the back of it, she will be turning herself in.

Without Sabine to finish telling the story, Rachel will have to follow it to its logical conclusion. She will read through all her material again, every report, every statement, every false lead and conspiracy theory. Everything bears looking at more closely, starting with copies of the photos that were taken from her office.

She pins the sheets in the empty space on the wall, in no particular order, as if she has never seen them before.

With an apprehension she hasn't felt in some time, she approaches them. Chest tight, extremities tingling. Nausea burns in her gut. How numb must she have been to see these grisly images almost every day for years and feel nothing? *See* nothing?

She moves along the montage, touching the picture of each victim.

Faith and Bram Mitchell: outside.

The Shoosmith family: huddled together under the table in their trailer.

Logan Billson: lying on the path.

The coffee on the table has gone cold when it finally hits her with breath-stealing force: the victims had all been *doing* something before they died, either to help their neighbors or to escape the flames. But Dee and Aria Kelly—they were both inside the van, prone on the bed, as if they had slept through the explosions.

Photos can be deceiving. It's been the longest day, and it's going to be an even longer night.

Now Rachel imagines their blackened bodies with flesh, heartbeats, their chests rising and falling. Sabine had mentioned that she and her sister slept in the bunks at the other end of the trailer, but here they are, Aria and Dee, together. Dee's hands are at her throat, her legs splayed. On closer inspection, Aria does not look like a sleeping cat curled at the foot of the bed, but like a flung doll.

Neither is in a natural sleeping position. They are positioned as if they were already dead.

2 0 1 9

—

SABINE

Just after nine, Sabine walks out to the gate connecting Malachi's Reach to the nearest main road.

It's still early, but her visitors on the other side of the spit have been packing to leave for an hour. She heard a ruckus at 3 a.m. and guessed it was the discovery of the waterbed leak; a shout at quarter past seven was a good indication one of them had counted the Jet Skis and found them short.

She laughs, wondering how far downriver it has traveled, and if it's still going.

Her foot finds a rock, and she stumbles. The driveway is a long-neglected track of potholes and dust about a mile long. An aerial view would show a ribbon of green behind her, snaking through the landscape, but out here she could be wandering in a postapocalyptic wasteland. No shade, the air hot and still. Only wheat stubble and flat, treeless land as far as she can see.

Good. She'll know when someone's coming.

It takes her just under ten minutes to reach the mesh gate and cattle grid. As expected, the gate is secured with a heavy padlock.

She checks it to make sure. A locked gate means she has either a ten-minute head start if the cavalry arrives or, given the rough state of the driveway, around two minutes' warning if the padlock is cut. If anyone approaches from the river, she has almost no time. But the tinny has enough fuel if she needs to make a run for it.

Sabine pulls the phone from her pocket and holds it up. There's a better signal here.

She opens the contacts and calls the number she entered last night. Eight, nine, ten rings, and then it goes to a computerized recorded message: *Sorry, we're unable to answer right now. Please leave a message after the beep and we will return your call.*

Frustrated, she hangs up without saying anything.

Who's *we*? What if it isn't his number anymore? She can't set anything else in motion until he responds; she has time, but the longer she waits, the more there is that could go wrong. Please let it still be his number.

She's almost at the house when a red-bellied black snake slithers from the wheat stalks and crosses in front of her, just meters away. She freezes as it passes.

Dee always said a snake crossing your path meant good fortune was coming your way, or that it was a symbol of protection. But Pop says a black snake is a warning: be careful who you trust.

Which is it? Maybe all three.

She redials the number. Again it rings out. This time she leaves a message.

"This is Sabine Kelly. I want us to meet. If you tell anyone I've made contact, I'll make sure everything comes out. This is your only chance to bring me in. Call me back."

Will he detect the tremor in her voice? He might mistake it for fear, but it isn't. She's not a skinny, frightened kid anymore.

Back at the house, she drinks a glass of tap water and cleans up any trace of her having been inside. When she's finished, she locks the door and places the key under the step. She's on her way down the hill toward the lagoon when the phone rings.

She checks the screen to make sure. It's him.

Her heart is pounding when she answers. "Hello."

"Why are you calling me, Sabine?"

His voice is exactly as she remembers: deep, authoritative, and reassuring. *Don't trust him.*

"I'm ready to turn myself in," she says. "But I need something from you first."

"What makes you think I have anything you need?"

"Hear me out."

"I'm listening," he says smoothly.

She sinks to her knees in the soft sand near the lagoon's edge. "I'm asking you to come." She hesitates. Once she gives her location, it's over. But she wants it to be over. "Start driving. Take the ferry across the river at Aerie Flat—it should take you around an hour and a half to get there. I'll send the full location then."

"Or I could simply arrange a trace on the phone you're using."

Keep focused and stay calm. "You could, but if you bring anyone else with you, I'll see them coming and I'll run. I'll find the only cop in the state that isn't bent and turn over the evidence with Logan's prints all over it, but you'll never see me in court. I'll disappear. If you want me in jail, you'll have to come and get me yourself."

"You're good at disappearing," he says. "I'll give you that."

"I've had a lot of practice." She hears the jingle of keys and a door slamming. He's already on the move. "Message when you're on the ferry, and I'll tell you where to go from there. When you arrive, leave your car at the gate."

"It might be better for you if you kept running, Sabine."

"Better for who? Is that a threat?"

"It's a warning."

"Make sure you come alone, and I promise I'll turn myself in," she tells him.

A beat of hesitation. *Is he scared? He should be.*

"Why the cat and mouse?" he asks. "Why now?"

Billson sounds tired. Tough. So is Sabine. If he had done right by her family, this wouldn't be happening—this is his reckoning too. She hopes he has suffered sleepless nights like her, wondering when the guillotine would fall. *She* is the cat. *She* is the guillotine.

"It's time," she says.

She ends the call, feeling flat. It wasn't as difficult or as momentous as she thought it would be. All this time, obsessing and worrying, and it was done in less than two minutes. Too easily. Why didn't Billson jump at the chance to bring her in? Why tell her to keep running—why warn her?

She gets up, brushing sand from her shorts.

There's no time for second-guessing. It'll be roughly two hours until he arrives. What will she do with her last hours of freedom? After the noise of the past twenty-four hours, it's blissfully quiet. Something isn't right.

She checks the *Kirralee*: intact, the cabin door closed and locked. The usual things she keeps on deck are in place, and nothing seems to have been disturbed inside. The gun is there, hidden in her top drawer. It takes her way longer than it should to stop looking at what is there and focus on what isn't.

The tinny is missing.

In a wild panic, she breaststrokes through the lagoon and scrabbles up the rock wall, onto the spit. There's a stinking pile of rubbish on the bank, but the *Endless Summer* has gone. No doubt towing a stolen tinny as payback, or else they've set it adrift and it's floating downriver.

You fucking bastards.

She curses herself, wishing she could rewind to the moments when she felt compelled to destroy, and instead just walk away. She has to be smarter than this. Twelve years, and she still hasn't learned the difference between justice and vengeance.

No Blue. No boat. No way of getting off the property. No going back, even if she wanted to.

———

As soon as she receives a text from Billson to say he's on the ferry, Sabine sends him directions for Malachi's Reach and makes her last call.

According to Ryan, everything they'd vowed to escape was happening to Taryn: stuck in Far Peaks, trapped in a shitty marriage, the drinking, the predictable and endless cycle of violence. But their friendship is tied to the past—it's not something they can ever fall back into, the way old friends do. They're different people now.

This will be the hardest call of all.

"Hello?"

She isn't prepared for the sound of Taryn's voice. For a second, she can't speak. Enough time has passed; she didn't expect to feel emotional.

"Taryn, it's me."

An intake of breath.

"Say something."

"I don't know what to say."

"I'm sorry. I didn't think I'd run into you like that. It took me by surprise."

Taryn snorts. "Yeah, me too."

"I think about you every day."

The sound of rustling paper. Then, "Where are you?"

"You know I can't tell you that."

"Sabine, why are you calling me?" Taryn's voice rises.

"I wanted to say I'm sorry. For everything. It's not the way things were supposed to be." That much is true. "I'd change it all if I could."

"I'm sorry too. But why haven't you been in touch until now?"

"It's hard to trust anyone," Sabine says. "You know, because of the reward."

There it is: a pin-drop silence as Taryn makes her choice. Sabine already knows what it will be, and she's gutted.

"Do you remember that time when Pop took us up the river?" she says lightly. "The place where there was a big old house and an enormous tree, and we were swinging on the tire and jumping in?"

Softer now. "I remember."

"We found the underground cellar."

Taryn laughs. "And we stole your pop's cigarettes."

"It was the best day ever."

Before they became different people.

Before Nan disappeared.

Before Dee and the drugs.

Before Aria.

Before Logan.

None of what's to come will be Taryn's fault. Sabine remembers what it felt like to be stuck in that town with no way out. Taryn has been eroded by greater forces, like the banks of the river, like Sabine herself. The thing about choices is you think they're decisions made in a split second at a precise moment in time, but they're not. They're the last domino in a long line of decisions, and the last domino always topples in the same direction as the ones that fell before it.

Taryn will screw her over, and that's okay. Sabine is counting on it.

She takes a deep breath. "Taryn, if you ever need me, you know where to find me."

2019

—

RACHEL

Rachel wakes to Blue licking her face. Groggily, she sits up and glances at the clock: it's just after nine. She never made it upstairs to her bed last night. She remembers lying down on the couch sometime around three, and the few hours of sleep she managed to get were disturbed by her overactive brain and the frequent sound of the dog's nails on the floorboards as he patrolled the house.

Blue leaves her side to prance by the door.

She keeps forgetting that he can't fit through the cat flap. "Sorry, mate."

After she unlocks the door and slides it open, he shoots outside to pee on every bush.

Rachel pours herself a glass of pineapple juice. No coffee for her today—half her sleep problem could probably be put down to the amount she consumed last night.

After Aidan left, the wall of photos and reports spread from the office to the dining-room table, which is now at full seating-for-twelve extension for the first time since Christmas. She read over her copies of the coroner's documents and inquest transcripts until her eyes were strained. Nothing jumped out at her. The toxicology reports on both Dee and Aria Kelly did not highlight anything out of the ordinary, although due to the intensity of the heat-related damage to their bodies, there was a noticeable lack of data on the levels of carbon monoxide in the blood. Urine was recovered and tested, showing nothing of interest in Aria's sample and moderate levels of methamphetamine in Dee's.

Not exactly a red flag, given Dee's long history of drug use.

She gathers four coffee mugs from the table and puts them in the dishwasher, squinting against the morning sun pouring through the kitchen window. Over the next hour, she finds other chores to do; she wipes the counters, cleans out the fridge, scrubs the oven.

Classic avoidance tactics.

If she's honest, her reluctance to face that epic paper trail isn't just because she has the beginning of another headache. It stems from her growing realization that her previous investigation was shaped by her belief that Sabine Kelly was guilty—her prime focus was on locating *her*, the suspect, not investigating the crime as a whole. She's a terrible journalist. She has judged and condemned Sabine in the same way that everyone else has. And why? Because she was looking for the most obvious answers, and what little evidence there was pointed to Sabine.

Sighing, she sits down at the head of the table.

She picks up a picture of Dee, smiling, full of life. Despite her problem with addiction, she had been a tall strong woman. Violence was in Dee's nature too: Sabine said her mother often fought back. The coroner's report showed there was no strong evidence of assault on Dee or Aria prior to death, but that didn't entirely rule out soft tissue injury like strangulation.

At a guess, Sabine would have been ten or twenty pounds lighter than her mother, at least a couple of inches shorter. And she had loved her sister. That was obvious. Arson can be a crime of passion and premeditation, but also of distance—it's easier to pour the fuel, light the match, then stand back and watch everything burn. Easier than it would be to, say, hold someone down and choke the life out of them while they stared back at you.

Even if Sabine *did* light the fires—and the timeline leaves that possibility open—it makes more sense that Logan Billson had already killed Dee and Aria Kelly. It fits with what Sabine has said all along, except now Rachel believes her. Sabine made the perfect suspect; she didn't stand a chance against the word of a police officer and the body of a dead hero.

Blue noses the door.

Rachel gets up to let him inside just as Mo slinks past her to go out. They sniff each other, but there's no animosity.

Given time, she and Sabine, despite their differences, might have been friends. She'll probably never know. They didn't get past the point of using each other—there was no trust between them, and that was mostly Rachel's fault.

She sits back down and moves papers around. The evidence—or lack of it—is interesting in itself. What's missing? She scratches her head.

Her hand stops on another photo.

She has very little on Sergeant Eric Billson. Over thirty years serving the same community, exemplary record. He took a step back during the fire and murder investigations, as is protocol, and returned to service a month later. Even Sabine can't say for sure if he was involved in the drug business, though he might have been complicit. If Billson is trying to protect his son's memory, he has a motive for warning Rachel off the story, and for the break-in at her house. But it doesn't mean he knew his son was a murderer.

She has a contact number for him, though it might be obsolete by now. At this stage, with Sabine in hiding and the investigation stalled, would it hurt to fire a warning shot? Warn him that if he continues to go after Sabine, Rachel will pick up the story again and expose his son?

She finds a copy of the historical trailer park map. It's freshly printed, unmarked. It doesn't matter—she knows the crime scene intimately by now.

Constable Tristan Doyle's report said Sergeant Billson was not present for either the fire crew attendance or Sabine's arrest. Billson only arrived at the crime scene shortly after Sabine was cuffed, put in the back of Logan and Doyle's vehicle, and taken to the station.

Something is niggling at her. She doesn't have a printed copy of Doyle's report on hand, so she pulls it up on her phone and rereads it.

Sabine Kelly exited the trailer park through the rear entrance, where I was parked and waiting for Constable Billson to respond to radio contact. By then I'd heard the second explosion and the fire had taken hold. I could see the flames above the tree line. I could also see Sabine Kelly had burns to her arms and scalp, but she did not react when I called out to her. As she walked closer, I asked her where Constable Billson was. She did not respond. She was catatonic.

Consistent with the statement, the coroner's report confirmed Logan and Doyle's police vehicle had been parked by the rear trailer park exit when Sabine was arrested. But other witness statements mentioned it was seen near the front entrance parking lot earlier, attending the fire in Dee's car.

Why move the vehicle to the rear unless, as Sabine implied, it was for "unofficial business"?

Unnerved, Rachel consults the map again.

She's not really looking at the map though—she's thinking of Doyle's statement, where he'd said Sabine Kelly had tried to evade arrest and he'd tackled her to the ground. Once restrained, she had confessed. Sabine herself agreed that she'd said it was her fault, but was it in a different context? Guilt, because she wasn't there to save them from Logan Billson?

Rachel can swallow that theory now. It makes more sense than Sabine leaving her boyfriend's bed in the middle of the night, visiting Taryn, then deciding to kill a bunch of people, including her

family—and people who were as good as family, who'd shown her
nothing but love and care.

What doesn't make sense is why the fire report says, based on the
burn pattern and multiple ignition points, that it would have taken
many liters of fuel to direct the flames to the surrounding trailers, yet
there was nothing to show how the fuel was carried? Nothing, not
even molten plastic or metal amongst the ashes and debris.

Rachel groans, stretching her stiff muscles. She smells like dog—
she desperately needs a shower.

She takes a clean towel and a change of clothes to the upstairs en suite.
It's been ages since she cleaned the cubicle; mold is beginning to bloom
on the grout, and the glass is cloudy with soap scum. She squirts bleach
on the tiles, letting it sit for a few minutes while she undresses. Aidan used
to make fun of her habit of scrubbing the cubicle while she took a shower,
saying it defeated the purpose. Rachel argued it was more efficient. Why
waste time doing one thing when you could accomplish both?

She runs the hot tap, then stops.

Her breath leaves her body.

It makes absolutely no sense how Logan Billson could be in so
many places in such a short period of time, unless he didn't act alone.
Unless there were two of them.

———

An hour later, Rachel has rearranged the papers on the dining-room
table into three piles and succumbed to her craving for caffeine. To
her left is a hefty stack with Logan Billson's police photo on top. In
the middle, pages of scribbled notes. To her right, just a few sheets.

She picks them up and reads through the report again. Compared
to other witness statements, it's short—lacking in detail and emotion,
but damning in its conflicted version of events.

What was it Sabine said? *I wasn't running away. I went to him. I thought he would help.*

Good cop. Doyle.

She has no photo at hand. Doyle was never of much interest until now. She picks up her phone, types his name in the search bar, then flicks back to the report.

Here's the thing: Doyle's statement is inconsistent. He stated that Sabine was catatonic, but in the same paragraph, he reported that she had to be subdued because she was running away, evading arrest.

Was it possible it was Doyle who lit the first fire to distract attention; then he drove around to the rear exit? The exit was the shortest route to the residents' section—assuming the fuel came from the police four-wheel drive, it would have been easier for Logan to carry fuel that way and avoid being seen. If that was how it went down, what happened to the fuel container? Could Doyle have removed evidence from the scene?

She thinks back. At no point did Arnie Willis say it was Sergeant Billson who set up the camera at the trailer park—if anything, he seemed confused when she mentioned him. Perhaps it's not Billson, but Doyle who poses the threat? Billson may have lost his son, but if Doyle *was* involved, he still has everything to lose if Sabine breaks her silence or turns herself in.

That's a lot of assumptions, and Rachel doesn't like making them without evidence. But when she opens the image tab on the search screen, her skin turns cold.

She recognizes his face instantly. Doyle has moved up in the world; he looks as fine in his uniform as he does in a tuxedo. *Sergeant* Tristan Doyle. Married to Lauren Doyle, Taryn's older sister, and unquestionably the same the man she saw in the wedding photo at Taryn's house.

She scrolls further, furiously clicking on photos and links, building a timeline before and after Doyle was a country cop slumming it in Far Peaks. A privileged upbringing. An expensive private-school education. His father is a federal court judge, his uncle a corporate counsel. Holy shit, he's well-connected.

She feels sick.

She might never know exactly when Doyle was tipped off, but Rachel knows she's responsible. *She* started it when she sent the pitches. *She* risked taking Sabine back to Far Peaks. *She* sat there in Taryn's living room, drank a beer with her, handed her a business card.

The police set trip wires, and people trip on them.

"I did that," she says to Blue, who whines as if to say, *What are we going to do about it?*

They have to find her. Sabine doesn't have all the pieces.

———

"Billson."

It's a curt and authoritative voice, one that ordinarily would prompt Rachel to take a softly-softly approach. Neither she nor Sabine has time for that.

"My name is Rachel Weidermann. I'm a journalist. Please listen— I've been interviewing Sabine Kelly to bring new evidence to light over the Trailer Murders case."

"You're writing an article?" he says.

"Yes."

She hears the distant sound of a radio and rushing wind.

"Are you still there? Please, I—"

"If by new evidence, you mean Kelly is ready to turn herself in and face the charges, I already know," he says.

She's gobsmacked into silence.

"The girl has to face the court like anyone else. The truth will come out then, not in some exploitative, sensationalist article."

"Do you *want* the truth to come out?" Rachel barks. "I find that very hard to believe."

"Believe what you want, but I do."

"And will she receive the same fair hearing as anyone else?" she says. "She was failed by the people who should have helped her."

"I know that."

"She needs to be in protective custody. If you arrest her—"

He cuts her off. "I'm not going to arrest her, Ms. Weidermann. I'm retired now, a civilian like you."

He hangs up.

———

It's only by chance that Rachel hears Ray Kelly's boat start up just as she's about to climb the fence to shortcut her way to the shack. Blue is already on his way when he hears the motor too. He changes direction and shimmies back under the fence.

She races to the end of her jetty to flag Ray down. "Stop! Wait!" He looks as if he's going to ignore her, but at the last minute he swings the rudder, turns a tight circle, and comes back. The tinny bumps against the jetty.

"You don't look well," she says. "Should you be heading out?"

It's an understatement; he's white-faced and sweating.

"The devil don't wait for nobody."

"Where're you off to?"

His presses his lips together. "Fishin'," he says.

"Where's your rod?"

If he weren't so pale, he'd probably be blushing. The tinge of pink on his neck gives him away. "All right, I got a tip-off."

"You know where she is?"

He nods. "The *Kirralee* passed through Lock Two yesterday morning. There's no log of her at Lock Three, so she's somewhere in between."

"What's in between?"

He thinks. "About seventy miles of river and backwater."

She raises her eyebrows. "And that means?"

"Needle and haystack situation." He gives a short whistle. "Get in."

Rachel looks down. She's still wearing a T-shirt and pajama bottoms. "I need to change."

"Not you, the dog."

Blue has ignored the whistle. He's watching Rachel, and Ray's watching him watch Rachel.

"Tamed the beast, have ya?" He laughs.

It sets off a fit of coughing that lasts a minute or longer. When it's over, he has to lie down in the bottom of the tinny until he gets his breath back.

"I don't think you should be going anywhere." Hanging on to the steps for dear life, she reaches in the hull for the tie rope. "You're no good to her dead, Ray. Tell me where to go and what to do."

Suspicion in his rheumy eyes. "For a quitter, you're all worked up. Where's the fire?" Another rasping laugh and coughing fit.

"I know who's after her. I think he's close."

He squints. "Got a boat license?"

"Yes."

It's not even a lie, but she has to concentrate on keeping her voice steady. The thought of navigating the river in a tin can terrifies her, and her hands shake as she ties the rope.

"I need to get changed. Tell me where to find her."

He stares at her for a long time, then nods. "A place called

Malachi's Reach. I used to take her there when she was a child. It's where we met when she escaped, when she came to the river. I reckon that's where she's gone."

"Is it on the map?"

He takes the hand she offers and pulls himself up onto the jetty. "You'll know it when you see it. Big old house on the left and a rocky spit. Take the dog. Like I told you, watch him close. He'll know when she's near."

"I can do this," she says, as much to herself as to him.

2019

SABINE

The plume of dust behind the car and the glint of sunlight on glass tells her Billson is coming.

Sabine takes cover behind an old rainwater tank to watch him make his way along the dirt road. At first he is just a shimmering mirage, then a dark blot on the landscape. When he's close, she realizes he's not in uniform, no weapon belt around his hips. It makes him less formidable than she remembers.

Dixon's gun hangs loosely from her right hand, heavy and slippery with her sweat. It occurs to her that an experienced police officer might be able to tell if a gun is loaded. Or, as in this case, not.

It's too late to do anything about that now.

When Billson reaches the gravel parking area, she steps from behind the tank and raises her arm. "Stop there."

"It's been a while, Sabine." He eyes the gun warily. "You're all grown-up."

"I'd say sorry for the long walk, but I'd be lying," she says.

He indicates the patches of sweat on his shirt. "I'd say never mind, but I mind."

"Keep your hands away from your pockets."

"I'm not armed."

She looks him over. "Where's the camera?"

He just blinks.

"The cop camera—the one that records everything."

He appears to grasp what she's asking. "Even if there was a camera, which there isn't, you have a gun pointed at my head—anything I say is said under duress."

"It's not what you say—it's what *I* say that matters!" It feels as if the ground is falling away under her feet. "So there's no camera?"

He shakes his head.

Sabine groans. She's so *stupid*.

When Rachel told her the police recordings were admissible as evidence, it gave Sabine hope that she could tell the whole truth. It couldn't be twisted. But she has seen her fair share of courtroom dramas—prosecutors asking questions to lead defendants into incriminating themselves, and the defense telling them to shut up so they don't incriminate themselves. How the fuck does anyone ever find out what really happened?

Her hope is fading. If the gun was loaded, it would take supreme self-control not to shoot Billson right now, point-blank in the face.

Choices.

"Take off your shirt, your pants, and your boots."

"I said I'm not armed."

"Just do it."

It takes all her concentration to keep the hand holding the gun steady while he strips down to his socks, singlet, and boxers. His limbs are tanned and muscly, but his torso is flabby and pale. He throws his clothes and boots in a pile on the gravel, then completes a slow circle to show he has nothing concealed.

"Phone?"

He looks up toward the gate on the hill. "In the car, like you said. Are you going to make me stand out here until I'm cooked? Is that the plan?"

"You can put your arms down." They fall to his sides. "Now you're going to take that path to your left." She follows ten steps behind as he picks his way along the stony path in his socks. When he reaches the cellar opening, she barks, "In there."

"What is this?"

"Go in the cellar and take a seat."

He shuffles down the steps. When he's sitting, he looks up at her standing outside the entrance, a meter above him. Sabine cops the full force of his steely glare.

"You can stop waving that thing at me. You're making me nervous."

And he's making her feel ashamed for treating him like an animal, but she's not about to tell him that. She closes the gate on him and retrieves the key to lock it.

"What's the point of all this?" he asks. "I came. Now tell me what you want."

"I want you to listen," she says through the bars.

He twists the top off one of the water bottles she has left there and drinks. When he's finished, he wipes his mouth. "Listen to what?"

She stands up straight, pulling back her shoulders. "I want to give my statement."

"Save it for the court and the jury," he says, shaking his head. "It doesn't matter right now."

She knows she should stay calm, but his placatory tone pushes her over the edge. "It matters to me! Your son destroyed my family!"

"I could say the same thing about you."

She gets up and paces beyond his range of vision. Her own vision is clouded—with rage or heatstroke, she can't decide. He's sitting in the cool dark while she's out here, blistering. And there's no camera. She really didn't think this through properly.

A hand reaches through the bars. He's offering her a bottle of water.

She walks back and takes it. Their fingers touch briefly before she snatches her hand away.

"Okay, I'll start," he says. "I know about Logan and the dealing."

She freezes. "Say it again."

Billson repeats, "I knew he was into something bad, but not until it was too late."

"Too late for my family, or too late for you cover it up?" she says bitterly. "The fire must have been very convenient for you. You got to bury him a hero."

"There's nothing *convenient* about burying your child." His face is drawn and haggard.

Sabine can't recall the difference between sympathy and empathy, but one or both are manifesting as a softening in her limbs.

She tightens her grip on the gun. "How much did you know?"

"I got an anonymous call about a week before the fires. A man said Logan was using Dee—your mother—to sell the drugs he got from busts, and she was selling it right back to the junkies he took it from. He said if I didn't do something, he'd take it higher."

Sabine recoils in shock.

"And what did you do?"

"Not enough," Billson says, as if he'd plucked the words from her mouth. "I was looking into it."

"Did Logan know you were *looking into it*?"

"I think he suspected, yes."

A week before the fire? *Oh God—Ryan.*

It tied in with the time she'd confided in him. He'd been upset and confused because she wouldn't let him see her while Dee was sick. After, to smooth things over, she'd told him what she knew about Logan, about Dee and the drugs. How Logan would come and drop off drugs, fuck Dee, knock her around a bit, and then come back later and take whatever money she'd made. And when Sabine and Aria got in the way he'd knock them around too. Logan was a cop. His father was the sergeant. Logan was untouchable, and Dee couldn't live without him because she needed drugs, and he was the only one letting it in and out.

Sabine wipes a tear that has rolled all the way to her chin.

She's not angry—Ryan couldn't have known what would happen. She didn't tell him everything, certainly not about the threats she had made to Logan. It was too late after the fires, hard enough dealing with her own regrets without telling him what she'd done. He was an idealist. He believed in the system. He still did. If anything, the guilt she has carried for so many years is a little lighter. Of course Logan wouldn't have felt particularly threatened by her, a junkie's kid with a reputation for lying. But a tip-off from within the community Logan thought he controlled, and his father, the sergeant, asking questions? It might have been enough to make him try to clean up his own mess.

Billson uses his singlet to mop the perspiration from his face and neck. "So where do we go from here?"

"I don't know."

"If you come with me now, I'll make sure you have every opportunity to defend yourself against the charges."

"You should have given me that opportunity twelve years ago," she says tightly. "Why should I trust you now?"

"At the time I was grieving and in shock. I was torn between being an officer and being a father." He raises his hands in gesture of helplessness. "You were the only one who walked out of that inferno alive. You showed no expression, no remorse, no tears; you gave no proclamations of innocence. I've seen the eyes of a killer before, Sabine. It's not something you ever forget."

The pit opens up inside her. "So you'd already made up your mind about me."

"What was I meant to believe?"

She laughs without humor. "And you all wonder why I ran."

"I still know people. I'll escort you in, and they can do this properly, the way it should have been done back then."

She waves the gun. "No. Enough talking. You'll listen."

2007

—

SABINE

S abine didn't question what woke her—she just sat up gasping, instantly alert. The digital clock on Ryan's side table read 10:54 p.m. She listened for sounds of disturbance, but the house was quiet.

Her compulsion to leave the warmth of Ryan's bed so late in the night was not so much a feeling that something was wrong, but an insistent tug toward home.

As she wriggled free of his arm, Ryan stirred and rolled over. He didn't open his eyes when she tucked the sheet over him and kissed his chin, nor when she stumbled around in the dark, feeling for her dress. When she found it, she pulled it over her head, picked up her sandals, and slipped through the door, closing it quietly behind her.

It wasn't the first time she'd snuck out of Ryan's room while his parents were sleeping, but it was the first time she didn't feel ashamed. The week before they'd delivered their judgment and given their blessing. Ryan was twenty. She was seventeen. Sabine was welcome, as long as they were careful with birth control, respectful of their rules, and discreet around Ryan's younger sisters. After several awkward family dinners and Ryan's steady urging that they accept her, she hoped they'd finally stopped seeing her as a younger version of Dee.

She and Ryan had already talked about leaving, of moving to the river. As soon as she turned eighteen and was of legal age to be Aria's guardian, they would. They didn't belong in this town. It was killing them, and though Logan had stayed away since the phone call, the threat of him still hung over her family.

She passed the Franklin family photo in the hallway: the perfect nuclear family of five, smiling, dressed in their best, with their hands resting on each other's shoulders like they were in a sitcom. Moonlight shot through the bathroom window, illuminating the picture. She'd teased Ryan about it often enough, the same way she poked fun at the Franklin household rules. The truth was she didn't mind the rules—they made her feel part of a family. And she loved that photo. She wanted to be in it.

She padded softly to the back door. Once outside, she listened for the *snick* of the dead bolt and slipped on her sandals. *Why leave a place where you feel safe, to go to a home where you're afraid all the time?* She wanted to turn around, let herself back inside the house, climb into bed with Ryan—but now the door was locked behind her. She could wake everyone up or go home.

She tiptoed down the steps to the deck by the swimming pool. The underwater lights made the water shimmer, cool and blue, and she paused to trail her fingers through it. The pool looked nothing like the river, but its touch was the same. When she was underwater, her lungs expanded, and strangely, she felt like she could breathe; when she floated on the surface, she was weightless.

On a whim she would never be able to explain, Sabine kicked off her sandals and stepped into the water. She kept going until her head went under at the deep end. When she touched the side, she turned around and walked back out, dripping. She left through the side gate, making sure it was properly latched behind her, because that was the rule.

The trailer park was a twenty-minute walk away. If she walked fast, she'd make it in fifteen. It took everything she had to drag herself away from Ryan tonight, or so she thought.

She didn't know yet what she was capable of.

———

Sunday night, everything was closed and the town was dead.

Sabine strode along the silent streets. Her dress clung to her like a wet sheet, and the ever-present dust settled on her skin, leaving a thin crust she couldn't brush away. It was a route she'd taken so many times she could have made it home with her eyes closed.

When she passed the alley leading to Taryn's street, her steps slowed.

They hadn't spoken in two months. Taryn was still avoiding her, hanging out with her new friends, and Sabine couldn't message her—after the night at the Queen, Dee had taken Sabine's broken flip phone, refusing to buy her another one.

If she could just talk to her friend, maybe Taryn would apologize. Or at least explain.

She turned and cut through the alley that brought her out near the train tracks. The streetlights were out. In front of Taryn's house, she could make out the shape of her dad's truck, parked like he'd stolen it, the front tires on the footpath and the rear tires in the gutter.

She went around the side and tapped on Taryn's bedroom window.

"Hey, Taryn," she called. "Are you in there?"

The distant sound of gunshots and swearing carried from the television at the front of the house. She sensed movement in Taryn's bedroom.

She pressed her hand against the glass. "It's me, Sabine."

A light blinked behind the curtain, then went out.

———

Sabine heard the explosion as she rounded the last bend before Windy Bridge.

Automatically, she ducked and covered her ears. Once the initial shock had passed and the reverberation stopped, she looked up. The night sky glowed bright red before fading to orange, and somewhere, somebody was screaming.

She ran, sandals slipping on the pavement, her dress billowing like a sail.

Later, she would remember what had woken her: a crimson flare behind her eyelids, the feeling of ghostly hands around her neck. So much red.

———

When Sabine reached the trailer park, the steel arch over the entrance gate appeared like a gaping mouth, and the driveway beyond it was like the dark pink flesh inside a throat. The air was foul with the stench of hot metal and melting rubber.

The first people she saw were Faith and Bram Mitchell, standing out on the road. Bram held Faith close, wrapped inside his dressing gown. They appeared incredibly old and frail as they gazed up at a twister of acrid black smoke.

Sabine skidded to a stop, heaving for breath. "What happened? Did anybody get hurt?"

Faith and Bram turned together—one body with two heads.

Faith struggled free, white with shock. She pulled Sabine into her arms. "Oh, thank God," she wailed. "We thought you were in there too."

Sabine looked around. The source of the explosion she'd heard wasn't obvious, but it was still burning. "In where?"

"It's your mother's car," Bram said. "Someone set it on fire. Emergency Services are on the way, but it could take a while."

Sabine backed away from Faith, confused. Over the stench of the smoke, she could smell herself: the fading notes of her cheap musk perfume, chlorine, the sweat of her fear.

"But they weren't in the car. Were they? *Bram, were they in the car?*"

Bram gripped her shoulders. "No, honey. They weren't in the car."

"Then where are they?"

Bram and Faith exchanged glances. Sabine had grown used to the way they were able to communicate without words. They knew something, but they didn't want to say.

"We called the police, but—" Bram said.

Faith finished his sentence. "They were already here."

Gravely, Bram nodded.

"Tell her," Faith said, turning away. Her shoulders heaved. "Lord help that sweet baby."

Bram nodded. "There was shouting for a while. You know, like there always is—but we heard Aria screaming, and then Logan left, and it was so quiet. We didn't know what to do."

"Stay here," Faith begged. "Wait for help. It's in God's hands now."

That's when Sabine knew something was very wrong, because Dee had never learned not to fight back. She would not have let Logan leave without throwing the last punch and taking a fistful of his hair. And Faith had mentioned God three times now when she'd never been to church in her life.

"Where is he?"

Bram tried to hold her back, but he was just an old man.

———

A growing mob of residents and guests surged toward the entrance to gather in the parking lot. There, they huddled in groups, watching

Dee's car burn. Sabine made out the lanky shape of Arnie Willis, silhouetted by the flames, as he fought to extinguish the fire with the office garden hose.

She ran as fast as she could in the opposite direction, pushing through the mass of bodies, searching their faces, some familiar, others strangers, and all filled with ghoulish fascination. None of the faces belonged to her mother or sister.

She passed the playground and the wooden fort where Aria was sitting that morning when Sabine had left the trailer park to meet Ryan. It had been a good day for lost and found: Aria was wearing an almost new Billabong cap, playing with a bubble wand and a bowl of soapy water, and Sabine had scored a bottle of Miss Dior perfume. They'd rejected an inflatable mattress with a slow leak, a *Muppet Christmas Carol* DVD and a screwdriver.

Take me with you, Beenie!

Not today, Sabine had said. *Next time.*

Too many images crowded her head. Her dress tangled with her legs; she pitched forward and fell. Gravel shredded her knees. She bit down on her tongue, tasting blood. Someone asked her if she was okay, and a man reached out to give her a hand up, but she scrambled to her feet on her own.

This is my fault. I pushed Logan too far, and all of this is my fault.

She zigzagged through the rows of cabins on the southern side, her breath wheezing in her chest. The smoke crept like an inky shadow between the buildings; it was in her nose and throat, stuck to the membranes like bitter-tasting medicine. Far away, people were shouting, but she couldn't understand what they were saying because all she could hear was Aria's voice.

Take me with you!

Not today. Next time.

When Sabine reached the residents' section of the trailer park, it was deserted. Eerily so.

Everything looked different in moonlight and shadow. The tall spotlight that usually lit up the area around the camp kitchen was out; when she looked more closely, she could see pieces of broken glass scattered on the grass underneath. The smoke was here too, hovering close to the ground like a fog in winter.

It dawned on her: nobody was around because they were all watching the fire.

She crouched low and approached from the Mitchells' side, cutting through their small garden. Faith's wind chimes tinkled in the breeze. The only source of dim light came from inside; in their hurry they'd left the doors open and the TV on.

She hid behind the trunk of the lemon-scented gum that separated the sites and checked the area.

Their annex door was fully zipped. The blackout paper Dee had insisted on taping over the windows prevented anyone from looking in. But if there was a light on, she'd be able to see it through the peephole Aria had made in the paper covering the window by her bunk. It was black.

Her sister's name was on her lips; then suddenly it was on the tree—*A R I A*, carved into the smooth bark, appearing like witchcraft. Sabine traced the letters with her fingertips, marveling that she hadn't noticed it before, wondering what Aria had used to wound the tree so deeply that the letters were bleeding sap. Anything to put off knowing what was inside the van.

She came back to herself the way she always woke after a dream: the jarring sensation of falling into her body while still not being in control of it.

The breeze dropped. She left the shadows and stepped toward the annex. If Logan had been here, he was gone now.

She wiped her eyes, unaware she was crying—no, it was a stinging vapor that was making them stream. What was that smell? Gas? Diesel? Whatever it was, the annex canvas was drenched in it. It was all over the ground too—when she lifted her feet, clumps of sandy dirt were stuck to the soles of her sandals.

Lightheaded from the fumes, she dug her thumbs into the veins of her wrists, as if she could slow her racing heart by pressing hard where her pulse beat. Covering her nose and mouth, she unzipped the flap and crept inside. As she tried to turn the door handle on the van, she realized it was locked. Hand shaking, she felt underneath the step for the magnet that held the spare, but it was gone.

She hit the trailer door with the flat of her hand. "Dee!" she called in a loud whisper. "Aria? Are you in there?"

No response.

She looked around for something to jimmy the door open. The few tools Dee kept in a box were inside. She thought of checking inside the Mitchells' van, but she wouldn't know where to start looking. She could smash a window, except all but the rear one were too small to climb through.

Lost and found. The screwdriver, a large heavy one with a green handle and a flat head.

As if on autopilot, she ran from the van to the residents' kitchen and found the screwdriver at the bottom of the milk crate. Back at the annex, she wedged the blade between the door overlap and the jamb, levering until her wrists ached and curls of paint came away. The aluminum buckled, but the latch would not give.

The skylight.

Sabine raced to the back of the van. She hoisted herself up on the spare wheel and scrambled onto the roof. Over the skylight was a plastic tarpaulin to keep the rain out. She stabbed a hole in the tarp until a jagged tear appeared, then pushed the tattered piece aside. The skylight, a plastic bubble, was already broken—she hit it hard with the screwdriver handle, chipping at the plastic pieces until they broke away from the screws and fell inside.

Smash. Then nothing.

She peered down, but it was too dark to see anything. Carefully, she slipped her legs through the hole and lowered herself into the void, landing on the shards of plastic with a loud crunch. She straightened up and felt along the side of the kitchen sink, then stumbled forward, hands outstretched, feeling her way until her knees hit the edge of the Dee's mattress. A shaft of pale moonlight came from above.

As her eyes adjusted, images emerged from the blackness. A coldness settled over her, and she held her breath. In the silence, a terrible stillness permeated everything.

They were there, Aria and Dee, lying on Dee's bed. Not moving, not breathing.

2019

—

RACHEL

If there's such a thing as river legs, Rachel has found hers by the time they reach Lock Two. She hasn't stopped being afraid of what's underneath, but as long as she stays on top of it, she and the river will get along just fine.

She adjusts the life jacket where the strap has slipped from the padding to cut into her skin. The dog looks at her with a peculiar expression, as if he feels embarrassed for her. Of course he does—he's more at home on the water than on land, his legs splayed for balance, a front paw on each side of the bow.

As they approach the lock and weir, the operator gives her a signal to wait. Blue wags his tail and turns a circle, setting the boat rocking.

"Bloody hell. *Sit down.*"

She pulls up short of the lock and holds steady to allow a house-boat to pass through first.

The last time she piloted a boat must have been ten or twelve years ago. More. The tinny has nowhere near the grunt of a speedboat, but she has made good time by gunning it in the stretches where there are no other vessels. According to Ray, when she reaches the cliffs, she should look for a man-made spit that runs parallel to the river.

The lock operator waves her through.

Strangely, she feels safer enclosed within the dark slimy walls of the weir than in the wide-open space of the river. If the most effective way to overcome a phobia is gradual and repeated exposure to the thing that scares you, she has just passed a crash course in under two hours.

The lock opens. She waves her thanks and continues upriver, avoiding the frequent hazard markers and dense thickets of reed.

She checks her phone, which has been suspiciously silent. Not much signal. Enough to make and receive calls in an emergency. For all she knows, her phone is being tracked right now, but there's no way she's throwing it in the drink.

The plan is to find Sabine, tell her about Doyle, and try to convince her to come with Rachel for protection. Beyond that, she has no idea.

A hysterical laugh bubbles up in her chest. *Protection? Who'd be protecting who?*

Billson might be able to help, if he can be trusted. She's still not convinced. And if Billson finds Sabine first, which was what he implied, Rachel is worried he doesn't know enough about his son's former partner to realize he's a threat. Billson could deliver Sabine straight to Doyle.

———

Twenty minutes later, the tinny rounds a bend in the river and a striking curve of ochre cliffs comes into view. On the opposite side, Rachel can see the square homestead that looks as if it has been carved from rock, set on a hill in a seemingly infinite stretch of golden wheat fields.

It's exactly as Ray described; she has the right place.

Blue knows it too. His tail settles into a lazy wag, increasing in speed until his rump wriggles from side to side.

"Be quiet," she says. "No barking."

There's the rocky spit, and a narrow opening between the end of the spit and the bank.

She cuts the motor. Using the oar, she propels the tinny through the gap like a gondolier, pushing off from the banks on either side. She worries she'll have to turn around; the water appears too shallow for a houseboat. But a little further in, she can make out the dirty-white shape of the *Kirralee*, moored at the far end.

She's almost dizzy with relief. Maybe the houseboat got beached— that's why Sabine hasn't returned.

Blue is quiet, but Rachel senses he's about to launch overboard. She grabs hold of his collar. Before the dog runs off and gives away their presence, she should check things out.

In the hull she finds a spare length of blue nylon rope. The water is a different color here, greenish and semiopaque above with a pale bottom, and probably only midthigh deep—far less terrifying than the murky water of the river. With some effort, she manages to keep hold of Blue while she flops inelegantly over the side and wades ashore.

She ties off the tinny to a low-hanging branch and hitches Blue to the trunk of a sturdy red gum. When she heads toward the houseboat, he strains at the rope, his alert gaze trained on the middle distance just past the house. A single sharp yap settles into a low whine.

"*Shh*," she says.

Her sodden sneakers leave sandy footprints onto the houseboat deck, but it doesn't matter—there's no one here. The doors and windows are shut.

An uneasy feeling swirls in Rachel's gut and sets her teeth on edge. *Is that a voice I can hear?*

After making sure the rope is long enough to stretch to the water in case Blue needs to drink, she follows a well-worn path through the trees leading toward the house. He almost strangles himself on the slip-chain choker in his attempt to follow her, but at least he isn't barking.

She moves quickly but quietly, avoiding the rocks on the path. When she reaches the wide front steps to the wraparound veranda, she stops to listen again.

The voice is louder here, but it's not coming from inside the house. Outside, somewhere to her right. No, two voices.

She heads up the veranda steps and turns left, passing an outdoor toilet and a collection of old furniture heaped against the exterior wall. She treads on the desiccated carcass of a dead mouse and shudders, flicking it away with the toe of her shoe before peering over the veranda wall.

Sabine is standing around twenty meters away, facing a stone entrance with a metal gate. Her back is to Rachel, and she appears to be talking to herself. She has a gun in her hand.

Rachel creeps along behind the veranda wall and crouches behind a wooden portico at the back of the house, trying to listen above the pounding of her blood.

"I'll show you where they are before you turn yourself in, if that's what you want," a man's voice says. "There was a collection—the community paid for their cremation."

"The *community*?" Sabine says. "Those people did nothing for Dee and Aria while they were alive, and neither did you." She lifts the arm holding the gun.

Reflexively, Rachel calls out. "Sabine!" Her arms raised, she strides from behind the portico. "Please don't."

Now the dog starts barking.

"Rachel? What are you doing here?" Her face lights up. "Blue—?" She nods. "He's been with me since you took off."

Rachel takes another few steps until she can make out a shadowy figure sitting just below ground level behind the metal gate. Billson.

Sabine is on her feet now, smiling. Her childlike delight is jarring, given she's holding a retired police officer at gunpoint.

"Rachel Weidermann, I presume," Billson says dryly. "I'd say it's a pleasure to meet you, but I'm not thrilled with my accommodation."

"I told him," Sabine says.

"And do you feel better?" Rachel says, shaking her head.

"Yeah, I kinda do."

"Well, congratulations. Now you'll have a false imprisonment charge as well."

Billson interrupts. "That's not how things will work out if you both get me out of here."

Rachel looks Sabine over. She's thinner, if that's possible, and filthy. Her hair is dull, her complexion sallow, but her blue eyes are feverishly bright.

"I want you to come with me. I've got your pop's tinny."

Sabine doesn't blink. "Thanks, Rachel, but I think my ride's coming, and I wanna see my dog before I go." At that, she gazes at the horizon beyond the wheat fields.

Rachel follows her gaze. You can see for miles out here, but she knows that the vehicle traveling at speed directly toward them is closer than it looks. Dust spews behind it, leaving a red haze.

"Someone's coming," Rachel says. "Unlock the gate. We have to go."

Billson gets up. He strains his neck to peer sideways through locked gate. "Sabine, who's coming?"

"Police," Sabine says. "The real ones."

"You called them?" Billson asks in disbelief.

"I'm not stupid," Sabine says. "If there's one thing I learned from that night, it's that I never should have trusted you. You would have done anything to protect Logan. You paraded me in front of everyone—you threw me to the wolves. So if you think I'm about to get in a car with you now so you can turn me in, you're wrong." She smacks her chest. "I'll walk in there all by myself."

"I did that so there would be *witnesses!*" Billson rattles the bars. "You've got to open the gate."

"Let him out," Rachel says. "I think something very bad is about to go down. Billson's not your enemy."

Sabine freezes in confusion. "What do you mean?"

"It's Doyle."

Sabine stares at the four-wheel drive racing along the driveway. "Doyle?" she says. "No."

Billson is so pale, Rachel thinks he's about to pass out.

"How did you get away that night, Sabine?" she prompts.

"Doyle felt sorry for me. He left the cuffs loose."

"He left them loose, or he took them off?"

"How…did you know?" she stammers.

"Why do you think he took off the cuffs, Sabine?"

She shakes her head. "Because he felt sorry for me."

With effort, Billson says, "He let you go so he could shoot you in the back when you ran, only he never got the chance."

"He's right," Rachel says urgently. "Doyle was in on it. He's been after you since the beginning. Come on, Sabine, where's the key?"

Sabine moves toward the cellar gate like an automaton. She lifts a rock to the side of the entrance and takes a handful of dust, sifting it through her fingers.

"I can't find it."

Rachel goes to help. "Are you sure you put it there?"

"It's here somewhere, but this stuff is like quicksand."

"Let me try."

Sabine has stopped looking for the key. She's standing, staring blankly at the rock, as if in some kind of dissociative state.

"We'll have to leave him," Rachel says. "It's you Doyle's after."

"No."

"What do you mean, no? What, do you want a fucking *duel* or something?" Rachel grabs her shoulder. "I'm not leaving you."

"And I'm not running this time."

Tires skidding on gravel. A cloud of dust.

Doyle is out of the car and striding toward them. A big guy, broad in the chest, his weapon raised and held in both hands. He moves like a soldier, but he's not wearing a uniform. Keeping the gun trained on Sabine, he takes them in one by one.

Rachel is vaguely aware of Billson heading back down the steps, retreating further into the cellar.

Sabine's arm still hangs limply at her side. Why the hell doesn't she *shoot*?

"Put it down, Kelly."

Sabine lets the gun slide from her grip. It dangles from her fingertips before hitting the ground with a thud.

Careful to keep away from a direct line to the cellar entrance, Doyle shouts, "You armed, Billson? Go on, make this easy for me."

"I'm not armed."

"What about you?" he asks Rachel.

Terrified, she shakes her head.

"Phones. Throw them here, *now*. Don't make me come and get them."

Sabine tosses hers first, and Doyle crushes it with his heel. Rachel's follows.

"Billson?"

"She made me leave it in my car."

Doyle pauses to assess his options. "Okay, Kelly. Slowly—now pick up your gun."

Sabine does as she's told. Doyle grabs her by the back of the neck and directs her to the entrance, using her body as a shield.

"There's no way out of this, Doyle," Billson says.

"Yeah, there is." He presses the barrel to Sabine's temple. "Shoot him. Go on. I know you must have been practicing."

Rachel collapses in the dust. The fear has taken hold of her entire body. Her organs feel like jelly and she's close to peeing herself, while Sabine is still strangely calm, pushing back against the muzzle so forcefully it indents her flesh of her cheek.

"Shoot me," Sabine says quietly. "Go on. You know you want to."

Doyle grimaces. He twists Sabine's body and smacks the gun across the bridge of her nose.

A sickening crack. Rachel gasps. A phantom pain shoots through her as if she has taken the impact herself.

Sabine's head snaps back, but her body seems rooted to the spot, her arms boneless. Dazed, she blinks. The split across her nose opens up and blood dribbles down her face. Her pretty features contort, turn ugly. Inexplicably, she smiles, and the spaces between her teeth are filled with blood.

To Rachel it's as disturbing as seeing an animal devour its young—unexpectedly violent, against the laws of nature. She scrabbles backwards on the loose gravel, trying to find her feet.

"Stay where you are," Doyle warns. Careful to hold Sabine by the wrist and keep his prints off the grip, Doyle lifts her slack arm holding the gun. With his other hand, he presses his own gun to the back of her head. "Get this over with. If we don't get you for the other murders, we'll get you for this one instead. Shoot."

Dully, Rachel realizes that if Billson is dead, that leaves one witness, so she isn't getting out of here either. Adrenaline races through her veins, but she can't make herself move.

Billson seems resigned to his fate. He closes his eyes.

Sabine puts tension on the trigger. Again, that bloody smile.
Click.

Click-click-click-click-click-click-click-click. Click.

Ten shots and nothing happens.

Sabine lowers her arm. "If you want me to do some murdering for you, you piece of shit, you'll have to give me yours."

There's a redneck twang in her voice that Rachel hasn't heard before. It's unsettling.

Billson slips sideways on his chair, clutching his chest.

Enraged, Doyle shoves Sabine in the back. She stumbles forward and rights herself, then puts her hands behind her head as if she has given up.

Doyle scratches his head. "Can't put my bullets in your gun, so… fine. I'll shoot your friend instead." He takes aim at Rachel. "Stand up and walk toward me."

Rachel ducks her head but stays where she is. She couldn't stand if she tried.

"Okay!" Sabine pleads. "There's ammo on the boat. I can get it."

"Where is it?"

She rolls her eyes like a teenager and deadpans, "It's a fucking *boat*. It's on the river."

"Start walking." He jerks his head at Rachel. "You too." To Billson, he says, "I guess you're not going anywhere."

Doyle walks several paces behind them as they head down the hill.

"I'm sorry, Rachel," Sabine says quietly. "I should've listened to you, but I wasn't—myself."

Rachel wants to dab at her poor wounded face with her shirt, but it's all she can do to put one foot in front of the other. "Are you yourself now? Otherwise what the fuck are we going to do?"

"Shut up," Doyle says. "So what's the point of an unloaded gun, Kelly?"

"I never planned on hurting anybody."

"Well. Your plans are about to change."

The sun is burning the part in Rachel's hair, and a million flies swarm and settle on her sweaty skin. She's certain she can feel them biting. When they reach the shade of the trees surrounding the backwater, she realizes it's late afternoon; the colors of the cliffs on the far side of the spit are changing from ochre to a sunset orange. Daylight savings—it won't be dark for hours yet.

As soon as they come into view, Blue races to the end of the rope, his tail wagging furiously. Sabine ignores him, and it breaks Rachel's heart to see his baffled expression.

"What's with the dog?" Doyle says.

"It belongs to the station. I tied it up so it wouldn't get in the way," Sabine says. "Shoot it—I don't care. The more bullets you spend, the more explaining you'll have to do."

Sabine is staring resolutely ahead, but Rachel detects the tremor in her voice.

Doyle takes a wide berth around Blue.

As they pass him, Sabine flicks up her hand. As Rachel anticipates, Blue drops to the ground and falls silent. To anyone else it would look as if she swatted a fly.

2019

—

SABINE

Three of them in the houseboat's tiny cabin: Sabine on the far side of the bed, Rachel at the foot of it, Doyle standing in the doorway.

Sabine takes the box of bullets from the bedside drawer. "Here." She tosses it at Doyle—he misses, and the bullets spill all over the floor.

He steps back onto the deck and points the gun at Rachel. "Pick them up."

Although Rachel's body shakes uncontrollably, her voice is steady when she says to Doyle, "It's not too late. You haven't killed anyone yet."

Typical Rachel—she thinks she can talk her way out of this.

Doyle laughs. "I'm not a killer. I've always had people to do that for me. Logan, and now you." He curls his lip at Sabine. "I've been clean for a decade. I have a wife and children—my character and reputation are spotless. This wouldn't be happening if you'd just stayed in whatever hole you crawled into."

How could she have fallen for his act? It's so obvious now. At least Logan was a predator she could see coming.

"You'll never be clean," she says.

Rachel hands him the box. "This is going to be one hell of a complicated crime scene. It won't be as easy this time. You'll get caught. Stop before it goes any further."

"Shut up, Rachel," Sabine says. *Never back a wounded animal into a corner and leave it no way out. Let it escape, and then go after it and put it out of its misery.* "You're not helping."

Doyle puts the box in his pocket. "Yeah, you're not helping, Rachel." He points to the upright cupboard behind Sabine. "What's that?"

"Storage."

"Open it."

She opens the latches, flings the door open, and steps aside.

"Take that stuff out."

She pulls the mop bucket and broom from the cupboard and tosses them on the bed.

"You, get in." He gestures at Rachel with the gun.

"What? Why?"

If it was just her, Sabine would take her chances, but she's helpless while Rachel's life is in danger. It took guts to bring Pop's tinny and come after her, to try to warn her about Doyle, when she could have just walked away. Unless Doyle plans to fire through the door so he doesn't have to look Rachel in the face, she'll be safer in the cupboard. It also means Sabine doesn't have to see her terrified eyes.

"Do it, Rachel."

As she steps inside, Rachel grabs Sabine's hand, relaying the tremors coursing through her body. It makes Sabine feel like crying. She gives her hand a tight squeeze and lets go.

"Lock it," Doyle says.

The latches on the cabin cupboards are the industrial kind, designed to stop the doors from flying open during transit. She secures them, hoping air will filter through the cracks to allow Rachel to breathe if Sabine doesn't make it back soon, or at all.

"Where do you keep your fuel?" Doyle snaps as Sabine turns away from the cupboard.

"There isn't any. I've been stuck here for two days. I'm out."

"Gas?"

With a sinking feeling, she catches on. "All solar electric and batteries." He won't pick up on her lie.

"Outside," he orders. "Move it."

He backs away and she follows him onto the deck. Keeping the gun trained on her, he opens the hatch of the below-deck storage unit, where she keeps things that need to stay cool and dry. Things like the two butane canisters he's now holding.

Her gut twists.

"Perfect." He tosses her one canister, then another. "Do your thing."

She shakes her head so hard her injured face throbs. "I won't."

"Burn it," Doyle tells her.

She moves toward the doorway. The second Doyle relaxes his shooting stance, she pushes past him, winds up, and throws the canisters overboard. They hit the surface and go under, only to bob up again a good ten meters from the houseboat.

Doyle is quick to recover. He grabs her by the arm before she can make it to the cabin and body-slams her into the wall. He's nearly a foot taller and almost double her weight—even if she could fight back, she'd offer little resistance. The breath whooshes from her lungs. Her vision goes dark. She slides to the deck and covers her face with her arms to protect herself from another hit.

It doesn't come.

Slowly, she regains her breath and opens her eyes, turning to peer through the doorway.

Doyle is in the cabin. He has found the matchbox she keeps on the windowsill; he strikes a match and touches the flame to the corner of a curtain. The flame smolders, then fizzles out. He lights another match. The second time it flickers before it catches, and a tiny dancing flame works its way along the hem.

She's dimly aware of Rachel, screaming her name and beating her fists against the cupboard door.

Sabine scrambles to her feet. "Stop!" she yells at Doyle.

She launches herself onto the bed and pulls a pillow from under the coverlet, but Doyle turns and yanks it out of her arms. She's prepared to beat the fire out with her bare hands, but now he has her by the waist, dragging her from the cabin. He punches her jaw, sending a fresh wave of agony through her bleeding face. Then he jabs the gun into her belly, and she doubles over.

"Please! You have to let her out!"

He pulls her up and shoves her outside until they're on the gangplank.

Sabine looks up. There isn't much smoke—just a slow creeping haze above the cabin, but once a fire gets going, it won't stop. The *Kirralee* is over fifty years old, with dry timbers and a brittle deck. The fuel tank is on empty, but the residual fuel and gas might be enough for it to explode.

She thinks of Rachel, locked inside, and it all rushes back. The heat, the smoke, the smell of burning hair and flesh—the difference is Rachel will be alive when the fire reaches her. She'll feel everything.

They're heading into the trees.

Doyle is red in the face, his breathing labored. He hasn't left as much distance between them this time—*Could I duck and swing? Kick his legs out from under him? How much time do I have?*

She chances a look back at the *Kirralee*.

The smoke has become a dense black plume. Despite the distance, Rachel's screams are getting louder. Blue, however, is lying on his side, strangely quiet.

When she glances back again, Blue is on his feet, a ruler's length of frayed nylon rope hanging from his collar. He has chewed through the rope. Sabine reads the tension in his hindquarters and the stiffness of his tail; he's alert, waiting for a punishment or a command. If she calls him now, Doyle will see him coming.

"Wait," she says loudly.

Doyle, assuming she's talking to him, says, "Keep walking."

"We can't leave her in there. It's inhumane."

"It's done. You'll shoot Billson, I'll shoot you, and it'll all be over. You won't even have to go to jail."

They're a quarter of the way back up the hill. The *Kirralee* is almost out of sight. Soon they'll be out of earshot too.

Deliberately, she stumbles over a rock and goes down hard, rolling into a crouching position—at the same time, she gives a sharp whistle.

Doyle, distracted by her fall, leans over to drag her up.

He must weigh a hundred pounds; Blue is a quarter of his weight, but he has taken down bigger prey. He covers the ground between them in seconds, emerging from the trees and hitting Doyle in the back with the full force of his momentum. Doyle rolls onto his stomach, the wind knocked out of him. Immediately, Blue goes for the arm with the gun and latches on, shaking his head in violent bursts the way Sabine has seen him kill a snake.

She watches in horror as they battle. She has never seen Blue behave so savagely. It's like she doesn't know him, but at the same time she knows exactly what is driving him because she feels it too.

Doyle shrieks and flips onto his back, kicking out with his legs and punching with his other fist. In contrast, Blue is silent and relentless as he shifts his jaw grip from Doyle's forearm to his wrist, preventing Doyle from getting a clear shot at either of them.

But the gun goes off. They all freeze. A wayward bullet. No injuries.

"Call him off!" Doyle screams.

"Drop the gun."

"*Call the fucking dog off!*"

"Drop the fucking gun!"

In response to her tone, Blue moves his grip to the base of Doyle's thumb. Despite the size and weight difference, he manages to drag Doyle a full yard downhill.

The gun slips from Doyle's broken hand.

Sabine crawls after it and picks it up. She takes aim. Every instinct is telling her to put a bullet in his head, but the smell of smoke has reached her. It reminds her of another time, another choice.

Blue's winning.

Rachel's dying.

"Hold, Blue!"

She runs, leaving Doyle on the ground, bleeding, and Blue hanging on for dear life. Her speed and the slippery path make for a treacherous descent, and she falls twice, scraping her knees and hands.

The *Kirralee* appears through the haze like a ghost ship.

If she was decrepit before, she's stricken now, taking on water and listing to the side. Her white timbers are blackened, and the gangplank has slipped; she has drifted several meters from the bank.

Sabine leaves Doyle's gun lying on the sand. She jumps into the lagoon, kicking hard to reach the rear deck, and hoists herself up. She takes off her wet T-shirt and wraps it around her face like a headscarf, leaving only her eyes uncovered. They're already streaming from the smoke.

"Rachel!"

The cabin wall is well alight on the port side, revealing a square of gray sky where the window has shattered. If it wasn't for the hole in the ceiling, the heat would be unbearable. Lazy flames lick the floorboards; a corner of the bedsheet is smoldering, but the doorway is clear.

"Rachel?"

No reply.

The image of Dee and Aria, their still bodies lying on the bed—if willing her to be alive is enough to make Rachel's heart beat, she'll be breathing when Sabine opens that door. If she's dead, Sabine accepts that her mind will tip over the edge. Madness. That's all there is on the other side.

She gulps air and lunges for the bed. The impact knocks the breath from her, and she sucks in a lungful of smoke. Through a bout of coughing, she reaches the other side and flips the searing latches, hissing as the skin on her fingers burns.

She opens the cupboard door.

Rachel is huddled in the corner. She fights as Sabine pulls her writhing body from the cupboard, throwing punches like a wild thing.

"It's me! Stop!"

"Oh, thank God!" Her face is bright red. The smoke hits her and she coughs.

Sabine shepherds her toward the bed. "We have to leave now—if the tank blows, we're gone."

"You first."

"Fine. I'm not here to argue with you. Go!"

Sabine scrambles across the bed, through the doorway, and onto the deck. Rachel is right behind her, but as she curls her toes over the edge, she realizes Rachel has stopped.

"Are you kidding me?" She grabs her hand and pulls her. "Hurry."

Rachel looks down. "Give me a second."

"Would you jump in if you were on fire?" She points. "Jesus Christ, *you're on fire, Rachel.*"

They both jump.

———

Sabine waits for Rachel to realize she's swimming in water that's only waist-deep, then picks up the gun and goes after Doyle.

When they come into view, it's clear that the situation has reversed: Doyle has managed to pin Blue down with his body. He has one hand clamped over Blue's muzzle. The other is a vice on his jugular. Though he looks spent and he's bleeding profusely from his arm and cheek, Doyle turns his head to watch Sabine.

She stops a few yards short, unable to process what's happening.

Doyle smiles. "Station dog, yeah?"

She's sure she can see the white of bone through Doyle's torn skin. She raises the gun. "Let him go."

"Go ahead, shoot. I'll break his neck first."

"Let him go, or I'll blow your face off, I swear."

Blue's hind legs kick feebly. His pitiful whine prompts a chemical reaction in her blood, and she moves closer. Her finger tightens on the trigger.

The hand at Blue's throat tightens too. "Get back, or you're going to need more bullets."

"I only need two," she says. "I'll kill him myself before I'll let you do it."

Doyle's eyes dart behind her.

"Don't shoot, Sabine." Rachel's face is streaked with ash and tears. "If you kill him, it's all over."

"That's what I want more than anything."

Doyle watches them both warily.

Blue has stopped fighting.

Rachel gently places a hand over Sabine's.

Time seems to slow down and fold back on itself. Sabine experiences déjà vu so strong she thinks she will be stuck in this loop forever. Perhaps they're all doing the same thing, over and over, and there is no way to break free.

More precious seconds pass.

Rachel moves first, advancing steadily to flank the strange two-headed beast that is Doyle and Blue, speaking the whole time.

"Everybody, calm down. Sabine, drop the gun. We can work this out—nobody else needs to get hurt."

She still thinks she can talk her way out of this.

But Rachel bends down in a single fluid movement, and in that moment, Sabine understands they're different. Rachel comes from another world, one Sabine can never be part of, and she would still say Rachel doesn't have a violent bone in her body. They have nothing in common, except this—and right now Rachel must be asking herself: *How will I survive today?*

Sabine lowers her arm.

Rachel raises hers.

They exchange a look of intense recognition, then Rachel brings a fist-sized rock down on the back of Doyle's head.

2019

—

RACHEL

The gravel parking area behind the homestead is jammed with vehicles, red and blue lights flashing. It's standing room only on the veranda, and Rachel's legs are throbbing. The portable lights hurt her eyes. She has endured over two hours of questioning—still no one has said she can go. Nobody has told her to stay where she is either.

Nervously, she approaches one of the police cars. Sabine is cuffed to the door handle. Blue lies at her feet, sleepy but watchful, seemingly none the worse for his near-death experience.

Rachel gives her a tentative smile. "I'm not sure if we're supposed to be talking. Are you...okay?"

"They're going to take me in soon," Sabine says, her expression unreadable. She tries to hold up her hands, but the chain yanks them back.

Rachel reaches down to stroke Blue's head. "I'll tell them every-thing. Billson will too. Once they recover the evidence and form the whole picture, they'll let you go."

On that, Rachel's voice cracks. It's wishful thinking. A lot needs to be unraveled before Sabine will see the outside of a cell. Given her history, it's not likely even the best lawyer will get her bailed out.

She drops her head. "I'll look after Blue until you come home."

"Rachel."

"I'm the one who should be in cuffs, not you."

"Rachel. Look at me."

Sabine's left eye is swollen closed, and the right is a red mess of broken blood vessels. The bridge of her nose is split, leaking watery blood, and the ends of her hair are fried. She could slip right out of the handcuffs again if she tried, her wrists are so thin, then melt into the trees and disappear, this time for good. She needs a hospital, not a holding cell. It's like witnessing animal cruelty, knowing there's nothing you can do but follow due process.

In comparison, all Rachel has is mild sunburn and sore muscles. And possibly the recurring nightmares of being locked in a burning cupboard and smashing someone's head with a rock. By the time the cavalry arrived, Doyle had come to; he was walking and talking when they took him away. Rachel wouldn't have minded if the damage had been worse.

"Don't look so worried—apparently I have a very expensive lawyer." Sabine's smile is grotesque in the ruin of her face. "This is how it's all meant to happen. I've come full circle."

Rachel's guilt and comedown after the adrenaline merge to form a fizzing ball of anger.

"This is my fault, can't you see? I didn't wait. I contacted people about the story—that's how Doyle knew you'd surfaced. You didn't stand a chance, because I didn't wait. The pendulum started swinging way before you thought it did."

Sabine shakes her head. "It's not your fault. I made it all happen. I did this."

"Doyle found you because of me."

"No, the snake slithered out of his hole, and you hit him on the head." Sabine frowns. "Everyone did what they were supposed to do—what I *expected* them to do—except you."

Rachel feels as if she is flailing under the water again. Her ears are filled with the ominous *whump-whump-whump* of a helicopter overhead. Everything slows down.

"I don't understand."

"You said sometimes there are no answers, but they're there, Rachel. I knew Billson would turn up alone—he's always wanted to know what really happened that night. I knew Taryn would call it in and claim the reward, and I knew you would try to sell my story before it was finished. But I didn't know who was coming for me, and I needed you to flush them out." She shrugs. "I'm good at reading people. I've had nothing but time."

"So everything went to plan," Rachel says flatly.

"No, the opposite." Sabine tries to stand, but the cuffs yank her back. "You, I got wrong. Two things I didn't see coming were you quitting on the story, and then coming to find me." Her one good eye is a blaze of blue. "I thought I could control everything, but in the end, we made such a beautiful mess together—now they can't ignore it or hide it anymore. Everything will come out."

Rachel looks around: the smoke, the ash, the frenetic energy of the firefighters down by the riverbank, the more dogged pace of the police marking the evidence. "So it wasn't meant to end like this."

"No. I would never deliberately put you in danger. It's your story now. You've earned it. Do what you want with it."

"I don't deserve anything," Rachel mutters.

"You did what I needed you to do. More than that—more than I can ever thank you for." She grimaces, as if it hurts to smile. "What happened to your fear of water?"

Rachel's body slumps in defeat. "Oh, I don't know. Maybe I was scared you were going to screw up my ending. This is way more cinematic."

Another pained grin.

"Are they treating you okay? Apart from the cuffs, I mean?"

Sabine looks away. "I think they're scared of me."

"They should be."

She turns serious. "You saved my life. And Blue's."

"As you did mine."

There's an awkward silence. Or maybe it's not awkward at all, but the comfortable kind when there's nothing left to say. Nevertheless, Rachel is not ready to walk away.

"What's the first thing you'll do when they let you out?"

"See Ryan," she says without hesitation. "There's so much he doesn't know."

With a heavy heart, Rachel remembers. "I went to his house."

"Yeah, he told me. I thought that was you."

She takes a deep breath. "A young woman answered the door. She had a baby, Sabine."

Sabine's confused expression clears, and she laughs. "I've done a lot of dumb things in my life, but falling for a married guy isn't one of them. Ryan is a better person than I'll ever be. Katie too. She's his sister."

"Oh, thank God."

"And I'm sorry I broke into your house."

Rachel blinks. "That was you?"

"I'll pay for the window."

"The insurance will cover the window, but I want my laptop back."

"I didn't take your laptop," Sabine says, frowning. "I only took what was mine. I have *some* principles."

So it was Doyle who stole the laptop, and Sabine who stripped the wall. Two robberies in a matter of hours. She shudders to think how close Sabine must have come to running into Doyle.

Blue raises his head. An officer is walking toward them.

"It's time, I guess." Sabine nods at the frayed rope attached to Blue's collar. "What's the first thing you'll do when you get home?"

Rachel spreads her arms. "Look at the state of me. I need a screaming-hot shower and a good lie-down."

Sabine laughs softly. "Remember when I said you needed rewilding, Rachel? I think you're almost there."

———

Rachel waits by the riverbank, damp seeping through her shorts. Fifty meters from where she sits, the smoking wreck of the *Kirralee* lies half-sunk, the spot where she jumped from the deck now submerged beneath the dark water. Someone has draped a gray blanket around her shoulders, and fine ash drifts like snow and settles on her bare legs.

Everything is happening the way it does in the final scene of a B-grade thriller—she half expects Bruce Willis to enter the scene, a cigarette dangling from his bottom lip.

She laughs and coughs, tasting mud.

"My wife—" Aidan is saying.

She doesn't hear the rest. She doesn't even know who called him, why he's here. His wet kiss on her cheek has left a dried patch of saliva; she can feel it crease when she moves her mouth. His hug was suffocating, and he smells *other*—a new soap, a different washing powder.

The only person Rachel wants to see is Sabine, but she's gone. If not for her, she would be a drowned husk inside the wreck. Where have they taken her? Is she still fighting, or has she given in? She can't picture Sabine strapped to a gurney or handcuffed in a cell.

Aidan is busy inserting himself into the narrative, answering the officer's questions about his "wife's" part in all this, nodding with a grave expression and a hand on his chin. The officer tells him Rachel should be taken to hospital, get checked over, something-something posttraumatic stress, and Aidan assures him she'll be taken care of.

"I'm surprised. This is not like my wife. Yes, she's brave. So brave. I'm proud of her, I'll take care of her."

Rachel cups her hands over her ears. *La-la-la.* Her love cools by another degree, and she welcomes it.

The constant strobe of red and blue light is giving her a headache. She touches a tender spot on her lip with a finger. Her forearm is grazed, and there's a raw scrape on her shin, but the thing that hurts most is the realization that Sabine hadn't trusted her from the get-go, that she expected Rachel would screw her over, and Rachel didn't let her down.

From the moment she sent the emails, fishing for a bite from an editor, she played right into Sabine's hands. Everything after that was about trying to stuff the worms back in the can she had opened, and Sabine was always a step ahead. She was never an objective narrator of Sabine's story—she is right in the middle of it. She's a fucking antagonist.

Something touches her shoulder. It's Blue, pressed close and quaking. She runs her palm along his back; pieces of singed fur break off in her hand.

The dog doesn't hate her, so she can't be all bad, right?

"Rach, they said I can take you now."

Aidan is holding his hand out to her, his perfect features crumpled with concern. In her old life she might take it, play the helpless woman, maybe coax him into bed for some ex-sex. That's how her revenge fantasies have played out before—sure as shit it would make her feel better.

But Blue gives a disdainful sniff, raising his muzzle as if he's caught the scent of something bad, and she cackles to herself.

She's one of the villains now.

"Just go, Aidan," she says, and echoes Blue's sniff. "I can find my own way home."

2019

SABINE

The other women in the jail complain about the food. Sabine finds it, like everything about this place, comforting in its sameness. The outside world is far away, and strangely, she doesn't feel locked up—the walls are a refuge, a respite from the fear. Here she has regular meals, hot showers, and predictable routines. No control. If she has nightmares, she can't remember them; she has slept more deeply than she has in years. She shares her room with three women, but she has kept pretty much to herself. She forgets their names and doesn't care to judge them for whatever they've done.

Her reflection in the stainless-steel mirror shows her scars have almost healed, leaving fresh pink skin. Her natural blond hair is growing back, and her eyes are tired looking but clear.

She fills a plastic cup with water and gulps it down to quell her nerves.

Sometime in the next hour she'll be released. Ryan is picking her up. Where she'll stay and for how long, she doesn't know. Her few belongings are laid out on her bed, and she's wearing the new outfit Rachel brought in for her: slim black pants, pumps, a blue cotton blouse.

Yesterday her solicitor told her the arson and murder charges had been dropped, and it would take another twenty-four hours to process the paperwork for her release. Sergeant Tristan Doyle has been remanded in custody awaiting formal charges. In his desire to avoid the worst of them, he threw Logan Billson under the bus.

There would be a new independent and thorough investigation.

On hearing the news, Sabine cried for the first time in weeks. It was a bittersweet moment, everything she had hoped for, but her life will be changed irrevocably from this point. She's not sure she's ready.

She has to take it a day at a time. One day to experience freedom knowing that justice for her family has been served. One day to hug Pop, to hold Blue, to love Ryan—without thinking it might be the last. One day to thank Rachel for saving her life, and to give her the only gift she can.

———

In the remand center's administration office, in the company of her solicitor and a justice of the peace, Sabine signs a sheaf of papers. She thanks her solicitor and shakes hands. From there, an officer hustles her down a long corridor to a rear exit.

"The press has the front entrance covered. It'll be easier this way," the officer says. "Good luck out there, Sabine."

"Thank you."

The door opens. For a terrifying moment, Sabine imagines herself wandering lost and alone in an empty parking lot, no one to collect her, the way it happens in movies.

The reality is cheesier, but perfect. Ryan is waiting with an enormous bunch of flowers that obscures his face. Blue is sitting by his feet with a yellow bow tied around his neck. It seems as if Blue doesn't recognize her at first, but then his nails are scrabbling on the asphalt, and he launches himself at her, tail whipping, slobbering all over her face and neck.

"I was going to tie Coke cans to the tow bar and write *Just out* on the rear windshield, but Rachel talked me out of it," Ryan says.

She stops in front of him, her hand on Blue's head to keep him from jumping up.

"Just so you know—I'm still mad at you," he says. "Lucky you've got the rest of your life to make it up to me."

He holds out his arms, and she moves into them. She feels his heat in her blood, his lips on her hair.

"God, I've missed you." He releases her and checks his watch. "We need to make tracks. Rachel wanted to come, but she's too busy cooking up a storm for dinner. We'll pick up your pop and head over to celebrate."

He takes her bag and opens the passenger-side and rear doors. Blue jumps in the back.

Sabine climbs in, and Ryan reverses out of the parking lot. She can't speak, but Ryan doesn't appear to notice—he has enough to say for both of them.

"Ray wanted to come too, but he wasn't up to traveling." He glances at her. "We might have to score some weed for him along the way."

Despite the emotion welling up, she laughs.

"Yeah, I figured you might have had something to do with his diminished supply." He creeps closer to the exit. "Get ready for the mob."

She hears the crowd outside the remand center entrance: a swell of voices, chanting. From the corner of her eye, she can see cameras, placards, people swarming toward the car as Ryan nudges out onto the road. A cyclist approaches in the bike lane, and he stops to give way.

"This is crazy—I've never seen anything like it," he says.

Sabine has. It all comes back: the suffocating press of bodies, the yelling, the hate. The feeling of dread that has kept her speechless turns into a wave of panic. Reflexively, she reaches for the door handle and pulls the release—if it wasn't for the child lock, she would be off, away and running as fast and as far as she can, but all she can do is squeeze her eyes shut and pray for it to stop.

The car starts moving again.

"It's okay now. It's over." Ryan covers her hand with his. "Say something."

The blood rush in her ears fades, and she can almost imagine the crowd isn't chanting, but cheering.

"Take me home," she says. "To the river."

———

Pop doesn't hug her when they arrive. Rachel doesn't either. There's a lot of face-splitting smiles as they stand around awkwardly, before Rachel ushers them to the table on the deck. She has prepared a homecoming feast of fragrant curry, steamed vegetables, fluffy rice, and naan.

Sabine is grateful there was no hugging. As much as she and Ryan want to climb inside each other's skin at times, platonic touch might bring her undone. It's enough that they're all here, and there's wine chilling in a bucket and fairy lights strung along the jetty. The river looks as if it has stopped flowing, it's so still.

Ryan and Rachel begin serving the food.

Sabine sits next to her grandfather. His face is drawn, but his eyes are bright.

"How are you, Pop?"

"Still kicking. Pain's manageable." He gives her a wicked look. "I'm still a boat down, though."

"I'm sorry—sorry for everything I've ever put you through," she says.

He holds up a hand. "Stop it."

"Just let me—"

"I'm only gonna say this once: you were a better parent for Aria than I ever was for Dee. You've got nothing to be sorry for." He looks down at his food. "Not sure I can do this spread justice. Can't taste much these days."

Sabine forks a mouthful from his plate. "I'll help."

"It's good to have you home," he says.

"It's good to be home." She lays her head on his shoulder, and he lets her.

———

"How are you feeling?" Rachel asks when they're alone on the deck.

"Half in one world and half in another," Sabine admits. "Like this is all a dream but I have to wake up now."

"You're wide-awake." Rachel smiles. "And I have some good news—the police traced Doyle's call and email to me, and they've recovered my laptop from his house. He was formally charged an hour ago. They're minor charges in the scheme of things, but there will be more to follow."

Sabine's stomach does a flip. "So soon?"

"Yes. There's something else I want to tell you," Rachel says. "But I'm not entirely sure this is the right time."

Sabine considers what it might be. Something about a book deal, maybe. If that's the case, she's happy for Rachel—it's only fair that she gets what she wants too. She's going to have a banger of an ending.

"How do we ever know how much time we have left?" she says lightly.

"Are you sure?"

"Yes."

Rachel takes a deep breath. "Okay. Don't run off," she says as she walks inside.

As if she'd be anywhere else. Pop is dozing on the floral couch in the living room. Blue is at her feet under the table. Ryan is doing dishes in the kitchen. This is as close to peace as she'll ever get—at least until she's old and gray, and Pop and Blue aren't around.

Rachel comes back, holding a yellow envelope close to her chest. After a few long seconds, she reaches inside to withdraw a sheet of paper, then slides a color photocopy across the table.

Sabine picks it up and cautiously turns it over. At first there's a disconnect—what she's seeing is so far removed from what she has always believed that she can't make sense of it. Slowly, the face she remembers, and this one, many years older, merge and come into focus.

"Oh," she says softly.

"I wasn't such a great journalist, but it turns out I'm pretty good at tracing missing persons."

Sabine feels as if she could float away. "Nan's alive?"

Rachel nods. "She's in an assisted living facility in New South Wales. She has dementia, but I sent a photo of you. The nurse said that on her good days she remembers."

Sabine wipes a tear away with her fist. She wasn't aware that she was crying. "What happened? How could she leave us like that?"

Rachel appears to choose her words carefully. "We both know how survival instinct can make us do things we ordinarily wouldn't do."

Rachel's frank stare implies they're thinking the same thing, that they're in this together. They're not.

"Has Pop seen this?"

"No. I don't think it a good idea, unless it's what your grandmother wants."

Sabine looks away. "I know what Pop was like. It wasn't just that one day. I think I always knew."

"You couldn't have done anything, Sabine. You shouldn't blame yourself."

"I don't blame myself," she says quietly. "I blamed Pop. I've always thought he killed her and buried her somewhere on his patch."

Rachel recoils. "How could you have forgiven him if you believed that?"

"I never forgave him. I *understand* him," she says miserably. "Because it's in me too."

"What's in you?"

"The bad blood." She shrugs. "The rage. Dee was the same—she never should have had kids."

Rachel covers Sabine's cold hand with her warm one. "That's why you chose not to have children?"

She nods.

"Well, maybe now you'll change your mind."

"It doesn't change anything, Rachel," Sabine snaps.

She gets up to pace along the deck. She needs to swim, and soon.

Rachel isn't done. "Well, what about this?" She hands her a sheaf of papers.

"What is it?" she says, distracted.

"It's a full confession for arson leading to the deaths of nine people, signed by your grandfather and witnessed by two justices of the peace."

"That's what was in the envelope? I thought it was about Nan." Sabine laughs, shaking her head. "It's fake."

"Of course it's fake." Rachel takes the papers and tears them right through the middle. "I just thought you should know, since you're the one who told me nothing is black and white, or even shades of gray."

After everything she has done, Pop's still trying to save her.

"Crazy old bastard," Sabine mutters. "I guess I can stop digging holes now."

Rachel gives her a quizzical look.

"Never mind."

Sabine kicks off her court shoes.

Blue, anticipating her next move, dashes down to the water and jumps in.

Sabine follows slowly. She craves the feeling of cool water against her skin, to have the river hold her. To be weightless. If she could, she'd stay right here forever.

The river takes, and the river brings back.

2019

—

RACHEL

Rachel wakes early. Something has stirred her from sleep—the dog barking, the rumble of an engine, or perhaps her thumping head.

She throws on a long T-shirt, heads to the kitchen, switches the coffee machine on. After swallowing two paracetamols, she goes outside to catch the colors of the morning, the best part of the day.

She's not alone. Sabine is already awake, sitting on the end of the jetty, kicking her bare feet in the rolling water. Occasionally, she tears away chunks of what looks like bread in her lap and flings it into the river. Her body no longer seems filled with the coiled tension that Rachel came to accept as part of her being.

As Rachel draws closer, she sees a swarm of catfish and shudders. She'll never get used to their gasping mouths, those horrific staring eyes.

She steps onto the jetty as Sabine gives a sharp whistle; across the water Blue turns, his V-shaped wake aimed like an arrow toward the riverbank. A houseboat passes—it's a big one, wide and sleek, its upper deck dotted with cheerful blue lounge chairs. Blue ducks under just yards in front of the bow as the boat emits a long blast of its horn.

Rachel claps her hand over her mouth, holding her breath until he pops up again. He makes it to the bank and dries off with a full-body shake that starts with his ears and finishes with his tail.

Sabine hasn't moved. "Will you keep him?" she says, without turning around.

Rachel doesn't understand. Maybe Sabine thought it was some-one else coming up behind her.

"It's me, Rachel. Keep who?"

"Blue. Will you keep him? If you're staying here, I mean." Sabine lifts her legs and swings her body around, cupping her knees. "I'd like him to be by the water."

"I'm not staying," she says, and she means it. "This place is far too big for me."

She decided weeks ago. She and Aidan had brought in a dozer to carve the riverbank into their own private beach; they'd pumped excess sewage into the water, believing it was not enough to do any real damage. They'd cut down a two-hundred-year-old tree. Damage is cumulative, through generations and over time.

She looks back at the house. It's excessive. Her entire life has been excessive. She wants to live more simply. A tiny house, or a fucking yurt.

"Blue should be with you," Rachel says.

"I can't take him where I'm going."

Rachel avoids the obvious question: *Where are you going?* "What about Ray?"

"Won't work." Sabine runs her fingertip over the raised burn scar on her calf. "He hasn't stopped dying."

"Are you moving in with Ryan?" That must be it. She needs to be with Ryan, but she doesn't want to take Blue from the river. "He'll adjust, surely?"

Sabine shakes her head. "What Ryan and I have has nothing to do with being together. What we have will last—doesn't matter where I am or where he is." She flashes a sweet, sad smile. "I've never been with anyone else."

Rachel suddenly feels like crying. She imagines the young lovers meeting in secret, never progressing in their relationship to the safe ledge of familiarity—marriage, a mortgage, bills, children, family holidays, photo albums full of memories, good and not-so-good—until the ledge crumbles away, leaving an ex-wife, alone. Sabine Kelly is stuck in a time warp where teenage love is all-consuming and forever.

It must be a nice place to be.

"You can be together now."

"Not yet. It's not over."

"It's done, Sabine," Rachel says bitterly. "You have everything you wanted."

Sabine raises her head and gives her a direct, unnerving stare. "You're supposed to be the smart one. Haven't you got ten fucking degrees or something?"

"Two."

"Whatever. Do you really not get it?"

"Get what?"

Sabine stands, brushing the crumbs from her lap, her mouth working, as if she's chewing gum.

"What, Sabine?" Rachel says impatiently.

"You said all along what was important to you—your *integrity*. You said the truth is bigger than all of us and justice takes care of the rest."

"That was just talk. I know better now."

Blue wanders over, covered in mud and whipping his tail. Absently, Sabine places her hand on his head, and the dog leans into her legs.

The looseness in Sabine's body, Rachel realizes, is resignation. Last night she seemed at peace; this morning she is tormented.

"It's just a word," Rachel says. "Truth is complex—so is the concept of justice. Why do you think we have volumes and volumes of law books? We don't always get it right." She's babbling.

Sabine is resolute. "Well, now we're talking about my *integrity*."

Her mouth twists. "You said I have everything I wanted. Well, what I want is to start over—I want to do my time and walk back into the world knowing I don't owe anything."

"What are you talking about? The world owes *you*."

A faint smile. "Was it easy for you to become a good person, Rachel? Or did you have to work at it?"

"You're a good person too, Sabine."

Please, stop talking. Don't say any more.

"I'm not. You know it."

Don't tell me, Sabine.

"I sat in the back of that police car; I saw the faces of all those people. I knew most of them my whole life and they hated me. They wished I had burned too. If people who knew me thought I could kill nine people and burn my home to the ground, what hope did I have in a room full of strangers?"

"Sabine—"

"No one was going to dig any deeper or ask the right questions. I ran because I knew there would be no justice for my family, and I vowed I wouldn't give myself up until there was."

Shut up.

"Well, now I have justice." She holds her palms upturned, weighing them like scales until they are level. "But is it really justice without the truth?"

Shut up shut up shut up.

"Everyone knew Logan was crooked, but he got buried like a hero. Guns and flags and his picture in the paper… Yeah, Dee was fucked up, but he was the one who got her on drugs. Aria and I dragged ourselves up, but we were okay, right? She was a good kid. Dee loved us. She did the best she could."

Sabine is crying—nothing like the racking, full-body sobs that overwhelmed Rachel on her worst days, but the silent, blank-faced kind.

"Dee tried to make it stop. She told Pop—that last time she went to see him after I threatened Logan—she said if anything happened to her, he needed to go after Logan. For her, for me, for Aria. She told Pop that if she wasn't around, he should protect us, even if he couldn't forgive her. And Pop promised."

A cool breeze picks up, ruffling Rachel's hair. Her legs feel weak—she has to sit down.

Sabine squeezes her eyes shut, as if trying to picture a scene. "I should have been there that night. I'm sure Logan planned to kill all of us, but I was with Ryan. I don't know why I woke up. I don't even know why I started walking—it's not like I had a premonition or anything; otherwise I would have *run*." She opens her eyes. "The trailer door was locked, and I couldn't get inside. There was no answer, so I climbed on the roof and smashed the skylight with a screwdriver. Petrol—it was everywhere, outside and inside. I didn't know where Logan was, and I didn't care about Dee. I just wanted to find Aria."

She goes somewhere far away. "They were on the bed. There wasn't any blood. I think he choked them." Her voice breaks. "The part that haunts me is that Logan would have killed Dee first. No way would she let him do that to Aria, and that means Aria had to watch what he did to Dee. The coroner should have known the fire didn't kill them."

Rachel doesn't want to hear any more. She wants to return to last night, when everything was over.

"I had to go back out through the skylight. I was on the top of the van when I saw Logan moving through the shadows of the trees—he was carrying a jerry can, like the one strapped to the back of the police four-wheel drive. He picked up the trail of fuel where it left off near the annex door and splashed a line that led to the gas canisters near the Shoosmiths' van. I had just climbed down from the roof when I heard a whoosh, like a train passing. Fire is loud, did you know that?"

"Yes."

Sabine collects herself. The tension in her body is back. "The coroner should have known the fire didn't kill Logan either."

Rachel exhales slowly. "What happened to Logan, Sabine?"

"He saw me coming. It's funny—he looked pleased to see me, but that was probably because he now had the chance to get rid of me too." She gives a manic laugh. "I let him get close—Dee taught me that. I stood there while he put his hands around my throat."

Rachel wants to back away, but her feet are rooted to the spot.

"I stabbed him in the eye with the screwdriver. For Aria."

I can't listen to this.

"I stuck it through his other eye. That was for Dee. He couldn't see to find his way out of the flames—he crawled to the path, thrashing and screaming. I would have stayed there and burned with him, but my dress was wet. I think it saved me. Only the skin on my leg burned and my hair caught fire. The next thing I knew, Arnie was there—I told him they were all dead. Arnie took the jerry can and the screwdriver. He took them, and he told me to run. I never really knew if he was covering for me, or if he planned to give them to the police, not until that day when you told me what he said."

Her words come faster now, like a river of pain breaking a levy.

"When the gas bottles blew, I was already out on the road. Doyle was there, and I trusted him—I didn't know he was in on it. I didn't know Bram and Faith had gone back for me and Aria. I'm sorry for that. They were good people. I'm sorry for the Shoosmith family, for all of them."

Sorrysorrysorry.

"You want the truth, Rachel?" Sabine doesn't give her a chance to answer. "Logan Billson bled out like a pig, and I watched. I have a million regrets, but I'm not sorry for that."

Rachel draws her knees to her chest. She twists her fingers through her hair.

Sabine's explosive anger, her sudden and violent fury—Rachel has seen glimpses of it. She has seen her change in expression, like a tripped switch; she knows from their conversations that Sabine has struggled with knowing this about herself. *Nature versus nurture? Bad environment or bad blood? Will she hurt the people she loves?* Now it's clear why Sabine says she will never have children.

"Does Ray know?"

"Not everything. He said what's done is done. Pop said the less he knew, the better off I'd be if they ever got him in court."

"Ryan?"

"You're the only one."

Sabine sighs so deeply she slumps forward. From her pocket, she takes a ziplock bag. Inside is a flat-head screwdriver with a green handle. The steel is black with old blood.

She hands it to Rachel. "I'm ready now."

Sabine is finished. Wrung out. Crying silently.

In that moment, Rachel misses her children acutely—not so much the well-adjusted, successful adult people they have become, but the wild, child versions who came running to her when they were hurt. Rachel could fix everything. She was superhuman, all-powerful. She has felt the urge to hug Sabine before, or at least to hold her hand, but she has already played through the scene: in it, Sabine rejects her comfort. Rachel feels the futility of it all—a hollow place inside. It's not possible to fix a person who has been so broken for so long with a simple touch.

She will call Lexi; she will sign the statutory declaration. She will lend Ben the money he needs. Fuck her integrity.

Sabine strokes Blue's head again, smoothing his damp fur. "So will you keep him? You'll have to lock him inside at night—he's been killing deer. I know it's wrong, but I don't have the heart to put him down. He thinks he's doing the right thing."

Rachel recalls the picture they used in the newspapers: a girl, mouth slack, her dress stained gray with ash, her long blond hair singed to the scalp on one side—defiant in body language but, inexplicably, horrifically, devoid of expression. Society doesn't trust a woman who doesn't grieve publicly.

Sabine Kelly is grieving now.

"You could have shot Doyle, but you didn't," she says. "You have to forgive yourself."

"No, Rachel, I would have killed him. If it wasn't the gun, it would have been my bare hands. The only thing that stopped me was you."

"Me?"

Her expression clears and brightens. "I've been so alone. But when you picked up that rock, when I saw your face—don't you see? At that moment, we were the same."

Rachel breathes out. "Deer are destructive," she says. "Blue's probably done the world a favor. I don't think he should pay with his life for that."

Blue hears his name and wags his tail, waiting for a command.

Sabine waits too.

All her working life, Rachel has tried to fight for justice from outside the arena—now she's in it. *Doing the right thing versus doing what's right.* Twelve years is a long time, almost half a life sentence.

"Could you live with yourself, Sabine, if no one ever knew?"

Slowly, Sabine nods. "You know. That's enough for me."

Rachel opens the bag and takes hold of the screwdriver, asking herself the same question: *Can I live with myself?*

She looks up. All along the river, the sky is streaked with purples and pinks. The trees bend and whisper; the current is smooth and easy. It was like this the day Aidan left—so beautiful it hurt.

But things can disappear forever down there. *Sure, it looks pretty, but it's a junkyard underneath.*

READING GROUP GUIDE

1. Throughout the book, there is the idea of "the river takes, and the river gives back." What areas of life can you apply this phrase to? What other relationships are cyclical or karmic like this?

2. Sabine reaches out to Rachel because she wants to tell her side of the story for the first time. Have you ever been in a situation where your side of the story differs drastically from another person's? How did you handle it?

3. At the beginning of the book, Rachel plays the role of the strict parent, refusing to pay her daughter's speeding ticket and her son's phone contract. What do you make of this parenting style? Is she being too strict? How does her attitude compare to parenting choices you have made or witnessed in your own life?

4. Compare Sabine and Rachel's upbringings. Despite ending up in the same physical location, how are their mannerisms and perspectives different because of how they grew up?

5. How is justice for the powerful different than justice for the powerless? Why is there a difference, and should there be?

6. Sabine is quite good at reading people, using this ability to make her plans. How good would you say you are at reading people, based on their facial expressions and gestures? How have you used this ability in your own life?

7. When Sabine points out a photo of Rachel's kids, Rachel notes that "photos can be deceiving," as the next day, both kids had fallen ill. How else can photos depict something that might not be the reality of that day?

8. Despite everything Dee did to make Sabine and Aria's lives difficult, Sabine still loved her. Why do you think she did? Can you relate to her situation?

9. Blue continues to be Sabine's steadfast companion throughout the novel. How does the friendship of an animal differ from that of a human? What kind of support can a pet give you?

10. Sabine has been living off the grid for many, many years. Do you think she will try to reintegrate into society after the events of the book? How difficult would that be for her, given changes in technology and societal norms?

11. How has Rachel changed throughout the course of the book?

12. Do you think Sabine is a good person? Was she justified in her actions, revealed to Rachel at the end?

A CONVERSATION
WITH THE AUTHOR

Where did the inspiration for this book come from?

It's always hard to pinpoint an exact image or idea that sets me off. I usually start with a big question or an interest that won't leave me alone, and from there I find a thread that pulls me toward something more focused and intimate. In the case of *The Backwater*, it was the idea that justice is neither equal nor accessible for the lower classes and, to take a step further, that society judges a woman accused differently to a man. Specifically, I looked at the cases of Lindy Chamberlain, Joanne Lees and Kate McCann, women who faced trial by media and whose lives were so public as they fell apart. A man is private in grief and trauma; a woman must be hiding something. A man is dignified; a woman is cold. Sabine Kelly's character evolved from thinking about gender-based miscarriage of justice, and through exploring the idea that we are less likely to judge or discriminate when we know another person's story.

How did writing Sabine's point-of-view differ from writing Rachel's? Did you have a favorite perspective character?

Every character I write feels real and important to me, so I don't have favorites or actively think about how to set them apart. By understanding a character—how they will react in certain situations—a perspective will always flow and make sense to me. I find plot challenging, never character, and it's not my goal to create like-able characters but to write relatable characters whose actions make sense with context. Sabine and Rachel are very different in lifestyle, class, history and psychology, and it's the point at which their divergent lives converge that provides the conflict and the backbone of this story. In writing Sabine and Rachel's characters it helped me to have lived experience of class disparity, so I found it easier to write two perspectives and to set one against the other.

What kind of research did you have to do for this book?

I fill the usual notebooks and amass links to reading and there are practical tasks like consultation and interviews, but much of my writing research is simply being in a place. I spent time in the Murraylands and Riverland districts of South Australia, watching and listening to the river and its people. I think you can learn more by not asking specific questions; fact-checking is necessary, but it can limit and deaden a story, like sticking to a script. Sometimes when I read through the final pages of a book I wonder, *where is all that fascinating stuff I researched?* Not a lot makes it into a book, at least not as pure fact or description. It's there in a less tangible way, conveyed through atmosphere and tone, and treating the setting as a character.

What is your writing process like?

My process is ever-changing, but I've come to accept I'm a slow and deliberate writer who needs to understand what brought my characters to the point where a story takes off. This involves a lot of thinking time. I'll construct past lives and build whole relationships in my head before I commit to the page, and my stories often have multiple timelines because I'm interested in how the past affects who we become. On average it takes several years to follow through from an initial idea or character study to a published novel, and I'm usually working on two or three books at once. I prefer to write at night, a habit formed when my children were young and finding time during the day was difficult. Writing daily is still a struggle. I tend to have bursts of intense concentration and, while the practical, methodical side of me needs to have a plan, it's the dreamer who usually takes over and gets the work done.

Which authors have inspired you most in your writing?

I've been an avid reader of horror, crime and suspense since I was a teenager reading Agatha Christie, Ruth Rendell (Barbara Vine), Patricia Cornwell, Martina Cole, King, and Koontz. Patricia Highsmith gives a masterclass in slow-burn character building, and I'm still enthralled by Thomas Harris's Lecter novels (though I've read them countless times over decades). Val McDermid and Karen Slaughter continue the tradition of keeping me reading their books in one sitting, and more recently there have been some excellent Australian crime fiction at the top of my reading pile: Shelley Burr, Hayley Scrivenor, Margaret Hickey, Sarah Bailey, Chris Hammer, Loraine Peck and Gary Disher.

ACKNOWLEDGMENTS

The Backwater's setting was inspired by the ecologically significant and extraordinarily beautiful Murraylands and Riverland regions of South Australia. I acknowledge the traditional owners of the lands and waters, the Ngarrindjeri and Nganguraku peoples, and their Elders past and present.

My thanks to Michael Heyward, Imogen Stubbs and the wonderful team at Text Publishing.

Penny Hueston—it's been such a privilege to work with you over thirteen years and seven books. Any accolades are as much yours as mine. The overwriting, poor tense sequencing, and sloppy syntax are all mine. (Can you please edit the previous sentence?) Thank you for everything you do to make me a better writer.

To Amanda Tokar, my agent, and to our community of writers, booksellers, librarians and readers—I'm so grateful for your support.

Hayley Scrivenor, Shelley Burr, Dinuka McKenzie and Michelle Prak—I have so much admiration for your work and endless appreciation for your words in support of *Backwater*. Thank you all.

Thank you to the Websters and their extended family for generously sharing their home on Murrundi, the Murray River, and their fascinating history.

Many thanks to Brett for patiently listening to my rambling, answering my endless questions, and for guiding me on all things crime and police procedure. I could not have found my way through this story without your help.

There are few people I trust to read my work before the alchemy of editing, proofreading and typesetting makes it, well…readable. Thank you, Allayne, Bec, Brett and Sue.

This book is dedicated to Allayne, because everyone needs a friend who will help you hide the body. Or find one. All that dog-walking—it's inevitable. Thank you, A.

As always, my love and thanks to my family. The past three years (the time it took to write this book) have been full of challenges, milestones, and change. We got through it the way we always make it through: together.

ABOUT THE AUTHOR

Vikki Wakefield writes fiction for adults and young adults. Her novels have been short-listed for numerous awards. *After You Were Gone*, a psychological thriller, was her first novel for adults and was published in 2022 to much acclaim. *The Backwater* is her second psychological thriller. Vikki lives in Adelaide, Australia.